Luke's Voice Sent a Shiver Down Her Spine.

But his resistance rose like a wall between them. She wanted to scream and shout and cry. She wanted to beg. But Honor Duvall begged no man. She lifted her chin and boldly, proudly, met his gaze, allowing her eyes to fill with the feelings she'd hidden in the past.

Luke Prescott actually flinched. His head dropped back and he gazed at the rafters. Seconds passed until he slowly lowered his face. With eyes as black as the devil's heart and hot as the fires of hell, he stared back into her soul.

She heard surrender in his voice. "Are you sure of this, Honor?"

"Yes, Luke, I'm very sure."

He closed the distance between them in two long strides. Taking her into his arms, he pulled her against his nakedness. "This has been the damnedest seduction I've ever seen."

His kiss was wild and hot, almost savage in its intensity. Even as she reveled in it, Honor realized her mistake. Luke hadn't surrendered. Captain Prescott, formerly of the Texas Rangers, never surrendered.

Luke Prescott took control.

Praise for Geralyn Dawson and Her Sensational Romances

"Geralyn Dawson is a masterful storyteller with an extraordinary talent for leaving her readers sated and begging for more all at the same time."
—Lori Wright, *The Literary Times*

"The very talented Geralyn Dawson writes a very humorous western romance [*The Bad Luck Wedding Dress*] with many superb characters!"
—Harriet Klausner, *Affaire de Coeur*

"[*The Bad Luck Wedding Dress*] was perfect! Five bells! This is a keeper!"
—Donita Lawrence, *Bell, Book, and Candle*

"Ms. Dawson is a refreshing new voice in the romance field."
—Christine McCollum, *Old Book Barn Gazette*

"Both uproariously funny and heart-wrenching in turns. [*Tempting Morality*] is the perfect read for both optimists and cynics alike."
—*Pen and Mouse Newsletter*

"Hilarious, warm, and witty! If this story [*The Bad Luck Wedding Dress*] doesn't put you in a good mood, I don't know what else will. It's a definite keeper."
—*The Time Machine*

GERALYN DAWSON

The Wedding Raffle

POCKET BOOKS
New York   London   Toronto   Sydney   Tokyo   Singapore

An *Original* Publication of POCKET BOOKS

POCKET BOOKS, a division of Simon & Schuster Inc.
1230 Avenue of the Americas, New York, NY 10020

ISBN: 0-671-00126-4

First Pocket Books printing November 1996

10 9 8 7 6 5 4 3 2 1

POCKET and colophon are registered trademarks of Simon & Schuster Inc.

Front cover illustration by Danilo Ducak

Printed in the U.S.A.

For Steven

In celebration of your sixteenth birthday.
Promise me you'll always drive safely, okay?

The Wedding Raffle

1

Republic of Texas—1843

A lanky, bowlegged cowboy burst through the swinging doors of the Golden Slipper Saloon and hollered out for quiet. "Listen up, boys," he said, excitement shining in his eyes. "You're not gonna believe this. She's up at the hotel. Gonna draw the winning ticket early. Gonna draw it *herself.* The Widow Duvall has done come to town!"

The piano player reached for a high C and hit a B flat. A dealer mishandled his shuffle, spewing half a deck of cards into the air. A gambler dropped his dice, a dancer snapped her fan, and a drunk lifted his head from the bar and drawled, "Well, I'll be dipped."

Luke Prescott eyed the generous bosom of the whore leaning over the second-floor banister and decided to raise his bet on a pair of aces.

Glasses hit the bar as the patrons of the Golden

Slipper made a rush for the doors. Two men in the game at Luke's table abruptly dropped their cards, pushed to their feet, and scurried from the saloon. Luke's friend, Rafe Malone, played out his hand, his concentration obviously suffering. When his attempt to draw to an inside straight failed, he folded his arms, settled back in his chair, and mused, "Honor Duvall here in Bastrop. Don't that beat all?"

His voice all but echoed in the nearly empty room.

Dust from the patrons' hasty exit floated in the air as Luke gathered up his winnings and deposited a thick stack of bills inside his wallet. The dumbfounded expression on Rafe's rugged face made him grin. "Sure seems like a lot of fuss for a raffle drawing. What's so special about Honor Duvall?"

Rafe brushed a smudge of dirt from the sleeve of his plaid gingham shirt. "Special? That's one way to say it, I guess. Notorious is the word that comes to my mind."

Luke arched a curious brow. "Notorious?"

"Haven't you heard about the Widow Duvall? And here I thought the Rangers kept close tabs on the suspicious characters who inhabit the Republic."

The words stung like whiskey on a raw wound. Luke hadn't been a Texas Ranger for six months, but Rafe didn't know how much that fact bothered him. Nobody knew. Luke had made sure of it. He hid his irritation behind a dry observation. "To do that, the Rangers would need a million-man army. Texas is overrun with suspicious characters, present company included."

Amusement gleamed in Rafe's green eyes. "Hey now, I'm a reformed man. You know that." Ignoring Luke's snort of disbelief, he added, "It's just that I'm surprised you're ignorant of the Widow Duvall."

"Ignorant? You'd best watch your language, Malone." In friendly retaliation, he offered up a fact certain to fire Rafe's curiosity. "Actually, I believe I may have had some contact with the woman," he said, scratching his eyebrow. "I was recently offered a job by a Mrs. Duvall who owns a place called Lost Pines."

Rafe's mouth dropped open and he leaned forward, a lock of dark auburn hair plopping down onto his brow. "That's her, all right. When did this happen? Why didn't you tell me about it? What did she want you to do? Did you meet her? Is she as beautiful as they say? What did you tell her?"

"Still curious as a calf in a new pasture, aren't you, Malone?" Luke smiled smugly as he slipped his wallet into his vest pocket. "She sent me a letter shortly after I arrived in Bastrop, before you talked me into moving from the hotel out to your place. That's been what, five or six weeks?"

"Something like that."

"Mrs. Duvall wanted to hire a gun for protection, someone willing to teach her and her family how to defend themselves. Seems that in the months since her husband died, all the men who worked for him have drifted on to other jobs."

"You mean it's just Honor Duvall, those two boys of hers, and their grandmother out at Lost Pines?" Rafe whistled softly. "Why, it's the most isolated homestead in this part of Texas. I hear it sits on a bluff above the Colorado River, smack dab in the middle of the pine forest. That was his business, you know, lumber. Duvall Pinery furnished wood for danged near every building west of here. The man had money. Raised racehorses on the side. So, what did you tell her?"

Luke shrugged, eyeing the bartender, whose ear was cocked toward their table. "I'm no babysittin' bodyguard or schoolmarm. I sent her Rip Tulk's name. He'll do it. He hires out his services all the time."

"I wouldn't mind servicing that one," the eavesdropping bartender observed with a snicker. He removed his apron and tossed it onto the bar before hurrying past them toward the door. "Saw her at her husband's funeral. I tell you what, keeping an eye on the Widow Duvall would almost be worth the risk."

Risk? What risk? Just who was this woman? Luke gazed around the vacant saloon and shook his head in wonder. "What did he mean by that?"

Rafe's chair tipped on its two hind legs as he shoved it back and stood. "She's had three husbands die on her." He lowered his voice. "People speculate about the coincidence of it. This last husband turned up his toes not long ago. Drowned in his own bathtub."

Duvall. Luke recalled the printing on the raffle ticket he'd purchased from a redheaded youngster earlier that day: One chance to win Starlight, the prizewinning quarter-miler offered by the estate of Armand Duvall. "Armand Duvall," he murmured.

"You know about him? Did the Rangers investigate his death, too?" Rafe donned a straw palmetto hat.

"How the hell would I know?" Luke replied, his control slipping as he thrust himself awkwardly to his feet. Eight months ago he would have uncoiled from his seat, as graceful and dangerous as a rattler. Six months ago he'd been ambushed by some east Texas horse thieves. Shortly thereafter, at the ripe old age of thirty-two, he'd been officially and forcibly retired when a doctor examined his bullet wounds and expressed doubt he'd ever walk again. Luke had made it his goal to prove the sawbones wrong and for the most part he'd succeeded. The limp had yet to totally disappear.

Rafe didn't pursue the question. Instead, he tugged

his hat low on his brow and led the way out of the saloon into the April sunshine. "Damn but I'm glad I talked you into coming into town this weekend. We'd have missed all the excitement if we'd stayed out at the farm."

"But we'd have gotten the doors hung and the windows put in on the new place. You'll be sorry if a family of 'coons moves in before you do." Luke was helping Rafe build a house on land he'd claimed as his headright west of town. After months of being laid up in bed, he both welcomed and enjoyed the physical labor, considering it therapy for both body and soul.

Rafe waved away Luke's comment. "Animals are preferable to some people I've shared a roof with over the years. Besides, I wouldn't miss this raffle drawing for nothin'. How about you? Have you purchased your tickets for the widow's raffle?"

Sucking in a breath of cedar-scented air and finding it pleasant after the smoky, stale odor of the Golden Slipper, Luke nodded. "A freckled-faced youngster browbeat me into buying one ticket. Actually, I wouldn't mind owning that horse. I saw her run in Austin last summer. She must be the fastest filly this side of Indian country."

"Yep. And I'm gonna win her, too." Rafe patted his vest pocket. "The odds are all on my side. I bought me fifty chances. Sorry, friend, but you wasted your money just buying one ticket."

Rafe kept his pace to an amble as he led the way up Main toward the hotel. Luke knew he walked slowly to accommodate him, and it annoyed him like hell. Damned leg. But at least he still had his brains, which, under the circumstances, was more than he could say about his friend. "You spent a hundred dollars on raffle tickets?" Rafe nodded and Luke shook his head. "You could buy a right fine horse for that amount."

"Not Starlight."

He was right about that, but a hundred-dollar gamble on a raffle drawing? "You always did have more money than sense."

"I'm gonna win."

"Win the prize for the biggest fool, maybe. The odds are still against you."

"Whoa!" Rafe made an abrupt stop and brought his hand to his chest dramatically. "This can't be *the* Captain Luke Prescott of the Texas Rangers talking to me about odds. This from the man who made a career out of playing long ones?"

Luke reached into his pants pocket and fished for the small tin of lemon drops he habitually carried. Removing a candy, he tossed it to Rafe, saying, "Suck a lemon, Malone. It'll keep your mouth shut."

Rafe popped the sweet into his mouth and grinned. The two men continued their stroll toward the hotel.

As he walked, Luke thought about the upcoming drawing and the lone ticket tucked inside his wallet next to his card winnings. Maybe Malone had a point. Maybe he should splurge on another ticket or two. A man couldn't ask for a better foundation for a breeding operation than the horse Lost Pines offered up for raffle.

He stepped on a rock, jarring his leg, and the slash of pain reminded him he might as well save his money. Horse ranching wasn't in his future, despite what he told those who questioned his plans now that his Rangering was done. Luke had other business to attend to. He had honor to reclaim.

Honor, hell. Had he ever known the meaning of the word? The old, familiar shame clutched at his gut, overwhelming the lingering pain in his leg. Every day he lived with the fact of his cowardice. Each night, the ghosts of those whom he had failed haunted his dreams: his wife, his children, the one-hundred-eighty-nine men who'd placed their trust in an unworthy man.

How did a man atone for such a sin?

Becoming a Texas Ranger had been an attempt. Serving the country for which his comrades had died had been a start, a small start, a penance. While others viewed his Ranger's star as a badge of courage, Luke knew the difference. He'd worn it as a daily reminder of his fear and foolishness, his cowardice and failure.

But now he no longer wore the star. His Rangering days were done, and he was forced to search for another way to earn his peace. It was all he'd thought about while lying up in bed. He'd considered and discarded a hundred different possibilities, but he knew in his heart that nothing short of extraordinary circumstances would do. He needed one great, monumental cause to fight for, one opportunity to make a genuine difference. For Texas—the country he loved so much. He would fight for her people, the strong, scrappy folk determined to carve a future from land that so often fought back.

Luke needed one chance to save lives instead of taking them. He needed to redeem himself even if it killed him, and at times he prayed for that sweet relief.

He inhaled a deep breath into his lungs and lifted his face toward the warm sunshine. Some of the chill left his soul as determination filled him. He'd find his opportunity. He didn't know when or how, but it would happen. He'd make it happen.

Ten yards ahead of him, Rafe hailed an acquaintance and forced Luke's attention back to his surroundings. People crowded the town's wide, dusty street. Perhaps fifty curious faces were now collected in front of the Bastrop Hotel. The air hummed with talk of the imminent drawing.

Snippets of conversation swirled around him like ribbons on the breeze. Luke listened in, rather than dwelling any longer on regrets and remorse, his forfeited career, and the fact that he could no longer physically keep up with his childhood friend—a friend he'd run to ground and arrested on three separate occasions.

A boy's voice sounded from behind him. "My pa says Mrs. Duvall buried her first husband in an abandoned silver mine up north of here."

"She killed her second husband stone cold dead," declared a feminine voice. "Put poison in his food."

"Same could happen to me if you don't quit fixin' those chicken gizzards," a sardonic voice replied.

"I cannot believe her name is Honor. How inappropriate!"

"I hear she's beautiful."

"Damn, I hope I win that horse."

"They call her the Black Widow."

"Those stepsons of hers talk nice about her. Her mother-in-law, too."

"Duvall's mother is still alive?" A grizzled older man blew a long whistle. "Hell, she must be seventy if she's a day."

"Luella Best is the second husband's mother."

"Surprised the Black Widow hasn't poisoned her off, too."

"If I win Starlight I'm gonna take her up to Nacogdoches and run her in the Summer Stakes."

The voices ebbed around them and Luke glanced at Rafe. "I'm beginning to understand why the lady has caused such a stir."

Batting a ladybug away from his face, Rafe nodded. "They say you can count on one hand the number of times she left Lost Pines to come in to town since she and Duvall moved here from east Texas three years ago. Folks have always wondered about her, but they never paid too much note until Armand Duvall died."

"Because of this raffle?"

"That and the dress." Rafe pulled a Havana from his breast pocket, rolled it between his fingers, and sniffed it. "It was the dress that did it."

"The dress?"

"Folk here in Bastrop simply did not approve."

Luke questioned him with a look.

"It was yellow."

"Yellow?"

"Bright canary yellow silk, I'm told. Lots of ruffles. Cut down to here." He made a deep scoop across his chest with his finger. "A real party dress. She wore it to her husband's funeral. Don't that beat all?'"

Luke burst out with the first honest laugh he'd had in months. "That must have gone over like a fly in the buttermilk."

As Rafe nodded sagely, Luke lifted his chin and gazed over the heads of the throng congregated in front of the Bastrop Hotel, not a difficult feat since he stood a good four inches taller than most men around him. Suddenly he was as anxious as everyone else in the central Texas town to spot the wicked widow.

He was intrigued. Beauty and daring. A dangerous lady. Honor Duvall sounded like the type of woman who played honey to a man's sweet tooth.

Rafe stuck the unlit cigar in his mouth and spoke around it while he checked his pockets for matches. "Don't know why she didn't just up and sell the horse. I know she received plenty of offers once she put out the news she intended to get rid of Starlight."

Luke thought about the ticket in his pocket and the

fifty in Rafe's. Eyeing the crowd, he completed a rapid series of mental calculations. "Did she sell tickets anywhere other than Bastrop?"

"Yeah. I heard a fellow from Austin talking about his chances earlier at the shaving saloon. I'm pretty sure he said he bought his chances at home." Rafe yanked the smoke from his mouth and frowned. "Since she sold tickets that far away, I wonder how many were bought? My fifty might not be nearly enough."

Beautiful, daring, dangerous, and intelligent, Luke amended with a grin. He'd bet she netted five times the sale price by staging a raffle instead of a sale.

Luke ignored the ache in his leg and walked a little faster. For the first time since the horse thieves shot him full of holes, he was interested, truly interested, in the events taking place around him. He couldn't wait to get an eyeful of the notorious Widow Duvall.

He wondered what color dress she'd wear to a raffle.

Honor Duvall plucked nervously at the bodice of her printed muslin gown as she pushed back the curtain of the second-floor hotel window and peered outside. Main Street was filled with people, and the sight caused her stomach to take a dip. "Oh, Luella, they will hang me for sure."

Seated at the vanity, Luella Best leaned closer to the mirror and smoothed an eyebrow with her fingertip. "No they won't, dear. Our plan is brilliant. Everything will work out fine."

"That's what you said when I went to build the coffin."

"So you're not a carpenter," the elderly woman replied. "That has no bearing on what happens here today."

Honor sighed and turned away from the window. Crossing to the bed, she gathered up her petticoats and kicked off her soft boots before climbing onto the mattress. Sitting cross-legged, she leaned back against the headboard and closed her eyes. "I can't. I can't quit worrying and I can't forget. I keep seeing it happen all over again."

"Oh, Honor." Luella sympathetically clicked her tongue.

"I'd never made a burying box before and it showed." Honor pictured the huge pine crate where it sat in the near north pasture out at Lost Pines. The coffin was a sorry construction of misaligned boards and bent nails. She had done a crude job of patching a board that split when they'd loaded the corpse. She blurted, "If not for the coyotes we could have used a tarp. But under the circumstances, what else could I do? And what if he wants to move it? I'm afraid the coffin will fall apart."

"Would you forget about the dad-blamed box!" Frustration filled Luella's voice. "Why, I swear, Honor Duvall. You are becoming downright morbid."

Honor glanced toward the mirror and met her mother-in-law's glaring gaze. "Not morbid, Luella. Afraid. I'm worried I've made a terrible mistake this time."

"Child, we have talked this to death already. What other option do we have? You've already sent the raffle proceeds to South Carolina. Despite all the pretties filling the house at Lost Pines, we don't have two coins to rub together. We wouldn't make it as far as Washington-on-the-Brazos if we tried to run now. What we do here today will buy you time to convert some more of your assets to cash."

"Will it? Money is scarce as hen's teeth in the Republic of Texas. I could trade a painting for a pig, but I can't sell it for the money I need to take y'all to safety."

Luella sniffed. "That may be so, but you have seven more mares and that magnificent stallion of Armand's. Texians might not spend their coin on parlor chairs, but fine horseflesh will wring the money from their hands every time. Look down in that street and tell me it's not true."

Honor rubbed her temples with her fingertips. "If only I hadn't spent the Starlight money, we wouldn't be in this mess!"

"Darlin', you can't think like that. You had a good plan for our future, one I didn't care for, maybe, but that's neither here nor there. I'm blessed that you'll take care of an old woman like me. My grandsons, ornery cusses that they are, are lucky you didn't wash your hands of them when their father died."

"Luella!" Honor straightened her back. "Don't start that with me. I may not have given birth to them, but those boys are my sons. And ever since I married your Philip nine years ago, you have been my mother."

The elderly woman flashed an impish smile. "I know. I just like to hear you say it."

"You're impossible."

"And you, Honor, are the head of this family. The decision to leave Texas was yours to make. Don't second-guess yourself now. The money is no longer available. The winning ticket must be drawn."

"It has been drawn. I put the real winning ticket in the Chinese urn in the parlor. I'll make it right someday, Luella. I swear. I don't like what I'm doing today."

"I know that, dear."

Honor watched as her mother-in-law grasped a silver-handled hickory cane and pushed slowly to her feet. It required great effort of will on Honor's part not to reach out a helping hand, but she knew better. Though all but crippled with rheumatism, Luella steadfastly refused assistance, snapping testily as she did so, claiming the fight helped make life worth living.

Silver-gray tendrils escaped the tortoiseshell combs placed artfully in Luella's hair and lines mapped the years across her face, but her blue eyes remained young, sparkling with intelligence and wit. Not only was she family, she was also Honor's best friend.

Luella moved to the side of the bed, lifted her cane, and rapped the end lightly against her daughter-in-law's knee. "You must put an end to this fretting, Honor. It's bad for your complexion. Remember, you're twenty-nine years old, now. Wrinkles are right around the corner."

"Thank you, Mother Best," Honor replied dryly.

"Well, it's true. And what's done is done. The dead are dead. No sense in you worrying about it now. Everything will work out splendidly. I feel it in my bones."

Honor sniffed. "What you feel in your bones is weather on its way."

"No, my bones feel *change* on its way. That's what Captain Prescott will be. Change. Change for the better. Now get off that bed. It's almost time to go downstairs, and you've wrinkled your dress."

Anger and despair surged in Honor's blood at Luella's words. "I don't want change. I want my family to be safe. I want to learn how to kill a man properly. That's all."

"I know, dear." Luella gave Honor's arm a comforting pat before grabbing her hand and tugging her to her feet. "And who better to teach you such a skill than Captain Luke Prescott, renowned Texas Ranger, war veteran, and bona fide hero? He's custom made for our purposes. Besides, he's handsome as sin and

I, for one, will enjoy having a man like him to look at over my morning coffee."

Honor couldn't help smiling. Luella constantly bemoaned the lack of men in their lives. It was one of the areas in which she and her mother-in-law disagreed. Honor had had her fill of men. She'd be perfectly happy if she never dealt with one of those creatures again.

That, however, wasn't an option. Her family—Luella, and Micah and Jason, the two stepsons Honor loved like her own—were in trouble, so deal with a man she must. "Do you think he'll attend the drawing?"

Luella laughed. "Of course he'll attend. Look down into that street, would you please? Every live body in town and probably half the ghosts are collected to witness this raffle. He'll be there."

"I wish I'd had the opportunity to meet him ahead of time. I should have sold him his ticket, not had Micah do it. I asked him what the Ranger was like and all he said was 'big.' "

"Micah is eleven years old, dear. You need to be specific with boys that age if you want them to pay attention to anything in particular."

Honor glanced toward the window. "I wonder if Prescott is a friendly type?"

"Hmm." Luella pondered the question for a moment. "You know, I've only seen him once from afar, but friendly probably isn't how I'd choose to describe Mr. Prescott. Bold, certainly. Courageous. Fearless." She paused, shuddered delightfully, and added, "Male. Very, very male."

Honor smothered a snort. "You spied all that in a single look? Without even speaking to him?"

"I know men, my dear." Luella's pale eyes took on a gleam. "And that man is extraordinary. Wickedly handsome. Big and solid and broad with dark hair and even darker brooding eyes. While I saw no evidence of it myself, I'm told his injury has left him with a limp. It will only make him more attractive, in my opinion. The hint of vulnerability provides a nice balance to that raw, virile lustiness he oozes."

"Luella Best!"

"Well, it's true, dear. I may be old, but I'm not dead yet." She patted her ample bosom over her heart. "Quite a specimen, dear. I was entranced."

Honor tilted her face toward the ceiling as if seeking divine assistance. "I think you should socialize more, Luella. You need a man in your life."

Luella leveled a knowing look at Honor and said nothing. She didn't have to. Honor knew she'd stepped right into that one. Not a week went by that Luella didn't argue with Honor's decision never to remarry. She'd even gone so far as to arrange for a parade of potential suitors to visit Lost Pines in the past few months: a debonair attorney investigating the possibility of breaking Armand's will, a dashing young tutor for the boys, even a brawny carpenter there to build a barn they didn't need.

Honor had not been fooled by Luella's conniving. She'd dispatched each man with alacrity, although when it came time to build the coffin, she'd wished she'd kept the carpenter around for a while.

Of course, this time was different. This time Honor was a full participant in the plot to lure a man to Lost Pines, and this time, marriage had nothing to do with it. No matter what Luella liked to think, this was no wedding raffle. She needed protection for her family and herself until they could manage to escape this Elysium of rogues and scoundrels called Texas. That's what this raffle was about.

That and preventing a hanging. Her own hanging.

She heaved a sigh. "I can't say you've allayed my fears where the Ranger is concerned. Big and solid and broad, you say? I'm more worried now than before. The Luke Prescott you describe doesn't sound like he has a forgiving nature."

The women's gazes met and Honor knew they both mentally pictured the coffin.

Luella licked her lips. "It'll be all right. He'll be impressed with you."

"Why? Because men, fools that they are, find me attractive? You know what I think about that. If Captain Prescott isn't intelligent enough to see past my physical attributes, then he isn't the right man for this job. Maybe you think he'll be impressed because everyone assumes I've inherited a fortune from three husbands? That's almost as bad. Or is it my reputation that will impress him? After all, I'm the subject of rumors wild enough to make a painted lady blush."

"Well, you certainly won't impress him with a gentle disposition," Luella replied with a sniff. "Or your coffin-building skills, either, if you want to be honest about it. Face it. You're as tangle-footed and butter-fingered as they come. That's why we need Captain Prescott. No one else has proved brave enough to stay the course."

"But Luella—"

"Hush now, I'm not done yet." She fussed with the sleeves on Honor's dress, making them puff. "Captain Prescott is a red-blooded man. He'll appreciate your beauty. I doubt he'll care one way or the other that you are wealthy—or will be once we've dealt with the problem of Armand's will. As for your reputation, well, I'll have to know the man better to see how he reacts to that. But what will impress the Ranger, Honor dear, is your courage."

"My courage?" Honor asked incredulously.

"Your courage. Rangers respect bravery above all else. Remember what they call Luke Prescott. The Bravest Man in Texas. He will appreciate the same trait in you."

"Pardon my language, but what in Hades is brave about me?"

Luella clicked her tongue. "Come now. It's not every day a man meets a woman who has nerve enough to do what you're doing. Texas raises tougher women than most, but you have to be the bravest woman I've ever had the pleasure of knowing."

Brave? Luella had finally lost her senses. The butterflies in Honor's stomach had butterflies. Grimacing, she rubbed her temples with her fingertips. "If you're trying to make me feel better, it's not working."

"Oh hush. Slip into your shoes and come along. The multitude awaits. And don't forget the ticket basket. You did bring the correct one, I assume?" She stopped and shook her head. "On second thought, I'd better check. Knowing your luck you've brought the basket with the real tickets in it. Hand it over, dear."

"It's the right basket." Honor had disposed of the authentic tickets after drawing a true winning number. She'd stored that coupon away, fully intending to make it right someday to the real winner. If she lived long enough.

Luella simply held out her hand and waited until Honor produced the gaily decorated basket. Choosing three random tickets, she perused the numbers then nodded crisply before returning them to the basket. "Very good. The numbers all match."

As the hotel room door closed behind them, Honor wondered if this was how the condemned felt while walking toward the scaffold. *Well, if worse comes to worst, at least I've had some practice.*

* * *

Luke popped another lemon drop into his mouth and enjoyed the sour bite of flavor as it mingled with the taste of whiskey on his tongue. He damned near swallowed the candy whole when the front door of the Bastrop Hotel swung open and Honor Duvall stepped outside.

He took one look at her and thought: Never trust a widow woman wearing a yellow dress.

As she glided across the boardwalk toward the front steps, he appreciated that a man need not trust a woman to find pleasure in looking at her. The Widow Duvall was exquisite, a classic beauty. Sunshine highlighted streaks of blond in her light red hair. Becoming color tinted her flawless skin as she took a position at the center of the hotel's front steps. Standing some ten feet away, Luke studied her, observing the long, curling lashes that framed deep brown eyes. He spied the faint dusting of freckles across her aquiline nose and thought that her bow-shaped lips looked ripe for a kiss.

No male could ignore that yellow dress. The muslin clung to her generous curves like skin on a peach, displaying the kind of figure that could raise steam from a frozen pond.

"She's a goddess," Rafe breathed. "I'd heard it, but I didn't really believe it." He struck his breast dramatically with his fist and declared, "I do believe I'm smitten."

Luke tore his gaze away from the widow and offered a wry look and a warning meant as much for himself as for his friend. "You sure you don't mean bitten? She is called the Black Widow, remember."

Rafe sucked in a breath. "That lady can bite me anywhere she pleases. I think I could stand a little of her poison."

Privately, Luke had to agree. Honor Duvall was

satin sheets and sultry afternoons. No wonder the Golden Slipper had emptied out quick as a hiccup.

The gathering quieted when the widow held up her shapely hands. The Ranger in Luke noted the cuts and scrapes that covered her palms. Well, well, he wondered. What had the lady been doing to cause such injuries?

"Good afternoon. For those of you who don't know me, my name is Honor Duvall."

Her voice reminded Luke of saltwater taffy—creamy smooth, slow and sweet. Wolf whistles and catcalls sounded from the back of the crowd, and the blush in her cheeks went brighter. Stoically, she ignored the disturbance. "As most of you know, we had originally intended to conduct this drawing at the next race day here in town. However, sales of our raffle tickets exceeded all our expectations."

Luke leaned toward Rafe and murmured, "Guess there must have been a number of hundred-dollar fools like yourself."

Rafe whispered a crude reply and Luke grinned.

The widow continued, "The fact is, we ran out of tickets. To keep matters simple we decided to end the contest early and conduct the drawing today. My son, Jason Best, will extract the winning ticket from the basket." She looked toward a towheaded boy Luke guessed to be eight or nine who stood near the front of the gathering. "Jason, do you want to come on up?"

Excited chatter skittered through the crowd as people pulled out their tickets, ready to stake their claims. The boy climbed the steps, and when Honor Duvall held out the basket, he began to reach inside.

Luke looked at her expression, and in that moment felt the familiar, suspicious itch at the back of his neck. "Wait a minute," he called out.

Jason Best froze and Honor Duvall's head whipped in Luke's direction. For just an instant, her eyes betrayed anxiety. "Yes?"

"Pardon me, Mrs. Duvall, but perhaps you'd be better served if someone other than family drew the winning ticket. You wouldn't want any appearance of impropriety, now, would you?"

"Certainly not, Mr. . . . ?"

"Prescott. Luke Prescott."

The world seemed to tunnel to just the two of them as she stared at him for a long moment. Then, flashing a secretive smile, she nodded and looked away. "Reverend Martin, would you like to do the honors?"

The preacher frowned. "I'm not exactly impartial, Mrs. Duvall. I bought a raffle ticket myself."

"I doubt if the people would object." Glancing back at Luke, she lifted an innocent brow and queried, "Would they?"

The crowd chorused their agreement. Luke folded his arms and gave her a nod. At his side, Rafe said, "What's the matter with you? You're acting peculiar again, Prescott." He dipped his head and began thumbing through his tickets. "How many chances do you figure she's sold? I thought I had the odds pretty well covered, but seeing all these people here makes me wonder. Damn, but I want that horse."

As the preacher made his way through the throng, Luke kept his gaze on Honor Duvall's face. She lifted her chin as their gazes connected and held. The boy stepped aside; the man took his place. She shook the basket, requested that Reverend Martin shake it, then asked if anyone in the crowd would like to shake it also.

The gathering erupted with *hurry up*s and *get on with it*s. Smiling, she held the basket above her head, looked Luke daringly in the eyes, and said, "Reverend

Martin, please draw a ticket and announce the winner of Lost Pines's most prized filly, Starlight."

The red tickets were similar in shape to playing cards, and the citizens of Bastrop, Republic of Texas, held their collective breath as Reverend Martin removed a single coupon from the basket. He attempted to read it, then frowned. Withdrawing a pair of wire-rimmed spectacles from his breast pocket, he hooked them over his ears, then tried again. "Number three, four, seven, six, two," he announced in his loudest pulpit voice.

Luke waited to hear the winner's cheer. All he heard were groans. Beside him, Rafe flipped through his tickets, muttering all the while. "My numbers all start with four. Every last one of them. Aw, hell, I wanted that horse."

Reverend Martin repeated the numbers. All through the crowd, scraps of red paper were being flung into the air. Luke looked from right to left, ahead of him, and behind him. No one called himself winner. Not a blessed soul.

Rafe, impatient as was his habit, called out, "Well, who is it? Who won the raffle? Who stole my horse?"

The thought struck Luke like sixteen-pound cannon shot. His hand went to his pocket. His gaze sought the widow's. She watched him just a tad too innocently.

Never trust a widow woman wearing a yellow dress.

Luke knew the answer before he read the numbers. Three four seven six two. "Son of a bitch."

"What?" Rafe asked.

"It's me. I'm it. I won the widow's raffle."

2

A wrought-iron sign arched between a pair of brick gateposts, swirls and scrolls forming the words Lost Pines. Loblolly pines hugged the road that slashed through the forest toward a large clearing crowned by a rambling, two-story manor built of pine, cypress, and native stone. Colonel Duvall had money, Luke thought as he gigged his horse and cantered up the lane. Lost Pines was one of the biggest homes west of the Sabine River.

Verdant pastures and fields surrounded the house on three sides. Behind and below it, the Colorado River flowed in a deep green ribbon toward the west. Luke spotted a corral, stables, and a barn, and anticipation sizzled through his veins. He tried to tell himself the cause was Starlight; he knew in his bones it was the widow.

As a Texas Ranger he'd played a number of roles:

soldier, gunfighter, peacekeeper, and, the function that had held the most appeal, sleuth. Now, six months out of the job, Luke found himself itching to solve the puzzle of Honor Duvall.

Of course, he had no business getting involved. Regaining his strength and stamina so he could get on with his search for redemption should have been his sole priority. Besides, he wasn't a Ranger any longer. He was here to pick up a horse—a very fine horse—not to delve into rumors of murder and mystery.

No matter how appealing the idea.

The thick forest formed a natural barrier on two sides of the pasture, a wood-railed fence enclosed the rest. Luke counted five grazing horses. Quarter-milers, all of them, he judged, but he couldn't pick out Starlight from this distance.

Riding nearer, he spied a white gazebo off to the west of the house. Bright red roses climbed its posts and Luke found it easy to picture Honor Duvall in such a setting. Dressed in yellow ruffles that emphasized her lush curves, she'd sip tea from a china cup as she gazed out at the Colorado. The air would be heavy with the fragrance of roses, her soft laughter music against the deepening dusk. Beauty amidst beauty. A little taste of the South here in central Texas.

He shook his head and lassoed his wayward thoughts. The horse, Prescott. Think about the raffle prize. You're here to pick up Starlight, that's all.

He took a closer look at the stables, hoping to spy his prize. Instead, he saw a flash of yellow gingham disappearing inside. Honor Duvall.

Anticipation skipped up a notch. She wasn't expecting him this early. Old training and new suspicions had led him to arrive more than an hour before the appointed time. Yesterday, the look in her eyes had been an outright challenge, and the raffle, well, something about that raffle smelled like an acre of onions. Maybe now he'd find out what had caused the stink. A little nosing around wouldn't hurt.

Luke turned his horse, a chestnut named Red Pepper, toward the stable. One of a pair of wide doors hung open and sunlight spilled into the gloom. Luke dismounted and secured his reins, then approached the building on silent feet.

Standing still as a sack of flour, he listened.

The raspy feminine laugh came from the far end of the building. The sound of it immediately brought to mind haystacks and nakedness and the musky, sultry scent of sex. So, he wondered, had the widow taken a lover? If she had killed Duvall, this could be the motive for murder.

Voyeurism not being his style, Luke turned to leave. An unmistakable exclamation of pain brought him up short.

"Stop it," Honor Duvall demanded. "Stop it, I'm telling you." A moment later, she squealed, "Yeow, that hurts! Let go of me right now."

Luke sighed. Oh, hell. He'd have to save her.

Dread flattened his mouth as he reached for his Colt Texas Paterson revolver. Interfering in domestic conflicts, so to speak, had always been his least favorite duty. A fellow never knew how the participants would take his intrusion. But he couldn't sit by and allow a man to hurt a woman. The widow was saying "Stop" so stop it would be.

The well-worn ivory grip slipped into his hand like an old friend, and Luke aimed the nine-inch barrel toward the roof. Chances were this time he'd need the gun for a club rather than for shooting.

"Ouch!" she hollered.

Like a panther approaching his prey, Luke moved

24

swiftly and silently. Light filtered through the cracks between the boards and illuminated his way. He listened hard for the rumble of a male voice, but heard only Honor Duvall's high-pitched noises, which he followed to the last horse stall on the right. Lowering the gun, he pointed it and said, "Let her go or I'll—"

She was alone. Alone, but twisting and twirling around, one hand stretched behind her head and down her back, the other slipped inside her unbuttoned bodice, reaching around her. Luke's chin dropped. Good God, what had he interrupted?

"Help me! He's loose and I can't get him out!"

Her skirts were fashionably full, but not nearly big enough to hide a man. "Who's he, Mrs. Duvall?"

She shimmied and Luke's eyes widened at the jiggle of her nearly bare breasts. "Ye-e-e-ow!" Her eyes flashed. "Captain, please, help me or leave. I need to get out of this dress."

"You want me to take off your dress?" Luke rocked back on his heels.

"He has half his claws sunk into me and the other half tangled in my chemise. I want him gone *now!*"

Claws. A critter. A quick glance around revealed a basket of kittens in one corner of the stall. Luke holstered his Paterson and released his tension with a laugh. "I'm at your service, Mrs. Duvall."

He immediately thought of the bartender's remark the day before. The twitch of his lips betrayed his amusement and seeing it, she fired a lethal look. "Never mind. I'll do it myself. Just leave. Now-ow-ow-ow."

"You'll squash him if you do," he said vaguely, his gaze sweeping over the hills and valleys of her curves, trying to identify the out-of-place lump. There, just above the dress's tightly fitted waist, Luke spied the telltale movement. Not knowing the variety and arrangement of her undergarments, Luke offered her a choice. "Shall I do this from above or below?"

Her face flushed pink, whether from embarrassment or pique he wasn't sure. "I don't want you under my skirts!"

Pique, he decided. "Careful what you say, ma'am," he said, stepping toward her. "You'll hurt my self-respect. I have a tender personality."

"Well, I have a tender and no doubt bloody back, and this poor kitten is frightened half to death. I feel him trembling."

"He's probably just excited, Mrs. Duvall. I'm certain I would be if I were in his place."

"Captain!" she cried, a definite note of scandal in her voice.

Considering her reputation, Luke found that curious.

Scents teased his senses as he closed the space between them. Vanilla and milk, not the spicy French perfume he'd have expected from the notorious Widow Duvall. Another curiosity.

With practiced skill he unbuttoned the rest of her bodice, making room for his other hand to slide smoothly down the back of her dress. Her skin was silk, as soft as the newborn kitten's fur. With one of his hands at her breast and the other inching down her spine, he felt need hit him hard and unexpectedly, and his body stirred.

Son of a bitch. It's been a damned long time.

Time hung suspended. The kitten continued to wriggle, but Honor grew still. The muscles beneath Luke's fingers tensed. Did she sense his arousal? Could she smell it on him? Did she feel something similar herself?

He almost groaned aloud at the thought.

Then needle-sharp milk teeth latched onto his middle finger and he let out a yelp. "What the—"

He yanked on his hand. The kitten yowled. The widow hollered. The yellow gingham ripped.

The gunshot stopped even the cat for a moment.

"Get your filthy hands off my mama." Jason Best pointed a single-barreled, muzzle-loading rifle at Luke's heart. The sulphur scent of black powder and youthful fear swirled in the air.

"Good Lord, what next?" Luke muttered in disgust.

He grasped the now squirming kitten and lifted him from inside Honor Duvall's dress. Then he spoke to the boy in a calm, informative voice. "An Indian can fire a dozen arrows in the time it takes to reload a long arm. That's why Texas Rangers value their revolvers so highly. Take it as a lesson, son. It's never smart to go against a man holding a superior weapon."

The boy advanced, his narrowed-eyed gaze locked on the hand Luke had around the widow's waist. "You—"

"It's all right, Jason." Honor shrugged off Luke's touch and clutched her dress to her chest. "This is Captain Prescott. He was helping me, that's all. I was playing with the kittens and Softy somehow managed to slip down my dress."

Softy? Luke swiped his mouth. Killer would be more appropriate.

The boy was having none of her explanation. "He had his hand down your dress, Honor. I saw it. Remember the trouble we had last time that happened?"

The last time that happened?

Honor blushed red as barn paint when a newcomer's voice said, "That was a different situation entirely, Jason. The carpenter misunderstood Honor's remark about his being good with his hands, and he attempted to take liberties she did not welcome."

The elderly woman he had met yesterday after the drawing stepped into view, and Luke's chin all but hit the ground. Luella Best was wearing pants. Men's pants.

What sort of family was this?

His imagination kicked into a gallop as he turned his head and gave Honor Duvall a measuring look. Did her wardrobe also include a pair of trousers—yellow trousers, of course?

Luella Best snorted, but when Luke met her gaze her eyes were filled with innocence. "It's lucky for us you arrived early, hmm, Captain Prescott?"

Distracted, he absently nodded. "Reckon so."

"Early by almost an hour. You must be eager."

Eager wasn't precisely the word for what he was feeling, but it was close. Despite his better judgment, Luke's gaze returned to the creamy globes of Honor Duvall's breasts. "Yes, ma'am."

Luella rolled her eyes and crossed the stall to Honor. Reaching out, she tugged up the gingham bodice. "Those are some nasty scratches, dear. I'll want to doctor them right away." Glancing at Luke, she said, "Captain, why don't you come up to the house for a lemonade while my daughter-in-law pulls herself together."

Before anyone could move, Jason asked, "Why was it different before? She was yelling then, too, and—"

"I'll explain it to you later." Honor's tone trembled with embarrassment. She brushed by Luke and headed for the door. Then she paused. "Oh, Jason. Would you please refill the water bowl I've put out for Mama Cat? I meant to do it first thing, but then I got distracted and started playing with the kittens, and Softy slipped and Captain Prescott—" She stopped abruptly, glancing back at Luke. Head held high and cheeks stained pink, she exited the stall.

Following the others outside, Luke rubbed his stinging finger as he watched her hurry up the slight hill toward the house, the hem of her yellow skirt dancing around slender ankles. Sunlight beamed down upon her, highlighting a glint of fire in the thick, wavy hair loosened from its braid by the skirmish. Yellow dresses, strawberry hair. Honor Duvall looked awfully bright for a black widow.

It made Luke wonder. Black widows didn't play with kittens, for one thing. But do they play with former Texas Rangers? Despite his better sense, he had a real hankering to find out.

Jason ran up ahead and disappeared into the house calling for his brother. Mrs. Best invited Luke inside, but he chose to remain on the front veranda. Needing to take the weight off his leg for a bit, he lowered himself into a white wicker chair and replayed the events of the past few minutes in his mind.

His mouth twisted in a crooked grin. Damn, but he hadn't felt this alive in months.

Mrs. Best brought him a lemonade, then excused herself to check on Honor. Luke sipped the drink, stretched out his legs, and tugged his wide-brimmed felt hat low on his brow. He waited almost half an hour before Honor Duvall reappeared.

"Another yellow dress?" he asked, rising from his seat.

She shrugged and donned a straw sunbonnet. "It's a good color for me."

Luke couldn't argue with that. In fact, he couldn't have spoken on a bet. The deep breath she inhaled all but popped the buttons on her bodice.

"Mr. Prescott, please accept my apologies for what happened in the stable. I am terribly embarrassed about the incident."

"No apology necessary, ma'am. I'm happy to have

29

been of service." The moment he spoke Luke wished he had chosen a different word. *Service* was popping up all too often in connection with Honor Duvall, and it didn't seem quite as amusing as before.

Her fingers plucked at a loose thread on the sleeve of her dress. Luke watched her, and in those fleeting seconds, he saw something that put him instantly on guard.

Honor Duvall was nervous. Not embarrassed nervous, but anticipating-trouble nervous. As if the widow wearing yellow had something black to hide.

Years as a Ranger had honed Luke's instincts. Now a sense of danger kissed the back of his neck and caused his hackles to rise. His blood was up and running, and despite the unknown threat, or more accurately, because of it, he grinned.

"I reckon it might help if we started all over." Tipping his hat, he said, "Mornin', Mrs. Duvall. I apologize if my early arrival has inconvenienced you in any way."

She nodded, accepting his effort. "Welcome to Lost Pines, Captain Prescott." She offered a timid smile, then said, "Would you care to come inside and finish your lemonade?"

Luke cocked his head to one side and considered the question. Why would she think he'd want to finish his drink inside when he'd been happy cooling his heels on her porch for half an hour? What was on the widow's dance card? Did she want him inside for some reason? Flipping a mental coin, he said, "Actually, I'd just as soon get right to Starlight."

Luke observed her closely as her smile, already on the feeble side, faltered. Interesting. Something peculiar was definitely happening here. Damned if it didn't feel good to be in the midst of an intrigue after a six-months hiatus.

She led him past the vegetable garden and detached summer kitchen toward a small pasture he hadn't noticed until now. Luke paid careful attention to his surroundings, including the woman at his side and the pair of horses cantering across the field, always aware of vulnerability at his back. "Those are fine looking mares, ma'am," he said, pretending to observe the small, chunky mounts with interest.

She nodded. "Those two and their brother in the other pasture are from Gold Dust."

Luke's brows rose at the name of the stud known all over Texas and a good part of the South, and his feigned attention became real. "Is Starlight—"

"No. Liberty Joe was her sire. Mr. Duvall always claimed she was Lost Pines's best sprinter, however."

Liberty Joe, Luke knew, was owned by Jack Batchler over in Jasper County and enjoyed a reputation second only to Gold Dust's. "I'm impressed. I knew your horses were good, but I didn't realize you had this caliber of bloodlines."

Honor shrugged. "Colonel Duvall kept his horses' pedigrees close to the vest."

Luke forgot to be wary as he realized the ramifications of what she'd just told him. Yesterday he'd won a filly from the second-best line of cow ponies in Texas. Today, if town gossip had substance and the widow was out to sell some horses, he stood a chance of securing a Gold Dust stud. He could build the greatest horse ranch in Texas. He could provide the Texas Rangers with the best mounts in the West.

Reality came crashing back. What was he thinking? He wasn't looking to breed horses. He couldn't allow himself to think beyond his quest. The horse farm business was simply a handy excuse he gave whenever anyone asked about his future plans. Damn shame, considering the circumstances.

Luke eyed the horses and pondered the problem. It'd be a crime to pass up such an opportunity. The Rangers needed good mounts.

Maybe Rafe would do it. A smile played about Luke's lips as he considered the idea. Raising horses might provide the former outlaw with a much-needed excuse to get on with living an honest life. Ever since that cursed woman threw him over, he'd been worthless as teats on a boar hog. He'd still be content living in that leaky-roofed shack if Luke hadn't pushed him into building a real house on the same property.

The more he thought about it, the more Luke liked the notion. Today he'd do some horse trading with Honor Duvall. Then, as his leg continued to mend, he'd talk Rafe into building a business. He'd be doing both his friends and his former comrades a good turn. A good saddle horse was a good saddle horse. It wouldn't matter to most Rangers if they bought their mounts from an old enemy like Gentleman Rafe Malone. Rafe would love the irony of it.

The Widow Duvall lifted her hands to retie the ribbon on her sunbonnet, and the movement arrested Luke's thoughts. Wait a minute. Never mind about his plans, what were Honor Duvall's? With horses like these, Honor Duvall already had the makings of the greatest horse ranch in Texas. Why would she want to get rid of her stock? Why the raffle? Were the rumors about her selling off the horses even true? And why the hell were her hands roughed up and shaking?

He gave her a pointed look and asked, "Are you chilly, ma'am?"

Her quick glance betrayed dismay, and her fists clenched as she lowered them to her sides. With a smile as false as county election returns, she drew a deep breath and said, "I'm fine, thank you. So tell me, what do you think of Lost Pines's assets?"

Given an opening like that, Luke decided to test the widow a tad and see what direction her designs would take. "Assets?" His gaze swept her figure then settled on her face. "Beautiful."

It was blatant flirtation and she obviously knew it, but her reaction wasn't at all what he expected. A notorious woman wold look at him with knowing eyes. An innocent would blush.

Honor Duvall snorted with disgust and her nervousness vanished. She approached the railed fence and gestured toward the animals. "What do you see when you look at my horses, Captain Prescott?"

Spunky woman, Luke thought. Damned appealing, too. Such a combination could be as dangerous as hell. No wonder his neck had been tingling.

As were other portions of his anatomy.

He turned his attention to the pasture. "I see compact builds, short necks, a heavy muscular development, and bulging jaws."

"Gold Dust lineage," she said, nodding. "These horses are intelligent, alert, and responsive to the rider's signals, qualities which make them ideal cow ponies. A better horse for cutting, roping, and branding cannot be found."

"You don't have to sell me, Mrs. Duvall," Luke told her, aware that was exactly what she was doing. Could this be why she'd been nervous? Nothing more sinister than the prospect of negotiating a sale? Perhaps she'd never done it before and she found the idea disagreeable.

For a long minute, she stood gazing silently out at the pasture, presenting Luke with a picture of such beauty he knew yet another strong surge of wanting. Then, drawing a deep breath, she turned to face him.

"I'm getting rid of my stock, Captain. Rumor has it you have an interest in acquiring fine horseflesh. I hope you're in the market for the best horses in Texas."

Luke folded his arms and studied her. This woman was up to something. The Widow Duvall had more on her mind than horse trading. "It never ceases to amaze me how fast rumor runs in the Republic. We don't even have telegraph lines yet. But you're right, Mrs. Duvall. I might be interested in doing some trading."

An orange butterfly danced across the air, dodging Honor's finger as she pointed toward a gray. "That's Scrappy Jill. She's probably the swiftest of all our quarter-milers, but Brown Baggage, over there," she pointed toward a bay mare at the far side of the pasture, "is the smartest, in my opinion. In fact, I think in time and with proper training, she might outshine Starlight. We have . . ."

She talked on about the horses for a good five minutes. Luke listened to what she said, but observed how she said it more closely. She wanted him to like her horses. She wanted very badly for him to like her horses. The question was, why?

"I'd like to see Starlight now, Mrs. Duvall."

She shut her mouth abruptly, and Luke's stomach took a plunge. Damn. Did she intend to give him trouble about giving him the sprinter?

The nicker of horses and the taunting chatter of a mockingbird filled the silence between them. Deep inside Luke, anger sparked and began a slow burn. If Honor Duvall thought to bait him with one horse, switch it with another, and tie it all up with a bow of seduction, then she'd drawn the wrong damned ticket out of that basket.

Hadn't she?

Remembering the silkiness of her skin, Luke grimaced. He studied the beauty before him. Once again, color stained her cheeks and her teeth tugged at her full bottom lip. She blushes more than a virgin in a whorehouse. Could it be she recognized her scheme was going awry?

Like any good investigator, he mentally ticked off his facts. She rarely came to town. Her husbands died under suspicious circumstances. She had a fondness for yellow clothing, a face to make Helen of Troy green, and a body to make a glass eye cry. They called her the Black Widow.

Luke had not been this fascinated by a woman in years.

"Starlight is in the front pasture," she said finally, turning away from the fence. "If you'll follow me."

Suddenly, she seemed in a powerful hurry. Tall for a female, her gait ate up the ground. Luke followed behind, doing his best not to limp, his gaze captured by the sway of her skirts. As they rounded the corner of the kitchen, she plowed right through the vegetable bed. Luke followed, doing his best to step between carrot plants and summer squash, onions and peas. Watching seedling after seedling fall beneath her stampeding feet, he wondered why he bothered.

As they approached the pasture, Luke spied the five horses he'd noticed earlier now huddled at the north corner of the field. The widow marched to the fence railing, halted, took a deep breath, then looked at him. Lifting her chin, she pointed toward the south corner and said, "There she is, Captain Prescott, your prize."

He looked. That section of the pasture was empty but for a crate and a large pile of dirt. "Come again?"

"Starlight."

Luke gazed from her to the empty pasture, then back to Honor. "I see five horses, Mrs. Duvall. Which one of them is Starlight?"

"Not up there, down here." She jabbed at the air with her finger. "Inside the coffin, Captain."

The coffin? Luke stared at the misshapen crate lying at one end of the pasture. "That's a coffin?"

She nodded.

A coffin. Luke considered himself an intelligent man. As a rule, he caught on to situations quicker than most. This time, however, it took a minute or two before the reality of what she was telling him finally filtered through his skull. His body jerked. His mouth fell open.

Never trust a widow woman wearing a yellow dress.

Well, son of a bitch. Luke slowly shook his head. The beautiful, notorious, thrice-widowed Honor Duvall had sure as hell put one over on him and everyone else in this section of the Republic.

Damned if the woman hadn't raffled off a dead horse.

3

Honor tried to ignore the furious pounding of her heart. She resisted the need to wipe her sweaty palms on her skirt and stifled the urge to babble. Minutes passed like hours and the Ranger didn't move. Not a muscle. He stood staring at poor Starlight's coffin and if he so much as blinked, Honor saw no sign of it.

When finally he did move, he scared her half to death. Honor took a step back as he climbed over the fence and hiked across the pasture toward the crate. When his steps faltered and he exhaled a disgusted *whoosh*, she figured he must have noticed the hole in the ground. He tossed a quick glare toward Honor, then scrambled down into the hole. Sunlight glinted off a silver pin on his hatband as he bent over. When he straightened he held a spade in his hand.

Honor groaned. Would those boys ever learn to put their tools away?

Captain Prescott was going to look. She'd known he'd probably do it, but watching it happen wasn't going to be pretty. Micah's voice echoed in her mind: *It'll be all right, Honor. It's not like he'll be squeamish or anything, him being a former Texas Ranger.*

Prescott climbed out of the grave and slipped the shovel's blade between the boards of the lid and side and levered the lid up, the screech of nails sounding to Honor's ears like chalk against a slate. He moved quickly and efficiently, and Honor watched him with a curious sense of detachment.

She prayed they'd done the right thing. They'd taken such a gamble on this man. Everything depended on the "Bravest Man in Texas" living up to his reputation.

Thanks at least in part to Honor's lack of carpentry skills, it took Prescott only a moment to pry open the crate. The lid rose, then lowered almost immediately. "Doesn't take him long to look at a dead horse," she murmured to herself.

Honor studied every visible nuance of Luke Prescott's manner as he used the butt of the shovel to pound the lid back onto the crate. *Thud, thud, thud.* Now he moved slowly. Deliberately. How she wished she knew what he was thinking.

On second thought, perhaps it was better that she didn't.

Her mouth went dry as he started to pitch down the shovel. Evidently, he had changed his mind. He looked from the shovel to her, then back to the shovel once more.

She lifted her chin and bravely squared her shoulders, telling herself she had nothing to fear. She reconsidered when Luke Prescott reared back and let the spade fly toward the middle of the pasture.

Honor's gaze followed the spinning shovel until

Luke turned the full force of his steel gray glare upon her. It was obviously time to explain. She climbed the fence and approached him, stopping well out of reach.

"You rode out here expecting to return with a race-horse, Captain," she rushed to say. "Your hopes of obtaining a true prize need not be ruined. As I attempted to show you earlier, Lost Pines has some wonderful animals."

"I should arrest you," he snapped.

That stopped her. Really, the man should at least give her the opportunity to tell her story. Raising a hand, she said, "I don't believe you have grounds for such an action, sir. I broke no law. I offered a horse, and there she is. I provided no guarantee as to the state of her health."

"What's the hole supposed to be, a grave?" When Honor nodded, he muttered an oath. "Figures. A woman who raffles off a dead horse wouldn't do anything so logical as to burn the corpse. Nope, she crates her up and digs a grave. It must've taken an entire day to dig a hole that big."

"Two, actually. The boys did most of the digging, although I helped a little. You see, Captain, my younger son has a strong aversion to the idea of burning Starlight's body, and he requested that we bury her instead. But it is your decision. You are the horse's new owner."

Captain Prescott shoved his hat back off his brow. "What am I supposed to do with a horse's corpse, lady?"

"I was hoping you'd help bury her. Micah doesn't do well with the oxen, and we had a tricky time of it moving her into the coffin. We need you to drive the team to pull the crate into the grave. I'm afraid we'll end up with it in pieces as it is. My carpentry work is not what it could be."

"You built the box? That's why your hands are all torn up, isn't it—that and the digging?" When she nodded, Luke slowly shook his head. "This is the craziest thing I've ever heard. What kind of person raffles off a dead horse, crates it up, digs a hole, then asks the lucky winner to bury the damned body?" He gave her a sweeping look from head to toe. "You are a cheeky thing, aren't you, Miz Duvall?"

She drew herself up and spoke in a voice filled with starch. "I'm not a thing, Captain. I'm a woman, and I have a proposition for you."

His gaze jerked up to meet hers, and Honor could have kicked herself. All that planning what to say and instead she comes out with something stupid and suggestive.

Prescott started to speak, but Honor forged ahead. "I mean that I'm offering you the two mares I showed you earlier. I'll give you the horses, Captain Prescott. It won't cost you a dime."

"Two horses to replace Starlight?"

"No. You have your prize. This is a different proposal entirely. I'm willing to offer two horses as payment for your services."

"My services?"

Honor was distracted from her purpose by the strange expression that crossed his face. "Uh, yes. Your professional skills. I'm told you're extra quick on the draw."

He choked. "Wait a minute. Are you talking about the schoolmarm job?"

"Pardon me?"

"You want me to teach you. Teach you how to shoot."

"That and provide us protection, yes."

"That's what this is all about?" At her nod, he blew

out an exasperated breath. "I've already refused your offer."

She worked to keep her tone pleasant. "But we never had the opportunity to discuss it. We can do that now. It's a good offer, Captain. I'm asking you to watch over my family, to protect them from any harm that might come their way, and to teach me how to handle weapons properly. I'm offering to pay for your services with fine horseflesh, two of Lost Pines's best mares."

"Why?" He drilled her with a look. "Why is it so dad-blamed important that you know how to use a gun?"

She shifted her gaze away, her teeth tugging nervously at her lower lip. Having already wandered from her prepared speech, she tried to think of a way to answer his question without telling him too much.

Captain Prescott stared at her for a long moment. Then his mouth snapped shut with an audible click. Anger kindled in his eyes.

Goodness. She had certainly made a bungle of the entire thing. Usually she was good with words, but today her bungling manner had extended to her tongue. What in the world was he thinking?

Much to her dismay, he told her.

"Are the rumors about you true after all? Are you looking to learn new ways to kill? Is that why you want to learn weapons?" Disgust laced his voice. "Change your dress, lady. A widow like you should always wear black."

He pivoted and took a direct line toward the house across the pasture, his limp obvious in his attempt to hurry.

"No! You're wrong, Captain. I stated it badly. Will you stop a minute and listen? I don't want to kill anyone or anything. I pray it will never come to that."

He dragged himself over the fence and kept on going.

Honor groaned in frustration. She picked up her skirts and hurried after him. "Please! Listen to what I have to say. Why are you assuming the worst?"

"Why shouldn't I?" he tossed over his shoulder. "Nobody offers a stranger that quality of horseflesh for nearly free. Even if you're not out to commit murder, you sure as shootin' want something more than what you've said. It's bound to be either illegal or immoral or both."

Going over the fence after him, she tangled a foot in her petticoat and fell awkwardly on the other side. She cried out and he turned and rolled his eyes with disgust. He retraced his steps and dragged her up like a sack of oats and plopped her on her feet. Glaring and tight lipped, he set off toward the stable again, plowing through the vegetable garden on his way.

"Captain Prescott!" She put on a burst of speed and caught up with him. She grabbed for his arm, her fingers, unable to get a grip on the band of taut muscle, grasping crisp cotton instead.

Smoke-colored eyes scorched down at her as she tugged on his shirt. "I want you to teach us because we need to know how to protect ourselves! I want to hire you, Captain Prescott, because someone is trying to kill my sons."

That brought him up short. "You want to run that past me again?"

Honor took a step away. "Someone has been playing tricks on the boys. Dangerous tricks. It started a few months back. At first I thought they were making it up. Twice they came in from playing and claimed someone had chased them through the woods. At the time I thought they were making excuses for being late. I changed my mind when they showed me the bear trap."

"Bear trap?"

She nodded. "Micah and Jason like to explore a cavern not far from here. Someone set a bear trap along the path they've forged through the woods and hid it with leaves. I've never seen a bear in these woods. Then Jason was thrown from his horse. We checked his saddle. The girth had been cut."

"That's when you tried to hire me?"

"No." She forced herself not to wring her hands. "I hired someone else, but he quit after two weeks. He said someone stalked him. He was afraid to stay."

"Who was it?"

"He never saw him."

"I find this difficult to believe. Why would anyone hunt a pair of boys? What did the sheriff say when you talked to him about it?"

"He told me he didn't have the manpower to chase after pranksters. He told me to hire private guns. Personally, I don't think he believed my charges. The sheriff and I are not on the best of terms. But that's neither here nor there. The fact is my family is in danger, and we're out here all alone. As much as I hate to admit it, I need a man around the house. We need protection, and we need to know how to defend ourselves if we are challenged. I can't shoot, Captain. I can't hit the ground if I'm aiming for it. I need you, Captain Prescott, just until I can make arrangements for us to leave Texas. I know your reputation. He won't scare you away. Please, sir. Please say you'll help us!"

His chest expanded as he sucked in a deep breath. Those steely eyes bored into hers, as if he could stare right into her soul. Honor's mouth went cotton dry and it took effort to swallow the lump in her throat.

"You're telling me the truth," he stated flatly.

She nodded. "Yes. Yes, I am. Please, say you'll help us? I love my family very much. I'm a desperate woman."

"I reckon you are." He paused a moment, then asked, "Tell me something. Why didn't you explain your circumstances in the letter you wrote me? Why this elaborate setup now? Why the raffle, for goodness' sake?"

"It's all a muddle, really. My initial problem was hardly one a person can reveal in a letter. Once I received your refusal, I intended to visit you and repeat my request in person. But then Starlight died—" She paused, massaging her forehead with her hand. "What we have are two separate issues that have overlapped. It's a very long story. Luella convinced me that once you saw the mares I planned to offer as payment for your services, you would agree to help us."

"You thought I'd put the value of horses above the safety of children?" he said, folding his arms.

"No, no." Honor waved a hand. "The horses part only came up after we decided you'd . . . I mean, after you won the raffle."

When his eyes narrowed Honor stifled a groan. Had he caught her slip?

"You rigged that raffle!"

He'd caught her slip. She wanted to scream. She dropped her head back and looked into the sky, vaguely noting the dark cloud hanging on the horizon. Luke Prescott was too smart for her. Honor didn't answer, nor did she meet his dagger-sharp stare. She'd really messed things up now.

"You did! You rigged the raffle." He braced his hands on his hips. "Now that *is* illegal, lady. That's stealing pure and simple. I'm obliged to send you to jail. You'll be lucky if they don't hang you."

Jail was certainly where she deserved to be, but she couldn't abandon her children and Luella. Lifting her chin, she said, "Well now, Captain, you have no proof of that, do you?"

His jaw worked angrily. "You have more nerve than a toothache."

"Luella considers it courage, not nerve."

When he snorted, Honor lifted her chin even higher.

"Careful there, Mrs. Duvall," he drawled. "If it starts to rain you're liable to drown." Before she could spit out an appropriate comeback, he continued, "All right. Tell me more about these threats against your stepsons."

Her breath caught. He wanted to know more. She hadn't ruined the plan entirely, at least not yet. "I don't use that term. They are my sons. I've raised them since they were babies and I love them like I'd birthed them myself." Knowing she needed time to gather her thoughts, she asked, "Would you like to go up to the house and sit down? Like I said before, it's a long story."

"I don't need to sit," he snapped back, jerking his hand away from his leg. He nodded toward the well. "I am thirsty, though. Think I'll get a drink while you're providing me with information."

He headed off for the rock wellhead and Honor trailed after him. He appeared willing to listen, and that was a good sign. She tried to organize her thoughts, but her mind fumbled around as her body often did. Instead of deciding what she'd say next, she wondered if she'd imagined the limp in his gait. He certainly showed no sign of such a weakness now.

In fact, he appeared quite, well, healthy.

Upon reaching the well, he turned the crank and lowered the bucket, his action drawing Honor's gaze to the breadth of his shoulders. She recalled her mother-in-law's description of the man—big and solid and broad.

Nothing wrong with Luella's eyesight, despite her advanced age.

Luke set the full bucket on the well's stone wall, removed the gourd dipper from its nail on the post, and offered her first sip. Honor declined with a shake of her head. He submerged the ladle then lifted it to his mouth, watching her while he drank.

Honor noticed the tendons in his neck work as he swallowed, and strangely, her own mouth went dry. The anxiety must be getting to her.

He wiped his mouth with the back of his hand and asked, "Tell me how Starlight is part of all this."

Her gaze had drifted to the dark splotches of moisture molding the front of his green cotton shirt to his chest. What else was it Luella had said? Very, very male.

"Mrs. Duvall?"

What was the matter with her? Honor licked her lips. She had no business noticing the captain's, uh, musculature.

"Mrs. Duvall."

This was all Luella's fault. That constant talk about men. She was a terrible influence.

"Woman, listen up! Did this prankster kill my horse?"

Honor jumped. "Something happened to your chestnut?"

"I meant Starlight."

"Oh." Heat stained her cheeks and she cursed her wayward thoughts. "No, that had nothing to do with our other troubles. Nobody killed Starlight. Well, I tried to, but Luella actually did it. It was awful."

"What happened?"

"I told you I can't shoot."

"You tried to shoot the horse on purpose?"

She shivered. "Yes. After the accident. It was a horrible mishap. Four days ago. We called the horses and they came running in. Starlight ran right through the fence." Honor sucked in a trembling breath at the memory. Her voice quavered as she finished it. "A board punctured her chest. She was suffering so. I tried to put her down, but I kept missing. I didn't want the boys to see her, so Luella finally took over the task even though her rheumatism was terrible that day, and she had to walk all the way out to the pasture. We all cried like babies afterward."

Prescott mumbled an oath, then returned the dipper to its place. Leaning against the well, he looked at her and asked, "And the raffle? How does that fit in?"

Honor shrugged. "It was a last-minute change after Starlight's death. Maybe it wasn't quite ethical, but I did obey the letter of the law, so to speak." She gestured toward the pasture where Starlight lay in her poorly built coffin. "Under the circumstances, going through with the raffle seemed to be the best idea."

"What circumstances?"

"It's a long story."

"So you said," he drawled. "Three times now. And so far I'm as confused as a mouse in a maze."

"I'm sorry. I'm not normally so confusing. You make me nervous, Captain Prescott."

He gave her a measured look. "Tell you what, Mrs. Duvall. Why don't you start at the beginning."

Honor understood that. It was something she herself had tried to do. "The beginning of the raffle or the beginning of the trouble?"

"The very beginning."

"We'd be here until Sunday if I went back that far." Honor lifted her face toward the sky as she organized her thoughts, and again she noticed the dark blue thundercloud billowing toward them from the west. They should start for the house. "He has bullied me for years."

Luke cocked his head.

"It's true. He still controls my money. Finally, though, I'm strong enough to resist him. He knows it, and because he's a snake he's chosen to strike where I'm most vulnerable. My family." She shuddered with a sudden chill and rubbed her hands over her arms. "He is using my sons to manipulate me."

The scent of rain sweetened the gust of cool wind that whipped over them. The captain turned his head, as if measuring the distance to the house or the truth to her words. "Just who is he?"

Honor's fists clenched as the old anger grabbed hold of her, churning like the cloud above them, dark and fierce and mean. Her voice trembled with the force of it as she met his gaze straight on. "I'm not certain who is actually committing these acts, but I do know who is behind them. It's Richard P. Armstrong."

The captain's expression remained blank.

"Congressman Richard Armstrong."

That made a connection. Surprise widened Luke Prescott's eyes as the first raindrops splattered against the ground. "The Congressman Richard Armstrong who wants to run for president?"

"Yes." Scorn dripped from her tone as she added, "He's my father."

The wind whistled in Luke's ears. He stared at Honor Duvall wondering if he'd heard her correctly. He had trouble finding his voice. "Richard Armstrong is your father?"

Caramel brown eyes snapped beneath the brim of her sunbonnet. "Yes."

"Congressman Richard Armstrong. From San Augustine."

"The same."

"And you're accusing him of attempted murder?"

She nodded curtly.

Hell, maybe murder runs in the family. A wagon load of questions hovered on his tongue, but Luke swallowed them as he glanced up at the sky. He cocked his head toward the house. "Let's take this inside. Looks like it's fixin' to—"

A bright flash and the immediate crack of thunder drowned out the rest of his sentence. The widow didn't so much as flinch. She appeared rooted to the spot, her eyes locked on his, demanding to be believed. Luke wasn't nearly ready to go that far.

Fat drops spatted down diagonally through the turbulent air. The rain was cold where it struck his skin. Luke placed his hand against the small of the widow's back and gave her a little shove. "Head for the house, Mrs. Duvall. I'll be right behind you."

She gave him one final questioning look, then picked up her skirts and dashed for shelter. Luke followed after her, his teeth set against the pain slashing up his leg as he moved faster than his healing injury wanted to allow. Halfway to the house, the cloud opened up. Cold spring rain blew against him in sheets, and by the time he climbed the steps to the front porch, he was as wet as a fish in water.

But it was Honor Duvall's accusation against her father that chilled his bones.

Luella Best met him at the door with a towel and a scolding. "I swear, Captain. What were you two thinking of, standing out in the middle of a pasture with a lightning storm dancing around you? I'm well aware Honor sometimes doesn't show a lick of sense, but Texas Rangers should be different."

She reached up and swiped the hat from his head, brushing beads of moisture from the felt. "Now, I won't have you tracking mud across my clean floor, so shed those boots and socks and come along. Micah is caring for your horse, and I've sent Jason to the attic in search of a change of clothes for you. I saved a trunk of my son's things to give the boys once they're grown, and I'm quite certain he'll find something in it for you to wear."

Barefoot, Luke followed her up the stairs to a room at the east end of a hallway on the second floor. Opening the door, Luella said, "This was Armand's room. It'll be yours while you are with us."

The woman talked as if his acceptance of the widow's proposition was a done deal. "I don't know what Mrs. Duvall told you, ma'am, but I haven't committed to staying here any longer than it takes for the weather to fair off."

She offered a patient smile. "Call me Luella, please. And of course you'll accept Honor's offer. It wouldn't make sense to do otherwise, and Texas Rangers are known for their good sense. You'll enjoy this room, Captain. If it weren't for my rheumatism, I'd live in it myself. I can't always climb the stairs." She flashed a regretful smile. "Anyway, the suite is simply too nice not to be in use. Just because Honor won't set foot in it doesn't mean no one else should."

Luke eyed the well-appointed room, his interest piqued. The widow didn't care for the place? Must be the absence of the color yellow.

The unusually large rosewood bed dominated the room. Filmy mosquito netting spilled from a half canopy lined in silver silk down onto a forest green counterpane. Heavy damask draperies framed the pair of French doors leading out onto the veranda, and the carpet beneath Luke's bare feet was thick enough to make his toes wiggle. Why did the widow shun such luxurious trappings? Was it grief that kept her away or a different emotion? Guilt, perhaps?

"Make yourself comfortable, Captain. The boys will be here directly with dry clothes for you. I'd best check on Honor. She seemed a bit overwrought when she came inside." The door latched with a click as Luella Best quit the room.

Rain pounding the roof filled the quiet left in her wake. Unbuckling his gun belt, Luke removed the revolver and checked the load. He glanced around the room, looking for something dry to use to wipe off his Paterson. He opened the top drawer of a marble-topped rosewood bureau and appropriated a man's handkerchief for the purpose. Stepping toward the French doors, he peered outside, where lightning did the sun's work in the cloud-dark sky.

The Widow Duvall's home sat perched atop a tall bluff above the Colorado River. The view from the master bedroom stretched toward the west far upriver, while the sloped bank of the opposite shore provided a clear vista far to the south. Even in the rain and the darkness of the storm, Luke could see for miles. He spied no firelight, no lamp burning in a window, not a sign of another soul. The lightning-sprayed isolation was total and complete. Perfect for a Black Widow woman.

The house fit her well, too. A wry smile lifted his lips as he turned away from the outdoor show and scanned the spacious room. Over the years he'd waited out more storms than he could count. He'd sought refuge in barns, bars, and brothels. He'd taken shelter under trees, inside caves, beneath nothing more than a gutta-percha poncho and his hat, and a time or two, even less than that. Never before had he waited out a toad-strangler in a setting as fancy as this. Or in one shadowed in quite so much mystery.

Luke returned his dry gun to his gun belt then looped it around the bedpost. Tugging his shirt free of his britches, he absently unfastened the buttons. Honor Duvall and Richard Armstrong. Was she telling the truth about the family connection? Did the pair bear a resemblance? Luke didn't remember Armstrong well enough to know. He had met the statesman once a little over a year ago in Houston, where he'd spoken in favor of the annexation of Texas by the United States. He remembered a tall, distinguished man who punctuated his arguments by banging his fist against a polished oak podium. Words like *determined, forceful,* and *zealous* flitted through Luke's mind. An Englishman by birth, the widow's father was an orator on a par with President Houston.

A rap sounded at the door. Micah Best's muffled voice called, "Captain Prescott? We have stuff for you to wear."

"Come on in."

Jason carried a complete set of gentleman's clothes, everything from a wide-brimmed planter's hat to socks. Micah carried a crystal whiskey decanter in one hand and a cigar box in the other. "Bath water is on the way, Cap'n," the older brother said. "Honor says the cold soaking likely pained your leg and you'd welcome a hot bath about now."

"I'm fine," Luke denied curtly, even though his leg ached like hell. He accepted the clothing from Jason as Micah set the decanter and cigars on the marble-topped dresser. "You can tell Mrs. Duvall that won't be necessary. I'm used to—"

Jason interrupted with a snicker. "You're not used to Honor, Captain Prescott. Arguing with her is a waste of breath. She's the most stubbornest lady in Texas, except for Nana, that is."

"I don't know, Jase." Micah frowned as he flipped open the lid on the cigar box. "I think Honor might beat even Nana as far as stubborn goes. Think about Charleston. We're all against her, but darned if it don't look like she'll win that battle." He lifted a smoke from the box and ran it beneath his nose.

"You have a point," Jason glumly agreed.

Luke couldn't remember the last time he had seen such a pair of hangdog faces. "Charleston?"

Micah explained. "Honor bought a hat shop in South Carolina. She's decided she hates Texas and wants to get as far away from it as she can. I think she'd go all the way to China if she could."

Jason added, "It's a darn good thing the only cash she has is what her daddy sends for monthly expenses or we'd be on our way today. These tricks that man plays on us are spooky as all get-out, but I'd still rather be here than in Charleston."

Luke studied the boys intently. Charleston, hmm? The widow had mentioned something about leaving Texas, but what was this about no money? Come to think of it, she'd mentioned it herself in a roundabout way when she said her father had control of her funds. But that made no sense. As a widow, Honor should have inherited at least half of her husband's estate. Damned if the situation didn't get more curious by the minute. "Mrs. Duvall mentioned y'all have been having some problems."

The boys traded a look. Jason's voice was troubled as he said, "Honor claims he is just trying to scare us. If that's true, it's darn well working. I hardly want to go outside anymore, Cap'n. I'm afraid I'll get a bel-lyful of grapeshot or something."

Luke tossed the dry clothes onto the bed and peeled

off his wet shirt, asking, "You share her opinion of who is behind this mischief?"

Both boys scowled. Micah said, "Her daddy didn't like it when Honor wouldn't do what he wanted. He was mean to her. You know, Cap'n, I was knee-high to a gnat when my daddy died, but I remember enough to know that fathers aren't supposed to treat their young'uns that way."

"What did he want her to do?"

Micah rubbed the back of his neck and grimaced. "Get married again. To a king or a duke or something from England."

"A viscount," Jason corrected.

"That's right. A fellow named Black except Honor's daddy calls him Lord Something-or-other and gets mad because Honor won't do it because she says she's a Texian and the only Lord she recognizes lives in heaven. Anyway, Black is gonna be here by midsummer, and that's why Honor intends to be long gone before then."

"So why doesn't Mrs. Duvall want to marry this gentleman?"

The younger boy shrugged as he crossed the room and opened a door built into the wall beside the fireplace. "Doesn't really matter, does it? It's what Honor wants. I reckon the water should be hot by now, Cap'n."

Inside the small chamber a large, inviting metal tub sat on a white tiled floor. Hearing the rasp of wood against wood, Luke moved closer and peered into the room. A dumbwaiter? First one of those he'd seen this side of the Sabine. Duvall sure hadn't skimped on his home.

Luke's lips pursed in thought. Perhaps that's where all his money went. Maybe his widow *was* broke. As

Micah poured a bucketful of steaming water into the bath, Luke said, "I'll do that, son."

"No thanks. Jase will help. We've done this so many times we could do it in our sleep. Colonel Duvall was a stickler for baths. Two, sometimes three times a day."

The younger boy nodded. "He was a strange bird. All those baths. We haven't done it since he died."

"You haven't bathed since he died?" Luke asked, curiosity tempering his teasing.

"I wish." Jason's long-suffering expression was all young boy.

Micah explained. "We use a room off the kitchen when Honor makes us wash all over. She and Nana bathe there, too."

That bit of information tugged Luke's mind in two directions. He shook his head against the image of the Widow Duvall at her bath and forced himself to concentrate on something Luella Best had said about this room. "Why is that?"

The younger Best accepted the bucket from his brother's hand and returned it to the dumbwaiter. While he sent it below, his brother answered, "Nana's room is off the kitchen so it's handier for her. She seldom comes upstairs 'cause of her rheumatism."

"And Mrs. Duvall?"

"She won't come near this room. The day ol' Duvall died she moved out lock, stock, and hairpins."

Luke twisted his head and eyed the bed. "He died in this room?"

"In the bath." Jason cocked his head, folding his arms and narrowing his eyes suspiciously. "You sure do ask lots of questions, Cap'n. That's considered downright rude behavior by a lot of folks in the Republic of Texas."

Luke couldn't argue with that. Half the folk living

here had come to Texas to avoid troubles in the States. "I apologize if I caused offense."

"Don't mind Jase, Captain Prescott," Micah interrupted, giving his brother a quelling glare. "We tend to be a tad protective toward Honor ever since a neighbor tried to hurt her a year or so ago. She managed to fight him off, but ever since then we like to keep a close eye on the men who come around."

Luke wanted to ask more questions, but the look in Micah's eyes stopped him. The next few minutes passed in silence as the boys filled the tub with hot water. When they were finished, the older boy stepped back and met Luke's gaze. "We hope you'll stay and teach us, Captain Prescott."

Jason glanced at his brother, then nodded rapidly. "Wait till you taste the dinner Nana has cooked up."

Eating didn't rate high on Luke's list of priorities at the moment. Learning answers from the Widow Duvall did.

"We're supposed to fetch your clothes so Nana can hang 'em by the fire to dry," Micah said, gesturing toward Luke's pants. "She said to tell you we'll eat in an hour in case you want a nice long soak. We'll keep water on the fire, too, so just ring the dumbwaiter bell if you want more."

Luke stared at the steaming water and considered his aching thigh. The bath did look inviting. Perhaps he should give himself a little thinking time before meeting up with the widow once more.

What the hell. Why not? Luke emptied his pockets, then shucked out of his trousers. As he handed the boys his damp clothing, he caught their quick glance below his waist and the subsequent shared look of admiration. As the boys left the room, he heard Jason murmur to his older brother, "I always heard brave men have big ones. Guess it must be true."

Luke chuckled as he opened the candy tin he had removed from his pants pocket and popped a lemon drop into his mouth. Padding out of the bathing room, he poured two fingers of whiskey into a crystal tumbler, then toted the glass and the decanter back to the bathing room.

He sank into the steaming water with a blissful sigh. Damned tub was so big he could prop his ankles on the rim and soak his entire thigh. Welcome warmth penetrated his skin and eased his stiffened muscles. Unconsciously, his fingers touched the dimples of the bullet holes that had changed his life. Luke rested his head against the high-backed tub, shut his eyes, and took a sip of his drink. The mingled sweet-and-sour taste of lemon and whiskey—one of his all-time favorites—was improved by the quality of Lost Pines's spirits. Added to the sensual pleasure of the moment was the aroma of roasting beef he scented on the air.

Maybe Lost Pines wouldn't be such a bad place to continue his convalescence after all.

For the first time, Luke seriously considered the widow's offer. He wasn't going anywhere until he could ride a horse more than two hours without his leg turning to jelly. Perhaps this would be a good use of his time, a way to ease back into action, an opportunity to practice skills growing rusty with disuse.

Solving the puzzle of Honor Duvall would require a thorough and comprehensive investigation. He could ask probing questions and analyze her answers. He'd ascertain the facts and determine a proper course of action, just as he'd done when he wore his Texas Ranger's star. Who knows? Maybe Honor Duvall would somehow lead him toward his quest.

Or maybe he was simply looking for an excuse to stay close to the woman who'd made him feel like a man for the first time in a very long time.

Better he hot-footed it back to Rafe's place and helped hang those doors.

Without opening his eyes, Luke sipped his drink and pictured the widow as she had looked when she'd accused her father of villainy. Her eyes had gleamed with conviction and the set of her chin had declared her strength. No coltish awkwardness about her then. So damned beautiful. His instincts told him she'd be a worthy opponent. In more ways than one.

It was more than just her breath-stealing beauty. Like any right-thinking man, he appreciated good looks on a woman, yet he could honestly say he valued other, less tangible qualities just as much, qualities such as the widow's spirit, her self-possession. The apparent loyalty she felt to children not of her blood, not to mention to a mother-in-law, impressed him.

But to level a charge of attempted murder on her very own father? A man who happened to be one of the notable political leaders of the Republic? He lifted his glass and spoke to the whiskey, "How can I believe anything Honor Duvall says?"

Her voice washed over him like ice water. "I don't lie, Captain Prescott. Not often, anyway. And not in this instance."

Luke abruptly sat up, sloshing water over the rim of the tub. Dressed in a fresh yellow gingham skirt and white bodice trimmed in matching yellow piping, his hostess stood in the bathing room's doorway, glaring down at him. Luke repressed the urge to cover his privates with his hands. "What in blazes are you doing?"

She stepped inside, steaming like a teakettle. "I think that's the question I should be asking. I realize my reputation is colorful, Captain Prescott, but you presume too much if you expect me to attend to you in your bath."

"What? Excuse me, Miz Duvall, but the only thing I expected was privacy."

"Then why did you tell my sons you didn't want a bath? Why did you demand I come upstairs and answer questions?"

"Your boys are cookin' up mischief. I didn't say any such thing."

Her gaze flicked over him and the color staining her cheeks grew brighter. A long moment passed in silence before she said in a strangled voice, "You threatened to leave if I didn't come answer your questions."

Luke's body responded to her look. She jerked her gaze away, staring everywhere but at him. Sensing the heat of his own embarrassment inching up his neck, Luke retaliated. "Honey," he drawled, his stare dropping to her bosom. "I don't send threats by way of boys, and I doubt you'd want to answer the kind of questions I'm of a mood to ask under the circumstances."

"What do you mean?"

Luke reached for a bar of sandalwood-scented soap and tossed it toward the widow. "You want to soap my back, Mrs. Duvall?"

She caught the soap reflexively. Her eyes widened, then immediately narrowed, signaling her comprehension. "Captain Prescott, you"—she spat the next word like an epithet—"man." She chucked the soap back at him.

In a froth of petticoat and peevishness, she pivoted abruptly and exited the bathing chamber. The bedroom door slammed behind her with a bang.

His lips tilted in a rueful smile, Luke downed the rest of his whiskey. "Guess that means soaping up my front is out of the question."

4

The tempest raging inside Lost Pines's library surpassed the intensity of the thunderstorm outside. Micah and Jason Best listened to their stepmother's displeasure with heads bowed and rear ends braced for what might be their first tanning in years.

"How could you do that to me?" Honor asked, her voice a full octave higher than normal. She paced the room, arms folded, fingers drumming against her arms as she railed at the boys. "I know you know better than to pull a stunt like that. You may well have ruined everything. Do you understand that?"

The boys nodded but she wasn't appeased. Her emotions were in a turmoil. Anger, fear, embarrassment. She wanted to scream, but she settled for a scold. "Captain Prescott is a guest in our home, boys. I'd hoped to convince him to help save your ornery hides. No telling what he'll decide to do now."

"But Honor!"

She ignored them, ticking off her next points on her fingertips. "As if interfering with my business with the captain wasn't enough, you chose to send me up to that room. You knew full well how I feel about Colonel Duvall's suite, yet you deliberately tricked me into going inside."

She glared first at one and then the other. "The lies still ring in my ears, boys. 'He doesn't want a bath, Honor. He wants to talk to you in his room immediately, Honor, or he'll leave as soon as the lightning quits. He's changed clothes and he's waiting on you.' Changed clothes? The man was *naked*, boys. Bare as a pecan tree in the middle of winter. And I walked in on him. I ask you, is that any way to convince a man to take a job?"

From her seat beside the fireplace, Luella looked up from her knitting. "Actually that might have worked if you'd been the one naked instead of the Ranger."

Honor speared her with a look, then redirected her attention to the boys. "Good heavens! What were you thinking of?"

Jason's head jerked up, his face flushed, eyes round and desperate. He burst out, "Honor, Captain Prescott is hung like a stallion!"

Micah groaned. "Aw, jeez, Jace."

Luella nodded. "I am not the least bit surprised."

Honor slumped against the desk, aghast, her face growing warm with embarrassment. How had this happened? Where had she gone wrong? When had she lost all control over her sons? And Luella. She was almost as bad. Despair rolled over her in waves.

Jason's expression was pleading. "Don't you think he's a fine-looking man, Honor? If he were a horse, he'd run the largest herd of mares on the range. Colonel Duvall always said you gotta judge a horse by his conformation, and Cap'n Prescott certainly has—"

"Jason Best, that's enough!"

Luella waved a hand, her eyes gleaming with interest. "Oh, let the boy go on, Honor. This is the most riveting conversation we've had in this house in months."

Micah gave his younger brother an elbow in the ribs. "Don't listen to Jason. You know all he ever thinks about is horses." He turned pleading and repentant eyes toward Honor. "I reckon we did wrong, Honor, but our hearts were in the right place."

Well, their eyes certainly weren't. *Captain Prescott's hung like a stallion.* Honor fanned her face, fighting off vivid firsthand impressions.

Micah held out his hands, palms up. "We know how you are about men, Honor."

"You don't like 'em," Jason piped up.

Micah shushed his brother and continued, "It's not that you don't like men. You just haven't had much luck getting a good one."

Honor hated to legitimize their argument in any way, but she couldn't allow that one to pass. "Your father was a very, very good man."

"Yes, my son was a fine man." This time, Luella's voice held none of her usual teasing. She grimaced as she pushed to her feet, and when she walked toward Honor, her face reflected pain from both her rheumatism and the memory of her loss. "A mother couldn't have asked for a finer son, or these boys a better father." She laid a hand on Honor's arm. "But Philip could have, should have, been a better husband to you. I fear I'm much to blame. Because I needed help caring for his babies, I pressured my son to remarry too soon after Ellen's death. He was still grieving, and I'm afraid you were the one to suffer for it."

Honor's throat tightened at her mother-in-law's words. Emotion buffeted her like a gale—sorrow, anger, grief. "But I loved him."

"I know, dear. And I firmly believe, had he not been taken from us so soon, he'd have come to love you, too. Just like the rest of us do."

Micah spoke up. "We do love you, Honor. That's why we did it. After what he saw in the barn this morning, Jase was pretty worried about you. Every man who has come to Lost Pines since the colonel died has tried to put his hands on you. We figured it doesn't matter where you live, Texas or South Carolina or even China, men are always gonna pester you 'cause you're so pretty. It only stops when you've got a man to take care of you. So, we reckon you need one. Then, when we visited with Captain Prescott, we realized he's different from the others. We thought he'd be a good choice."

"Oh, Micah. I can take care of myself. It's you boys who give me fits." Honor closed her eyes and massaged the bridge of her nose. Weariness weighted her words as she said, "Why is it that every time y'all start thinking, I wind up with trouble on my hands?"

"We don't cause trouble on purpose, Honor," Jason added.

"They were trying to help, my dear. Don't you see?" Luella's pale blue eyes grew serious. "Captain Prescott *is* different from the others. He is man enough to stand up to your father. He's brave, honorable, and courageous. He's smart and he's handsome and he's strong, or at least he will be once his leg heals."

Jason added, "He knows horses, and the scar on his leg isn't too ugly, either. Did you notice that, Honor? We hoped you would."

"Was that why you sent me to his room?" she squeaked. "You wanted me to see his scar?"

Micah replied, "Luella says you never look at men, Honor. That you look right through them. We figured not even you could look past Cap'n Prescott's, uh, manliness."

Honor whipped her head around to look at her mother-in-law. "This is partially your fault, Luella. The way you talk around these boys."

"They're right." Luella nodded. "Captain Prescott is a hero, Honor. We could use a hero around the house. You could use a hero in your bed! Heaven knows you've endured enough of the other kind."

Cold panic clutched Honor's heart. Memories threatened to burst through the self-protective walls she'd erected in her mind. "That's enough. I've heard enough from all of you." She rushed toward the door.

Micah's voice followed her. "No you haven't, Honor. If you had heard us, you wouldn't be forcing us to move away. This is our home. We love it here. We love Texas! We don't want to move to Charleston!"

She whirled around, frustration and fear and fury sharpening her voice. "I'm trying to save your lives!"

"Then marry Captain Prescott! Marry him and stay in Texas! Marry him before your father makes you marry someone else."

"Marry Captain Prescott?" she screeched.

"Marry Captain Prescott!" Revulsion vibrated in Luke Prescott's voice.

He stood in the doorway.

Honor groaned softly. She had thought she was embarrassed when she walked in on the Ranger at his bath. That feeling was but a drop in the tub compared to the humiliation drowning her right now. She forced herself to straighten her spine and square her shoulders, even though what she really wanted was to curl into a ball and cry.

Disgust laced Luella's voice. "Well, there goes the surprise." Addressing her grandsons, she said, "Boys, I am sorely disappointed. Time and time and time again I have tried to teach you patience. You've acted prematurely once more. I had specific plans on when to mention marriage. Honor is not yet ready to hear that marriage is her best protection." She swept from the room in a cloud of righteous indignation, pausing beside Captain Prescott to offer an aside. "Children these days have no sense of proper timing."

The boys looked at Honor. She closed her eyes and waved them away. "Go, just go. I'll deal with you later." They escaped the library in a flash, leaving Honor alone with her embarrassment and the captain.

She turned to face him. He wore Philip's shirt with the sleeves rolled up to the elbow. His feet were bare, the trousers too short. "How much did you hear?"

"Plenty." His smile was grim and didn't reach his eyes. "You know, Mrs. Duvall, I've been misled, maneuvered, and manipulated up to here." He held his hand chin high. "Rigged raffles. Dead horse prizes. Peeping widows. All that, I could handle. But this, this marriage talk. Y'all have gone too far. I'll be damned before anyone—and I mean you or those boys or that busybody, pants-wearing woman—will try to add a wedding to the list. I'm calling an end to it, here and now. I've had my fill of Lost Pines."

"An end? No, you're not leaving." Panic clawed at Honor's stomach and she forgot about being embarrassed. She stepped toward him. "You can't. This has nothing to do with marriage. Please, think of the children."

"The children?" Luke hooked a thumb over his shoulder. "You mean the young rapscallions who appear willing to do anything to keep your family in Texas? If—and I emphasize the word—*if* these incidents of danger are actually happening, I wouldn't put it past that pair to stage them."

Honor's knees went weak and she sank into a nearby chair. "Staged? The boys wouldn't do that to me." She considered the idea for a moment before shaking her head. "No, you're wrong, Captain. They may be guilty of shenanigans today, but I saw their faces when they were chased through the woods. I saw the bear trap. They're telling me the truth. You must believe me."

"Come on, now, Mrs. Duvall." Luke folded his arms. "After what I've witnessed here today you expect me to believe you? To believe that Richard Armstrong, a well-known, well-respected man of unimpeachable reputation, is out to murder a pair of not-so-innocent boys?"

"It's true!"

"Why should I believe anything you say? Setting aside my own experience, you don't have a reputation to inspire trust in a man, Mrs. Duvall." He crossed to the oversized walnut desk sitting in the center of the room. Propping a hip on its top, he shot Honor a challenging look. "Three dead husbands. Do you know what they call you in town? The Black Widow. People think you killed 'em."

She wrinkled her nose. "Surely a lawman knows better than to set store in unproven rumors."

"Or unsupported accusations," he snapped back.

Like yours against your father. The unspoken words hovered between them.

He'd scored a point and she nodded in acknowledgment. Luke continued. "Under the circumstances I'm surprised Armstrong hasn't tried to squelch the talk about you. Having a suspected murderess as a daughter can't be good for his own reputation."

"No, it isn't." A surge of satisfaction warmed the chill of negative feelings inside her. She rounded her eyes innocently and laid a hand against her chest. "It's a terrible thing for a politician to have such a wicked daughter. I'm afraid someone keeps stirring up those old rumors despite all his whitewash efforts."

Prescott slowly shook his head. "Someone? Someone by the name of Honor Duvall, I'll bet. What sort of family is this?"

"My family is all under this roof, Captain."

He lifted a brass paperweight from the desk and tossed it from hand to hand, studying her all the while. Abruptly, he scowled and said, "Rumor has it that President Houston will support Armstrong's candidacy to follow him in office."

"I wouldn't know. I have no interest in such matters, Captain Prescott. For all I care, every government official in Texas could take a running jump into the Rio Grande."

He arched a brow. "You don't enjoy the world of politics, Mrs. Duvall?"

Anger spurted like a fountain. "I don't enjoy being a political pawn."

"Now that's an interesting statement for a presidential candidate's daughter to make. Are you a political pawn or a player? An accusation like the one you've made to me could play havoc with your father's campaign."

"I don't care enough about the election to trouble myself with interfering in it, Captain."

He swore softly and Honor looked up in surprise. His expression had gone cold and mean. In a clipped tone, he said, "Your indifference pokes a nerve, Mrs. Duvall. I'm a Texian in every sense of the word. I've

fought for this country in the revolution, in the inva-
sion of '42, and in too many Indian skirmishes to
count. My patriotic pride is so thick one of Rezin
Bowie's knives couldn't cut it. I firmly believe that
political apathy can be as dangerous to a country as
a plague. It makes me crazy to run up against it anywhere, but especially in Richard Armstrong's daughter. We're talking about the future of Texas."

"No, Captain Prescott," she said, vaulting to her
feet. "We're talking about the futures of my two sons.
About whether they'll have futures or not."

"I don't believe you," Luke said flatly. "I'm not
certain what it is, but I know you have something on
your mind, Mrs. Duvall. The stink of a setup perme-
ates this place. Now I'm not exactly certain how I
figured into it, but it doesn't really matter. I won't
play your game. Just because my leg is lame doesn't
mean my mind is. Go find another sucker, madam.
I'm not it." Turning away, he exited the library.

Honor couldn't let him go. Heels playing a staccato
against the marble floor, she followed him into the
entry hall. Desperation rang in her voice. "I'm telling
you the truth! I knew nothing of this talk about marriage. The very last thing I want is another husband.
Think about it, Captain. I've already had three and
each one of them made my life more difficult than it
was before. This is no scheme of mine. I need protection for my family. My father is trying to kill my sons.
I swear it!"

She grabbed his shirtsleeve. Her voice broke as she
cried, "Please, Captain."

He paused and turned around. The barest hint of
compassion flickered in his eyes and gave her a moment of hope. "All right, Mrs. Duvall. I'll accept that
you're probably innocent of this marriage talk. But as
for the rest of it, it simply makes no sense. The presi-

dency of the Republic of Texas is within your father's reach. I find it impossible to believe he would risk his political neck by terrorizing his family."

"But he is."

"You haven't told me why, Mrs. Duvall. Why would he do something that evil? It's not that I don't believe a man of Richard Armstrong's stature capable of nefarious deeds. Texas politics has attracted villains from the start. But trying to kill family—children related by marriage if not by blood—goes a step beyond what even Texians would tolerate. If you want me to believe he'd go this far, you must give me a real good reason why. And marrying some British lord isn't reason enough."

How did he know about Marcus Black? Micah and Jason, obviously, telling tales out of school once again. Those boys! "But it's the truth," she declared firmly. "Can't you simply take my word for it?"

His jeering laughter echoed in the high-ceilinged hallway. "This from the woman who raffled off a dead horse?"

So he wouldn't take her word. He wouldn't believe in her father's evil. He wanted a reason why Armstrong would hurt her children. Stubborn man. Honor licked her suddenly dry lips, feeling as if she stood poised atop a precipice, and either way she jumped would send her flying into trouble.

She had a reason to give him, a reason certain to appeal to the patriotism he so eloquently declared just moments ago. But dare she reveal it? She'd made a conscious choice years ago to remain uninvolved in that side of her father's life. Her feelings for Richard Armstrong were convoluted and illogical. She hated him. She loved him. She'd never truly wanted to destroy him, just to escape him.

But in the past, his actions had affected only her.

This time he'd gone too far. This time he'd endangered her children.

For her sons, she'd send the man to hell herself. "If I ever learn to hit the things I shoot at," she mumbled, stepping away from Captain Prescott.

"What was that?"

Honor drew a deep breath in an attempt to calm her trembling. "I started to explain this earlier. Part of it, anyway. My father is threatening my boys because, for the first time in my life, I've refused to cooperate with his plans for me. He is striking at my most vulnerable spot, my family, in order to put an end to my little rebellion, as he calls it."

"What are you rebelling against? This marriage?"

"Yes. He wants me to marry another man of his choosing. I've refused. I'm no longer allowing him to dominate my every action, and he is threatened by it. He needs me under his thumb, you see, because I am a pawn in his political game."

Interest gleamed in his eyes. "What political game?"

She looked away as a myriad of images bombarded her mind. Richard Armstrong laughing and tossing his squealing six-year-old daughter into the air. She and her father standing over her mother's grave. Repeating wedding vows to a man forty-five years her senior. A game of hide-and-go-seek she'd shared with Philip Best and his sons. Armand's special bath salts.

The bear trap that would have mangled her son's leg.

She put the chill of winter in her words. "Espionage, Captain Prescott. My father is a spy for the British."

East Texas

Richard Armstrong watched in idle amusement as the dancers at the Spring Ball attempted to revive the sole available fiddler, the victim of an overdose of inspiration from his whiskey bottle. Directed in their actions by the proprietor of the Tavern and Travelers Inn hosting the affair, the frolickers rolled the drunken man across the floor, propped him into a seated position against a barrel chair, rubbed his head with vinegar, and crammed the better part of a jar of Underwood's pickles down his throat. When their efforts proved unsuccessful and the fiddler slid back to the ground in a drunken heap, the proprietor, a crusty old Irishman named Gallagher, took up the instrument and gave the strings a general rake with the bow. To a chorus of cheers, the old man sawed away on the fiddle, stamping his foot with a flourish, and began to call the figure.

The titian-haired beauty standing next to Armstrong sighed. "My da cannot tell a tune from a tornado, I fear."

Wincing, Armstrong agreed. "They sound about the same. I believe you and I are the only persons present sober enough to notice."

Smiling, she nodded and spoke in a voice that was a pleasing blend of Southern drawl and Irish lilt. " 'Tis been a successful party, to be sure."

Armstrong thought of the money he'd won from his bets on the day's races and agreed. Before he could continue his conversation with Gallagher's beautiful daughter, a stumbling, free-handed fool attempted to drag her off to the floor for a dance. Acting the gentleman, Armstrong started to intervene. His efforts proved unnecessary, because the lady dispatched the drunken reveler with a quick slap and a thorough scolding.

Pretty thing, Armstrong thought, as she excused herself to dance with a young boy who had politely requested the favor. High-spirited. She'd be a hard one to break to halter.

Having eavesdropped on earlier conversations, Armstrong had learned, among other things, that Gallagher's daughter, Katie Starr, was a widow who'd recently lost her only child. Watching her now, he was vividly reminded of another willful widow. The Widow Duvall. His own dear daughter.

God curse her.

Honor had developed backbone and it was causing him nothing but trouble.

Richard pushed his way through the throng of people to the long oaken bar where mugs of ale were lined up for the taking. Forgoing the ale, he moved behind the bar and appropriated a bottle of Irish whiskey and a glass. As he poured his drink, he watched the widow dance, his eye attracted by more than her beauty. Despite an obvious effort to appear cheery, her face bore signs of infinite sadness that set her apart from the ardent revelry surrounding her. It was in her eyes and in her smile. Grief. Deep, heart-wrenching, soul-shattering grief.

The sight gave Richard an idea.

He sipped his whiskey, and as it scorched its way down his throat he thought perhaps Honor deserved a dose of the Widow Starr's trials. Maybe he should raise the stakes and actually kill one of those boys. Which one should it be?

A buxom woman wearing too many ruffles and a suffering grimace snatched the fiddle from Gallagher's hand, stopping the music. Before the crowd of dancers could protest, she'd launched into a recognizable rendition of "Molly Cotton-Tail." The improvement in the music led to raucous cheers and the din of clattering feet. Richard made his way to a corner table, took a seat, and considered his idea.

By stubbornly refusing to marry per his instructions, Honor had provoked the threats he'd made against her family. Despite the incidents, she had yet to falter in her defiance. Her latest message to him had been filled with vituperative language and wild threats of her own.

The game had become tiresome and time was growing short. He needed his daughter's cooperation. Marcus Black, Viscount Kendall, was due to arrive from London any day now and their agreement hinged upon the Englishman's marriage to his daughter. With his dreams finally within reach, Richard refused to allow anything or anyone to stand in his way. If he had one child killed, Honor would undoubtedly do whatever was necessary to protect the other child.

He tossed back the rest of his drink. He'd send a letter with the post coach tomorrow.

A harmonica joined the fiddler and the music eased into a waltz. With his decision made, he felt like joining the frolickers. Moving onto the dance floor, he approached the Widow Starr and tapped her buckskin-clad partner on the shoulder. "Cutting in, sir," he said, sweeping the beauty away from the scowling frontiersman.

The spitfire frowned, but didn't refuse him. Richard didn't speak as he led her in the dance, just enjoyed the feel of a beautiful young woman in his arms. As the music filtered through his mind, he heard other strains instead, transporting him to another place, a time soon to come. No longer was the fiddler an overdressed, overage woman, but a violinist of superb talent. The ballroom was not a puncheon-floored tavern in the middle of nowhere, but the glittering gilt-and-crystal ballroom of Larksbury Hall in Kent.

A grand English country home, Larksbury Hall was the unentailed estate that neighbored the Armstrong family lands. Currently owned by none other than Viscount Kendall, it was but a part of the purse due Richard upon the execution of their agreement.

Larksbury Hall was much bigger and richer than the Armstrongs' Thornhill, and Richard's twin brother, William, had always coveted the grand mansion. Richard didn't remember a time he hadn't hated his brother, favorite son and heir to the barony on the basis of having been born six minutes before he.

For most of his childhood Richard had attempted to compete with his brother for his parents' affections, to no avail. Although he learned to live with the inequitable situation, he never accepted it. When he was eighteen, his parents forced him to marry a rich cit's daughter in order to replenish the family coffers with her dowry, and for Richard this was his limit. He'd taken his wife to America, eventually joining Moses Austin's colony as one of the Old Three Hundred.

Texas had sounded as far from his father as he could possibly get.

Now he had a chance to show them all. Taking his own parents' example to heart, he'd made certain that each of his daughter's marriages brought substantial financial reward. This wedding would top them all. It was the first step in an intricate plan he'd contrived with the viscount.

Lord Kendall wanted Honor. He wanted the lumber rights to the Lost Pines forest and other investment rights in Texas. Most important of all, he coveted the political power he'd garner at home by placing the presidency of the Republic of Texas into British hands.

In return, Richard Armstrong would gain the means to rub both his brother's and his father's noses in Larksbury Hall dirt. Because along with wealth, a grand estate, and political power, his negotiated reward for service to the crown upon the completion of his three-year term as president of the Republic included a title.

A heavy hand landed on Richard's shoulder, jerking his thoughts back to the present. John Gallagher offered a wide smile and said, "I'll be a-dancin' with me daughter, if you please. Seeing the two of you steppin' out into the waltz put me in mind of her dear sweet mother, God rest her soul." To the widow, he said, "You're the spittin' image, Katie mine. Will ye do me the honor?"

Richard gracefully stepped aside and wandered toward the buffet table set along the far wall laden with both plain fare and delectables. He lifted a slice of turkey from a platter and took a bite of the succulent meat. A smile spread across his face as he chewed. Richard Armstrong, the Earl of Lindley. Lord Lindley. It had a particularly nice ring to it.

He swallowed the meat and said a quick, silent prayer for his father's continued good health. More than anything, he wanted the bastard to live to see his underrated son a rich, landed earl. "I want the old goat to die of apoplexy."

Honor pushed aside the drapery covering her bedroom window and peered out into the rain. Sleep eluded her this long, dreary night as the events of the day ran through her mind like nightmares. She'd named her father as a spy to the premier lawman—retired or not—in Texas. What kind of a daughter was she?

What kind of a father was he?

Honor gave a bitter laugh. Richard Armstrong had earned whatever grief came his way.

Outside, lightning flashed and thunder boomed, violent like the storm in her soul. Naming her father a traitor had been an impulsive gambit, an idea that grew from the seed planted by the captain with his speech about patriotic pride. When the moment turned dire, she'd gone with her instincts and revealed the secret she'd harbored for years.

Richard Armstrong had spied against his country, and his own daughter had levied the charge.

Honor allowed the drapery to fall back into place and turned away from the window. Her gaze fell upon the necklace lying on her dressing table. Crossing the room, she lifted the locket and flipped it open, revealing the miniature of her mother. What would Mama say if she knew what her daughter had done?

Tears stung Honor's eyes as she traced the beloved face, hauntingly similar to her own, with her fingertip. Everything had been different then. They'd been happy. They'd been a family. Oh, Mama, how everything changed after you died.

When Penelope Armstrong miscarried and bled to death on the south Texas savannah, it seemed that whatever good existed in Richard died with her. He built a wall between himself and his daughter, shutting himself off from love and filling the emptiness with destruction. He turned away from ethics and principles and embraced greed, ambition, and corruption.

Honor didn't know exactly when he'd turned to spying. She lost close contact with her father three months after her mother's death. That's when he'd married her off to a very wealthy Franklin Tate in exchange for rich cotton land in east Texas and specific financial provisions in the old man's will. Franklin once told Honor he pictured her father as a buzzard circling the sky waiting for him to die. He said it strengthened his will to live.

Remembering her first husband, Honor smiled sadly. For the most part, Franklin had been kind to her, more grandfather than husband, and she'd genuinely grieved when he finally gave Armstrong his wish. The manner of his death haunted her to this day. Sometimes she wondered what her life would have been like had she not felt so responsible for Franklin's demise. Had she not been wallowing in guilt, she might have resisted her father's pressure to marry Philip.

But then again, probably not.

Honor snapped the locket closed and returned it to the bureau. Philip had been a young, handsome widower with two adorable little boys her empty arms ached to love. Childless after eight years of marriage, Honor had jumped at the opportunity to wed a man with a ready-made family who offered the promise of more babies to come. Her father had been rewarded with Philip's influential support in the infant government of the Republic of Texas, and Honor had been given Micah and Jason to bounce on her knees and Luella to laugh with. But Philip never gave her that which she desired most of all. He never gave her his love. Or any new babies.

When he died, she had gone a little crazy, which was not surprising under the circumstances. She'd been ripe for the plucking when her father had come to call with Armand Duvall on his heels.

Shuddering, she crossed the room and crawled into her bed. She punched up her pillow, snuffed out the candle, and snuggled down into the sheets. Sleep remained elusive.

Her feelings toward her father were so complex. On one hand, what he'd done to her was no different from what fathers had been doing for ages. Arranged marriages were a way of life in many parts of the world. His own marriage to Honor's mother had been arranged to further Armstrong family interests. Why should he expect his daughter's to be any different?

"Because I have acceded to his wishes three times already," she muttered into the darkness. Three arranged marriages should have satisfied her obligation to her parent. He should have accepted her refusal to marry his precious Lord Kendall and looked to achieving his goals another way. He shouldn't have threatened her. He never, ever should have threatened her children.

That's when he'd crossed the line. That's when he'd proven himself a villain of the highest order.

Some would say, Luke Prescott included, that he'd done it the day he started spying against Texas. Personally, after today, Honor was grateful for the meeting she'd inadvertently witnessed in Austin between Richard and a representative from the British embassy a little over two years ago. She'd sought out her father to seek deliverance from the hell of her marriage to Armand and instead overheard a conversation destined to affect more than the politics of a nation.

It just might save her boys' lives.

Honor threw back the sheets and lay stiff as a corpse in her bed as she dealt with the reality of the moment. Her father had betrayed his country, and now, by telling Prescott, she had betrayed her father.

Nausea churned in her stomach. The Republic of Texas would hang a traitor. Could she live with that?

She sat up and sucked in a deep breath. She'd have to live with it. He'd brought it on himself with his wicked, evil acts. This wasn't her fault. She had tried her best to balance her own needs with the duty of a child to her father. She hadn't gone out of her way to bring trouble down upon his head. The planned move to Charleston proved it.

Honor exhaled with a sigh. Refusing to marry Marcus Black had been well within her rights. She'd fulfilled a daughter's obligations to her father long ago. She deserved to live her own life her own way, and that meant never again marrying without love.

"I won't feel guilty," she whispered. "I won't!" Richard Armstrong had forfeited any right to her protection when he moved against her sons. Her first duty was to Micah and Jason. She would defend those boys at all costs.

Slowly, Honor melted back against her bed. She rolled to her side, tucked her knees to her chest, and pulled the covers up to her chin. Luke Prescott had asked for proof of her father's treachery and all she'd had to give him had been her word. When that hadn't been enough, she'd promised to provide something more. Just what that proof would be, she had no idea. But she'd find it. She had to find it. "I'll do anything to protect my babies."

How big a liar was she?

Luke asked himself the question as he stood at the French doors in Lost Pines's master suite gazing out into the rain. The afternoon thunderstorm had been followed by a late-night fury that lit up the sky, shook the heavens, and dragged him from the luxurious comfort of the late Armand Duvall's bed.

Not that he'd been asleep before the storm broke. He'd lain awake for hours attempting to decide just how to deal with the Widow Duvall and her claims. He'd yet to arrive at an answer.

After dragging him back into the library, the woman had told a wild tale of a clandestine meeting between her father and his British spymaster and the overheard conversation that indicated a relationship between the two men that went back for years. Luke had listened in amazement, the obvious desperation in the widow's tone lending credence to her claims. By the time she'd finished speaking he'd been certain of only one thing. Whether the story was true or not, Honor Duvall honestly believed it was.

Luke realized right away that her allegation against her father couldn't be ignored. The charge, valid or not, could prove harmful to Luke's beloved country. He shuddered to think of the potential damage to the Republic should the people of Texas elect a British spy to the country's highest office. On the question of annexation alone, the ramifications were enormous. The last thing England wanted was for Texas to join the United States.

While the British didn't wish to add Texas to their empire, they did want to prevent America's westward expansion. They hoped to reap commercial advantages from Texas trade and to tamper with the American tariff system.

But what if Honor Duvall's allegation of espionage was false? What if Richard Armstrong was innocent? He was a strong supporter of annexation, which Luke believed was essential for Texas to survive and prosper. If the widow took her father out of the race by making her accusation public, and it resulted in an anti-annexation candidate's election to the presidency, then the threat to the Republic was the widow who nursed a vendetta and was capable of altering the politics of a nation.

It was a hell of a conundrum, one he could not, in good conscience, ignore. Thinking it best to stay close to the widow until he'd decided how to deal with the problem she presented, he agreed to stay the night at Lost Pines.

The question remained. How big a liar was she?

Sighing heavily, he turned from the window and returned to his bed. Shucking off his pants, he climbed between the sheets, punched the pillow, and stretched out, determined to finally find sleep.

Visions of the widow lying naked, here in this very bed, interfered. His loins tightened, hardened, and he cursed the natural reaction even as he welcomed it. The bullet that had hit so close to his groin had caused him to question whether his manly capabilities had survived the shooting. The doctor had told him not to worry, but for months he'd gone without knowing for certain.

Honor Duvall had certainly answered the question. Several times over. Of course, he still needed to put himself through his paces, so to speak. Somehow, he didn't think the widow would want to help him solve his problem.

And what about her problem? Was her family truly in danger? He couldn't leave the question alone. He heard the clock strike three, then four. His mind drifted on a fog of confusion and debate.

It was sometime after that, in those dismal hours before dawn when dreams of past happiness so often wrenched him from sleep, that the light of revelation burst in his brain.

Luke sat up straight in bed. His heart pounded. Why hadn't he seen it before? Honor Duvall had given him a gift. The greatest gift he could imagine.

His mouth went dry and his breathing quickened. This was it! This was an opportunity to do something meaningful for Texas. Uncovering the truth might well be the greatest service Luke could ever perform for his country. But would it be enough to finally atone for his failure seven years ago?

Possibly. If anything could ever be enough, this might be it.

Luke lay back upon his pillow and marveled at the ways of chance. He had found his opportunity in a most unlikely place—Lost Pines—and with a most unlikely person—the beautiful, fascinating, notorious Honor Duvall.

Never would he have guessed that the widow could be his redemption.

5

Rafe Malone's ramshackle cabin sat nestled against a hill. Towering burr oaks and live oaks shaded the roof, while a lightning-split cedar pointed the way toward a front door hanging crookedly from a single hinge. Rough logs of loblolly pine formed the walls and the wide, deep chimney was fashioned of sticks and clay. With clarified rawhide instead of glass covering the lone window, the structure was dilapidated and dingy, the quintessential bachelor's abode. It offered basic shelter and little else. A particularly cold winter made it easy for Luke to persuade Rafe to begin construction on the new place that lay just beyond the hill.

Luke whistled beneath his breath as he drove the wagon up the rutted lane and waited expectantly for one of the women to comment on the cabin's run-down state. Seated beside him, Luella took a final drag

3

on her pipe, then set it aside. "Pretty spot y'all have here."

A wry grin touched Luke's mouth. He should have guessed Luella Best wouldn't do the expected. She and her daughter-in-law were two of a kind.

From the bed of the buckboard where she sat with the boys, Honor Duvall motioned toward the cabin. "Look at the yellow roses, Luella. I haven't seen such glorious bushes in all of Texas. Aren't they beautiful?"

"Gentleman Rafe Malone grows roses?" Jason's tone swelled with disgust. "An outlaw fussing with flowers? Who'd a thunk it? Of all the sissified things to do."

Ignoring his younger brother, Micah thumbed his hat back off his brow. "Is this your real home, Cap'n Prescott?"

His real home. Luke flinched at the memory that ambushed his brain. A small log house with blue gingham curtains on the window. The colorful wedding-ring quilt on the bed. The scent of cinnamon from a hot apple pie fresh from the oven. The laughter of children. Oh, God, the laughter of children.

Luke cleared his throat before answering. "More or less. Mr. Malone was kind enough to offer me a place to bed down while my bullet wounds healed." With his gaze resting on the roses, he added, "And Jason, he's a *former* outlaw who retired from his profession with a full pardon from the president. The flowers are Rafe's handiwork. I'd advise you to take care when bandying about the term sissy."

The boy gazed toward the cabin, his eyes growing wide. "Would he shoot me?"

Luke rubbed his jaw and pretended to ponder the point. "I doubt it. More likely he'd hand you a pair of shears and tell you to get to pruning."

"Not this time of year, Captain Prescott." Amusement colored Honor Duvall's tone. "Roses are pruned in January."

It was the first time all morning she'd spoken to him directly. Luke glanced over his shoulder. Today's yellow dress was floral-printed cotton, buttercups on a deeper field of gold. What was the reason for the choice of a solitary color in her fashions? It was just one of a profusion of questions he entertained where Honor Duvall was concerned.

"That's right," Jason observed. "I remember 'cause it was January when you sliced open your pinkie finger with the shears." To Luke, he said, "Honor is smart enough, but at times she's clumsy enough to fall off a stick horse."

Clumsy? Luke thought about it as he pulled the wagon to a halt in front of the cabin. He wasn't sure he bought that one. He had trouble picturing such a smooth liar as a bumbler.

That the woman was a liar was an established fact. The rigged raffle proved it. But the charge against her father, well, he'd get to the bottom of that, one way or another. It was why he was here, sitting in front of Rafe Malone's old cabin with a wagon full of women and boys and a shopping list for hard-to-come-by weapons in his pocket.

Luke secured the reins, more than ready to stretch his legs after the forty-five-minute ride from Lost Pines. Because Rafe's habits leaned to late nights and late risings, he expected to find him still asleep. He instructed his companions to wait in the wagon until he'd made certain Malone was decent. His first clue that was not to be the case came with Honor Duvall's softly whispered, "Oh my."

Luke followed the path of her gaze to a clear-water

creek some twenty yards away. What was it about the widow and naked men?

Rafe sat on a stump beside the water wearing nothing more than a towel across his lap. Water dripped from his slicked-back hair and a bar of soap lay beside him on the ground. He sat slumped over, elbows resting on his knees, a long-necked bottle filled with caramel-colored liquid dangling from his hands.

Luella leaned forward and peered toward the trees. "I knew I should have brought my spectacles along."

Honor's voice had a bite to it as she declared, "Captain Prescott, I won't have my sons subjected to a drunkard's idiocy."

"Malone doesn't drink," Luke said without hesitation. "It's cider." Swinging carelessly from the wagon, he bit back a curse as his leg jolted against the ground. He limped toward the creek, praying he'd not inadvertently lied. Liquor did nasty things to Rafe, bringing out the meanness that had fueled his life on the wrong side of the law. But he'd given up spirits when he'd given up thieving, and Luke had known him to backslide only once—the day Elizabeth Perkins married Joseph Worrell.

A twig snapped beneath Luke's boot and Rafe looked up at the sound. Pain radiated from his deep green eyes. "Three last names," he said. "Can you imagine that? Elizabeth had her baby. A boy. She gave him three last names. Harrington Perkins Worrell. What's she thinking, her and that lawyer of hers are too important to give the kid a real name?" He paused and took a long swig of his drink. "Pretentious. Damned pretentious, I'm telling you."

Luke reached out and snagged the bottle. Lifting it to his nose, he sniffed the contents and was relieved to find his suspicions correct. Cider. With Elizabeth

Worrell a new mother, it could just as easily have been whiskey.

He didn't know what to say to the brokenhearted Rafe. Finally, awkwardly, he filled the silence. "Maybe it's a family name."

Rafe turned his head and spat at the ground. "Her daddy's name is Sam. What, that ain't good enough? It was good enough for our president, by God. Sam Houston. There's a good man's name. Strong. Powerful. Hell, if I ever have a boy, I think that's what I'll name him. Sam Houston Malone. Sounds good, doesn't it?"

"You hate Sam Houston."

Rafe took aim on a stone near his foot and kicked it into the creek. "That I do." His voice dropped to a near whisper, but Luke heard it. "Three last names and mine ain't one of 'em."

Luke took a swig of cider. "It's a hell of a deal, Rafe. I know this thing with Elizabeth has twisted your guts, but you've got to let it go. She's married, Rafe. She has a baby now. You gotta forget her."

"But I love her!"

"Love gets a man nothing but trouble, Rafe. You know that."

"I don't know that," Rafe said, spearing him with an angry look. "You talk about love like it's a disease, but it's not. Even with the way things turned out, I wouldn't give up the months I spent loving Elizabeth for all the gold in Jim Bowie's lost mine. I know you suffer over losing Rachel, but you're a fool to blame what happened on love."

Luke's gut clenched. He very deliberately set the bottle on the ground. "Shut up, Malone. You really are in bad shape to bring that subject up."

"Maybe. Or maybe I'm spoiling for a fight. Of

course, it could be I'm feeling brave enough to say something I've wanted to say for years."

Luke growled a warning.

He never even paused. "Better than being a fool. Love is wonderful, grand, stupendous. It's what makes life worth living." Holding the towel around his waist, Rafe pushed to his feet, his gaze shifting to peer past Luke's shoulder. Dropping his voice, he added, "And maybe it's time I gave it another shot."

He unleashed the reckless, roguish smile that had attracted women all over Texas and called, "Good morning, Mrs. Duvall. Welcome to my home."

"Thank you."

Luke's stomach sank like a stone. He whipped his head around. Honor Duvall stood no more than twenty paces away and damned if the woman wasn't staring at Rafe's bare chest.

With as much swagger as a man dressed in only a towel could manage, Rafe approached the widow. "We haven't officially been introduced. I'm Raphael Malone, Mrs. Duvall. Please, call me Rafe. All my friends do. I'm hoping we can be friends ourselves."

Honor's smile was shy, but the look in her eyes was too damned bold in Luke's opinion. "Only if you'll return the favor by calling me Honor," she replied.

Luke scowled. She hadn't given *him* leave to use her first name. Clearing his throat, he stepped up beside her. He knew Rafe Malone like a brother, and he had seen the man in action more times than he could count. Rafe had a self-destructive streak as wide as the El Camino Real, and as snake-bit as he was feeling today because Elizabeth Perkins Worrell had given her husband a son, he was liable to cozy up to the widow and do something stupid.

Like talk Honor into having *his* baby.

Luke decided to nip any potential trouble in the bud. He laid a proprietary hand on the widow's shoulder and said, "Remember that job I told you about, Malone? Honor convinced me to take it. We've come by to pick up my things."

She stood stiffly silent while, for a long minute, Rafe remained quiet. Luke waited, softly stroking his thumb across the woven texture of her dress as the sound of boyish bickering drifted from the wagon. Finally, Rafe raked him with a knowing gaze before looking back toward the widow, his manner a symphony of regret. "I see," he said with a sigh.

"I doubt it," Luke replied dryly.

Obviously aware of the undercurrents of the conversation, Honor bristled beneath Rafe's look and shrugged off Luke's touch. "You are mistaken in your assumptions, Mr. Malone. The truth is my family is not safe, and I have retained Captain Prescott's services in order to make it otherwise. We traveled with him today only because he insisted we not remain at Lost Pines unprotected."

Actually, Luke hadn't wanted to leave her alone because he didn't trust her. Until he proved her accusation one way or the other, he planned to stick to the widow like the yellow on her dresses.

Holding herself as regally as a queen, she turned her snapping brown eyes in his direction. "Luella and the boys would like to break out the fishing poles. Apparently you mentioned something about a likely spot?"

Rafe answered for Luke by hooking a thumb upstream. "Two hundred yards thataway. Best white bass hole in the county. Let me get into my britches—"

"Please," Luke drawled.

"—and I'll show you. We can—"

"You and I have a few things to discuss, Malone." Luke motioned him toward the cabin. "I'll show you the fishing spot, Honor. Rafe and I will join y'all after we've finished our business."

"Very well. I'll tell the others."

Both men watched her walk away. Rafe glanced at Luke and drawled, *Very* well. Her eyes are pure Kentucky whiskey. A man could get drunk just staring into them."

"Let it go, Malone. We have more important things to discuss." He was gratified to see the teasing glint in Rafe's eyes die.

"What's this about? Why isn't her family safe?"

"She says someone's been playing some nasty tricks on the boys. Listen, Rafe, I need a favor. I'm hoping you'll let me shop your old-age fund."

Rafe's sudden stillness betrayed his surprise. "You want guns?"

"I have a list. I need to string trip wire for a couple of priest guns, lay some man-traps. Defensive moves."

"I'm intrigued." Rafe gave the activity at the wagon a measured look. "You know, I expected to see you back here with Starlight, not the Black Widow and her kin. Something tells me you have a hell of a story to tell." When Luke remained silent, he added, "I reckon that'll have to be the currency in use here this morning. If I'm gonna let you raid my weapons stash, you're gonna have to satisfy my curiosity."

Luke laughed. "You always were a bartering man, weren't you, Malone?"

"No, I was a thief. Used to be, I took without giving in return." He moved toward the cabin. "Go on. Show your widow where to fish while I get dressed. You can fill me in on the details when we're picking out your pistols."

His widow. Now there was a statement that could

be taken a couple of different ways. Both of them made him grimace.

As Luke led Honor and the Bests toward the fishing hole, he realized the significance of something Malone had said. Picking out pistols meant showing Luke his stash.

As soon as the hooks were in the water, Luke hurried back to Rafe. "You're going to show me where you keep your stuff?" he asked as he entered the cabin.

Having donned pants and shirt, Rafe sat in a chair and pulled on his boots. "Reckon so."

"But I've been looking for that for years. Why now?"

"You're not a Texas Ranger now."

He wasn't a Ranger now, and damn Rafe for the reminder. "Why does that make a difference? The pardon we negotiated allowed you to keep everything you stole."

Wickedness gleamed in Rafe's eyes. "Yeah, but you never knew just what a cache I had. I didn't want to make things awkward for you." Luke snorted at that and Rafe gave a wide grin. Standing, he moved toward the cabin door. "C'mon, lawman. I've been waitin' to show you this for years."

He led Luke to a path leading from the cabin up the hill. Luke watched as his friend halted beside a clump of thorny blackberry vines and gingerly pushed them aside. "Well, I'll be damned," Luke drawled when Rafe's efforts revealed a round opening in the wall of rock. "Passed right by it every visit to the outhouse."

Rafe glanced at his friend, his eyes alight with humor. "Within pissin' distance."

A reluctant smile tugged at Luke's lips. "All those years I searched for your stash it was right beneath my nose. Literally. Shoot, Malone, I hate to admit it, but of all the desperadoes I chased you were definitely the best."

"Thank you," Rafe said, dipping his head in a bow. 'Of course, by saying that you compliment yourself, you realize. You were the only Texas Ranger who ever managed to catch me."

"Three times."

"Don't brag, Prescott, or I won't show you my old-age fund." He ducked inside the opening and disappeared.

"I'll be damned," Luke repeated, then followed behind him.

The cavern was the size of a small cabin, allowing Luke room to stand upright without fear of bumping his head. Sunlight beamed through a handful of small openings scattered above them, providing sufficient light to illuminate the cache of chests, boxes, and barrels stacked against the rock walls. The scent of black powder hung heavy on the air.

Luke eyed the stash and gave a low, slow whistle. "You were a thief right up to the end, Malone." Before him sat the proceeds of Rafe's five-year stint on the wild side of the law. The cash, weapons, and other valuables had been ceded to the bandit as part of a negotiated settlement with the Texas Rangers. Rafe's infiltration of a vicious band of killers had been Luke's idea, one that had allowed his friend to end his life of larceny without fear of legal retribution. By the time the renegades had been dealt with, everyone up to the president had agreed that Rafe had earned his clemency.

"Nobody guessed you had near this much stuff."

"I've gotten rid of quite a bit of it, actually."

Luke touched the butt of the gun he wore strapped to his thigh. The Colt Texas Paterson five-shot revolver decorated with gold inlays and engravings had been a gift of thanks from Rafe after Luke arranged his pardon. Luke never asked how his friend came to possess such valuable weapons, but the Texas navy would be a good guess. He honored their friendship by carrying the gun, and he'd used it in defense of his life more times than he could count.

His hand drifted toward his gun belt and he thumbed the mother-of-pearl-ornamented stock. "I tried like the devil to find this place."

"Oh, I knew. And I knew why you wanted to find it, too. You wanted to use it to blackmail me into going legal. In the end, you found another way to do it. You're a sneaky bastard, Prescott. And you have that look in your eye again. So, tell me. What scheme of yours has you stealing from my stolen goods?"

"I intend to pay for what I take." Removing a slip of paper from his vest pocket, Luke handed it to Rafe. "I need quite a bit. The only weapon they have on the place is an old squirrel rifle. Apparently when the hands deserted the widow they took her guns along with their own."

"Guns are second in value only to horses here in Texas. Easy to steal, too." The former outlaw was grinning as he stepped beneath a beam of sunlight and read the list out loud. "Four shotguns, two revolvers, two derringers, four bowie knives, a pair of knuckle-dusters, and ammunition for everything." He glanced up, his expression serious. "You planning on starting a war, Prescott?"

"No. But there's a chance I might need to prevent one." Luke took the weight off his leg by propping a hip on a crate. "What do you know about Congressman Richard P. Armstrong?"

Rafe's brows lifted. "The fancy talker from San Augustine?" At Luke's nod, he continued. "Not much, really, other than that he's declared with the majority in favor of annexation. I believe right now he does work for the secretary of state. Of course, that's liable to change as the election draws closer." He shrugged, adding, "That's about all I can tell you, Luke. Armstrong and I don't exactly run in the same circles, if you know what I mean. Why do you ask?"

"He's Honor Duvall's father."

Rafe whistled in surprise. "Well, don't that beat all. I had no idea. Of course, that's probably how he wants to keep it. A family connection to the notorious Black Widow Duvall can't be too good for getting votes." He flipped the latch on a trunk and opened the lid to reveal a stack of shotguns. Metal clinked against metal as he pulled four weapons from the box and offered them to Luke.

"Wait till you hear the rest of it, Malone," Luke said, accepting the guns. "Theirs is not a happy little family. The widow has accused her father of being a spy."

"What?" The trunk lid slipped from the former outlaw's hands and slammed shut with a bang.

"She claims he's been passing information to the British for years."

Rafe sat on an ammunition crate, an incredulous expression on his face. "I don't believe it!"

"I'm not certain I do, either, but the question needs to be settled one way or another." A ribbon of excitement curled inside Luke's blood as he recalled the Widow Duvall's accusations. "Honor claims to have overheard a meeting between her father and an Englishman in which strategies for the defeat of annexation were discussed."

"Wait a minute. That makes no sense. England is violently opposed to Texas becoming part of the United States. Armstrong is *for* annexation."

"Is he? Or has he taken the position in order to place himself at the point where he can glean the most useful information for the Brits?"

Rafe rubbed his jaw with the palm of his hand. "Could she be telling the truth?"

"I have to find out."

Nodding, Rafe said, "That's why you're taking the job she offered." Rafe snagged a set of knuckle-dusters from an open box at his feet and tossed them to Luke. "She's hiring you to protect her family. From who, the British?"

"Nope," Luke replied, tucking the knuckle-dusters inside his pocket. "Her father. She claims he's threatening her sons in order to coerce her into doing something she refuses to do. According to her, such threats are an old trick of his. And get this. She's not hiring me solely for protection. She wants me to teach them how to protect themselves. It seems to be an important issue with the woman."

Honor had been rabid about it, in fact. As she'd told her tale she'd worn out his ears talking about how she refused to allow a man to have power over her life ever again. "If I need someone shot, I'll shoot him," she'd said, her voice trembling with the force of her emotion. "If I want to leave a bed or a house or Texas itself, I'll darn sure do it and no one will stop me. And I will never, ever, as long as I have breath in my body, get married because someone else wants me to do so."

Rafe looked up from his perusal of Luke's list and asked, "So what does her father want her to do? A little spying of her own, perhaps?"

Luke shook his head. "Armstrong wants her to remarry. She's trying to escape her father by running away to South Carolina. But one thing that makes me doubt her story is that she hasn't picked up and left already. If her children were really in danger, why would she hang around?"

"No money?" Rafe gestured at a stack of ammunition boxes, silently instructing Luke to take his pick.

"That's what her boys say, but you should see Lost Pines. Between the house, land, and her horses, her wealth puts this little treasure trove of yours to shame. I need to pin her down about a passing comment she made that her father controls her money. If it's true, she could be short of cash. We know the pinery shut down operations after Duvall's death. She has no ongoing source of income from what I can tell on first glance."

Luke checked inside a box labeled Percussion Caps to verify its contents. "Honor Duvall is a real curiosity. Every answer I get from her gives rise to three more questions." As he thought about it, his mouth curled in a slow grin. "And I think I'm going to have a hell of a time uncovering all the answers."

Rafe snorted. "I knew it. You want her. You want under the Black Widow's yellow skirts."

Luke didn't meet his friend's eyes. "I don't trust her. It could all be a pack of lies. It's not real smart to bed a woman who might stick a knife in your back."

"Let me get this straight," Rafe said with an incredulous laugh. He hefted a Texas Paterson in the palm of his hand. "You don't trust Honor Duvall well enough to bed her, but you're willing to put a five-shot revolver in her hands?"

Luke accepted the gun from his friend. "What if she is telling the truth? If the residents of Lost Pines are in danger, they need to have decent weapons and the knowledge of how to use them. According to the widow, not a one of them can shoot worth a damn."

"So you're gonna teach the Widow Duvall how to shoot?"

"Yep."

"Umm." In the dim light inside the cavern, Rafe pretended to study his fingernails as he spoke in a nonchalant voice. "Teaching a lady to shoot is close work. You gotta put your arms around her. Bend real close to her face. Bet she'll be all warm and sweet smelling as you help her take aim." He cleared his throat. "Come to think of it, I'm not doing much these days. Why don't I help?"

"I should have let you hang, Malone."

Rafe laughed and scooped a sheathed bowie knife from inside a leather trunk. "Living with the Widow Duvall. Tough work if you can get it."

Crack. Honor's shoulder took the recoil as the shotgun exploded. She kept her gaze locked on her target as smoke rose from the gun's barrel and the acrid scent of gunpowder permeated the air.

Nothing. Another miss. With a scatter-gun. Lord love a duck.

Micah's voice rang out. "Hey, look at that! You got a bird's nest, Honor."

"She was shooting at a bottle on the fence post," Luke said, in a long-suffering voice. The amber glass bottle sat untouched way to the right and much lower than the tree branch where the bird's nest had rested.

"Maybe you should set a bigger target, Captain Prescott," Jason said, snickering.

"Like the broad side of the First Baptist Church," his brother added.

The church was the largest building in Bastrop County. Honor childishly stuck her tongue out at her son as she lowered the gun and rubbed her aching shoulder. The boys giggled at her response, she bit back a sigh. They were right. She had to be the worst shot this side of the Gulf of Mexico.

Luella peered at her over her spectacles and spoke to Captain Prescott. "I hope you're not planning to teach her to shoot a revolver, Luke. We'll be here till Christmas."

She had a family full of jokers. Honor lifted her chin. "I just need a little practice. The captain has spent the majority of his time instructing the boys, and Luella, you're one to talk. You're not doing that much better than I am. I'm beginning to suspect your success in putting down poor Starlight was a fluke."

Luella tapped her lips with a finger. "You know, dear, you may be right." Turning her head, she smiled guilelessly at the Ranger. "I believe we should go over it once more, Luke. Please, show me how to aim one more time?"

Honor almost groaned aloud. The woman was at it again. If a sixty-seven-year-old woman could be termed a hussy, then Luella Best was it. All morning long she'd played the bold and brazen flirt. Honor halfway wondered whether nature or the excessive batting of Luella Best's eyelashes created the breeze swirling about her skirts.

All that *oohing* and *cooing* made Honor sick to her stomach. She loved Luella fiercely, and in many ways they were a lot alike. Not, however, when it came to men.

Captain Prescott didn't help matters. His wicked grin and playful banter encouraged Luella. It was shameful. The scoundrel was at least thirty years younger than her mother-in-law.

As Prescott wrapped his arms around Luella to demonstrate, again, the proper way to aim her weapon, Honor turned away and prepared to reload her shotgun. Luella's giggles made her roll her eyes. It was obviously time to invite a gentleman to Sunday dinner. If she must flirt, let her do it with men her own age.

Come on, now, Honor, be honest. You'd giggle too if Luke Prescott held you in his arms. Why, you'd melt like butter on hot cornbread if he turned that wicked smile on you. And if he kissed you—

Honor dropped the measuring horn. Good heavens, what was the matter with her! Where had such thoughts come from? She refused to think about Luke Prescott that way.

You are thinking about Luke Prescott that way.

Oh no, she silently moaned. Maybe she was more like Luella than she liked to believe.

Mentally distracted, Honor paid scant attention to her actions as she attempted to reload her shotgun. With the gun pointed heavenward, she prepared to dump her charge down the barrel directly from the powder horn.

"Good Lord, woman!" Luke Prescott exclaimed. Quick as a minnow, he snatched the gun from Honor's hand just when the first grains of black powder spilled from the horn. "Are you crazy or just stupid? This gun is still hot. The flash will burn up the barrel into the powder horn. Do you want to blow off your hand? Never, ever, *ever* pour a charge directly from the powder horn to the barrel. Use the measuring horn. That's why you have one."

Honor knew that. An embarrassed blush heated her cheeks. She hated to be called stupid, especially when she deserved it.

"Did I not go over every safety caution, one by one, before I put the blasted gun in your hands?" Luke asked, thunderclouds in his eyes. "Did I not make a specific point of warning you against that?"

"Yes," Honor said softly. She wanted to disappear, to dissolve in a puff of smoke and blow away.

He loomed over her. "What were you thinking, girl?"

Girl? That put the starch right back in her backbone. She was no girl, but a woman. She'd been thinking like a woman and that's what had gotten her into trouble. "I think I've had enough practice for today."

Shaking his head, Luke propped the shotgun against a tree. Frustration added a bite to his words. "Well, it's a good thing that I'm making that call and not you. Your sons are right. You couldn't hit the broad side of that church if you were inside the building. But I know what you're doing wrong, and we're going to stay here until we fix it."

He motioned toward Luella and the boys. "Y'all check out just fine. Jason, that gun's about as big as you are, but after seeing you handle it today, I'm awful glad you didn't decide to take a shot at me in the barn the other day. And Micah, you did especially well shooting from the hip. What you need to do now is practice on your reloading speed."

Luella gave Honor a knowing wink, then beamed a smile at Prescott. "And what about me, Luke? Did I do something especially well?"

The steam drained from the Ranger's expression. He gave a soft laugh and slowly shook his head. "Luella, I think you know exactly what you do especially well."

"Ah, Captain, you should have known me forty years ago."

Honor shut her eyes. She couldn't take any more. She didn't want to watch Luella make eyes at men, and she didn't want to catch herself doing the same shameful thing. So what if she found Luke Prescott . . . appealing. Hadn't fourteen years of marriage and three husbands taught her that men brought a woman nothing but trouble? She had no business thinking about Luke Prescott's arms or his smile or remembering the way the bath water had slicked down the hair on his chest.

But she did think about them, and it sharpened her voice as she said, "What is it I'm doing wrong?"

He slanted her a glance. "You flinch."

"Flinch?"

"Yep. You shut your eyes and jump as you pull the trigger. Yanks your aim every single time."

"I don't shut my eyes."

"Yep, you do. You shut your eyes and flinch. You shot a bird's nest, Honor. Twenty feet above your target. What I aim to do is to teach you not to flinch."

"Now, that will be a change for our Honor," Luella observed. "Men have been teaching her *to* flinch for years."

"Luella!" Again, the rosy heat of embarrassment crept over Honor's body.

Luke's narrowed eyes studied her, and Honor ducked her head, hiding her face beneath the broad brim of her sunbonnet. The Ranger had learned enough of her secrets, her shame. He did not need to know any more.

Luella handed her gun to Luke Prescott. "If you don't need us anymore, Luke, I'll take my grandsons back to the house. This morning's instruction has reminded me we've neglected their academic lessons of late."

"Ah, Nana."

"Hush now. Jason, I left my cane propped against that tree. Fetch it for me, would you?"

Honor noted the white lines of pain bracketing the older woman's mouth, and concern washed through her. Luella had been on her feet too long. "Let me run up and get the wagon. You can ride back to the house. Or better yet," she glared a demand at Prescott, "the captain can carry you up."

"It would be my pleasure," Luke said, stepping forward.

"Of course it would." Luella lifted her chin. "But I don't require your assistance, Luke dear. No matter what my daughter-in-law thinks, I am no invalid and I'll not be treated as such. If you want me in your arms, you'll need a better approach." With a flick of her wrist, she dismissed Prescott and Honor. A quirk of her fingers beckoned the boys and they shuffled sheepishly to her side.

"Luella—" the Ranger began.

Honor stopped him with a quick shake of her head before turning to her mother-in-law with a teasing grin. "You're not fooling me one bit, Luella Best. We're due a delivery from the mercantile today, and Mr. Wilson always sends two men to unload the supplies. The odds are more to your liking up at the house, aren't they? Two men as opposed to one?"

A distinct twinkle lit the older woman's pale blue eyes. "Perhaps it is a case of odds, I'll grant you that. But not the ones you think." In a voice as dry as west Texas in July, she added, "I've watched you with the shotgun this morning, dear. I figure my odds of surviving to the afternoon are vastly improved if I absent myself from the range of your gun."

She winked at Captain Prescott. "The Bravest Man in Texas. See why I wanted you for the job?" With that, she offered Micah her arm and started stiffly toward the house, leaving silence in her wake.

Luke began to prowl, reminding Honor of the mountain lion that had preyed upon her stock last winter. "I wish she wouldn't call me that," he muttered.

"And I wish you wouldn't use my given name."

"I didn't."

"Did too. A few minutes ago you called me Honor and I never gave you leave."

He stopped midprowl and cracked a laugh. "My apologies. But considering how we're all but betrothed, don't you think it's rather strange for me to call you Mrs. Duvall?"

"You're not very funny, Captain."

"You're right. Marriage is never a laughing matter. I know that little detail of your plan got lost in all the talk of treason the other day, but—"

"Wait a minute." Honor folded her arms. "It's not my plan."

"Luella's, then. You know all this nonsense this morning was for you, don't you? She was looking to get a rise out of you. Then when that didn't work, she plotted to give us time alone together. I think you've learned your scheming skills at the feet of a master."

Honor could argue with little of what he said. Still, loyalty to Luella made her say, "She *was* feeling poorly."

"I realize that."

Honor massaged her temples with her fingertips. "You must understand about my mother-in-law. For all her peculiarities, she has a heart as big as Texas. The other day you heard Luella say she believes marriage is my best protection from my father. Well, she believes that to the core of her being. She has paraded men through Lost Pines for months, hoping I might change my mind about remarrying. It's obvious she considers you the next man in line."

"Well, she is bound for disappointment in that case."

"You'll get no argument from me, Captain Prescott," she quickly agreed. His brows rose and he jerked his head backward. Had her swift agreement stung his pride a bit?

She smiled at the thought, then explained. "I'm free for the first time in almost fifteen years and I intend to stay that way. All I want from you is to watch over us while I gather the means to move my family to South Carolina. You have my word you'll see no marriage schemes from me." After a moment's hesitation, she added truthfully, "You should know, however, that I can make no promises for Luella."

He flashed her a rueful grin and Honor felt it clear to her toes. "All right. On this matter, I'll accept your word. Now, what about your father?"

She frowned, annoyed at his conditional response. Neither did she follow his train of thought. "I beg your pardon?"

He fished in his pocket and tugged out the ever-present bag of lemon drops. She accepted the candy he offered, its tartness somehow appropriate for the moment.

"You said your father wants you to remarry." He rolled his sweet around his mouth, measuring her with his look. "I have to ask myself whether this charge of treason you've made against him isn't simply an effort to thwart a parent's efforts to see his daughter secure in a good marriage."

Bitterness churned in her stomach. She gave him a long look. "I could tell you about the other *good marriages* my father has arranged for me, but I won't. I promised you proof, Luke Prescott. You'll have it."

"When?"

Honor schooled her expression into a smile and lied, "Soon."

In truth, she had no good idea of how to prove her father's treason. In the past couple of days she'd given the matter a great deal of thought, and every possibility she'd considered had one unthinkable drawback. Each involved inviting her father to Lost Pines.

She really, really, really didn't want to do that.

It was time to change the subject. Pasting on a bright smile, Honor said, "So, Captain, are you ready to continue our lesson? I'm at your service."

Luke Prescott grimaced. "There's that word again."

6

Service. Hell. All morning long, Luke had tried his very best to keep his thoughts on the business at hand and off of Honor Duvall. The task proved monumental. She drew him as a child was drawn to a firefly on a warm summer night.

Her physical beauty was classic, golden and ethereal. Her inner appeal was just the opposite. Spirited and spicy. Bold. Earthy. Her character breathed life into the goddess, and the combination created a woman few men could, or wanted to, resist.

Luke both wanted and resisted. Now was not the time for the distractions of sex, no matter what his body suggested. Today he planned to teach Honor Duvall to keep her eyes open and her aim steady when she pulled the trigger. Period.

Besides, Rafe had all but dared him to do otherwise

and Luke had never backed down from a challenge. At least not in the past seven years.

"All right, Honor. Let's get down to work."

Luke opened the satchel he'd filled with weapons at Rafe's. Removing a revolver and loading supplies, he motioned for Honor to watch. "Do you know how to load a Paterson?"

She shook her head. "No, *Luke,* I don't."

He smirked at her snippy tone and handed her the gun. Removing his own Paterson from its holster, he said, "I figured as much, so I emptied mine earlier. I want you to copy what I do, all right? Exactly. No pouring from the powder horn this time."

"I learned the first time you yelled at me. I'm not slow, Captain."

"Never thought you were, ma'am, and I'm mighty glad of that. There's a lot to be said for a fast woman."

Her aim with a gun might be poor, but her lethal glare was right on target. Luke's lips twitched with a grin as he prepared to load the cylinder. "Place an equal amount of black powder into each chamber of the cylinder."

Honor mimicked his motions, pouring powder into each of the five holes. Luke nodded his approval. "Now, take a bullet from the pouch and place it on the mouth of one chamber. Once that's done, you rotate the cylinder until the ball is under the loading lever." He paused, holding his up for display. "There you go. You've got it. Now, ram it home."

At that, the gun slipped from her hand and tumbled to the ground, spilling the powder from the cylinder. Luke gave a long-suffering sigh as she quickly bent to pick it up. He didn't speak as she repeated her previous efforts, and this time when she rammed it, she managed to keep her hold on the revolver.

"Now, do it again for every chamber," he instructed. "Unless you're in a real hurry, put a little grease over each ball in the chamber to eliminate the danger that when one chamber fires, the other chambers fire too. It doesn't happen often, but it's a standard precaution."

Honor nodded and bent herself to the task. Luke readied his gun before she'd finished with her second chamber. Quelling the impatient desire to reach out and do the job for her, he returned his Paterson to its holster, then resolutely folded his arms and observed her actions.

The woman's head kept twitching. What was wrong now? Her head dipped and twisted and arched. Finally, he realized she was having trouble seeing past the drooping brim of her bonnet.

Women and hats. He would never understand why females took the side of fashion over form so very often. He reached for the ties on her sunbonnet and said, "Here. This is in your way."

His hand brushed silky hair and he knew a natural urge to bury his fingers in its thickness. Thank God a hairpin gouged him, poking some sense back into him. He jerked the bonnet off and started to back away, but before he completed a step, Honor dropped the gun a second time. He dove to catch it.

So did she. Their heads collided. "Good Lord, woman," he growled, lifting a hand to the fast-rising lump on his head. "What did you do, wash your hands in butter this morning?"

"Oh, give me the blasted gun." She swiped it from his hand and held it in a trembling grip. Reaching for the bullet pouch, she fished inside for one of the round lead balls. When she fumbled with the pouch and a hundred lead balls spilled into the thick green grass at their feet, Luke had had enough.

"Stop. Don't move another muscle." He commandeered the gun and with swift, efficient movements, completed the loading process by placing small brass percussion caps one at a time on the nipples at the back of the cylinder. Grasping her arm, he dragged her twenty paces closer to the target, then positioned her in front of him. "I reckon the only safe place out here is directly behind you."

Her chin went up. "That shows a blinding lack of sensitivity, Captain."

"Blind? Now there's an appropriate word for the moment. Grip the gun with both hands. The Paterson is designed so that when you cock it, the trigger drops. Try it." When she managed that much without mishap, he said, "All right, go ahead and shoot, Honor. You have five shots. See how well you can do."

She fired a scathing glare over her shoulder, then pulled the trigger.

The gun kicked, smoke rose from the barrel, and Luke drawled, "We're not duck hunting. Wrong time of year. Again."

Cautiously, he moved beside her to observe her as she shot. Damn, he thought as the gun exploded. He'd hoped the two-handed grip would solve this problem. "That was wide right and still above the trees. Shift your aim left and do it again. Keep your eyes open this time, Honor."

"I don't shut my eyes!" she exclaimed, turning her head to glower at him even as she pulled the trigger.

The bullet ricocheted off a nearby tree. "Honor! Now you're murderin' trees. I'm beginning to wonder if you aren't better off without lessons, lady. You're plenty dangerous the way you are."

The truth of his statement struck him as he stared into her whiskey eyes. The Widow Duvall was dangerous all right. She was trouble wrapped in an angel's package.

Framed by nature's myriad shades of green, she lowered her arm and held the Paterson pointed toward the ground. The glint of sunlight turned her hair the color of fire, and the vision of her lit a flame inside Luke.

So damned beautiful. She was a liar, a cheat, and God knows what else, but he wanted her. He wanted to pull all the pins from her hair and plunge his fingers into the silken mass. He wanted to bare her body to his eyes and touch and taste those bountiful, tantalizing breasts. He wanted to bury himself between her thighs and lose himself in the wild heat of a primal mating.

Luke's sex grew hot and heavy. Blood pounded in his veins. He imagined laying her on the blanket of grass and doing what his body urged him to do. He forced himself to look away.

Hell. If she knew what he was thinking she'd use those last two bullets on him. He'd give fifty-fifty odds that at this close a range she just might hit him.

And now, if he had any hopes of teaching her how to shoot—a skill everyone who lived on the frontier should possess—he had to touch her.

He sucked in a deep breath, then exhaled in a rush. "I need to show you what happens when you pull the trigger." He moved behind her, reached down and wrapped his hands around hers, then lifted their arms into position. "Grip it firmly. Both hands, Honor. That's it. Now, line up your target. I'm just going to steady your aim."

Her head came to just below his chin. Luke inhaled her scent. Ginger this time, and vanilla. She'd baked molasses cookies this morning before their lesson. "Squeeze the trigger, Honor," he said in a rough voice.

She seemed to weave on her feet. "Is this necessary?"

"Just squeeze the trigger."

Her finger moved and as the gun fired, Luke's hold prevented her hand from jerking. This time, the bottle shattered.

"Feel the difference?" he asked as the sound of the shot echoed across the pasture.

She held herself stiff as a fence post and she didn't immediately reply. Luke suddenly realized that with her backside pressed up against him she was bound to have noticed his arousal. Dropping his arms and taking a backward step, he hurried to make his meaning clear. "I didn't let your hand move. I kept my eyes open. The gun stayed steady."

"My eyes stayed open."

"I doubt it." He appropriated the gun from her hands and tucked it into his waistband. At her curious look, he explained, "Just to be on the safe side while I set up another target." He snagged a cracked earthenware jug allotted for the purpose and started across the pasture, glad for the chance to put some space between them.

He needed the cooling-down time. "You are a sad case, Prescott," he grumbled beneath his breath.

Raffling off a dead horse had proved Honor Duvall a liar and came close to making her a thief. And lest he forget, rumors of murder followed her name. Murder. Blessed hell. Was there any truth to the gossip?

Based on his short acquaintance with the widow, Luke had a hard time giving credit to the charge. He couldn't picture her as a killer. She'd told the truth when she said she couldn't shoot. Exactly how had her husbands died? If Honor had shot them, it damn sure wasn't murder. Accidental death. Rotten bad luck for the fellow in range of her gun.

Luke bent over to balance the jug on the log where the bottle had previously stood. Straightening, he gazed back at the widow. She looked hotter than a pot of boiling collards. Pretty as all get-out, but angry. He'd do some checking and find out what he could about the deceased spouses. He'd question Luella first, perhaps, then check with the sheriff.

Of course, he couldn't ignore the possibility that Honor had him fooled. She might be a damn good actress.

He breathed a sigh and started back toward her. Reaching her side, he pulled the revolver from his waistband and handed it, butt first, to Honor. "One shot left. Let's go through it again. Remember how it felt, Honor. I won't hold you as tight this time. You need to do it yourself."

"Are you certain this is the best way to teach me to shoot, Captain?"

She looked as if he'd given her a spoonful of castor oil rather than a gun. Luke didn't look forward to the next few minutes any more than she apparently did. She went stiff again as he put his arms around her. "Not at all," he grimly replied. "But I'm afraid if I waited for you to figure it out yourself we'd be here until dark."

"You are such a wit, Captain." Sarcasm dripped from each word.

She cocked the gun and the trigger slipped into place. He firmed up his grip, saying, "Hold still, now. Concentrate, sweetheart."

She twitched worse than ever and the bullet kicked up dust a good twenty yards from the target. Grimacing, Luke shook his head in disgust.

"Well, that one was your fault," she said, glaring up at him.

"My fault?"

"Yes, your fault."

"Why?"

She opened her mouth, closed it, then repeated the action twice more before saying, "Because."

"Because?" Luke folded his arms.

Squaring her shoulders, she tossed her head. "Because you called me sweetheart."

"I did?"

"You did."

"Oh, well. Don't take it personal. Usually when I have my arms around a woman it's expected."

The look she sent him could have melted pig iron. Luke held out his hand, palm up. "Give me the gun and I'll reload for you. You can practice that later on." He had an idea in mind, an old Ranger method for curing the shuddering fits. He suspected Honor might have just the temperament needed for this training technique's success.

He'd tried being patient and as agreeable as he could manage, but that had gotten them nowhere. The time had come to shake the lady up. A little spit in her shine might be just the thing she needed to focus her concentration.

Using his body to shield his actions from the widow's sight, he loaded the gun. Sort of. "Follow me, Honor. I want to make this easier on you. Let's get you up close to your target, all right?" He stopped a mere fifteen feet from the jug and glanced over his shoulder. Honor hadn't moved from her spot. "Come on, gal. I thought you wanted to learn."

"I do. I just don't like looking the fool."

What she looked like was a man's favorite fantasy, Luke thought as she finally joined him. Disgusted with himself, he said harshly, "Quit flinching and keep your eyes open, and that'll solve your problem." He handed her the gun, then stepped aside. Bracing his legs wide apart, he folded his arms and demanded, "Two hands, now. Pay attention to what you're doing."

She set her teeth, took aim, cocked the revolver, and jerked her hand when she pulled the trigger.

"It's not a flinch," she declared hotly. "It's the kick of the gun that makes my arm move. Maybe I'm not strong enough to shoot a gun."

"Maybe you're too stubborn to admit what you're doing wrong and fix it. Again."

Crack. Another miss. She wouldn't look at him, but he could tell by her expression that anger and frustration had her in their grip. Good. "Again."

Her mouth flattened in a thin line and she inhaled a fortifying breath. As she took aim, Luke noted that her hands were as steady as he'd seen them all morning.

Honor's finger twitched on the trigger and slowly began to squeeze. *Click.* No explosion. Honor slowly opened her eyes. She held the Paterson pointed just above the treetops. "I flinched," she said softly, her expression bordering on forlorn.

"And closed your eyes."

Her voice trembled as if she'd taken a painful blow. "I swore I'd never flinch. It's a matter of personal pride for me, Captain."

Never flinch at what? Luke sensed he wouldn't like the answer. Shades of darkness hovered around her, and he found himself wanting to chase the shadows away. In this case, anger was his weapon. He knew just what to say to make her mad all over again. "You have to quit anticipating. Learn to concentrate. Try to overcome your handicap."

"My handicap? What handicap?"

Luke dredged up a superior smirk. "The fact that you're a woman, of course."

Honor froze. She bit off her words. "What does that have to do with it?"

"It has everything to do with it. Let's face it. Women are simply inferior to men. They're not as smart or as shrewd or as strong. They sure don't have the stomach men do for living out here on the frontier. You can't argue about that. You're the one who's all ready to run away back east. Now, aim the gun and shoot."

Sputtering, she began to pivot toward him.

"Not at me, dammit!"

Her smile was vapid but her eyes shot bullets. "Oh, I'm sorry. I'm so stupid, that's what I thought you meant."

Good. Anger is what she needs. "At the target, Honor. The jug. See if you can't come closer this time. At least in the same county."

She took aim, fired, and missed again.

Staring out at the gouge in the earth where the bullet hit, Luke said, "I don't know. It might be that you're not teachable."

Aim, squeeze, *click*.

Glare.

Luke reloaded the gun. "Again."

Aim, squeeze, *crack*. Miss.

"Dangerous day for birds to be flying."

Aim, squeeze, *click*. "Damn you, Luke Prescott!"

"Well now, Honor, I am appalled. What kind of language is that for a lady to use?"

"Go stand out in the pasture, Prescott. I'll hit my target." Aim, squeeze, *crack*.

Tufts of grass sprayed into the air some fifteen yards short of the target. She growled in exasperation.

Better, much better, Luke thought. He didn't want to say it, of course. The object here was to keep the widow riled to focus her concentration.

Aim, squeeze, *crack.*

Now, that one was pretty close. "I think this afternoon I might ride over to Rafe's and stock up on powder and bullets. Looks like we'll need twice as much as I'd figured."

She took a deep breath, gripped the gun in two steady hands, and aimed at the target. *Click.* This time the empty chamber didn't faze her in the least. Aim, squeeze, *crack.*

The earthenware jug shattered.

Honor whirled to face him, her expression radiant with victory. Her eyes sparkled. Her smile gleamed. And when she gave a triumphant laugh, Luke knew a stab of desire so sharp and sweet that he groaned with the force of it.

"I did it!" She threw her arms wide. "I did it, Luke!"

Luke wasn't so far gone with lust that he failed to recognize the hazard of the moment. Wearing a lopsided grin, he closed the distance between them and reached for the Paterson that dangled dangerously from her hand. "Of course, you did it," he rumbled, twisting the gun from her grip. He tucked it inside his waistband at his back, saying, "All you needed was to concentrate."

"You made me angry on purpose," she said, sudden certainty flaring in her eyes.

His gaze dropped to her mouth. "Yep."

She licked her lips. "You don't really think I'm stupid."

"Nope." Rosy and wet, her lips beckoned. All dressed in yellow, she glowed like the sun in the sky. Luke's resistance melted. He slipped his hands around her waist and dipped his head. In a silky-soft tone, he swore, "You're bright, so bright you blind me, Sunshine."

He touched his mouth to hers.

Honor Duvall was whiskey straight. Intoxicating heat. Delicious. Just a taste, he told himself as he moved his mouth against hers. Just a taste to quell the flames scorching his blood.

Honor placed her hands against his chest as if to push him away, but instead her fingers grasped his shirt and held him. Luke growled deep in his throat and yanked her tight against him. One hand slid up her body to plunge into the silken flame of her hair. The other stroked downward, caressing the curve of her hip.

She moaned faintly, and the needy sound raised a shudder across his skin. He slipped his tongue past her lips, stroking her sweet velvet softness. Honor responded in kind. Her tongue danced a sinuous ballet against his own. With every second that passed, his need spiraled. Again and again and again he plundered her mouth, tasting victory and vice, mystery and madness.

The flames burned even hotter.

His lips released hers as he trailed his mouth downward to the elegant length of her neck. He wanted her. Oh, how he wanted her. He wanted to bare her breasts to his questing kiss, to bury his need in the core of her womanhood. Here. Now. On a quilt of spring grass and wildflowers beneath the brilliant blue Texas sky.

He slid both hands down to cup her bottom. Lifting her, he flexed his hips, pressing and seeking and cursing the barrier of cloth between them.

"No. Oh, please, no!"

Lost in his masculine craving, Luke heard her voice from miles away.

"Let me go!"

She struggled in his arms and the words fell into

place. Immediately, he released her, setting her away from him with a frustrated thrust. She stared at him, hands steepled over her mouth, her hair in wanton disarray. Emotion swam across her dark whiskey eyes. Passion. Confusion. Fear.

Aw, hell. Breathing heavily, Luke lifted a hand to rake his fingers through his hair. "Honor, I uh, I'm sorry. I didn't intend—I only wanted—" He exhaled sharply. "Just a kiss. One little taste. I didn't mean to take it so far so fast."

Her body shuddered. Her eyes were round and fearful. "Stay away from me!"

Trying to catch his breath, Luke knew a twinge of annoyance. He hadn't done a damn thing to warrant shudders and fear. What did she think he was, some sort of monster?

Maybe. At his side, his fists clenched. And maybe she had the right idea. It took all his control not to cross the distance between them and finish what they'd started. What *they'd* started. Not just he. The merry widow had been right there with him during that kiss.

"Don't be giving me the evil eye, lady," he said gruffly. "I stopped, didn't I?"

She sucked in a breath and squared her shoulders, visibly summoning control. A veil descended over her eyes and Luke could no longer read her emotions. "Captain Prescott," she said, the faintest hint of a quaver in her voice. "I think it would be best if we pretended these last few moments didn't happen."

"Yeah, well, you're real good at pretending, aren't you, lottery lady. I wouldn't get your bloomers in a twist over this if I were you. It was just a kiss."

She wouldn't meet his eyes, staring instead at a spot over his shoulder. Her color, already high, flushed brighter as the silence between them lengthened. Suddenly, she said, "Shall I reload the Paterson?"

Luke snorted. "I reckon I've had all the fun I can stand for this morning. You head on back to the house. I'll gather up our things and follow along directly."

Her relief was palpable. With a nod, she turned and commenced a dignified retreat. Grudging admiration filled Luke as he watched her hurry toward the house, sunshine painting ribbons of red-gold fire in her hair.

Left alone, Luke began to gather the weapons and supplies. As he bent to retrieve the measuring horn Honor had left lying upon a rock, a strong sense of foreboding overcame him.

He straightened. His trained eyes searched his surroundings, but he knew the trouble brewed inside of him. One kiss. One little taste.

He had made a grievous mistake.

Standing alone beneath the brilliant blue sky, Luke recognized a simple truth.

One taste of Honor Duvall would never be enough.

A three-quarter moon rose in the eastern sky and bathed Lost Pines in silvery light. Honor sat at the worktable in the kitchen, absently cracking pecans. The others had long ago sought their beds, but she was edgy and restless, haunted by memories, recollections of days long past and of hours as recent as today.

Honor brought her hand to her mouth and two fingers absently traced lips still tender from the pleasure of Luke Prescott's kiss. When had a man last kissed her with such sweet passion? Had she ever been kissed in such a manner?

Not by Armand, certainly. In three years of marriage he'd never once tasted her mouth. Thank God. Their marriage bed had been bad enough the way it was. And Philip? Honor gently tugged a nut free from its shell. How many times had she dreamed that Philip would take her in his arms the way the Ranger had? Hundreds? Thousands?

But for all of her imaginings, she'd never suspected she could feel the sensations she'd felt when Luke Prescott touched her mouth with his.

Her body still hummed. An anxious yearning held her in its grasp. Questions filled her mind. Questions about the Ranger, about herself. About Armand, and Philip, and even Franklin Tate. Three husbands. Three marriage beds. Countless fast-handed suitors in between. She should be as knowledgeable and experienced as her reputation suggested.

Instead, with the press of his lips against hers, Luke Prescott had proved just how little she truly knew.

Maybe you should ask him to teach you.

Startled by the wayward thought, Honor pushed to her feet and walked to the kitchen door, pushing it open. She stared out into the moonlit darkness where a misty fog had begun to collect low to the ground. Silent and spooky, it was a good night for ghosts. If the spirits of the men she had married and buried walked those eerie fields of darkness, she should probably spend the night in the kitchen. No telling what terrors her husbands might play upon the woman responsible for their deaths.

A harsh laugh escaped her. They didn't need to catch her alone outside in a fog. They managed to haunt her quite sufficiently in her dreams.

"Enough of this foolishness," she scolded herself. Feeling sorry for oneself was useless and unbecoming. She turned away from the doorway and returned to the worktable where she stored the shelled nuts in a tin. She'd make a pie later in the week when she wasn't so fretful.

Her mood was all Luke Prescott's fault. The former Texas Ranger with his storm-cloud eyes and seducer's kiss made her think about things that couldn't be. Not now, when she was so close to escaping her father and the dangers he presented. Not ever. Because she could never be certain history wouldn't repeat itself.

And she absolutely, positively refused to kill again.

At that, Honor blew out the lamp and left the kitchen, hurrying down the foggy path toward the house. Once inside, she moved toward the staircase, managing to avoid most of the squeaky floorboards in her attempt to be quiet, but not all. As she passed her mother-in-law's doorway, Luella called out, "Come share a cup of tea with me, dear."

The woman had the hearing of an owl. Moments later, both women sat in front of the bedroom's fireplace, sipping tea generously laced with brandy.

"You were unusually quiet at dinner," Luella casually observed as she brought her cup to her mouth for another sip. "The cobbler was fine, you know. Different, certainly, but quite delicious once one's tongue adapted to the heat of it."

"I knocked over the cayenne when I was reaching for the cinnamon."

"We should move those spices to another shelf."

"At least when I'm cooking."

Cedar logs spat and crackled, filling the silence that fell between them. Honor pushed the rocker with the tips of her bare toes, debating the wisdom of asking Luella for her advice.

Luella made the choice for her. "So, what happened between you and Luke this morning? He was a bear with a thorn in his paw when he came back from the range."

Honor replied without answering. "He spent the afternoon riding the boundaries, familiarizing himself with the land. He's taking our safety quite seriously."

"Of course he is." Luella set down her cup. "You knew he would, surely? The man is, or was until recently, a Texas Ranger. You can tell just by looking at him he's a man to take care of his own, and that's what we became when we talked him into accepting your offer."

"That's what I'm afraid of," Honor grumbled.

Luella pursed her lips. Leaning forward, she sat like a puppy waiting for a bone. Honor sipped her tea. She didn't know how to explain what had happened out there in the pasture this morning. "Captain Prescott is different, Luella."

"Different from what, dear?"

"I don't know." She searched for words to express her feelings. "He paid more attention to my shooting than to my breasts."

Luella arched a brow, a slight hint of a smile playing about her lips. "He didn't want to get shot."

Honor stiffened with offense. "I wouldn't shoot a man for staring at my breasts."

"I never thought you would," Luella said, looking over the tops of her spectacles.

"Oh." Honor caught on to Luella's line of thinking. "But I don't think it's because he was afraid I'd shoot him, accidentally or not. He's just different, Luella."

"How so, dear?"

She searched for a way to put her feelings into words. "The men in my life have taught me that my looks are more curse than asset. None of them ever saw past my features to who I am inside. None of them even considered trying. I get the feeling Captain Prescott isn't like that."

Luella frowned. "Honor, if you think Luke hasn't noticed your beauty, then you are fooling yourself.

Why, some of the looks he sent you over dinner nearly lit the candle wicks."

"I know he's noticed." The memory of his kiss flashed in her mind as she sipped her tea. "It's just that he seems as interested in my *lack* of form when I try to fire a gun. That's nice, Luella. Very, very nice."

"I worry about you, Honor."

"I know you do."

"Pour me a little more tea, would you, dear?"

Honor did her mother-in-law's bidding, twice adding extra brandy when Luella complained of the weakness of the brew. They spoke of the older woman's joint troubles for a time until, totally without prior thought, Honor burst forth with the confession, "He kissed me."

A delighted smile spread across Luella's face. "And?"

Honor drank half a cup of tea before answering. "Oh, Luella, I'm afraid I liked it."

"That's wonderful!"

"That's terrible!"

"Oh, Honor, hit me again with the brandy. I'm afraid I'll need it to listen to this."

Honor gave her a disapproving look. "Please, Luella. This isn't a joking matter. I'm so confused."

"What are you confused about?"

"Me. He made me feel . . . fuzzy. Why? What with Franklin and Philip and the suitors unleashed on me over the years, I've been kissed by upwards of a dozen men. At times, I even encouraged some of those kisses. Not a one of them turned me to mush."

"And Captain Prescott did?"

She nodded. "I finally hit the target and I was so excited, so happy. I don't know exactly how it happened, but all of a sudden we were kissing." She paused, recalling the moment and the storm of sensation he'd stirred to life within her. "It was so wonderful. I've never felt anything like that before."

"It's zizzle," Luella sagely observed.

"Lust."

"No, nothing that simple. Lust is basic. It's butterknees and dizziness, heat and need. Zizzle is all that plus the magic, the sizzle with added zest. The something extra I could never put a name to, so I named it myself. It's what I had with Mr. Best, God rest his soul, and I never found it with another man. Zizzle is why I never remarried, Honor. I never found another man whose attentions gave me zizzle."

"You're talking about love?"

"No." Luella waved a hand. "I'm talking about zizzle. It's very rare. People can love one another, have a true, deep, abiding love, and not have zizzle. But when you have both—" She stopped and stared at the fire, her usual sharp-eyed gaze gone dreamy and soft. "When you have both, Honor dear, the world is heaven on earth."

They rocked in silence for a bit, both lost in thought. Then Luella said, "I admit I had my hopes where Luke was concerned, but this is more than I counted on. You cannot ignore it, Honor. Zizzle in a marriage is the greatest treasure you'll ever know. You must give this a chance."

"Marriage?" The teacup clattered in its saucer as Honor roughly set it down. She shoved to her feet. "Marriage has been my greatest nightmare. It has nothing to do with this! Good heavens, Luella, will you never give that nonsense up?"

"What did Duvall do to you? Can't you talk about it after all this time? Don't you think it would help to get it out?"

Honor shook her head violently. She couldn't explain what went on in Armand Duvall's bedroom, not to Luella. She'd feel responsible, and besides, it didn't matter anymore. She exhaled a shuddering breath. "I will not marry Luke Prescott or anybody else. I am leaving this godforsaken country and moving to Charleston. You cannot change my mind on this, Luella. Not you, not the boys, not my father or Luke Prescott or all the zizzle on the planet! I won't get married again. If nothing else, I won't be responsible for another man's death."

Luella's nose wrinkled and she spoke in a snippy tone of voice. "If that's the case then why did you hire the captain to teach you to shoot?"

"That's different and you know it." Honor paced the room. "Self-defense isn't murder. My marrying again would be precisely that. I'm hard on husbands, Luella. I've killed three of them."

"Don't be stupid, Honor. You are not cursed to kill your husbands. Don't forget, technically you killed only two of them."

"And one of those was your son." Tears spilled down Honor's cheeks at the memory of Philip Best gasping his last breath.

Luella shook her head. "That was an accident and as much Philip's fault as yours. How many times have we discussed this? You didn't know cooking the leaves along with the stalk made that plant poisonous. It's ludicrous for you to believe that just because your first three husbands met untimely deaths your fourth would face a similar fate. You are thinking with your heart, not your mind."

"Well, at least I'm thinking," Honor snapped back.

Hurt flashed in Luella's eyes and Honor immediately felt contrite. She sank onto her knees beside her mother-in-law's chair. "I'm sorry. I didn't mean that. I'm just so confused."

Luella patted her hair. "It's all right, child. Don't

fret about me. If you're thinking it, you can say it. I'm a tough old bird. We've always been able to talk to one another and I don't want that to change. You understand? You agree?"

Honor nodded.

"Good. Then hear me out."

Sighing, Honor shut her eyes as Luella forged ahead. "I know this fear you nurse about killing off your men is only part of the reason why you're so dead set against marriage. Freedom is all well and good, but it won't keep you warm at night. It won't give you babies."

Honor flinched inwardly at the blow. Luella knew her too well. "I have children."

"Yes, and I'll always love you for thinking that way. But Micah and Jason should have a sister. You should know the joy of having your own babies, Honor. Babies given you by a man you love."

It hurt too much to talk about this. "Luella, please."

"Don't interrupt, dear. Now, what you've told me tonight only reinforces my opinion that Luke Prescott is the perfect man for you. Despite your prejudices, I want you to give the idea some thought. Look at me, dear." Luella waited until Honor met her gaze. Her wise blue eyes staring deep into Honor's, she continued, "You are a courageous woman, Honor. Don't allow your fears to rule you. Don't be afraid to explore the feelings you have for Captain Prescott. Tell him the truth about the husbands if it makes you feel better. The Ranger is the Bravest Man in Texas, after all. I doubt if he'll be swayed by your arguments any more than I am."

Honor wanted to scream. "It was just a kiss, Luella. Even if I weren't opposed to marriage, what makes you think Captain Prescott would entertain the thought? He was as appalled by the idea as I."

"Yes, but that was before the zizzle. Don't underestimate its power. And if it were just a kiss, you wouldn't have come squeaking past my door so late tonight."

Unwilling to argue any further, Honor picked her teacup off the floor and rose to her feet. So what if she did enjoy being in Luke Prescott's arms? So what if she did long for babies? Maybe she didn't need to be married to have them. Luella was wrong, she wasn't ruled by fear. Not any longer. Not ever again. Maybe it was time to live up to her reputation.

"Perhaps you're right, Luella. Perhaps I should explore this zizzle phenomenon further." Setting her cup and saucer beside Luella's porcelain teapot on a tray, she added, "Marriage is not necessarily a requirement, now that I think about it."

Luella's head snapped up. "Honor Duvall, don't you get sassy on me now. A little exploration is all right. Just make sure you stop short of awarding him the treasure. A ring on the finger before a fling on the bed."

At the doorway, Honor paused. "I'll do what I can, Mother Best. But you, yourself, warned me not to underestimate the power of zizzle."

7

Afternoon sunlight beamed through the trees and dappled the bank of a shallow creek some three hundred yards upstream from its confluence with the Colorado River. Luke sat with his back propped against the rough-barked support of an elm tree, his legs stretched out and crossed at the ankles. He chewed the end of a straw as he cast his line into the rock-formed pool for another try at the fish growing fat from stealing his worms. "He's a slippery son-of-a-gun," Luke observed. "Almost hate to catch him."

Jason stood balanced on a pair of rounded gray rocks jutting out into reddish water. "Doubt that'll be the problem, Cap'n. Not the way our luck's been running." He reached for the stringer at his feet and pulled it from the water, his young muscles flexing from the weight of the day's lone prize.

Luke eyed the fish wriggling at the end of the chain

and saw dinner. Three pounds, tops, but a tasty three pounds. Catfish was his favorite.

The boy studied the fish, his expression perplexed. "Why do you think God made catfish so ugly? Do you think he was trying to do them a favor? Make 'em in such a way to turn a fellow off to eatin' 'em?"

"A man can't know what the Maker had in mind, squirt. But if that's the case, the crawdads you've corralled in that pail of yours must be one of His favorite creatures."

The boy's straw hat dipped as he nodded sagely. "Well, me and Him have something in common, then. Just wait till you taste the gumbo Luella will cook up with the crawdads I snagged. You'll think you died and went to heaven."

Luke wasn't about to naysay the boy. The truth was, he'd felt that way every night for the past two weeks when he shared a meal of Luella Best's making. The woman was the best pot wrangler he'd ever had the pleasure of knowing. When a man sat down at Lost Pines's table, he was in for a savory treat. Not only did his taste buds get to wallow in pleasure, but his eyes got to feast on Honor Duvall.

Luke's fishing pole bowed as something took his hook. "Got him," he said with satisfaction. Keeping his line taut, he climbed to his feet and prepared to land what felt like a good-sized fish, but it turned out to be driftwood.

"Good-sized snag you caught there, Cap'n," Jason said, his face wreathed with an ornery grin.

The look made Luke think of Honor. Of course, most everything these days made him think of Honor. Hell, if he stared long enough at that ugly old catfish, his muddled brain would probably find something beautiful about it to compare to the Widow Duvall.

Seemed like nothing but stump water filled his head whenever she was around.

And she'd been around a lot. It was as if she'd made up her mind to torment him. A flash of ankle here, a plunging neckline there. Witty conversation. Laughter that sent shivers up his skin. If she were someone other than Honor Duvall, he'd accuse her of flirting with him. And doing a right fine job at it.

He wanted her. Badly. He kept blaming his prolonged abstinence, but he knew it was more than that. He counted it a victory that he'd not laid a hand—or anything else—on her since that kiss two long weeks ago. It was best that way. Nothing had changed. Proving or disproving Richard Armstrong a traitor must take priority over everything else, including the itch he dreamed of scratching with the beautiful widow.

Luke had learned that lesson the hard way. Never again would he allow concern for a woman to interfere with his duty.

Luke worked off his sexual frustration with hard work. It was damn near impossible for one man to defend a spread the size of Lost Pines, so he'd concentrated his efforts on protecting the people who lived there. He'd laid down hard and fast rules for the widow and her family to follow. He'd set up a variety of man-traps in a number of appropriate locations. He rode Lost Pines's perimeter three times a day, searching for signs of trespassers. As long as the Bests and Honor Duvall followed his instructions, they should be safe enough from the malicious trouble they'd suffered up until now.

The shooting lessons continued, but always in a group. The boys quickly developed a proficiency with the weapons, and even Honor gave a decent showing with a shotgun. Putting a knife in her hand had proved more dangerous than he'd anticipated. He learned right quick to choose his words with care when telling her which way to move. A two-inch slice on his forearm testified to the fact that the words right and left sometimes twisted in her feminine brain.

Unless she did it on purpose. She'd had a bee up her britches about something at the time, and Luke had to wonder. The woman was smart. Clumsy, true, but truly intelligent. Her ciphering talent put his own to shame. Watching her work Lost Pines's books, he'd been amazed at the speed of her calculations. And he dared not forget the raffle. It was definitely the most innovative bit of thinking he'd ever seen, dead horse or no.

Yep, there was more to Honor Duvall than a beautiful face and mouth-watering body, and Luke had better not forget it. He glanced at Jason. "You 'bout ready to head back?"

"Reckon so." The boy retrieved the stringer. "Did you bring a knife, Cap'n? Honor's not squeamish about many things, but she hates cleaning fish. She makes us clean 'em before we bring 'em home."

Luke shook his head. "I want him for supper tonight so let's not kill him yet. We can leave him here. The water's cold enough this time of year he'd stay alive for days unless a cottonmouth gets him. One of us can fetch him later."

"All right."

They gathered up their supplies and made the short trek through the woods back to the house. Jason took the tackle and poles down to the storage shed, while Luke stopped first at the kitchen to leave the pail of crayfish, and then at the pump to wash. Entering the house through the back door, he was surprised and a little disconcerted to hear the rumble of a male voice and a decidedly feminine laugh coming from the front parlor. The abrupt cessation of all sound bothered him even more. Something smelled fishy and it wasn't his hands.

What mischief was the widow up to now? The only way a man could have safely gotten inside the house was if she'd let him in. Hand hovering near his gun belt, Luke moved silently down the hall toward the parlor. At the doorway, he halted, listening hard.

The silence was deafening.

Finally, Honor said, "Oh my. You could tempt an angel to sin with that."

A man chuckled softly. "I'm real good at temptation, angel. One more time?"

"Mmm."

Luke's stomach soured. He didn't like the sound of this. It put pictures in his mind he didn't like seeing, and the fact he didn't like seeing them made him even sicker. *Never trust a widow woman wearing a yellow dress.*

Who the hell was she with? The low, deep-pitched murmur had a familiar ring, despite its being more rumble than words. Cautiously, he leaned forward, preparing to peer around the door and find out. Then reason stopped him. A man often learned more by listening than by looking. Besides, looking might make him lose his lunch.

The ticking of the clock echoed in the quiet. "Enough," Honor said with a sigh. "You're a wicked man. Please, no more. I'm a mess."

"Lick it off, angel. Or better yet, let me lick it off."

She laughed. "You are an exceptionally wicked man."

"Thank you," he replied, his voice louder than before. "I do try."

Luke recognized the voice. Rafe Malone, the damned bounder. Son of a bitch, you can't trust a horse thief, either. Luke stepped into the parlor.

They sat next to each other on the horsehair sofa. Rafe's hand was lifted to Honor's face, his thumb sliding across her lower lip as he said, "You missed a spot."

"Well now," Luke drawled, not a hint of friendliness in his tone. "If y'all aren't as cozy as two fleas on a one-haired dog."

He caught the expression of surprise on Honor's face as she sprung away from Rafe. She lost her balance and tumbled off the sofa, her calico-clad behind hitting the floor with a thud.

Rafe tossed Luke a dark look before offering the widow a helping hand up. "That's a rude way to say hello, Prescott."

"My manners are just fine. It's yours that need some work." Narrowing his eyes, he added, "We shoot poachers in this part of Texas."

"Poachers?" Rafe slumped back against the sofa. A glimmer of amusement played across his face. "Excuse me, but I wasn't aware you'd claimed a headright."

Rafe obviously wasn't referring to the league-and-a-labor land grants made to settlers by the Republic of Texas. His reply disputed Luke's right to the land—the land being Honor Duvall.

Luke eyed the widow, wondering if the color in her cheeks resulted from embarrassment. The glare in her eyes suggested otherwise. Her assertion proved it.

"I own my own league-and-a-labor, Mr. Malone," she said, challenge ripe in her tone and in the uplifted tilt of her chin. "I determine who can and cannot hunt on my land, no one else."

The men shared a put-in-their-places look. Hell, no sense speaking in innuendo around her. A man might as well come out and say, keep your damned hands off my woman. Except she was right. She wasn't his woman.

But she sure as hell wasn't Rafe's, either.

"Honor knows what she's talking about. Of course, she did hire me for protection and you know how seriously I take my duties. So tell me, what brings you to Lost Pines, Mr. Malone?"

"Bonbons."

"Pardon me?"

"I brought bonbons." Rafe returned his attention to the widow. "Candies to share with a beautiful woman."

Luke scowled. Maybe the circumstances weren't as guilty as he'd imagined, but they weren't entirely innocent either. Over the years he'd seen Malone romance a goodly number of women. This was the first time he'd been bothered by it. The nausea churning his gut had yet to disappear.

The clatter of a walking stick proved a welcome distraction. Luke glanced toward the doorway, where Luella stood beaming at the scoundrel on the sofa. "Rafe Malone, you flatterer you. I must say it does my heart good to hear you speak that way to an old lady like me, but I'm afraid I know your game. I'm not sharing my sweets with you. They are now tucked away safe and sound in my bedroom."

She swept into the parlor, pausing to lift her pipe and tobacco pouch from a table before taking her customary seat in a rocker by the fireplace. "My, my, my," she said around her pipe stem. "How nice it is to see such pretty menfolk in my parlor."

Rafe's brows rose and he cut a look at Luke, who gave a wry grin, his ill humor fading at the sight of his friend's astonishment. He'd grown so used to Luella's male mode of dress and direct manner of speech that he didn't even notice it anymore. "So, I'll ask again. What brings you out this way, Malone?"

"Uh." Rafe's attention returned to the elderly

woman as an aromatic cloud rose from the barrel of her pipe. "I picked up mail in town this morning. You have a letter." He reached into his jacket pocket and removed a letter sealed with red wax. Fluttering it like a fan, he tore his gaze away from Luella long enough to shoot Honor his infamous Gentleman Rafe Malone wicked-wolf smile and added, "I couldn't pass up the opportunity to visit with Honor, so here I am."

"Lucky us," Luke said dryly as he accepted the letter. He recognized the handwriting before he read the name. The Raven. Luke hadn't heard from him since being discharged from the Texas Rangers. What did Sam Houston, president of the Republic of Texas, want from him this time?

He hoped to hell it wasn't something to interfere with his job here at Lost Pines.

"Thanks." He slipped the sealed letter into his pocket. "Now that you're here, how about we take a little walk. I want you to take a look at a horse."

Interest lit Rafe's eyes. "Starlight? I've been wanting to see her run again."

Luella choked and coughed on her pipe smoke. Honor's rosy complexion bleached white and her smile turned sickly. For Luke, their obvious discomfort was a welcome, entertaining distraction from the letter burning a hole in his pocket. "No, not Starlight," he drawled. "Her running days are over, I'm afraid."

"Really? Why's that?"

"We've put her out to pasture," Honor piped up, holding Luke's gaze, silently willing him to keep the raffle results secret.

He didn't know why he should. He'd certainly enjoy informing Rafe he'd spent a hundred dollars trying to win a dead horse. After that scene in the parlor, Luke found the idea especially appealing until he thought about telling his friend how he'd spent an entire afternoon burying the carcass.

Rafe would never let him hear the end of that.

Luke cocked his head toward the door. "Come on, Malone. I'm taking my pay on this job in horseflesh and I want your opinion on my choice. If you'll excuse us, ladies?"

Outside the sun was shining and the hint of heat in the slight breeze carried a warning of the summer to come. Luke limped his way toward the stable, his leg muscles more stiff than sore. That salve Luella had given him was working. This time, Rafe actually hurried his step a bit to keep up.

As they neared the stable, Rafe tossed Luke a sidelong glance. "So, do you really have a horse to show me, or was it an excuse to give me grief about sharing my sweets with the delectable Mrs. Duvall?"

"I don't need an excuse to give you grief, Malone. And as long as it's sweets you're sharing with the widow and not something meatier, then I don't care what you do."

Rafe planted his feet in the dirt. "Why would you care at all? Because of this espionage business? Or is it because you want her for yourself?"

Luke pursed his lips. Did he know the answer? Did he want to know? He blew out a breath. "Just leave her alone."

Rafe gave him a long look, then shrugged. "Whatever you want, Luke. If you can figure it out yourself. I think—"

He broke off abruptly, pursing his lips. Then he began to nod. "But then, maybe this isn't about the widow, at all. Perhaps you simply wanted to read your letter from the Big Drunk in private."

Luke grimaced at his friend's use of the Cherokees' name for Houston. He and Rafe stood on opposite sides of the fence when it came to their opinion of the leader of the Republic of Texas. Any discussion between them about Houston or his policies invariably led to argument. Rafe held a mean, personal grudge against Houston, and he was quick to voice his opposition to anything the man proposed. Luke knew few particulars about the trouble between the two men, other than it had its start at the Battle of San Jacinto. Whatever had happened, Rafe couldn't see past it. Hell, he'd almost refused the pardon for his crimes just because President Houston had issued the blasted thing.

Covering his vest pocket with his hand, Luke asked, "What did you do, read my mail? Is it something I should peruse in private?"

"I don't know. I didn't read it. Wouldn't waste my time." Rafe kicked a rock with the tip of his boot. The stone hit a water trough with a thump. "I have suffered some correspondence from the Raven myself. I recognize his handwriting."

Luke didn't comment as he led Rafe around the corner of the stables. A fenced corral came into view, and the long-legged stallion trotting around the perimeter temporarily pushed all thought of Sam Houston and his letter from his mind. Luke cocked his head toward the corral. "Look at him."

The sturdy mount might have sensed he was on display because he lifted his head and trumpeted. Furrows creased Rafe's brow as he frowned. "I've never seen a horse like that. What's wrong with his face?"

"Not a damn thing. He's a desert horse, and they all have that dished face. Micah told me Colonel Duvall had him brought over from Egypt shortly before he died. His name is Saracen."

Rafe studied the animal with a critical eye. "He's

not as big or as heavy as the quarter-milers. Can he run as fast?"

"Nope. Saracen won't earn the purse on quarter-mile tracks around Texas." Luke used his thumb to nudge his hat back off his brow as he glanced from his friend back to the horse. "But that's not why he's valuable. A man in my company owned a dished-faced mount until it got shot out from under him. I've never forgotten the animal. That Arab could run forever. Had more endurance than any I've seen before or since."

Rafe eyed him speculatively. "So what are you thinking, Prescott?"

Luke propped a boot on the fence. He searched his mind for the right words to present his idea to his friend. Rafe had a tendency to make snap judgments, and once he made a decision on something, it took all but an act of God to get him to change his mind. Luke began slowly. "For Rangers who sometimes ride a hundred miles without stopping, endurance makes all the difference in both man and mount."

"So you've been telling the truth about wanting to start a horse ranch? It's more than just talk to keep folks off your back about your plans? You've decided to give it a shot?" Rafe leaned against the fence, his arms outstretched and propped on the top rail.

Luke noted the interest in his expression and made a point to keep his voice casual. "Actually, I thought you might want to consider it."

One of Rafe's arms slipped off the rail. "What!"

"Think about it, Malone." Luke faced his friend, his voice intense. "Your land is perfect for raising horses. A natural range of good grass, plenty of water. You don't have Indian trouble up your way. Actually, I'm amazed this place hasn't been picked clean by the Indians."

"They haven't raided this far east in years."

"Must be they don't know about these horses. It's the only reason I can think for them keeping away."

Luke watched Rafe as he scrutinized the stallion. "You know horses as well as I do. You'd be good at this, Rafe." After a moment's pause, he spoke to the heart of the matter. "Besides, the house will be finished soon. You'll need something to do."

Malone's face turned dark as a blue norther cloud. "I have plenty to do."

"Sure. Like sitting around and moping about Elizabeth Worrell's new baby."

"Bastard," he said with little heat. "I could learn to hate you, Luke Prescott."

"No, you couldn't. Not when you know I'm right." He gestured toward the Arab. "Spanish horses are plentiful and cheap south of the border, and with a stud like this, we could breed horses to suit Rangers' needs to a T. Just think, Malone. How would it make you feel to have a Texas Ranger come begging to you for the perfect horse, offering money for something within your power to give. Or refuse."

Rafe's lips tilted in a slow smile. "Refuse, huh? You do have a way with words, don't you, Prescott? I must admit you paint a tempting picture."

A puff of breeze sent the moist scent of fresh manure drifting past them. Luke waited, observing his friend closely. When he judged the moment to be right, he said, "We could go partners, Rafe. The widow has offered me two of her mares, but I've a mind to convince her to substitute the stallion instead."

Rafe's brows arched in surprise. "Never thought I'd see you taking advantage of a woman, Prescott."

"This is Honor Duvall we're talking about," Luke said with a grimace. "Besides, I doubt it'll matter to her one way or the other. She's leaving Texas. She's moving back east to sell hats."

"Hats?"

"Hats." Luke shrugged. "Anyway, what do you think? Any chance at all you might consider it?"

Rafe hooked his thumbs in his back pockets and watched the ground while he kicked the dark soil with the toe of his boot. Three, four, maybe five minutes passed before he drew a deep breath, then exhaled in a rush. "I don't know, Luke. I'm not saying no, but I can't rightly say yes, either. Much as I'd enjoy seeing Rangers come begging to me, if I raised horses, I think I'd prefer the racing variety."

"Now why doesn't that surprise me?"

"Guess it's the disparity in our backgrounds," Rafe said with a grin. "I always needed the speed to get away and you needed the stamina to track me down."

"And which paid off in the long run?"

Rafe made a crude hand gesture. As the sound of Luke's chuckle died away, the horse thief's expression grew serious. "Do you want an answer today?"

"No." Luke shook his head. "I want you to think about it, that's all. I've some business of my own to attend to first."

Business that might or might not succeed. He'd answer the treason question one way or another, but if that didn't rid him of the black storm in his soul, he'd move on to something else. And it wouldn't be raising horses.

Rafe gestured toward Luke's pocket. "I reckon you mean government business. Still a Texas Ranger in your heart, aren't you, Prescott. I'll leave you to your letter. I want to see Starlight. Where do you keep her?"

"The near pasture behind the house." Luke knew a sense of satisfaction at the thought of sending Rafe on a dead-horse chase. Grinning, he turned his attention to the message in his pocket. Removing the paper, he slid his finger along its edge. He found himself curiously reluctant to open it and read the letter inside.

Luke respected Sam Houston, both the man and, especially, the office he represented. For all the chin music Rafe and like-minded individuals indulged in, few could deny the Raven's success on behalf of Texas. No one else knew that seven years ago Houston's gruff assurances had saved Luke's sanity. He was Luke's president, his general, and in a strange way, his friend. Sam Houston owned Luke's undying loyalty, and almost any time the president set a task before him, he accomplished it. It was either that or die trying.

Either result would have suited Luke just fine.

This was not one of those times. Not now. Not since the widow's raffle. For the first time in seven years, Luke wasn't prepared to drop everything and rush off to do the Raven's bidding. That's what a message like this usually meant.

Briefly, he wondered at this change of heart. Flirting with death had earned him most of Houston's accolades, even though it never banished the dark torment in Luke's soul. He eyed the letter in his hand. How would he explain that change in the status quo to Houston? Not without implicating Honor before he'd proved her innocence. Or her guilt. Muttering a curse, he broke the seal.

The paper crackled as it unfolded, and Luke braced himself to read the broad, bold scrawl of the Hero of San Jacinto.

Good Lord. Luke's stomach dropped like a hammer. This was no summons or charge to duty. Sam Houston was coming to visit. The president of the

Republic of Texas had heard about Luke's raffle win. He wanted to judge the abilities of his own quarter-miler by pitting him against the famous Starlight. He trusted Luke would make arrangements for a race.

"This is good. Real good," Luke mumbled, meaning just the opposite. Then another thought occurred to him. He pondered the idea for a good two minutes before his lips slid into a slow grin. He'd been right the first time. This *was* good. He couldn't have planned it better if he had tried.

Returning the letter to his pocket, he fumbled for a lemon drop and slipped it into his mouth. An image shimmered in his mind of him in his dress boots and Honor in yellow silk. They waltzed beneath a glittering, star-filled sky.

Luke glanced at Saracen and said, "Good thing Luella's salve is helping. I'd hate to host the social event of the season and not be able to dance with my hostess."

"You want me to do what?" Honor slammed the cornmeal barrel's lid onto the worktable and glared up at Luke. The man obviously had lost his mind. "What is in those candies you're always eating, locoweed?"

The spicy aroma of gumbo permeated the air in the kitchen as Luke set the catfish on her worktable. He held up his hand and said in a placating voice, "Now, Honor."

"Don't you 'Now, Honor' me." She picked up a cleaver. "I'm not a child to be . . . pacified."

Wariness flickered in his smoke-gray eyes as he devoted his attention to the chopper. "Put it down. You're coming along fine on your lessons, but I'm not ready to turn you loose with a knife yet."

"I'd like to turn you loose," she grumbled.

Though his gaze remained fixed on the chopper, his voice rumbled with wicked amusement. "Oh, I do wish you would."

How was it he made her want to hit him and curl up next to him at the same time? Frustrated as much at herself as at him, Honor grabbed the fish by the tail and slapped it onto her cutting board. "Thank you for your contribution to tonight's meal. Since we have a guest, it comes in handy. But next time, Prescott, clean it before you bring it home, all right?"

She whacked the catfish in two with a single hard swoop. The bewhiskered head scuttled across the board and over the edge and plopped onto the table. She wished she could put an end to his ridiculous suggestion just as easily. "Lost Pines hosting a party in honor of Sam Houston," she scoffed. "Of all the lamebrained ideas. Why would you think I'd even consider it? Even if I had the money to host such an affair, which I don't, I wouldn't want any low-down political snakes slithering across my land, not even the president of the Republic. Besides, have you forgotten we're in danger here? You want to explain how opening the gates to a passel of strangers wouldn't leave us open to risk?"

Luke frowned at the headless fish. "Why did you do that? That's not how you clean a fish."

"Do you plan to answer my questions?"

"Only if you gnaw on your tongue for a minute and give me a chance to speak." He lifted the head by a whisker and tossed it into a waste bucket. "I'll cover all the expenses for the jubilee. I have money put aside, and it's only right since it's my idea. But you and I made a bargain when I decided to remain at Lost Pines, Honor. You promised me proof of your father's treason, and you're taking your sweet time providing it. I get the impression you've conveniently forgotten about it."

"I haven't forgotten."

"Oh? You have something for me?"

"Not yet, no. But you've seen me going through Armand's papers. It wouldn't surprise me to find he'd been involved in my father's shenanigans, also. If that doesn't pan out, I'll keep looking until something does."

"It's a shot in the dark. My plan is a whole heck of a lot better."

"A party? What does hosting a party have to do with finding proof of my father's treason?"

"It's the best way to bait my trap. If your father is the slime you say he is, he'll make a play for the prize I intend to offer. If he's innocent of your charges, he'll leave my bait alone and I'll know you're the one I need to deal with."

"Deal with," she scoffed. "Why, you—" Honor broke off her sentence as her blood ran cold. "You think you're going to invite him here? To Lost Pines?"

"I knew you were quick."

Honor was quick enough to carry the thought a step further, too. She shuddered. The cleaver slipped from her hand, the blade slicing half the tail off the catfish before biting into the cutting board. "You want to use my family as your bait."

"No, not at all. Not really." Grimacing, Luke reached for a smaller knife. "Move over, Honor. You're about to ruin my supper. I should have known not to let you near my fish. Jason told me you weren't much for cleaning them. Why are you here at all? I thought Luella was cooking tonight. Jason bragged about her gumbo the entire time he collected those Louisiana lobsters."

"Not really? Not really!" Nearly bursting with rage,

Honor backed away from the table. "Have you lost your mind? Two little boys. Luella's half-crippled. How can you even consider putting them in danger?"

Calmly, Luke sliced the fish lengthwise and pulled the meat away from the bone. "Wash off the war paint, Honor. What I have in mind won't put them in any danger. In fact, if you are telling the truth about your father, my plan will likely make life safer for your family."

"About as likely as that catfish to swim again," she snapped back. Bitterness swelled within her. "Sure, Captain, invite the bobcat right on into the henhouse. Let the cat come play with the mice. Throw a rattler in with the rabbits, why don't you?"

"You certainly have animals on the mind tonight, don't you? Fish and chicken and rabbits. What happened, did you skip a couple of meals?"

"I'd like to take a bite out of your hide, Captain."

"Lord knows I have fantasies about that myself," he drawled. He pinned her with a knowing gaze. "You should have told me, sunshine. Ever since you kissed me I've had a hell of a time keeping my hands to myself. If I'd known you felt the same, I wouldn't have tried so hard."

The heat of her temper seared the words on her tongue, leaving them in ashes. How dare he! She wanted to hit him. She wanted to hurt him. All she managed was to stand in a frozen, speechless fury while he skinned and filleted the blasted catfish.

"This is how we'll handle it," Luke said, scraping the discards into the bucket. "President Houston plans to look me up in just over a month. That'll give us plenty of time to put this together. We'll have the picnic in the afternoon, then a dance at night, and the race the next morning. The women and children we'll put up in the house; the men can camp."

"Hold on, Prescott," Honor demanded when she finally found her voice. "You're getting a little ahead of yourself, aren't you? I'm the notorious Widow Duvall. No one will attend a social event I host."

"Sure they will. Curiosity will bring 'em if nothing else. Shoot, between the draw of your name and Sam Houston's, we'll have so many guests, there won't be room for all the tents in the pastures."

Desperation filled her. "No. You don't need my name. Use yours. You're the Bravest Man in Texas. Tell you what, advance me a loan and I'll take my family and leave here. You can use Lost Pines for your party. You can have Lost Pines if you want. I don't care. Just let me go before my father arrives."

"I'll protect you, Honor, I promise. I'll import so many Rangers for this event that this'll be the safest place in North America. You don't need to run off." Luke dumped cornmeal into a bowl for batter, then rummaged around until he found salt, pepper, and an egg. "Now, we'll make it a public party, but we'll send invitations to those we especially want to be here— the Brits and your father. I know the British chargé d'affaires, Charles Elliot. He visited me a time or two when I was laid up after the ambush. He's a good man and if he's your father's contact, it'll take some shrewd strategy on our part to pull off our plan."

"Your plan," Honor croaked, forcing words past the lump in her throat. "Not mine."

Luke glanced up. "I don't suppose y'all keep any ale, do you? I like a little beer in my catfish batter."

Honor shook her head, suddenly drained of both anger and energy as her emotions tugged in a dozen different directions. How would she ever win an argument against a man who spoke of picnics and treason in the same breath?

"Didn't figure you would. I've had Luella pegged

as a hard whiskey drinker from the first, but I'm not one hundred percent positive about you. Sometimes you're ratafia, but other times you're white lightnin'."

Cocooned in her own misery, Honor ignored his nonsense. The thought of inviting her father to Lost Pines terrified her. But in all truthfulness, hadn't she known this was coming? From the moment she grabbed Luke's sleeve to stop him from leaving and named her father a traitor, deep in her heart hadn't she known she'd be forced to face Richard Armstrong? Sure she'd made a token attempt to search for Luke's proof, but had she ever truly expected to find it? No.

Luke cracked the egg into a second bowl. As he whipped it with a fork, he said, "This isn't just another ball I'm aiming to host, you realize. The horse race is the main event. Texians would pay a visit to hell to watch a good horse run, so I reckon they'll show up to Lost Pines to see Starlight."

"Starlight!"

His grin was wicked as sin. "You're gonna like this, Honor. This scheme's right up your alley."

8

Honor served supper early to accommodate Rafe, who insisted he must return home that evening rather than accept her invitation to stay the night. The meal proved to be a merry affair as Rafe rhapsodized about the taste of Luella's crawfish gumbo, then took a bite of Luke's fried catfish and declared it passably fair. One bite was all he got, however, because Luke speared the fillet right off his plate, declaring he wouldn't waste good food on bad company.

The boys paid rapt attention to the banter between the two men, and bittersweet emotion tugged Honor's heart at the sight. At nine and eleven, Jason and Micah were of an age to need a male influence in their lives. Positive male influence. They'd suffered enough of the other kind, which was one more argument in Honor's case against marriage. Never again would she marry to provide her sons a father. Experience had taught her how benevolent intentions sometimes cause more harm than good.

Armand Duvall had fooled her completely. He'd promised to be a good father to Micah and Jason, and she had believed him. Instead, from the moment the vows were spoken, he'd ignored the boys entirely. At first, her husband's inattention had infuriated Honor. Later on, she was grateful for the way matters stood. As long as Armand looked right through her sons, he didn't hurt them.

Throughout the three years of her third marriage, Honor wondered how she'd failed to see Armand for his true self before they had wed. Like scarlet flags against a bright blue sky, the signs had existed for anyone to see. Her blindness caused Honor to question her judgment, yet another reason to refuse remarriage.

Finishing his second helping of ginger pudding, Rafe leaned back in his chair and patted his stomach. "Delicious, ladies. Absolutely delicious. I declare, I am stuffed to the gills."

"Best stay away from Honor, then, if she's carrying a knife," Luke muttered.

Honor ignored the slight as Luella suggested an after-dinner drink and smoke. "You'll have plenty of time to get home before dark, Rafe. Stay awhile, please. I might even share one of my bonbons with you."

"How can I resist," the rogue replied.

The boys escaped to their bedroom while the adults adjourned to the parlor. After the day she'd had, Honor decided to indulge in a glass of dewberry wine. She sat beside her mother-in-law on the horsehair sofa and sipped her drink while Luke proposed his plans for the Lost Pines spring jubilee. Upon hearing the details of his intentions, she considered switching to Luella's whiskey.

Rafe rubbed his jaw with the palm of his hand. "Sounds good, Luke, all except for the speeches. You're gonna ruin a good party by inviting politicians to air out their lungs. Shoot, I'd rather listen to a hellfire-and-brimstone preacher. They're at least entertaining. Politicians will put you to sleep. Either that or get you killed."

Honor nodded toward Rafe. Stirring the fire with a poker, Luke shook his head in disgust.

"You and Honor have something in common, Rafe," Luella observed, her impish gaze flicking between Honor and Luke. "She hates politics."

"Actually, Luella, I don't care enough about politics for such a strong reaction."

"That's just plain stupid." Luke shoved the poker back into its brass stand and rounded on Honor. "The job of our government, any government, for that matter, is to defend life, property, and basic liberties. We darn well better care who and what those men are."

The passion in his voice yanked Honor's thoughts off the subject and onto the man standing before her. Luke's eyes gleamed with self-confidence. He stood tall as his own reputation and as broad and strong as a log cabin wall. Here among the expensive furnishings of Lost Pines's parlor he wore his frock jacket and black string cravat as easily as the frontier buckskins he favored.

He's so much like Texas, she thought. An extraordinary blend of valor and swagger. He belongs here, like no one else I've ever met.

Envy, and something else, rumbled up inside her. To be so confident, so sure of oneself, was an ideal to strive toward. As he expounded his political views, the air around him vibrated with his zeal, his pride, his potent masculinity. The man was devastatingly appealing and he captured Honor in his spell.

Her blood warmed as she watched his hands move, emphasizing his words. Large hands. Strong. She recalled how they had held her, and her breathing quickened. She quit listening to his words, hearing only his voice, a deep-pitched rumble that seemed to stroke across her skin. A raw, aching yearning swelled within her. She was drawn to Luke Prescott like smithy shavings to a magnet.

"Back in thirty-three," he said, "Colonel Travis wrote to a newspaper in the East. He said that Texas is composed of the shrewdest and most interesting population of any new country on earth, and that the people sent to exhort them must be respected and talented. Well, that hasn't changed in the last decade. Our leaders must be respected, must be talented. It's our duty to pay attention to what candidates for that leadership say. To hold them up to scrutiny. To do otherwise abdicates our responsibility as citizens of this great country."

"I reckon I can respect the president," Rafe interrupted, smirking. "I can respect the amount of white lightning he can put away, anyway."

The new voice freed Honor from the captain's spell and a mixture of embarrassment and anger washed through her. She was acting the fool, and the very thought of it drove her crazy. Zizzle, indeed. Luella was wrong. This ... this thing between Luke and her was nothing more than basic lust. She knew it well. The men in her life had painted its leer upon her memory.

It was lust that fueled Luke's teasing words and put the heated look in his eyes. Lust fed his kiss. In that regard, he was like many other men she had known. Men like him reserved deeper feelings, love and loyalty and devotion, for more lofty concerns than women. Zizzle, hah. Luke Prescott saved his grand passion for Texas.

She glared at the former Texas Ranger. "You are blind as a post hole when it comes to your regard for this godforsaken country."

Luella shook her pipe stem at Luke. "I think you put your finger on part of the problem a minute ago. You said, 'Politicians are the *men* who make decisions for the country.' Well, it's my opinion that a few *ladies* should be thrown into the mix. We'd get problems straightened out in half the time it takes you boys."

Rafe choked on a smothered guffaw.

Honor never took her gaze off Luke. "I do believe you're right, Luella. A woman wouldn't wade into the verbal muck with the heroes of San Jacinto. Sam Houston and his Peace Party and Mirabeau Lamar's War Party—what a joke! That entire campaign for presidency turned into a debate over who was the bigger liar, drunkard, and public thief."

Luke pounced like a panther. "So you do pay attention to politics!"

She wrinkled her nose. "Just enough to learn that neither party represents me."

"How can you say that?" His eyes flashed with frustration.

Experiencing an overwhelming need to put him in his place, Honor took a moment to organize her thoughts. "The laws of the Republic were based on Jeffersonian Democracy, correct?"

The men nodded.

Honor continued. "This means that in Texas, every male family head is entitled to land and is expected to work it and defend his rights on it. But also in Texas, as a residue of Spanish law, the property rights of married women are also guaranteed."

"See?" Luke folded his arms. "Because of politicians, you're better off in Texas than you'd be in the States."

"Not hardly," Honor said dryly. "Do you know who framed the constitution of the Republic?"

"Property-holders, mainly."

She shook her head. "Lawyers. And when a lawyer writes a law, he always knows how to pen another document to get around that law."

"Now wait a minute," Rafe protested. "I resent that. Before I immigrated to Texas, I practiced law in Tennessee. And I never—"

"You were a lawyer?" she interrupted. "No wonder you were such a successful thief."

Rafe sat back in his chair abruptly. Admiration glimmered in his eyes as he shook his head and said, "The woman could fillet fish with that tongue."

Luke ignored his friend. His narrowed dark eyes studied her keenly. "Honor, is your father, perchance, a lawyer? Were any of your husbands lawyers?"

Honor's stomach dropped like a stone. Curse the man's perception. Abruptly, she stood. "Excuse me, I need some air."

Rafe's shrewd glance shifted from Honor to Luke, then back to Honor again. She wondered just what it was he thought he knew.

"Before you go, I'd best say my good-byes," he said, rising to his feet. "I have a few things that need tending to at home. Never expected to stay gone so long today." He thanked both Honor and Luella for their hospitality, then took his leave.

Thank goodness, Honor thought. She'd exhausted her capacity for the exchange of pleasantries. She hadn't looked forward to the end of a day this much since Jason caught the chicken pox and bedtime meant a welcome end to his whining. While Luke walked

Rafe out to his horse, she gathered the empty glasses and escaped the parlor. Old ghosts and current insecurities went with her.

Honor shivered as she walked the path to the kitchen, more from the memories plaguing her mind than from the late afternoon air. She washed and rinsed the supper dishes, bitterness welling up inside her as she considered Luke Prescott's insightful question.

God plague her father and the men of his kind who wrote laws to ensure that power remained in the hands of those already in possession of it.

With the kitchen set to rights, she hung up her damp dishtowel and stepped outside, where languid sunbeams slanted across pastures sparkling with brilliant wildflowers. The bucolic scene proved too happy for her mood, so she turned away, following the path down toward the creek and the shadowed woods that hugged its bank.

The quiet foliage wrapped her in pine-scented melancholy. She headed for her usual perch, the large, flat limestone rock that jutted out over the water at perfect toe-dangling distance from the surface. Once there, she removed her shoes and rolled down her stockings before sinking to the stone with a sigh. She dipped one toe into the icy water and shivered. Still, the winter cold in her soul surpassed the springtime chill of the creek.

The captain wanted his proof. He intended to invite her father and his schemes and threats to Lost Pines, and she saw no way to prevent it. She had yet to gather the financial means to escape.

For just a moment, she reconsidered the wicked idea of selling off her assets without permission of the trustee. She could take the money and run. It was a tantalizing notion, but one she could not in good conscience indulge. Her father had warned her of the consequences should she attempt such a thing. He'd track down every last item, from manor house to crystal vase, and repossess it. Legally, God curse him. The buyers who trusted her honesty would be the ones hurt.

That's if she could sell her holdings at all. Coin wasn't exactly plentiful these days, and paper currency—Texas currency, worth only cents on every dollar—would do her little good.

Nope, unless something changed, and quickly, she'd have to stay at Lost Pines and face her father at Luke's jubilee. She'd have to try to trick him into revealing his true self. Her desperate promise had come back to haunt her.

Stretching her foot toward the water, she muttered, "I'd hoped not to pay my share of the bargain at all."

"Now why doesn't that surprise me?" Luke emerged from the woods like a specter.

Honor jumped, teetering on the edge of the rock for a long moment until she finally caught her balance. One glance at Luke made her wonder which was preferable—getting wet or facing Luke Prescott. Judging by the expression on his face, the man was on a mission.

She eyed the cold water. No, she'd never make it. She wasn't much of a swimmer and besides, Luke would come after her. At supper Rafe had related the tale of how the Ranger once pursued him through a range fire, never turning back despite clouds of white smoke that hung like death over the land. And it would have been death—Rafe's death—had Luke given up. As it turned out, slapping handcuffs on the smoke-snorting horse thief succeeded in saving his life.

But at this moment, her life was not being threatened. Her peace of mind was something else. "I came out here to be alone," she told him.

"Too bad." Luke chose a nearby fallen log as his seat. "I think it's time we had a talk."

"We've been talking off and on all day."

"Then your tongue ought to be warmed up and ready." He removed his hat and tossed it to the ground.

Honor shot him a glance. Luke had a way of accenting the word tongue that always made her think he was saying one thing but meaning another. This time he appeared innocent, about as innocent as any predator ever could, that is.

"Tell me about the money, Honor."

It was a quick, hard jab to the stomach. "Pardon me?"

"Tell me what a lawyer did that affects your property rights. If you are so desperate to leave Texas, explain to me why you don't sell your assets and skedaddle out of here. Tell me why you can't."

She stared, unseeing, at the opposite creek bank. "What makes you think I can't?"

"Because that's the smart thing to do and you haven't done it. Therefore, there's a reason why you can't."

Mockingly, she replied, "Aren't you just chock full of flattery."

"Tell me, Honor," he demanded. "Tell me what your daddy did to you."

Resentment shadowed her laugh. "Do you have until Christmas?" Luke opened his mouth to reply, but she interrupted. "No, that sounds self-pitying and I don't mean to do that. I've promised myself I won't."

He flicked at his thigh with a small cedar twig. "Has he legally restricted the use of your funds?"

"You are an intelligent man yourself, Captain Prescott." Her eyes slowly closed as the fight drained out of her. "Each time I wed, Father insisted on marriage contracts and new wills. He or one of his cronies served as the attorney who drafted the documents. He made certain that provisions went into each will that gave him control over my husbands' estates."

"Your husbands knew this?"

Honor nodded. "Franklin and Philip believed my father, being a man, was better equipped to deal with business affairs than I. I don't think Armand cared much one way or the other."

"Does your father own Lost Pines?"

She shook her head. "I own it. I just can't sell it without his approval, and since he seldom gives me such license, I'm pretty much stuck. I'm horse poor, Captain. Horse poor, house poor, land poor, fancy-rugs-and-furniture poor. The only cash I have is what we can manage to earn and the living allowance my father sends on a monthly basis. It wouldn't carry us to Galveston, much less to Carolina."

Luke whistled softly. "The raffle."

Honor's lips twitched in a crooked smile. "I'm rather proud of that idea, I'll admit. Barter is not specifically prohibited by Armand's will."

Luke drew in the dirt with his stick and Honor watched the sketch take shape beneath his hand. A coffin. Man sized. Not like the burying box she'd built for Starlight. She shuddered.

The former Texas Ranger asked, "So, Honor, how did Duvall die? How did all your husbands die?"

The question hung on the air like the smell of rotted fish.

Luke lifted his head and studied her, searching for

an apt description of her complexion. White as wheat flour? Pale as a waning moon? Peaked? Sickly?

Guilty.

His stomach clenched and he wished he had a lemon drop to take the sour taste from his mouth. He'd had to force himself to ask the question he didn't much want answered. "Did you kill Duvall?"

Honor flinched. "No," she said softly. "Not Armand." Sincerity shone in her eyes as she looked at him and added, "I didn't kill Armand."

Now what did that mean? Had she killed one of the others? Both of them? Luke arched his brows, encouraging her to continue.

She looked away. "He sort of drowned."

"How does someone sort of drown?"

Dusk crept over the woods like a fog. Or maybe it wasn't dusk. Maybe it was Honor and the trouble she wore like a shroud. She spoke in a voice reedy thin and ghostly. "He had an accident while bathing."

"What happened?"

She shrugged. "It's a long story."

"Now where have I heard that before?" Luke tossed away the stick he'd used to draw in the dirt and folded his arms, waiting expectantly.

"It's rather private, Luke. Suffice it to say he bumped his head and slid beneath the water."

"Did you cosh him over the head?"

"No. I told you I didn't kill him. Not unless I can be blamed for not being there to save him. Normally, I attended Colonel Duvall at his baths. That night, I refused."

"Did he need your help? Was he crippled up?"

Her expression changed, growing hardened and cold. "I guess that depends on how one defines crippled. Physically, my husband was quite healthy."

Luke narrowed his eyes and studied her. He was

learning to read the Widow Duvall and he reckoned he had a glimmer of what she wasn't saying. "This has something to do with that bedroom of yours and why you won't go near it, doesn't it?"

Her blush both answered him and gave rise to a number of new questions, questions that boiled in his gut. "What happened, Honor, love play get a little rough?"

Her whiskey eyes went dull and scorn laced her voice. "What Armand Duvall required of me had nothing to do with love, Captain Prescott. He was a sick, perverted man, and I'm well rid of him."

"Sounds like you had a motive for murder."

She tossed a leaf into the creek and watched it float downstream toward the bubbling white foam where water met rock. "I admit I thought about it. I admit I wished for his death." A bitter smile twisted her lips. "But I'm afraid I couldn't make myself kill another husband."

Another husband? Oh, hell. He really wished she hadn't said that. Trying to read her secrets, Luke studied the woman before him. The gentle breeze played with golden tendrils of hair loosened from her braid, and she lifted a graceful hand to smooth them back away from her face. She was classically beautiful, possessed of an angel's face and a temptress's body. But deadly? No, he simply couldn't see it. He didn't believe it. He didn't want to believe it.

But she'd just admitted it.

Luke scooped a stone off the ground and tossed it into the river. The water rippled in ever-widening circles, symbolic, somehow, of the intrigues multiplying daily at Lost Pines. He'd put it off long enough. "What do you mean, Honor? How did your other husbands die?"

She seemed to go limp, melting backward onto the

rock. She lay with her fingers laced over her breasts, staring through the canopy of leaves toward the graying sky. "It is my fault Philip is dead. Luella would tell you differently, but it's the truth."

Luke wanted desperately to believe this story had nothing to do with murder. Another accident, he hoped, knowing Honor's bumbling ways. It wasn't too big a stretch. She'd come close to doing him in on one or two occasions since the shooting lessons commenced. "What happened?"

She shut her eyes and shuddered. A full minute passed in silence. Then softly, in a voice aching with grief, she said, "It took him a whole day to die. I killed him with dessert."

Luke surely had misheard her. "Come again?"

A tear slipped from the corner of her eye and trailed slowly across her temple. Emotion clogged her voice as she cried, "I killed him with a rhubarb pie!"

He said the first thing that popped into his mind. "Piecrust that heavy?"

"No, Captain. Poison that strong." Her eyes flew open as laughter spilled from her mouth, giggles brimmed with hysteria's razor edge.

"Tell me."

She rolled to her side, her back turned toward Luke.

That wouldn't do. He wanted to see her face. She stiffened slightly as he moved to sit close to her. When he lifted her bare feet into his lap and began rubbing her chilled toes between his warm hands, she simply turned her head and stared at him. Tears slowly filled her eyes and she blinked repeatedly. Luke gave her foot a gentle squeeze. "Tell me what happened, sunshine."

Grief, profound and terrible, quaked across her face. She pulled her feet away from him and sat up, hugging her knees. For long moments the only sound to be heard was the high-pitched whine of insects swarming over the water.

"Philip was a cotton planter," she said, her head dropping back as she gazed toward the sky. "We lived in east Texas not far from Nacogdoches. Twice during our marriage he made business trips back east. The last time someone served him rhubarb pie for dessert and Philip adored it. He requested the recipe and brought a few plants home with him, hoping the rhubarb would grow in Texas."

She paused, and Luke prompted her by saying, "I'm not familiar with that plant. Did it grow here?"

"We never had a chance to find out. The first day home he gave me a rhubarb and asked me to make a pie." She closed her eyes. "It was such a strange plant. So sour." Her mouth pursed as if tasting the memory and she shuddered. "Thank God none of the rest of us cared for the flavor. Luella and I and the boys ate but a bite. Richard had three pieces."

Luke grimaced. While he'd never heard of rhubarb, he'd seen the results of food poisoning before. Most likely, Philip Best's death hadn't been easy. "Look, Honor, I'm sorry I brought it up. You don't need—"

"Yes, I do." She stared him in the eyes. "I cooked the leaf blades in with the rhubarb stalk. I later learned only the stalk is edible. I killed my husband with my cooking and it was a horrible death."

Her voice trembled. "Such pain in his stomach, nausea and vomiting. He could barely breathe. It went on for hours and hours. When finally he hemorrhaged, his death came as a merciful release."

"Don't you think you're being a bit hard on yourself? It was an accident, a horrible accident to be certain, but you didn't kill him, Honor."

A single tear slipped from her eye to trail slowly

down her cheek. "In my head I know that, but in my heart ... it's another matter."

Luke's desire to pursue the question of her first husband's death faded in the face of her distress. Instead, he lifted his hand to Honor's face and wiped away the tear with the pad of his thumb.

It wasn't enough. He shifted toward her, leaned forward, and pressed a kiss to the salty trail. Her quavering sigh was all the encouragement he needed to seek out her lips. A single taste of the sweet heaven of her mouth drove all thought of husbands and death and despair from his mind.

He kissed her with tenderness and an offer of comfort, his touch against her cheek a gentle, soothing stroke. Nothing harsh or wild or savage, nothing at all like the first kiss between them. This was a delicate passion. A sharing. He'd almost forgotten what it was like.

"Mmm," he sighed against her mouth as he wrapped her in his arms. She was warm and soft and womanly. It had been so long since he'd enjoyed such a simple pleasure as holding a lady in his arms.

A lady. Or the Black Widow. Which was she? Maybe both? Luke wasn't certain. All the rumors and hints of scandal led a man to expect the hard edge of a whore. Instead, he discovered innocence faded but not erased.

Luke trailed little kisses across her face and down her neck, finding a spot that made her shiver. Grinning, he nipped her there for good measure.

"Yeow," she purred.

"You taste good, lady."

"You make me forget myself."

"Is that a problem?"

She hesitated, her gaze searching his, and Luke was lost in the glistening, stormy soul of her deep brown eyes. "No," she finally murmured. "Actually, I think it is a blessing. Kiss me again, Ranger."

Luke obliged.

The mood of their kisses shifted, altering with the reality of her response. Her hands lifted, touched his arms, slid up his shoulders, and clasped behind his neck. She slipped her tongue into his mouth even as she pulled him toward her, pressing the hardened tips of her breasts against his chest.

Luke groaned as need grabbed him, hard and hot and hungry. It clawed at self-control already weakened by weeks of proximity and years of self-denial.

The Widow Duvall spun her web around him. Did she know what she was doing to him? Was she the Black Widow rumor claimed her to be? Was she out to trap an unsuspecting man in the silken splendor of her delights?

Or was she as lost in the web of raw, aching want as he?

As the twilight deepened, he glanced into her face and saw the glitter of arousal in her eyes. Luke concluded that for now, anyway, they spun together.

Impatient for her weight against him, he rolled onto his back, bringing her with him. His hand covered the fullness of her breast even as the other found her rump and pressed her against his aching erection. She moved just a little, rotating her hips one time, and Luke thought he might explode. Lady or liar? Which was she? Did he care?

He should care. He had his redemption to think of. He couldn't allow his mission to be compromised. Not again, by God.

"We need to stop this," he said.

"Probably." Then she denied the word with another circling of her hips.

The urge to take her, to bury himself deeply in the

pleasure of her body, drove him to the limits of his self-control. It was too much, entirely too soon. He had to stop but, dear God, he didn't want to. Maybe just a little more. He was strong.

He was so damned weak.

"Sit up, sunshine," he coaxed. "Let me look at you. Just look."

She did as he asked, straddling him, her knees on either side of his hips. Luke lifted his fingers to her bodice and deliberately popped the first button on her yellow-checked gingham gown.

She uttered no protest. He clamped his teeth against the craving clawing at his gut and carefully worked her gown loose and pushed it off her shoulders.

Honor wore no stays beneath her dress. Her embroidered chemise covered the swelling of her bosom, but Luke found the thin, revealing lawn more provocative than bare skin.

At least, that's what he believed until she boldly bared her breasts.

He let out the breath he'd been holding in a harsh *whoosh*. God bless experienced women.

Full and round, her breasts were crowned by taut nipples colored the pink of ripe peaches. More than anything, he wished to taste them. "You bring me to my knees, Honor."

She smiled then. Crookedly. Tremulously. "Actually, Captain, I've laid you flat."

He ran his hand up the side of one globe, cupping its weight. Soft, silky, smooth. Because he was weak, because he teetered on the very brink of losing control, he asked, "And is that what you want, Honor? To lie with me? Here and now?"

"Yes. No. I don't know. I can't think because of the zizzle."

The anguish in her voice was like a spray of cold

water on the fire inside him. Zizzle? Relief mingled with severe disappointment as Luke dropped his arm back to his side. "I think that's a pretty clear answer."

"No! I mean . . . it's just that—"

"It's all right, Honor." Luke put his hands around her waist and lifted her off him.

She stared toward the ground as she hurriedly put her clothes to rights. Luke sat up, then pushed to his feet. His body ached with unappeased desire, but the unexpected pang in his heart hurt him worse. It pained him to see Honor looking so miserable, and that realization left him uneasy.

"Best be getting on back," he said gruffly. "It'll be full dark soon."

As she pulled on her shoes sans stockings, Luke noticed the trembling in her hands. Well, hell. His runaway attempt to comfort her had only made matters worse.

She never met his eyes as she stood and started toward the path through the woods leading back to the house. At the trees, she paused. "I apologize for leading you on, Luke. It was wrong of me. It wasn't intentional. I want you to know that. You see, I've never . . . it's just . . . it's different with you. You're different."

Luke saw her shoulders rise and fall with a deep breath. Then she pivoted and her soulful eyes locked on his. "You make me feel good, Luke Prescott. No man has ever done that before. I've married three men. Bedded three men. None of them ever touched me like you do." With that bald confession, she turned and fled.

"Son of a bitch," Luke muttered.

Bending over he retrieved his hat, then harshly brushed the clinging leaves from its brim. As he plopped it on his head, he heard Luella Best's voice from the cover of the trees. "You should marry her, you know."

Luke's spine snapped straight as a loblolly trunk and he spat a curse unfit for a lady's ears. Of course, Luella Best was no lady. "So, you get a kick out of voyeurism?"

She left the concealment of the trees. "I wasn't spying on you, Captain. I came looking for Honor. I didn't know you were with her. Once I happened upon the scene, I couldn't very well make my presence known. Honor would have been horrified."

"What you should have done was hightail it back to the house."

"I considered it, but I decided Honor might need my protection."

"Your protection!" Luke braced his hands on his hips. "What kind of a man do you think I am?"

Luella folded her arms and stood right up to him. "The kind of man Honor desperately needs. Not, however, in the manner in which you were about to indulge her."

"You are making me angry, Luella," Luke warned.

The shadows deepened to near dark and a cricket's chirp marked the coming of night. Luella's features faded with the light, but her eyes continued to glitter. "I'm not particularly happy with you, either. I had thought better of you, Luke. That you would take advantage of that poor child on the very heels of plunging her into her worst nightmare purely sets my temper ablaze."

"Pull up on the reins, there, woman. I didn't take advantage of her. Shoot, I could make a good argument for it being the other way around. And, what do you mean I'm plunging her into her worst nightmare?"

"Her father, of course." Luella threw her hands out

wide. "Inviting him to Lost Pines? What if Black has arrived from England by then? Armstrong's bound to bring him with him. No telling what Honor will do then. She's liable to up and run away, leaving the rest of us behind. I can't say I'd blame her if she did."

"Tell me about this Marcus Black. Who is he?"

"He's the reason why you are here, Captain Prescott. According to her father, Black's crazy-obsessed to own her, but our Honor would rather run away to Carolina than stay in Texas and marry him. I can't blame her one bit."

Luke scowled as Luella continued. "Personally, I don't put it past Armstrong to go and fetch her back. That's why I believe the only way she'll be safe is if she marries someone else, someone as strong as Richard Armstrong. A man able to protect and defend her. I've suspected all along that you are the perfect candidate, but now that I've seen the zizzle I'm certain of it."

Luke shook his head, confused. Zizzle again? What language did these women speak? "Luella, I think you've slipped an oar. I'm not about to wed your daughter-in-law. I doubt if even a double-barreled gun could get an 'I do' out of me now."

Luella sniffed. "Well, I'm warning you, Mr. Texas Ranger. If I catch you unbuttoning our Honor again, we'll darn sure put it to the test. I'm a good shot, as you well know."

"Hoisted on my own petard," he wryly replied as he studied the elderly woman. Here she was, hardly able to walk, old enough to have one foot in the grave, and she didn't hesitate to rake the Bravest Man in Texas over her coals. "I like you, Luella Best. I truly do."

"Of course you do." She took his arm. "Now, escort

me back to the house, please, Luke. You are not the only wolf on this riverbank, I hope you realize."

Wolf? Luke laughed to himself at that one. Pigeon was more apt. Honor might have hired him for protection, but he'd bet his last Mexican gold coin that Luella Best had had marriage in mind when she helped to orchestrate his presence at Lost Pines.

"Tell me about the raffle, Luella."

She gave him a sidelong look. "Now there's a curious change of subject. What do you want to know?"

"Honor admitted it was rigged. How did you make sure that my ticket number was drawn?"

"Oh, well, she worked that out with Micah. When he sold you your ticket he noted the number. It was the only number Honor put in the basket."

"She is such a little larcenist. No wonder she and Malone get along."

"Now, Luke," Luella scolded. "She didn't want to do it, you know, but her hands were tied. She didn't have another horse the equal of Starlight, and she hesitated to offer a lesser horse as the prize, fearing the reaction of the winner. Horses are serious business in Texas. No telling what a normal man would have done when he learned the truth."

Luke stopped short. "And I'm not a normal man?"

"Oh, no. You are special. Very special." She patted his arm. "I knew it when I suggested you for the winner of the raffle, and you have proved me right. You are exactly what Honor needs. You're the Bravest Man in Texas. You'll show her how to face her fears."

"Luella, I'm afraid you are sadly mistaken." Captain Luke Prescott, the man whose reputation hid the yellow stripe running down his back, would never have *cojones* enough to marry the Widow Duvall. Whatever terrors she faced, his own surely outstripped them. He'd married once. He'd failed a wife once. He didn't have the guts to risk going through that again. He'd rather face the entire Mexican army alone and unarmed than fasten wedding shackles around his ankles once again.

He'd been head over heels for Rachel when they married. He'd liked being a husband, loved having a home and family. When Rachel gave birth first to Daniel, then to little Sarah, Luke believed himself the happiest, luckiest man on earth. But it hadn't lasted. War had come to Texas, and Luke had destroyed his life, his love, and his self-respect.

"I can't help her, Luella," he said softly as they approached the house. "I'm not at all certain I can even help myself."

The day's events haunted him as he lay in bed that night. He tossed and turned, unable to slumber, until the break of dawn when sheer exhaustion allowed him the surcease of sleep.

Which was why he was still in bed shortly after nine o'clock when Honor's scream split the air.

9

The instant she spied the blood Honor screamed and started running. "Jason!" she cried, dashing across a clearing brilliant with bluebonnets and Indian paintbrush, her skirt hiked to her knees. As she drew closer to the boys, horror joined the fear.

The shaft of an arrow protruded from her son's shoulder.

Oh, Jason.

Micah supported his younger brother's weight as they stumbled toward her, his freckled complexion as pasty and pained as Jason's.

"What happened?" Honor asked when she reached them, her voice trembling with the question.

"We sneaked out to the caverns," Micah said. "He caught us by surprise. We never should've disobeyed Cap'n Luke's rules."

"It hurts, Honor. Am I gonna die like my mama and daddy?"

The fear in his voice nearly sent her to her knees. "Oh, baby. No." Forcing a smile, she stared her injured son straight in his pain-glazed eyes and declared, "You'll be just fine, Jason. I promise. Cross my heart."

"But you're gonna have to rip the arrow out."

Micah wiped the perspiration from his brother's face with his sleeve. "Won't be any rippin', Jase. Honor will do it nice and gentle. She's always gentle. You know that."

"Yeah." Jason's eyes closed. The bloodstain seeping across his blue chambray shirt continued to grow.

Honor sniffed the metallic scent of blood and almost gagged. Her gaze locked on the stain, her thoughts whirling like a dust devil. She didn't know what to do. She couldn't apply pressure to the wound to stop the bleeding with the arrow embedded in his shoulder, but she was afraid to pull it loose. What if that only made the bleeding worse?

My baby! My sweet little boy!

Think, Honor. Think. Spiderwebs and soot. That's it. She needed spiderwebs and soot to stop the bleeding. Luella. She needed Luella's help. No, not Luella. Luke. He'd know. He'd know what else to do. Oh, Luke, I need you.

She opened her mouth to shout his name when the sound of his voice pierced the muddle in her mind. "What happened?" Luke called, hurrying toward them. He was shirtless, wearing only buckskin pants and leather moccasins. His right hand clasped his Texas Paterson. Honor's gaze latched onto him like a lifeline. "Help us, Luke," she pleaded.

His raking gaze assessed the situation in seconds. "We're lucky. It went all the way through."

171

She hadn't thought to check that. Dear Lord, she hadn't been thinking at all.

"Let's get inside. I'd be surprised to see a full-fledged attack come this time of day, but we can't take any chances." Taking care not to jar Jason's shoulder, Luke scooped him into his arms. Jason let out a moan and his body went limp.

Honor's heart stopped. "Jason!"

"He's fainted, Honor. That's all." Luke started for the house. "It's better this way. That arrow needs to come out and it won't feel good. Micah, you run on ahead and tell your grandmother what's happened."

Micah raced across the pasture toward the house. Honor scurried along beside Luke. "Jason will be fine. He will, Luke, right?"

He glanced down at the boy. "Yeah. If you gotta get hit, the shoulder's a good place for it to happen." Anger simmered in his voice as he demanded, "Why haven't you mentioned Indian troubles to me before?"

"We don't have Indian troubles."

"That's a Tonkawa arrow sticking out of Jason's shoulder."

Honor sucked her bottom lip and shook her head. Indians had not done this, but she wouldn't argue with him now. Later, once Jason was better, she'd argue with him. "Do you know what to do to help him?"

"I was a Texas Ranger on the western frontier for the better part of seven years. I've seen an arrow wound or two."

Jason let out an unconscious moan as Luke climbed the stone steps to Lost Pines's front porch. Micah held open the heavy door. "Nana's in the kitchen heating up water. What else can I do, Luke?"

"I need your grandmother in the house more than I need hot water. Get her inside, then lock and bar the doors. Bring the guns and ammunition upstairs. We'll keep watch up there."

He carried Jason upstairs. Honor ducked around him, racing to the boys' bedroom where she yanked back the bedding and fluffed the pillow.

"Sit down and hold him, Honor. We can't lay him down until we get the arrow out."

She did as he asked and he lowered the boy into her arms. "I need my knife. I'll be right back."

Honor nodded, unable to speak past the emotion clogging her throat. He limped as he left the room, and Honor realized then it must have hurt him to move as quickly as he had while carrying Jason. He'd never exhibited any pain. "The Bravest Man in Texas," she murmured.

A warm wetness dripped onto her arm and she glanced down. Blood. Bright red and ugly. "Oh, baby."

Tears slid down her cheeks as she gazed at the iron point protruding from a dogwood shaft. "I'm so sorry I brought you to this."

It was her fault. She knew it in her soul. This was her father's doing, not the Tonkawas'. Richard Armstrong was behind this villainy. She knew it.

Luke returned and Honor held her breath while he went to work. After slashing away Jason's shirt, he cut the arrow's shaft as close to the boy's skin as he could manage. Still unconscious, Jason thrashed in her arms.

"Hold him still, Honor. This will hurt him." Luke gasped the arrow just below the hawk-tailed fletching, took a deep breath, and yanked the arrow free.

Honor knew she'd hear that sucking sound in her dreams for years to come. Jason's scream would haunt her for the rest of her life.

Blood spurted from the wound both front and back. Panicking, Honor jerked her head up. "What do—"

Luella came forth with bandages and warm water just as Micah dashed into the room, crying, "I brought spiderwebs from the attic. Got a big ol' ball of 'em."

"Excellent," Luella said matter-of-factly. She was a vision of efficiency as she instructed Honor to lay Jason on his good shoulder and move away from the bed. "After I wash him up we'll pack the wound with webs and bandage it, front and back. Tomorrow we'll make a prickly pear poultice to protect him against infection."

Honor gazed questioningly at Luke and he nodded his agreement with Luella's treatment. "Why don't you go on to your room, Honor. Take up watch at the window. If the Tonks are coming, they'll likely come from that direction."

"The Tonkawas aren't coming," she replied, her gaze on Luella as she ministered to Jason. "Micah, I think you'd better tell Captain Prescott exactly what happened."

"No, I think you'd best go keep watch," Luke snapped.

"The Tonkawas did not do this."

"Honor's right, Cap'n Prescott." Micah laid a comforting hand on his brother's thigh. "The Tonks leave us alone because of what Honor did for 'em a few years ago."

"What Honor did for them?"

The boy nodded, a spot of color returning to his complexion as Luella concealed Jason's wound with a clean white bandage. "It wasn't long after the Colonel moved us out here. Honor saved a little Indian boy from drowning in the Colorado. Turned out he was family to the chief. They've left us alone ever since."

Luella glanced up. "They've been rather friendly, actually. They've brought us meat upon occasion."

"They would never have hurt Jason. Never." Honor's voice throbbed with loathing as she unfolded a brightly colored quilt to lay across her son. "This is Richard Armstrong's doing. I'm certain of it."

Luke speared her with a look as sharp as the bloody arrowhead that now lay on the nightstand. Between them hung the reality that, if she were correct, Luke had failed in his charge to protect the boys. "Tell me," he demanded of Micah.

"We did wrong, Cap'n. We disobeyed your rules. Remember Jase and me telling you about the new tunnel we discovered in the sinkhole cavern? Well, after Nana said we wouldn't have to study our lessons until this afternoon we decided to get up early and do a little exploring. When we got there we saw that somebody else found it, too."

"Not the new tunnel," Jason said weakly from his bed. "The main part."

"Jason!" Honor cried.

They spent the next few minutes inquiring after his health and rejoicing in the fact that he had awakened. Then Micah continued his story. "We stumbled on a campsite not far from the cavern's entrance. Bedroll and coffeepot, the usual stuff. We didn't see anybody, so we went on to the sinkhole."

"That's where he winged me." Jason closed his eyes, his mouth dipping in a pained grimace. "Indians don't use coffeepots, Captain. Honor's right."

"I see." Luke's words held a depth of meaning.

Watching him, Honor swallowed hard. The change in his appearance was both subtle and intimidating. He stood a little straighter, a tad broader, but it was his face that revealed the most. It reflected nothing at all.

175

Texas Ranger Captain Luke Prescott stood before them now. Honor thought of things she had heard said about him. Mean as hell with the hide off when he's riled. So hard he could kick fire out of flint with his bare toes. She looked for the man who'd held her so tenderly the night before and saw only the man she'd hired to protect her family. The mixed feelings she experienced surprised her.

Micah obviously noted the difference, also. His voice was eager as he said, "I had my shotgun with me though, Cap'n, and I aimed toward the place where the arrow came from. I got off both barrels. Chances are I winged him right back."

"Where is this cavern?"

Micah provided vague directions that Luke pinned down with crisp, precise questions.

"You're going after him?" Honor asked.

"That's how I'm supposed to earn my keep, isn't it?" He addressed Luella and Micah. "I want y'all to stay in the house till I return. Preferably upstairs with an eye toward the windows, all right?"

Honor waited expectantly for her directions, and when he cocked his head toward the door, she nodded and followed him out of the room and down the hall. She paused just outside the master suite, standing uncomfortably in the doorway while he strapped on his gun belt and buckled his knife sheath around his thigh. Sunlight beaming through the front door glinted off the knife blade as he slipped it into place. Honor shivered as old ghosts rose in her mind to haunt her.

"I want you to think it over good before I leave the four of y'all here alone, Honor. Take a minute and consider everything. Are you certain of this story? When I go I'll be leaving you unprotected." One side of his mouth lifted in a scornful smile. "Not that I did you much good this morning. I apologize for my failure. It won't happen again."

Honor shook her head. "It's not your fault. The boys shouldn't have gone to the caverns alone. I'm as much to blame as anyone. If I hadn't defied my father—"

"You're positive Armstrong is behind this?"

She gave him the minute of thought he'd requested, not because she needed to but because she respected the logic behind his plea. "Yes, I'm positive, Luke. The Tonkawas wouldn't hurt us. I'd bet my life on it."

Luke lifted his hat from a chair and set it on his head, yanking it low on his forehead as he moved toward her. He stopped a mere foot away, his steel gray eyes staring at her from beneath the hat's wide brim. "That's exactly what you're doing, you know," he said softly. "Betting your life and the lives of your family."

"Yes." Honor touched his arm. "But the person I'm betting on is you."

Honor watched from her own bedroom window until Luke's form blended with the forest. Pressing her fingertips against the warm glass, she said, "God go with you, Captain."

When she returned to the boys' room, she found Jason asleep and Micah speaking softly to his grandmother. "We've been exploring a new passageway through the caverns. I wish your knees weren't so bad, Nana. You'd love to see it! The rock formations are so fine. Jason and I figure out what they look like and give 'em names. There's the Fisherman and the Frog and the Christmas Star. We're fighting over what to call this new one we found. Jace likes the Ghost, but I think Crazy Horse fits it better." A lock of red hair plopped down on his forehead as he glanced at his

177

brother's sleeping form. "Maybe we'll go with the Ghost after all."

After testing the temperature of Jason's forehead with her hand, Honor sat beside Micah on his bed. "I'm going to have to punish you, you realize. And even if Luke catches whoever did this today, I still want your word you'll stay away from those caverns."

"I promise. I'll probably be too scared to go back for months, anyway."

Honor didn't bother to remind him they wouldn't be living at Lost Pines for months to come. At least, that's what she hoped, now more than ever.

Luella asked, "Micah, did you see anything in the culprit's camp that might help to identify him?" To Honor, she said, "Your father smokes a particular blend of tobacco. The aroma is quite distinctive."

Micah scrunched his face as he thought. "I know that tobacco and I didn't smell it. All I can remember is the hat. The hatband caught my eye. I halfway remember seeing one like it before, but I can't remember where or when."

"Describe it for us," Honor said.

"It's whistles. Tin whistles all strung together."

Tin whistles. Honor sucked her teeth. She'd seen that hat before, herself. But who? Someone in town? A friend of Armand's? Maybe—

It came to her then, and fury fountained up inside her. "Wild Horse Jerry Mullins."

Luella snapped her fingers. "That's it. You're right, Honor. I remember that hat myself."

Mullins hadn't worn the hat the day he'd attacked her almost two years ago, otherwise she'd have made the connection immediately. Suddenly, so many things made sense. "I could kick myself. I should have realized from the beginning that Mullins did Father's dirty work." Vaulting to her feet, Honor paced the bedroom, ticking off each point on her fingers. "He lives in Bastrop County. He's done work for my father in the past. He certainly has reason to hate me—that scar of his healed poorly. He's a perfect pawn for Richard Armstrong to use."

Luella drummed her fingers on the arms of her chair. "You didn't mention something else. He's a nasty, mean son of a buck, Honor."

Micah said, "Cap'n Luke will have to track him through the forest. Bet he doesn't catch up with him until tomorrow. Hope it doesn't rain and wipe out his trail."

Silence settled over the room like a shroud. Three pairs of eyes fixed on the boy lying wounded on the bed. Jason's head tossed on the pillow. He let out an anguished groan.

Luella grumbled, "I'd like to shoot the man dead, then shoot him again just to keep my barrels clean."

Honor looked at her son. "I can shoot a gun when I'm angry. I don't flinch. You know what, Luella? I'm very angry at Wild Horse Jerry Mullins."

Muggy spring heat wrapped the earth as Luke tracked through the forest. The scent of pine hung heavy on the air along with an unusual silence. A hot afternoon loomed on the horizon, suggesting perfect conditions for a thunderstorm late in the day.

Wonderful, Luke thought. Just what he needed—a toad-strangler to wipe away the bastard's trail. Rain made his job more difficult, but not impossible. Nothing would prevent his finding the bastard cowardly enough to hide in bushes and shoot a child.

Luke was in a foul mood. The morning's events had made him mad enough to chew leather and at the same time pricked his pride. While the boys he'd promised to protect went and played with danger, he'd been laid up in bed asleep. He'd failed in his duty, once again, because a woman had him tied up in knots. It made him mad enough to chew bullets.

But the person I'm betting on is you.

Honor's words echoed through his mind. God, it was happening all over again. Once before, others had wagered on his abilities and lost, paying the highest possible price. He hoped like hell that this time he'd live up to expectations.

He hoped he hadn't made a fatal mistake by believing Honor knew what she was talking about, and that the Tonks weren't raiding Lost Pines this very minute.

Although the boys' path through the forest was obvious, the going proved slow. The density of the trees made travel by foot preferable to horseback, even for a man with a gimp leg. Besides, he might be willing to bet his life that Honor was right and the Indians weren't about the wood this morning, but he wasn't willing to bet his horse. Any tribe nearby, friendly or not, wouldn't think twice about stealing such prime horseflesh.

Atop a slight knoll he paused and sniffed a deep lungful of air. He'd learned to read the wind long before joining up with the Rangers and he'd utilized the skill often. Slowly, carefully, he separated the parts of the breeze. From nearby, the bite of dung. Rain to the southwest. Pine sap all around. Luke tasted the air, worried it. The wind shifted and he caught a burst of wood smoke and rabbit grease, but not his prey. Not the particular human stink of a man who'd shoot a young, unarmed boy.

He whooshed out his breath and started back down the hill, picking up the boys' trail again at the bottom. Within minutes he'd entered a section of the forest grown thick with hardwoods, loblollies, and underbrush. Here the path Micah and Jason had taken was more obvious; so, too, was the opportunity for ambush. His senses alert, Luke moved cautiously and carefully forward.

Even in his concentration, he thought of Honor. So, she'd saved an Indian child. Somehow that didn't surprise him. Most Texians agreed with the vicious Indian policy President Lamar had established in his administration, but Honor lived by her own set of rules. Popular opinion wouldn't mean squat to the notorious Widow Duvall.

Luke liked her for that.

In fact, Luke liked Honor for a lot of reasons. Maybe that was why the idea Luella had planted continued to niggle at the back of his brain, even in the midst of today's troublesome events. Marriage. Him and Honor Duvall.

No. It was a crazy idea. "Luella's butter has slipped right off her cornbread," he muttered.

Luke's senses told him he was alone in this section of the forest. He moved quickly, hoping to pick up the archer's trail and get business accomplished fast. He was anxious to return to Lost Pines, to check on the boy and to reassure himself that his belief in Honor's suspicions had not been misplaced.

He came upon the sinkhole abruptly. So abruptly, in fact, that he damned near fell into it. He stood at the very edge of an oval-shaped aperture some fifteen yards across and ten yards wide. Near the center, a narrow, natural bridge of limestone spanned the yawning break in the earth. Someone—probably the Best boys—had tied a rope at its narrowest point. Luke leaned over the precipice to see it dangling to the ground some sixty feet below. "Couple of monkeys," he observed, noting the dark, shadowed entrance to the cavern at the back of the sinkhole.

Bloodstains at the foot of the bridge indicated Jason's position when hit. Luke clenched his jaw as his determination to apprehend the culprit soared to new heights. By the looks of it, the boy easily could have tumbled over the edge when the arrow struck.

That thought heavy on his mind, Luke smiled with grim satisfaction when his search found evidence that Micah had, in fact, winged the son of a bitch. Luke touched his finger to the splash of red on a gray rock, then glanced back toward the spot where Jason had been shot. A definite ambush, this. The fellow obviously had lain in wait for the boys.

Luke's nose led him to a campsite not far from the blood spatters, and what he discovered answered a couple of interesting questions. Honor had been right. This was no Indian camp. Second, the bastard had left the area bleeding and mounted, most likely on a mule. Good. He'd make better time on foot.

He'd have his prey in sight before the noonin'.

Picking up the trail, he traveled steadily for the better part of an hour. The shadowed stillness of the woods surrounded him, calling to mind similar stretches of land in eastern Texas, and other manhunts. Gentleman Rafe Malone had stolen his last horse in east Texas. The ambush that had come so close to ruining Luke's leg had occurred in a thicket much like this.

Memories, more bad than good, kept Luke company on his trek, and he smiled with gratitude when warm sunlight struck him full in the face as he broke through the edge of the forest. Luke recognized the spot right off. He was close to Castle Hill, some five or six miles from town.

"Bet he's gone for a doctor," he murmured to himself.

A glance off to the north suggested he'd wagered

wrong. Fifty yards away at the top of a hill, a mule munched grass in front of a small log blockhouse. At the animal's feet, in danger of being trod upon, lay a bow. Luke had run his prey to ground.

He hardly noticed. The hundred-dollar horse tied to a post on the far side of the mule arrested his attention.

Luke knew that horse. He knew her very well. He'd groomed her the day before yesterday, and he'd seen her earlier this morning munching spring grass in the pasture at Lost Pines.

Fear kicked him in the gut. What the hell was Honor's horse doing here?

Honor trembled like a kitten up a tall tree as she held the Paterson trained on Wild Horse Jerry Mullins. Light spilled into the structure through eight narrow loopholes in the walls and illuminated a fearsome sight. Wild Horse Jerry Mullins lay mortally wounded on the floor, his lifeblood steadily draining from his cursed body.

Fear and fury battled for supremacy within her. She'd ridden her horse dangerously fast on the Indian trail through the forest, flying across the clearings and the meadows until she'd located the prey she'd sought. She'd come here to kill him, to shoot him dead, but now she felt the urge to stanch the flow from his wound. What was wrong with her? Wild Horse Jerry was gut shot and begging her to put him out of his misery. Why didn't she just do it?

"Ain't nothing can be done," he said weakly. "I knew it as soon as that boy of yours plugged me. Finish me. Do it now. Ain't that what you came after me for?"

She didn't reply.

"Damn you, Honor Duvall, you owe me."

183

"I don't owe you the time of day," she snapped.

"That's a lie." A spasm of pain racked his face. His voice quavered. "I lost everything because of you— my land, my woman. My very best horse. You marked me!" He rolled his head to display the ragged scar that tore across his cheek from his temple to his chin.

The barrel of Honor's gun jerked wildly as the shakes intensified. "You tried to rape me!"

His colorless skin appeared white against the crimson packed-dirt floor. He closed his eyes. "I was just funnin' with you. You didn't have to slice up my face."

Funning with her? One of the most terrifying moments of her life and he was funning with her? Honor's eyes narrowed and her aim steadied. "I was aiming for your jewels at the time, Wild Horse. I lost my balance."

"Always were a damned clumsy gal," he mumbled, his voice weakening. "Do a better job of it now, all right? Knowing my luck, you'll foul this up too."

"Maybe I want you to suffer. You tried to kill my son."

A ghost of a smile touched his bloodless lips. "Reckon I'm no better with a bow than you are with a knife. I wasn't aiming for your boy. Meant to shoot over his head. Killing one of the young'uns was to be a last resort. I didn't figure we'd gotten that far yet."

Honor clasped her gun with both hands as Luke had taught her, hoping to steady her aim or at least calm her shakes. "You deserve to hurt, Jerry Mullins. You've terrorized us all. Jason could have died, and we still must worry about infection setting in."

"Bitch." He spat the invective weakly as he attempted to pull up his blanket. "It's gettin' cold in here, ain't it? Or I reckon it's the dyin'." His voice drifted lower. "I damn near made it home. Did my best to get there. Didn't cotton to the idea of spending my last hours on the cold hard ground, but it looks like that's what'll happen. God damn, it hurts!"

He fell silent and Honor wondered if he'd lost consciousness. She took a couple steps toward him, trying to decide what to do.

His voice was a specter's whisper. "You gonna let that boy be a killer, Honor?"

She shuddered. "Don't say that."

"It's true. If you don't pull that trigger, your Micah's gonna be the one with my blood on his hands. A boy has a hard time washing 'em clean."

"You, not my son, are responsible for your own predicament." But even as she said it, she recognized he'd read her right. Even if she found the will to deny her natural compassion for someone who suffered, she refused to allow Micah's bullet to be the one that killed this man. Not when the means to prevent it lay within her grasp.

Honor dropped her arms to her sides, the gun hanging limply from her right hand. She wished she'd never come looking for him, never discovered his empty cabin, never remembered the blockhouse that sat on a direct path between the boys' caverns and Mullins's home. Built by early settlers for defense against the Indians, the small fort undoubtedly had seen its share of death. Another life would end here today. She would take it.

"Dammit, Honor. Get it over with. The waitin' is as bad as the hurtin'."

"Give me a minute, would you?" Tears gathered in her eyes. Her gaze locked on his bloody hands cradled against the wound just above his belt. She searched for the courage to do as he asked and found that killing proved much more difficult than she ever imagined.

"Shit." His strength seemed to fade with the word.

"Sure am thirsty. If you won't kill me, at least give me some water."

"I didn't say I wouldn't do it. I'm thinking about it."

"Well, while you're thinking, give me a drink. I dropped my pouch by the door."

Sighing, she glanced around for the flask. A thought tugged at her mind, something about giving water to a belly-shot man. She couldn't remember whether one should or should not offer it. For all her anger at Mullins's actions, Honor's heart was torn by his suffering. Locating the leather pouch, she carried it toward the bed. "I'd go easy on this. It might not be good for you."

"What's it gonna do, kill me?"

Honor lay down her gun to help him lift his head. After two small sips he dropped back against the mattress with a groan.

She gazed into his chalky white face and saw the handsome man he once had been. "Why did you do it, Jerry? Why did you go after my boys?"

"Revenge." He sucked in a breath, grimacing. "It's a powerful motivator. Money ain't bad, either."

"My father paid you."

"Yeah. You really . . ."—he panted twice—". . . got his dander up." His face contorted and tears slipped from his eyes. "Too long. This is taking too damned long." A vile curse rumbled off his tongue.

And a bloody hand reached for the gun she'd left untended.

Honor froze. Light returned to his eyes and his lips lifted in an evil, maniacal smile. "Your squeamishness is gonna kill you, gal. You shoulda done me in when you got the chance. Hell, you shoulda killed me that time I got beneath your skirts."

Had she not been so angry, she'd have been scared

witless. What a fool she'd been to leave the gun within reach. "Look, Wild Horse—"

"Shut up. You had your chance. I'm dying and I don't feel like going alone." He cocked the pistol and the trigger dropped.

He pointed the Paterson straight at her heart.

10

Luke had a real bad feeling in his gut. His neck itched something fierce. Nudging up against the fort's southern wall, he listened intently for any sounds coming from within. Honor's gasp was the first noise he heard. The deeper-pitched male rumble was more difficult to make out, so he eased closer to the loophole.

"You owe me, Honor. I did everything you asked. Every goddamned thing. You stood there battin' those eyelashes and flashin' that smile. You knew what you were doin', what you were promisin'. Admit it, Honor."

Son of a bitch, who was this man? Luke's thoughts rushed like the wind. Was Honor in on this man's plot? Had Luke been set up from the first? Was she the liar he had feared?

No, she'd never hurt those boys. Her fear this morning had been real. Had her partner acted against orders? Was that what brought her here?

"All right," she said harshly. "I admit it. I promised to trade my favors in exchange for your help."

Good God, she'd confessed. A yawning hole of pain seemed to open up inside of Luke, but anger quickly rushed in to fill it. His breath came in shallow, silent pants. The woman had played him like a barn dance waltz, and he'd acted as though he had gunpowder for brains. Richard Armstrong a spy? What a crock. Honor Duvall was a lying, cheating, scheming witch.

"I did it all," the man inside the fort said. "Didn't I?"

"Everything. You did everything I asked."

Her voice sounded breathless. Wait a minute, was that fear?

"And you double-crossed me. Just like you're doin' with that Ranger, now. Didn't fool me. I knew from the moment he turned up what was goin' on. What did you promise him, Honor? Have you paid him yet? Has he plugged you yet? If not, he's too damned late. I'm ahead of him in line. Only problem is, I'm gonna have to plug you different from how I wanted."

In a flash, Luke's face was at the loophole. He saw Honor. Pale and afraid. No angle for a shot at the man. The door was on the north wall. Move, dammit!

"Jerry—"

"Say your prayers, gal."

"Drop, Honor!" Luke shouted, kicking open the door. Seconds passed like hours. The man wasn't where Luke expected. There, on the floor. Squeezing the trigger. Honor still on her feet. *Too late! I'm too late!*

Luke heard the other gun click as his own exploded. Once, twice. The man fell dead.

The echo from Luke's shots reverberated through the small room. Honor stared down at the body, then up at him, her doe eyes dazed and bewildered. "I forgot. I was in a hurry and I didn't pay close attention. I forgot to load powder into the gun."

Disgust rolled through him in waves. He shoved his Paterson into its holster and turned on his heel. Damned if he hadn't forgotten something, too. Never trust a widow woman wearing a yellow dress.

The physical exertion of digging another grave for the widow took the edge off Luke's anger, but only the edge. Honor showed enough sense to steer clear of him while he planted the man he'd killed on her behalf. He broke a sweat while filling in the hole when what he really wanted to break was Honor Duvall's neck.

The words he'd heard her say screamed in his mind. *I admit it. I promised to trade my favors in exchange for your help.*

The thinking half of him wanted to kill her. To his utter dismay, the rest of him still wanted to bed her.

"Son of a bitch." He tossed down the shovel and drilled a glare toward the blockhouse where the Black Widow sat on the stoop, her arms crossed, her foot tapping, and her own glower every bit as angry as his own. She'd started right in with the chin music, trying to jaw her way out of the corner she'd hemmed herself into. Luke hadn't been in a humor to listen to it then, nor was he of a mind to attend to it now.

Wind swirled around him, heavy with the scent of rain. He glanced toward the sky and his mood blackened. Twenty minutes before it opened up if they were lucky, and the greenish tint to the cloud indicated hail. His choice loomed before him. Leave and get soaked by a cold spring rain and possibly beat up by ice, or stay and share shelter with the wicked Widow Duvall.

Determined strides carried Luke toward the horse. As he slipped his foot into the stirrup, she jumped to her feet and asked, "What do you think you are doing?"

"Going into town."

"What about me? That's my horse you're climbing onto, Captain."

"You can use the mule." Luke cocked his head toward the brand-new grave. "He won't be needing it."

Her eyes shot bullets. "That's my horse and if you try to leave here with it, I'll have you arrested for stealing."

Luke cracked a laugh. "Now that's a good one. Like anyone in the Republic would take your word over mine." He prepared to hoist himself into the saddle, but a hundred-pound cannonball launched herself at his body.

He had one foot in the stirrup and she caught him off balance. Luke hit the ground with a thud, Honor landing on top of him. By the grace of God alone he pulled his boot free without breaking his ankle. The horse shied and Luke rolled them away from the flailing hooves, finally stopping with Honor beneath him.

Pain radiated up his bad leg as he shoved up on his arms and glared down at her. "What, do you have a death wish today? That horse could have killed us both."

Her eyes flashed. Her cheeks glowed with color. Her lips. Oh, Lord, her lips. Time hung suspended as a fierce shaft of longing pierced the shell of Luke's pain and anger and distrust. "Damn," he muttered, instinctively lowering his mouth to hers.

But Honor wasn't having any of it. She caught his lower lip between her teeth and held on till he yelped. "Get off of me, Prescott." She pushed ineffectually at his chest. "You have the nerve of an abscessed tooth."

"Me!" He tasted the coppery tang of blood as he

ran his tongue over the wound on his lip. "You're one to talk."

The first cold spatter of rain hit the back of Luke's neck, distracting him long enough to glance up at the sky. Well, great. His sense of timing reeked today. "Come on. Let's get inside."

Honor shook her head. "I'm not going in that fort. The blood . . . I can't."

"Fine. Get wet." He got to his feet. "Maybe a hailstone will hit you and knock some sense into you. It's fixin' to come a gully washer, and I aim to stay dry."

Honor stood and brushed off her skirt. "I never took you for a fool before today, Captain Prescott. I could have explained everything had you offered me the opportunity to be heard."

"Oh, I don't doubt that." He started for the blockhouse. "You, Mrs. Duvall, have lying down to an art form." Thunder rumbled and the rain fell harder. He expected Honor to follow, but instead she ran for her horse. Cursing the frequency of springtime thunderstorms in Texas, Luke stood in the doorway and watched as the hardheaded woman guided the horse down the hill.

Then the crack of lightning nearby sent him right back outside into the rain. "Damn fool woman."

The need to protect Honor Duvall was a living, breathing monster inside him. He glared at the spot in the trees where she'd disappeared, then headed after her, cursing the indignity of riding the dead man's mule. Within moments he was soaked to the skin.

Honor's flight through the forest took an obvious path. Luke trailed her, angry at himself and even angrier at Honor. Why was the woman forever outside during rainstorms?

He smelled lightning on the air just before it struck

too close for comfort. He kicked the mule, ignoring the dull ache in his leg, hoping to catch up with her soon. "Then I'm gonna drag her by the hair back to that blasted fort before we both get struck dead by a thunderbolt."

A long ten minutes later, he exhaled a grateful breath. There, through the trees, sat a cabin. Honor's horse was tethered beneath a lean-to outside. She was safe.

Luke dismounted to approach the cabin. Halfway down the slope, his foot found a muddy spot and slid out from beneath him. He went down hard on his knee, jarring his bad leg. He clenched his teeth against a groan and silently cursed the woman he pursued.

He all but dragged himself the rest of the way, muttering as he sheltered the mule with the horse. He'd done too much walking today. That, along with the cold rain and the spill, had made his leg muscles one big bundle of nerves. Finally, he reached the cabin door. Pushing it open and ducking inside, he spied a shivering, water-soaked figure stacking logs in the fireplace.

He was proud that his voice reflected only disgust and not a hint of pain as he said, "Damn fool woman."

Honor looked up with world-weary eyes. "Why did you follow me? Why won't you leave me alone?"

It was a hundred-dollar question and Luke's answer came straight from his heart, skipping his mind entirely. "I can't."

"Why not?"

Luke shrugged. He had no answer for her. He had yet to figure that out for himself.

Raindrops drummed against the shingles as he crossed the small room. His leg was telling him to sit, but he refused to listen. While Honor fiddled with the measly fire, he broke the lock on the trunk at the foot of the bed and rummaged through it for dry clothing.

What he found was only half his size. He'd wait for the fire Honor nursed to life to dry his own things.

Long minutes passed with neither of them speaking. Eventually, thunder boomed and Honor jumped, a question exploding from her mouth like an accusation. "You overheard me talking to Wild Horse?"

Luke scowled at the fledgling flames and nodded. "I must say you're slicker than boiled okra, Honor Duvall. You all but had me convinced your story about your father was true. Tell me something. Are Luella and the boys in on it, or are you tormenting your family for the fun of it?"

Loathing filled the look she shot him. "You play yourself for a fool, Luke Prescott. I would have thought Texas Rangers knew better than to jump to conclusions."

"I'm not a Ranger."

"But you are a fool. I'd have said anything under the circumstances and besides, the lies I told referred to an incident that happened two years ago. I'd just as soon not bother to share the details." Turning back to the fire, she dismissed him. "Believe what you want, Captain. I truly don't care."

The sneer in her voice told him she meant it and for some strange reason that rankled. Luke didn't want to dwell on her words. He was too miserable to think at the moment.

A shiver raked his bones. He was as cold as a well digger's boots. Honor couldn't build a fire worth beans. His fingers jerked at his laces as he tugged his shirt open. The heavy, wet buckskin peeled from his skin as he stripped away his shirt and tossed it on the floor. "I should have stayed in that fort and kept dry," he muttered.

Honor glanced over her shoulder, her gaze locking on his bare chest. "Feel free to use the blanket from the bed to cover yourself, Prescott."

"If you insist," he snapped back. He'd be damned if he'd feel guilty about taking the blanket, he decided as he wrapped the scratchy wool around his bare torso. It was her fault he was wet. He wouldn't be half frozen and his leg wouldn't be killing him if he hadn't chased after Honor Duvall. Why had he bothered? Why should he care about her safety after what she had done?

The voice of reason whispered in his head. *And just what did she do?*

She whored her favors and played the double-cross, that's what. Luke had heard her say it.

Under the gun, she'd said it. You can't hold that against her.

Luke growled low in his throat, his mind jerking away from such thoughts. His gaze raked the widow, the man in him unable to ignore the way her sopping dress clung to her curves. Emotions rumbled inside him, knowledge he didn't want to face. Grabbing up his shirt, he marched across the room toward the fireplace, gritting his teeth against the pain in his leg and the turmoil in his soul. He spread his shirt across the back of the rocking chair pulled close to the hearth, then appropriated the poker from her hand. "Let me do it. We'll freeze to death with you in charge of the fire. If you have any smarts at all you'll get out of that dress before you catch a chill."

She rolled her eyes. "That, Captain Prescott, is a line as old as black pepper."

"You can leave off being snippy, Mrs. Duvall. I don't want you naked." In his mind, he gave a bitter laugh. It was the biggest lie he'd voiced in years.

"How reassuring," she said dryly. "I'm fine dressed as I am, thank you very much."

Even as she said it she moved away from the fireplace and toward the wooden chest. For his own sake he hoped she'd find something to wear, something big and thick that didn't plaster itself to her skin the way that thin dress did.

Luke devoured her with his gaze as she bent over the chest. I'm fine, she'd said. The epitome of understatement, that. Honor Duvall was more than fine. She was the kind of woman to make a Texas Ranger forget his horse.

Instantly, with an intensity that left him breathless, arousal clawed through him, hardening his body. Wonderful. Just what he needed. One more ache to go with all the others.

She pulled a white linen shirt from the trunk and held it up, judging its size. Her fingers moved to the buttons at her bodice and she gave him a pointed look. Luke turned away and devoted his attention to the fire, using the poker to shift the logs and allow for better air circulation. He heard the damp fabric plop soggily to the floor and an image of Honor's naked body flashed in his mind.

He blew out a sigh that sounded similar to the hiss of the kindling fire. Why did she do this to him? Knowing what he knew, why did this woman, this liar, affect him as she did?

Because in your heart you know she's not a liar. You believe her. You believe in her. She'd told the truth all along. Honor Duvall is no enemy to you or her family or even Texas.

Luke groaned softly and shut his eyes. But he couldn't hide from the truth. It *was* true. He could trust the widow. The person he couldn't trust was himself.

The reality of the moment washed over him. She'd called it right. He had been a fool. The minute he'd spied her horse where he hadn't expected it and heard her admit to something he should have known was coerced, his brain had taken a siesta. Well, hell. The worst lies a man told were the ones he told himself.

Honor was aptly named. Everything he'd seen in the weeks he'd spent at Lost Pines proved it. Love for her family shone in her every action. She displayed her courage, loyalty, and sincerity daily. He'd jumped to a conclusion today and literally got a soaking for it. A well-merited soaking. Honor had deserved a chance to explain. He'd have to apologize.

The idea managed to dampen his desire, somewhat anyway. Luke jabbed at a burning log with the poker and summoned the will to say he was sorry, not an easy feat, by any means. "Honor, I'm—"

He turned around to face her and damn near swallowed his tongue. Look at the legs on that woman!

The man's shirt she wore hit just above mid-thigh. She'd taken the braid from her hair and stood wringing the water from the long red tresses. Her dress and petticoat lay draped across a ladderback chair, her undergarments spread across the top of the trunk.

She had to be naked beneath that shirt.

The fire tool slipped from his hand and clattered against the puncheon floor. Good Lord, he was in trouble. He was hot. Leaving the poker where it lay, he moved away from the fireplace and cleared his throat. "Your turn, Honor. You'd best get warm before you catch your death."

Her gaze was frosty. "I suppose you're right. I almost caught my death once today. Once is enough."

He winced, knowing once would never be enough with Honor Duvall.

Hail pounded against the roof as Luke finally eased

the ache in his leg by sitting on the edge of the cabin's narrow bed. A nasty storm whipped around outside. The one brewing inside the cabin was no slouch, either, he thought. Might as well face it and hope it blows over fast. He fumbled around for words to ease into his apology and finally asked, "Who was that man?"

Standing in front of the fireplace, Honor bent at the waist and turned her head, allowing her hair to fan toward the floor while she combed it with her fingers. She met his stare. "Wild Horse Jerry Mullins."

"How did you come to be there?"

She turned her head away from him and fussed with the other side of her hair. "After you left, Micah described the attacker's hatband. I recognized it and realized Mullins was the culprit."

"So you decided to go after him yourself?"

"Yes."

Frustration rushed in like water, strangling Luke's voice. "You know, Honor, if I didn't know better, I'd accuse you of being smart." She jerked upright, but he pressed on. "What were you thinking of? You almost got yourself killed. I may not walk real good these days, but I can track the devil in the dark. I'd have found the bastard."

"I'm the boys' mother."

"So?"

"It's my job to defend them."

"But that's why you hired me."

She shut her eyes and shook her head. "I know. It's just ... I can't explain. I'm their parent. I should defend those boys."

"Like your father defended you?" Luke snapped.

She whirled around and faced the fire. The cedar log spat and crackled. Like Honor in a temper, Luke thought. "Was he following your father's orders?"

At first she didn't respond and Luke waited, massaging the cramping muscle in his leg through his wet wool trousers. "Honor?"

"He said my father paid him. Killing was to be a last resort."

"Richard Armstrong would murder his own grandson?"

She offered him a bitter smile. "They're not his blood kin. He's an Englishman, Luke. Blood is everything."

Luke didn't know how to reply to that. He did know the time had come to pursue the truth about the candidate for president. The jubilee was the first step. After today he better understood why Honor didn't want her father anywhere near Lost Pines, but the opportunity to trap Armstrong passing secrets to the British was too good to pass up.

He'd make sure she and all the Bests remained safe. No more slipups like today's. He'd given his word to protect her and that hadn't changed just because Wild Horse Jerry Mullins lay six feet under. He would protect Honor with his very life.

The thought made him shudder, took a swipe at his gut, and Luke blinked in surprise. Son of a bitch, the idea of dying actually bothered him. Why not? His gaze went unerringly to the long-legged beauty standing before the fire.

Honor Duvall.

That's what had happened. She had happened. He cared about Honor Duvall and her family. She and the Bests had slipped past his defenses. They'd scaled the walls and settled into the hollow where his heart once dwelled.

Oh, Lord. Luke felt cold again. So very cold. Without conscious thought he tugged off one boot, then the other, and grabbed his wet socks by the toes and peeled them from his skin. He stood, and his fingers worked the buttons on his pants. In moments he was naked with the gray woolen blanket wrapped around his waist. He was drier, but he wasn't any warmer. He cared about this woman and her family, and the fact made him icy from the inside out.

"Luke?"

Her eyes were so beautiful. "Hmm?"

"Now that I've calmed down a bit, there is something I want to say."

Her hesitation garnered his total attention. Bracing himself for her scorn, he replied, "Say it, then."

She cleared her throat. "I want you to know that the reason I came after Mullins had nothing to do with you. With your abilities, I mean. I know you would have caught him. I know you'll keep us safe."

He felt as if all the air had been sucked from his lungs. Where had this come from? "How, Honor? I sure didn't do it today."

She waved her hand, dismissing his words. "You have to sleep, Luke. The boys weren't supposed to be out alone like they were. They know that. Anyway, I didn't want you thinking I don't trust you, because I do. You're the Bravest Man in Texas. You'll keep us safe."

Her show of confidence knocked him flat, made him want to hit something. Luke eyed the ceramic pitcher beside the bed and his fingers flexed with the need to throw it against the wall. She didn't know him. Nobody knew him, not even Rafe. Hell, since moving from Rafe's place over to Lost Pines, even *he* had begun to forget just who he was. Today reminded him. Young Jason Best showed him the truth of it. The Bravest Man in Texas was actually a yellow-bellied failure.

He raked his fingers through his hair. He had no

right to forget, none at all. Remembering was his duty, his personal battle cry. Sam Houston said it first, and all of Texas had taken it up. No one alive said it with more fervor than Luke. *Remember the Alamo! Remember Goliad!*

Remember Rachel and the little ones.

The pain, the shame, was a cannonball to his gut. He closed his eyes and reeled from the emotional blow.

"Luke, are you all right?"

His fists clenched. Hell, no, he wasn't all right. The thunderstorm had moved inside him. Pummeled by guilt, whipped by remorse, singed by shame, and drenched with sorrow, he was lost in the soulless winds. *Remember.*

How long he stood without moving, he had no idea. The sound echoed softly at first, from far away.

"Luke? Luke! What's the matter? Luke?"

Hers was the voice of the rainbow, vibrant and colorful, filled with peace and with promise. She called him back, vanquishing the storm. He focused his eyes and looked at her. Looked hard.

Framed by the firelight, draped in white, Honor Duvall was an angel come to life. Beautiful. So damned beautiful. Not just on the outside, but inside, too, where Rachel had been beautiful.

The knowledge rocked him. Honor was like Rachel. Different as night and day in most every way, but in respect to their hearts, their inner goodness, Honor Duvall and Rachel could have been twins.

Oh, hell. He was in bigger trouble than he'd thought.

An image of Rachel's face shimmered in his mind. Though watery with fuzzy edges, it was the clearest picture he'd had of her in years. They'd grown up on neighboring farms in Tennessee. Rachel was as plain of face as a pecan, but as sweet on the inside as pecan pie. He'd figured out early on in their acquaintance that physical beauty couldn't hold a candle to a divine soul. He'd fallen in love with the real Rachel, the inside Rachel. He'd never known such a beautiful woman as she.

Until now.

Rachel's image faded, replaced by the very real vision of Honor Duvall. Beautiful inside and out. He could love ...

His mind slithered away from the idea. Good Lord, the rain must be spiked with locoweed. His thoughts were crazy, all over the place. Thunderstorms and rainbows and pecan pie. And love.

The words burst like a confession. Or a defense. "I'm married."

She reared back, outrage rounding her eyes.

"She's dead," he hastened to correct. "I'm a widower."

"You never mentioned a wife."

He seldom did. Talking about Rachel and his babies invariably invited other queries, questions he couldn't bear to answer. This was different. Today he needed to answer the questions. He needed the reminder. Remember the Alamo. Remember Goliad. Remember his children. "Rachel and our two little ones died during the Runaway Scrape."

Honor's mouth rounded in a silent oh and compassion softened her liquid brown eyes. "I wasn't in Texas in the spring of thirty-six," she said. "A member of Philip's family had passed on, and we all were in New York. It wasn't until we came home that we heard about the Scrape and how horrible it was."

Luke turned his head. He stared through the cabin's grimy window and into the past. "Folks left everything they owned, just picked up and fled in front of the advancing Mexican army. It was a wholesale panic. Afraid of both the Mexicans and the Indians. Half of Texas headed pell-mell toward the Sabine River and the safety of the States, using any form of transportation they could find. For most that meant only their feet."

"You were with them?"

Luke swallowed hard. "No. I was with Sam Houston's army. It was a month after the Alamo fell, a couple of weeks before San Jacinto. Houston had us in fast retreat. I'll never forget coming up on the stream of refugees. It was like walking in snow. Feathers floated all around us. Goose feathers, pin feathers. Rich folk and poor. When they found they needed to lighten their load they dumped their belongings on the run."

"Mattress feathers," Honor murmured.

"Went on hundreds of yards at a stretch. Just like snow. The army walked through them and caught up with some of the refugees. Hundreds of women and children, emaciated and ragged. Begging for food and medicine that the army didn't have." He paused as memory assailed him. "Couldn't hardly hear for all the coughing. Malaria had every other person shaking like a tree in a gale."

"Your family was there?"

Luke shook his head. "I knew they left our farm. I couldn't find them. I looked and looked and looked. They should have been there."

She crossed the room and reached out, touching his arm.

Luke knew without her speaking what she wanted to know. "It was two months after San Jacinto before I found out. A neighbor came back to the farm and told me. They drowned crossing the Colorado on March sixth."

Compassion softened Honor's voice. "The same day the Alamo fell."

Lightning struck the cabin with a flash, a crack, and a boom. Honor gasped and jumped. The cabin shuddered. Luke didn't move so much as a muscle.

When the sound died away, he slowly nodded. "The same day the Alamo fell."

They hung their clothes closer to the fire to dry. Honor expected to feel embarrassed by the condition of their dress but she didn't. The wall he'd erected with the talk of his wife and family separated them as surely as fifteen layers of cloth. Honor need not fear his advances.

As if she would under any circumstance.

Seated in a chair pulled up close to the fire, she fanned her fingers through her hair in an effort to speed its drying and sneaked another peek at Luke. He stood staring into the fire, poking it occasionally, apparently unconcerned that most of him was bare to her gaze.

Honor had to force herself not to stare. She halfway wished Luella were along to enjoy the view.

Luke's shoulders were as broad as the Brazos. His corrugated torso flaunted a light mat of dark hair narrowing to a line that disappeared beneath the blanket. The thin layer of skin displayed muscles to perfection, and his every movement created a rippling effect that left her mouth dry and her fingers itching to touch.

It must be the zizzle, Honor concluded. None of her husbands had caused such a reaction, not Philip, whom she'd loved, nor even Armand, a most handsome man to whom she'd been attracted before she'd learned to despise him. And Franklin, well, she'd been so young when she'd married him, more concerned with dressing up dolls than undressing men.

She'd grown up. Surreptitiously, she eyed the blanket and imagined what lay beneath it. *Honor Duvall, you're a wanton woman.*

Sarcasm weighed heavily in Luke's voice as he spoke for the first time in half an hour. "Here we are—the notorious Widow Duvall and the Bravest Man in Texas."

She jerked her gaze upward, heat flushing her cheeks. Had he noted the direction of her stare? "I didn't earn the notoriety," she snapped, embarrassment adding sting to her words.

"My point exactly. Just goes to show what fools people are to make judgments based on reputation alone."

After pondering his statement for a moment, Honor said, "Are you saying you are not the Bravest Man in Texas?"

"What do you think? I noticed you eyeing my yellow belly off and on."

Tan. It was a light golden tan. Honor opened her mouth to correct him, but fortunately she comprehended the real meaning behind his question before she spoke. "Yellow belly? As in cowardly? Really, Captain, do you take me for a fool?"

He sucked in a breath, then pinned her with his stare. "Ah, Honor, that's exactly what I'm afraid of—taking you."

Her mouth went dry as valley cotton as he destroyed the wall between them with a single sentence. But instead of pursuing that line of thought, he took the conversation in a direction that left her slackjawed in surprise. "I reckon I'm living proof that horses' asses outnumber horses," he said. "I owe you an apology, Honor."

"Pardon me?"

"No, pardon me." He flattened his mouth in a grim

smile and watched the fire. "You were right earlier. I acted the fool back there at the fort. If I'd bothered to stop and think, I'd have known better than to suspect you of being in cahoots with that scoundrel. But I wasn't thinking and I offended you and I'm sorry."

Honor's thoughts and emotions whirled in confusion. Unable to make sense of her feelings, she defended herself by retreating into pride. Regally lifting her chin, she said, "Would you repeat the first part of that, please?"

"What, the part about me being a fool?"

"Actually, I meant the part about me being right. However, if you feel the need to name yourself a fool again, please feel free."

With his hands held palms out toward the flames, Luke twisted his head and gave her a narrow-eyed stare. "You like to see a man grovel?"

"I like to see you grovel, Captain Prescott."

"You don't have to be so smug."

"But it's so much fun. Now, you were saying?"

He studied her for a long moment. The firelight cast flickering shadows on the planes and angles of his face. His gray eyes glinted like sunlight off a pistol barrel, and when he aimed them in her direction Honor declared them just as dangerous.

He spoke in a soft, hoarse voice. "I said I'm sorry for not believing you. About Wild Horse. About your father."

Liquid silver, she thought. Heated liquid silver and pain. Old pain. She recognized the feeling and responded to it, the tears welling up from deep inside her, a reaction to this terror-filled day and to events of long ago.

Luke reared back, his expression horrified. "What did I do? Why are you crying? You don't cry."

Curiously, his reaction only made the tears come

faster, rolling silently down her cheeks. She didn't answer his questions because she didn't know how. All she knew for certain was that he touched a chord buried within her.

Maybe she reacted to his apology. Luke had no way of knowing how much his simple expression of regret meant to her. She could count on one hand the number of times a man had spoken those words to her before. Actually, she could count it on one finger. Philip had said them once, the first time he'd cried after making love to her. Guilt had consumed him. The pleasure he had felt in taking his new bride to bed had failed to override his sense of disloyalty toward his late first wife.

Honor gasped in a breath. Through blurry eyes she gazed at Luke and a great swelling of emotion rose in her chest. She felt ... she wasn't sure what. Some knowledge, some certainty, hovered at the edges of her mind.

"Honor, what is it? What's wrong? What can I do?"

She spoke from the bottom of her heart. "Hold me, Luke."

Luke closed his eyes and dragged a hand across his face. "I can't hold you, Honor. Not like this. Not with you wearing nothing but a shirt and me wrapped in a blanket."

"You want me to get dressed?"

He paused for what seemed like days before saying, "You'd better."

But Honor didn't want to get dressed. She felt reckless and needy and daring. She sucked in a breath, licked her lips, and asked, "Why?"

Flames flared in his steel-gray eyes, scorching her skin and giving Honor the answer she'd already sensed.

Luke reached for the article of clothing nearest to

him. It happened to be her drawers. His tanned hand was like strong, polished golden oak in contrast to the sheer white cotton. He held the garment out to her. His voice was controlled. "Our stuff is mostly dry. I think that would be for the best."

Honor stood. Her tongue slowly circled her lips. Their gazes held as she accepted the garment from him, recalling their kisses, remembering the feel of his hands upon her skin. She wanted to know his touch again. Dear Lord, how she wanted it.

A wicked spirit whispered in her mind. *So, seduce him. Take what you want. This one time, Honor, do what you want. Live up to your reputation. Find out about zizzle. It won't hurt either one of you.*

Honor listened. She looked at Luke, saw the need that mirrored her own, and the last of her resistance took flight. She spoke in a breathy whisper, "You want me to put this on?"

He cleared his throat. "Yeah."

"All right."

She pivoted, giving him her back. She felt weak and warm and gloriously alive. A little voice of reason urged caution, but it was silenced by the thrum of her blood. She glanced over her shoulder, caught him watching her, his expression as hard as granite, heat burning in his eyes. She shivered as though he had touched her. Honor slipped her drawers slowly up each leg, slithered them over her hips, and turned to face him.

For a long moment, he stood without moving. Then he reached for her chemise. He tossed it to her.

She caught it and once again turned away from him. Her fingers unfastened the shirt buttons. Honor licked her dry lips, shrugged her shoulders, and allowed the shirt to fall.

The sound of Luke's sharply drawn breath made her

close her eyes in responsive need, and she relished her femininity as never before in her life. She slipped her hands through the sleeves of her chemise, then lifted her arms above her head and shimmied her shimmy into place.

Luke's almost inaudible groan was music to her ears and gave her confidence to continue. Spine straight and shoulders back, Honor turned to face him.

"What are you doing?" he asked in a raspy voice. His gaze never lifted above her neck.

"I'm getting dressed like you told me."

"I never—" His throat bobbed as he swallowed hard. Ignoring the petticoat, he made a grab for her dress. He tossed it to her. Honor thought she might have heard him say, "Please."

She took her time about it. Holding the dress by the shoulders out in front of her, she gave it a shake. She tested its state of dampness by stroking its length. After casting a secret look toward Luke, she decided to step into the dress rather than pull it over her head as she normally would have. Spreading the bodice, she leaned forward and lifted one knee high. The leg of her drawers slid up her calf and the chemise gaped. Cool air caressed her breasts as she offered up her bounty to the former Ranger.

She met his gaze again when she stood. The heat in his eyes made her blood hot. Her breasts swelled with aching and her woman's parts throbbed with need. She ever-so-slowly pulled the dress up over her hips. One arm through a sleeve, then the other. Covering one shoulder, both shoulders. All that remained were the buttons on her bodice.

She dropped her gaze and spied the telltale proof of his reaction pushing against the blanket he wore. Never before had she felt so feminine. His name burst instinctively from her lips. "Luke?"

"Finish it, Honor."

The rasp in Luke's voice sent a shiver down her spine, but his resistance rose like a wall between them. She wanted to scream and shout and cry. She wanted to beg. But Honor Duvall begged no man. Never again. She lifted her chin and boldly, proudly met his gaze, allowing her eyes to fill with all the feelings she'd hidden in the past.

Luke Prescott actually flinched.

At his sides, his hands opened and closed on empty air. His head dropped back and he gazed at the rafters. Seconds passed like hours until he slowly lowered his face. With eyes as black as the devil's heart and hot as the fires of hell, he stared into her soul.

She heard surrender in his voice. "Are you sure of this, Honor?"

"Yes, Luke, I'm very sure."

He closed the distance between them in two long strides. Taking her into his arms, he pulled her against his nakedness. "This has been the damnedest seduction I've ever seen."

His kiss was wild and hot, almost savage in its intensity. Even as she reveled in it, Honor realized her mistake. Luke hadn't surrendered. Captain Prescott, formerly of the Texas Rangers, never surrendered.

Luke Prescott took control.

11

Luke knew kissing her was a mistake, but his body wasn't listening. Something had changed between him and Honor Duvall. Luke couldn't put his finger on what, but he knew it had happened. He knew that weeks ago he wouldn't have thought twice about taking what the widow so creatively offered. Today he'd made a valiant effort to decline her invitation, but his extended stretch of celibacy had taken a toll on his ability to resist. Or maybe it didn't matter. Maybe it was just her. Maybe Honor Duvall would lay him low no matter what.

As the heavens rumbled and rain pounded the rooftop, Luke kissed her. He took her mouth with all the pent-up passion of the preceding weeks. He kissed her like a hungry man starved beyond patience. His tongue explored her, savored her, gloried in the warmth and wetness of her mouth. So sweet. So right.

His mouth fit to hers with a satisfying sense of homecoming.

His hand stroked her impatiently. Down her back, over her buttock, along her thigh. Again and again and again. When she sighed into his mouth his loins clenched with a need so fierce and hot, so elemental, that he groaned low in his throat.

He broke off the kiss, sucking air through his teeth as her fingers trailed boldly down his spine and dipped beneath the barrier of the blanket. He stared into her whiskey eyes, communicating without words. He asked, she accepted.

When she smiled he forgot how to breathe. *Honor.*

He stripped away the covering, baring himself to her gaze. She whispered his name and he clutched the sound to his heart before scooping her into his arms and carrying her to the bed. The silken sheet of her red-gold hair brushed his sore thigh, both soothing and inflaming. Luke ached to drape it all around him.

She gave a soft sigh of pleasure as he lowered her to the mattress and the hot throb in his loins intensified. Honor smiled up at him, a little nervous, a bit afraid, but the warmth in her eyes bade him continue. He straddled her, drinking in the vision of her beauty, staring down at the gingham-clad bounty in heated anticipation.

She spoke in a wobbly voice. "I sorta like this."

Reaching for her bodice buttons, his hands froze. "Sorta?"

Her skin glowed with a tint of color as she nodded. Luke planted his hands on either side of her shoulders and loomed above her. Allowing a hint of peevishness to sound in his voice, he said, "Let's not make snap judgments here, sunshine. We just got started."

Her smile dawned slowly but brightly, like sunrise

over the water. "I meant I like being dressed and you
. . . not."

He knew a quick stab of pleasure at her words.
Luke grinned and nipped at her neck. "Oh, really?"

She nodded. "My husbands—"

"No." He planted a quick, hard kiss on her mouth,
then slid his knees back and deliberately lowered his
hips. "Not now. We'll not speak of others. This is you
and me in this bed, Honor Duvall." The soft cotton
of her dress both cradled him and barred him from
the prize he so fiercely desired. He pressed himself
against her. "Just us."

"Yes."

He shuddered at the silky-soft sound of her whisper.
Damn, but a man liked hearing that word from a
woman. Inhaling deeply, filling his lungs, he savored
the rain-washed scent of her and recognized a simple
truth. Never again would he hear or see or smell a
thunderstorm and not be reminded of this day, this
woman, and this time.

"I want . . . I wish . . . May I touch you?"

Luke rolled onto his side. "I'll probably die if you
don't."

She lifted a tentative, teasing hand that bypassed
the part of him that most ached for her touch. Her
palm swept across his chest, her fingers combing
through the hair that adorned him. His muscles
clenched as she grazed his nipple.

"You are so different."

Good Lord, the woman was full of surprises. "I trust
you mean that as positive comment?"

"Oh, yes. Definitely positive. Definitely very good."

"In that case, I'll do my best to be bad from here
on out." He rolled her onto her back and his head
hovered just above her bosom. "I suspect you'll like
my version of bad, Honor."

He covered the peak of one gingham-clad breast with his mouth and laved and nibbled and sucked until the cloth was once again wet and her nipple hard. In a similar manner he bent his attention to her other breast, and her soft whimper of need fired his passion to even greater heights. Her hands stroked his back and he knew a combination of pleasure and pain as her nails sank into him. Lifting his head, he kissed her lips once, hard and fierce, before sliding down her body to nuzzle her womanhood. She sucked in a breath.

The cloth was rough like his tongue. He slipped his hand beneath her dress and stripped off her drawers. All the while his mouth paid homage to the core of femininity through the thin gingham barrier of the widow's yellow dress.

She arched upward, seeking, offering. Demanding. Out of the corner of his eye he saw her hands claw the sheet beneath her. "Luke? Luke!" Her thighs clamped against his head and she began to shake. Recognizing her pleasure, Luke growled a low sound of triumph.

"Oh, Luke."

His name slurred on her tongue and the sound was an erotic shot of whiskey to his blood. He could play no more. He stood beside the bed and with a fluid motion, he stripped off her dress and her chemise. Her perfection nearly knocked the breath from his lungs. He heard her voice through the haze of his desire.

"I'll never forget you, Luke Prescott. Not the look of you, the scent of you, the taste of you."

The sound of his name on her lips flowed over him like warm honey. If some tiny part of him recognized a message he didn't like in the declaration, it was swamped by the tide of craving that had him parting her legs with his knee. Her hands reached for his hips as he probed at the gate of her womanhood, holding him, pulling him closer. It felt so damned good to be wanted.

The heat of his hunger drove him, and Luke thrust into Honor's welcoming wet heat. Again and again and again he plunged his body into hers. He couldn't think, could only feel. Her arms holding him tight. Her legs intertwined with his. Her hair a fiery veil of silk spilling across his skin.

At the brink, he forced himself to slow. He gazed down at Honor Duvall, willing her to open her eyes, demanding she join him. Her lashes fluttered and their gazes met. The moment stretched, its significance silently acknowledged.

Honor lifted her hips to meet him. Once, twice. The exquisite sensation pulled a groan from his throat. *Honor,* cried his soul. She gave a little whimper, her body milking him as she found another release. Just before Luke joined her in the throbbing, pounding, pulsating rush of pleasure, an absolute certainty of knowledge burst in his soul.

He'd tasted a hint of it in her kiss. The joining of their bodies, the mingling of their spirits, confirmed it.

Making love with Honor Duvall was like coming home.

The rain ended by late afternoon, allowing plenty of time to get home before dark. With Honor perched atop the mule and Luke riding her horse, they took the longer route back to Lost Pines, avoiding the densest part of the forest. The rain-washed air smelled sweet and clean and a rainbow painted the western sky. Honor barely noticed. Her thoughts were in a whirl, her emotions in a jumble. She had finally lived up to her own reputation.

Why? Why now? Why him? She'd seduced the poor

man. She, Honor Armstrong Tate Best Duvall, who'd never seduced a man in her entire life! The same Honor Duvall who made it a point to dispatch would-be suitors at first flirt. What had made her do it now? What had made her listen to the imp of wickedness inside her and finally act the wanton widow with Captain Luke Prescott, former Texas Ranger?

The answer burned like lighting in her mind. Love. She loved him. Lord help her, she'd gone and fallen in love with Luke.

Honor slipped sideways in the saddle, almost losing her seat on the mule. How could she have done it? How could she have been such a fool? The thought of loving Luke gave her the shakes—an entirely different variety from the trembles the man, himself, gave her.

Yet, in her heart, she wasn't terribly surprised. She must have sensed the truth on some level or she'd never have been so bold as to offer him her body. She drew a deep breath, then exhaled an audible sigh. But sensing her love for Luke vaguely and admitting it outright were two separate matters, as different as buttermilk and strong coffee. Either could be pleasant, depending on one's mood. At the moment, Honor wanted only a stiff shot of whiskey.

She sighed again loudly. Up ahead of her on the horse, Luke twisted in his saddle and their gazes met and held. Was that uncertainty she read in his storm-cloud eyes? Did Luke feel as unsettled as she in the aftermath of their lovemaking?

"Sure," she muttered with disgust, tearing her eyes away from him to focus on the nearest loblolly pine, "and it will snow in Bastrop County in July."

The man had been awfully cheery when they finally rose and dressed. That in itself had been a new experience for Honor. Armand never spoke to her after he dismissed her from his bed; Philip often cried. Franklin simply patted her head and sent her on her way. Luke's reaction had unnerved her.

So had the fact that he'd made love to her three times before the rain stopped.

Actually, he had not unnerved her. He'd made her one big bundle of nerves. Tingling, sizzling, *zizzling* nerves. Luella certainly had known what she was talking about.

No, the light in Luke Prescott's eyes this afternoon had nothing to do with any insecurity over what they had shared. He certainly wasn't riding along realizing he was in love with her. And heaven knew he couldn't be questioning his success as a lover. Maybe he was having second thoughts about asking her to ride this dad-blamed mule. Or maybe his leg hurt and he was too proud to say so. He had to be sore from all the walking and . . . other exercise.

"Honor?"

She started. He'd spoken from right at her side. When had he wheeled his horse—her horse—around?

"Honor, I've been thinking."

Now why did that make her stomach fall to her feet?

Luke thumbed his hat off his brow and gripped the saddle horn with both hands. His dark-eyed scrutiny made her breath catch. "It makes a lot of sense," he drawled. "It's the perfect solution for you, and I reckon I'll be able to stand it." He shot her a grin as dangerous as the Paterson riding at his hip. "The fringe benefits are incredible."

"What are you talking about?"

"I didn't say?"

There was that light again, Honor thought, her own eyes narrowing as she stared into his. Doubt? Apprehension? The man made her teeth-chatteringly nervous. "No, you didn't say."

"Oh. Well. All right." He reined the mare to a halt and Honor followed suit. Reaching into his shirt pocket, he tugged out his small candy tin. After offering her a lemon drop, which she declined, he popped a piece of candy in his mouth. "It's like this, Honor. I've made up my mind. I think we should get married."

Honor twisted sideways at the word marriage. She lost her balance and slid right off the mule's back, landing with a wet plop on her backside in the mud. "You what!"

Giving her an amused look of affection, he climbed down from her horse, took her hands, and pulled her to her feet. He brushed mud off her behind, then lifted her back onto the mule. Remounting the horse, he nudged it into a walk and motioned for her to follow.

Finally, he spoke, launching into a justification that sounded suspiciously like one of her father's campaign speeches. "With us married, you won't have to leave Texas. Think about it, Honor. The boys and Luella will be happy as coons in a cornfield. Then there's the money consideration. Chances are good our marriage would free up your funds."

His gaze remained on the road ahead as he paused a moment, frowning. "Remind me to have Rafe take a look at Duvall's will. I don't doubt he's familiar with every shady trick in the law books. Not that it will matter, of course. I may not be as plump in the purse as Colonel Duvall, but I have money enough to support you and the Bests."

Honor finally found her voice. "But Luke—"

"Now, I know you might be thinking you don't need me around any longer since Wild Horse Mullins has gone over the river, but my leaving Lost Pines now would be premature. We can't know that your pa didn't hire more than one outlaw to do his dirty work, or won't hire somebody else once he learns about Wild Horse. Besides, there's the jubilee to consider. I won't be talked out of proving Richard Armstrong's treason."

He gave her a quick, sidelong glance and added, "And, we can't forget we may have made a baby this afternoon. I'd want to be married to you if you were having my child."

Honor glared at him. If she'd had a rock she'd have chucked it at his smug expression.

"It's a possibility, Honor. My wife got caught with our Daniel the first time we were together. Little Sarah came along almost as quick. I guess I'm just a potent man."

She eyed his gun, wishing she could grab it and shoot him.

"So, what do you say? We could ride on into town now and find us a preacher."

She was wearing a dress with mud caked across the behind! The man truly had lost his mind. Not that she was any better. Thoughts tumbled around her brain like rocks in a butter churn, making little sense at all. One fact was clear, however, and it was enough to have her shaking in the saddle. Honor couldn't forget her instinctive, immediate reaction when he'd said they should marry.

Joy. A warm flood of exultant, delirious, incredulous joy.

She'd recovered in an instant, of course, as soon as the panic set in. "I appreciate the offer, Captain Prescott, but I'm not a ruined young virgin. It was quite gentlemanly of you to extend a proposal, but it certainly wasn't required. You can go on your way, now, secure in the knowledge you acted properly."

His expression chided her. "I don't give a damn

about acting properly. I asked because I honestly want you to marry me."

She yanked back on the reins. When the mule stopped, she watched Luke closely as she asked, "Why? Do you love me?"

Despite Luke's uncanny ability to make his face a mask, he couldn't hide the reflexive wince of muscles around his eyes. Seeing it, Honor kicked the mule hard.

"I care about you, Honor," Luke said as the mule rambled forward.

She snorted in a most unladylike manner.

"Now, Honor—"

"Don't you 'Now, Honor' me. I hate Texas! I won't stay here. Especially not with someone who proposes marriage by saying, 'I reckon I'll be able to stand it.' Your mother didn't spank you enough when you were a boy."

"Well, you can make up for that now. That sort of thing can be enjoyable if done properly." As she let out a squeak of rage, he forged on. "Listen to me, Honor. Maybe I could have been a bit smoother with the question, but you can't deny that marrying me is the smartest thing you can do."

Short of attacking her family, there was nothing worse he could have said. Honor went cold. She'd heard similar words before. Her father had used that argument every time he'd forced her into marriage.

Curse you, Luke Prescott. Why couldn't you have been the hero you are reputed to be?

A hero would have saved her. A hero would have championed her. A hero would have loved her.

Luke wasn't different at all. More fool she, for forgetting the lesson drummed into her for years. Despite rumors to the contrary, Texas didn't have any heroes. Opportunists and scalawags, yes. Adventurers and scoundrels aplenty. Heroes must be backed up at the border.

Well, she couldn't wait around for one to find his way across the Sabine. She'd always known she'd have to save herself. That meant getting away from Luke Prescott now. He, more than any other, more than her father, even, had the power to hurt her. Because she had handed him that power. She had given him her heart, wrapped up with a pretty little bow. Thank God he was too dense to realize it. Still, even a man could figure out the truth if it stared him in the face long enough.

Reacting purely from emotion, Honor slid from her saddle and planted her feet in the damp green grass. "Marrying you would be the dumbest thing I could do, Prescott. You just ride on back to Lost Pines and gather your things. You're dismissed. I want you off my property by nightfall."

"What?" His fingers clenched the reins.

"You heard me. You are dismissed. Your services are no longer required."

"The hell you say!" Luke's eyes narrowed to angry slits, and he looked as if his jaw might break from the pressure of his gritted teeth. Saddle leather squeaked as he dismounted. He braced his hands on his hips and his voice dripped with menace. "Dammit, woman. Didn't you hear anything I said? You need to marry me."

Honor folded her arms, lifted her chin, and stifled the urge to take a backward step. "I heard it all quite clearly. I simply choose to disagree."

His pulse pounded at his temples. The man was a cannon about to explode. He leaned down into her face. "Don't you have a lick of sense, Honor Duvall?"

"I am an intelligent adult woman, Luke Prescott. That's all I need to be. I'll not give a man authority over me again for any price. I'm leaving Texas just as soon as I can manage, and no man will ever again control my time or my money or my life."

"I don't want to control you and I damn sure don't want your money. I'm trying to protect you."

She knew that. Luke was not a man to take advantage of any woman. She knew it as surely as she knew her father would exploit any creature that breathed, given half a chance. Yet, she was so afraid. The love she felt for this man was too new, too vulnerable. She'd known unrequited love with Philip and the thought of living that way again made her crazy. Heaven forbid he should ever discover her feelings. Being pitied by Luke Prescott would destroy her.

So, too, she might destroy him. Three times a widow. Leave it to the Bravest Man in Texas to want to risk the long odds of survival as husband number four.

With that thought weighing heavy on her mind, she lashed out, wanting to hurt him, to put him at arm's length. "Protect me? Like you protected Jason? My son easily might have died. I expected better from a Texas Ranger."

Honor regretted the cruel words the moment they left her mouth. Shame washed over her as Luke's mask slipped back into place, but not before Honor saw her accusation hit him where it hurt.

His voice came low and cold. "I'm not a Texas Ranger. Don't blame my failings on the corps." He grasped her upper arm and dragged her over to the horse. "Go home, Mrs. Duvall."

An empty, yawning sensation gripped her stomach. "Luke, I'm sorry. I didn't mean—"

"Get on the goddamned horse, Honor!"

Seconds dragged by in silence. It was best she leave him, Honor knew. Before she hurt him any more. Before he recognized the love burning in her heart. The mare nickered as Honor took the reins and swung into the saddle. Tears stung her eyes. She blinked rapidly, willing them not to fall, wanting to say something but not certain what. "Luke, I . . . What about the mule?"

"I'll ride the mule," Luke replied grimly. "He suits my mood. You see, Mrs. Duvall, you can dismiss me all you want, but I'm not leaving Lost Pines. Not until the horse race." He slapped the horse's rear, and added, "After that, however, I'll make boot tracks just as fast as I can manage."

The widow and the former Ranger steered clear of each other as much as possible during the days that followed, each going out of his way to avoid the other. Honor stayed in the schoolroom helping Luella teach the boys their lessons, while Luke took a trip into town to report the circumstances of Mullins's death to the sheriff. The lawman agreed to keep the details of what happened quiet, and Luke was pleased when the local newspaper mentioned only that Wild Horse Jerry Mullins had passed along.

Upon his return, Luke spent the better part of every day on horseback patrolling Lost Pines's perimeter and fretting about Honor Duvall. Nine days after their interlude in the cabin, he was still riled up.

And the widow had quit wearing yellow.

The late morning sun climbed a bright blue sky, puffy white clouds riding a gentle easterly wind. Luke sat on the front porch steps, sipping cool well water from a crystal glass and tossing pebbles at the fragrant pink blooms of a rosebush growing some five yards from where he sat. He wasn't in the mood for flowers. He wasn't in the mood for much of anything besides brooding. Honor Duvall had plumb messed with his mind. What message was she trying to send with her choice of wardrobe?

He still couldn't believe she'd thrown his proposal back in his face. Why had he even bothered? He'd tried to do the right thing and gotten reamed for it, despite the fact that every reason he'd given in support of the idea had been a good one and she had to recognize it.

Luke pinged a flower head-on with a stone, then frowned when petals flew off. He chose an ugly milkweed for his next target. Widow or not, he'd done the honorable thing by asking for her hand. If beneath his righteous indignation he sensed a deeper, more meaningful reason for the proposal, he wasn't about to admit to it. Honor was ornery-mule stubborn and he was tired of it.

"Bullheaded woman," he grumbled to a black beetle climbing toward him up the stone steps. "Let her uproot her family and drag them off to Carolina. Doesn't matter to me. I don't give a flyin' fig what she does, not as long as she waits until after the horse race to do it." Not as long as she wasn't carrying his get with her when she went.

Movement at the edge of the clearing caught his attention. Luke stood, his hand drifting to the gun strapped at his hip as he watched the horse and rider lope toward him. He identified the bay first and excitement filled him. Rafe Malone had returned from the capital.

Luke descended the steps and met his friend with a handshake and a question. "How did you fare at Washington-on-the-Brazos?"

"Well, hello to you, too, Prescott." Rafe secured his horse to the hitching post and brushed travel dust from his brown frock coat. "Invite me in and offer

224

me something to drink and I just might tell you all about it."

Luke grimaced. "Sorry. We've had an incident since the night you stayed for dinner, and it's made me a tad overanxious. Come on in and wet your whistle, and I'll tell you all about it." In the parlor, Luke poured water from a pitcher into a glass and offered it to Rafe along with an abbreviated version of the events surrounding the attack on Jason. "You see why I'm impatient to put our plan into motion."

Rafe nodded. "Well, that much has been done. Honor's invitations have been sent, including the ones I hand-delivered in Washington-on-the-Brazos."

"And the response?"

"Armstrong will be here, but we've run into a little problem with Charles Elliot. I don't think he'll make the trip the way matters stand now."

Luke's grip on his own glass tightened. Why? He was certain the reason had nothing to do with Honor's reputation. Elliot wasn't a fool. "What did he say?"

"Very little. Vague excuses mostly. I did some snooping around and learned that his relationship with your man Houston has been a bit strained of late. Talk is the two nearly came to blows during an argument."

"Charles Elliot and Sam Houston quarreling?" Luke set his glass down hard on the marble mantel above the fireplace. "That's hard for me to believe. I know Elliot. He's a damn fine diplomat. I can't picture him losing his composure, not with the president of the Republic, especially. What were they arguing about? Annexation? Texas's relationship with Britain? How to deal with Mexico City?"

"A horse race."

"Serious business, then." Luke scowled and heaved a sigh.

"Houston was drunk as a skunk—now that's a surprise—and apparently said something totally inappropriate and unpolitic to Elliot. According to the rumor, it stung the Brit's pride, and while he'll do his job, he's not inclined to attend a party intended to honor an insulting son of a bitch."

"Do you agree?"

Rafe shrugged. "I liked Elliot, Luke. He struck me as an honest-hearted man. I don't see him allowing a personal slight to interfere with duty. To answer your question, no, I don't agree with the gossips. I wouldn't bet my horse that a falling-out has even occurred. I know that since his arrival in Texas last August, Elliot and Houston have grown tight. It wouldn't surprise me if the two of them cooked up a false story for some reason we haven't yet guessed."

Luke flattened his mouth in a grim line. He hated being politically out of touch, and he cursed the injury that had made it so. He hadn't a clue to what Houston and Elliot might be in cahoots about. The British chargé d'affaires must attend the barbecue. His presence was integral to the scheme.

Was Luke's plan a fool's dream? Was he too uninformed to even attempt to trap Armstrong into revealing his treason? Did he even have a prayer of accomplishing such a coup?

I'm not a quitter. I'll make it work.

He glanced at Rafe. "What about the other diplomats. Did they accept the invitation?"

"Both Eve of the United States and Cramayel of France said they'd be delighted to attend a jubilee given in the president's honor."

Luke nodded thoughtfully. "I doubt if Elliot would want to be the lone member of the diplomatic corps in Texas who failed to join us. Whatever his game is with Houston—either real or political farce—what we need to do is give him an excuse to come, to take some of the attention off Houston."

"Now ol' Sam will love that," Rafe responded, his tone dry as July.

Luke ignored him. "We need to somehow expand the scope of the barbecue, broaden its purpose and give Elliot an excuse to attend."

"That makes sense, but what else can you do? You're already having a horse race and a dance. What other event could you stage at this late date?"

Luke had a glimmer of an idea. He ambled over to the candy dish on a table beside the sofa. Removing a lemon drop, he popped it into his mouth, sat on the sofa, and pondered the problem.

He was vaguely aware of Rafe's long and curious look, and he partially noted his friend's softly spoken observation. "He's gettin' one of those looks again. That Captain Luke Prescott predator's gleam. Somebody's goose is about to get cooked. Hope it ain't mine."

Luke stretched out his legs and crossed them at the ankles. He folded his arms and nodded once sharply.

Across the room, Rafe lifted the water pitcher to refill his glass and pressed him. "What? What scheme has that brain of yours conjured up now?"

Satisfaction melted through Luke like fine French brandy. "No scheme, Malone. Just another draw for the jubilee."

"Which is?"

"Me. Captain Luke Prescott, celebrated former member of the Texas Rangers. I'm the Bravest Man in Texas, you know, and if that's not enough, we have the beautiful, engaging, renowned-in-her-own-right, politician's daughter, Honor Duvall."

"I don't mean to be insulting here, Luke, but I don't know that your presence at the party makes such a difference. It's not like folks don't know about it already. True, we've kept it quiet that you're living here, but I made sure the word is out that the jubilee's horse race will be between Sam Houston's nag and your"—Rafe paused and cleared his throat—"Starlight. People assume you'll be here for that."

"You're right. But I mean to give them a real good reason to come see me."

Rafe waited, and waited some more. As he lifted his glass to his lips, he cursed. "Damn you, Prescott, I hate it when you do this. Quit dragging your tongue. Spit it out."

Luke sat up. He propped his elbows on his knees, his chin in his hands, and flashed his wickedest grin. "I'd like to ask a favor of you, Rafe. Would you do me the honor of being my best man?"

Rafe's hand jerked, spilling water down his front. "You mean?"

"That's right." Luke shot to his feet. "A wedding. My and Honor Duvall's wedding. It's a perfect excuse for Elliot to show up, and President Houston won't be offended to share the limelight with a wedding. Since some folks are calling him the Father of Texas, we'll even ask him to escort the bride down the aisle. Armstrong will go along with it because he's supposed to be Houston's man."

Rafe wiped dazedly at his shirt with a handkerchief. "You're gonna marry Honor Duvall? When did this happen?"

"It hasn't. Not yet." Luke smiled with unholy glee at the thought of informing the stubborn widow of the change in plans. "I'll tell her this afternoon."

Rafe's brows arched and his mouth dropped open. "You'll *tell* her?"

"Yeah."

"That ought to be rich. What if she says no?"

"She can't." Luke headed for the door. "You might say I'm holding all the raffle tickets."

Since the day of the attack, Honor had made it a practice to escape to the barn each afternoon for an hour of play with the kittens. She needed time to herself, she found, and her time with the kittens proved soothing. They'd grown quite a bit in the weeks since Luke's arrival at Lost Pines. Two of the litter were missing from the barn, presently settling in to their new roles as Micah's and Jason's house pets.

Honor scooped up a calico and a gray and carried them to a corner stall spread with clean, sweet-smelling hay. Sunlight beamed through the cracks in the walls, highlighting dust motes drifting slowly on the air. She pulled a ball of twine from the pocket of her oldest faded gray homespun and rolled it toward the cats. As they pounced on the string, she tugged the end and tried desperately not to think about Luke or love or loving.

She failed miserably.

Reaching out to the calico, Honor's fingers stroked the luxurious, silk-soft fur. She'd made a mistake when she listened to Luella talk about zizzle. She'd made a bigger mistake by not listening closer. "A ring on the finger before a fling on the bed," her mother-in-law had said. If she'd paid closer attention, she wouldn't be wallowing in heartache. "I wouldn't have known what I'm missing."

One of the kittens mewed as if in agreement.

"Not that I want the ring on my finger," she hastened to explain as the gray kitten halted its play and stared up at her. She didn't. Not without love. She had plenty of experience with that sort of marriage, thank you very much. But for all the arguments she'd presented against the idea, despite having sworn never to marry again under any circumstances, she knew she'd wed Luke Prescott in a heartbeat if only he loved her.

If only. They had to be two of the saddest words in any language. Gloom settled over her soul and she lifted the calico and cuddled it against her cheek. Softly she hummed a lullaby, singing more to comfort herself than the playful kitten.

That was how Luke found her. He emerged from the shadows like shade and he raked her with an angry stare. "What the hell are you wearing?"

Tension crawled up her spine. She clutched the kitten to her breast. "Hello, Luke."

"That dress is gray. There's not a speck of yellow on it. The blue and brown were bad enough, but gray?"

It was the most he'd said to her since the cabin. Honor stared at Luke for a long moment. The sorrow in her heart weighed on her, putting her in a pensive mood. "Yellow is nature's color of caution."

"Yeah. So what?"

"The first year my family lived in Texas, we faced some of nature's fiercest challenges. Flood, range fire, storms the likes of which I'd never seen before. But the only time I saw my mother truly afraid was when I ran barefoot through the kitchen and disturbed a snake behind the cornmeal barrel."

"A rattler?"

"Milk snake, but Mama thought it was something else." She said no more, watching him think it through. When his eyes widened she knew he'd put it together.

Luke muttered a soft curse. "Coral snake. The difference is in the pattern of the bands. 'Red and yellow, kill a fellow; red and black, poison lack.'" A pair of long strides carried him to her. He hunkered down before her and stretched out his hand, twisting a curl of her hair around his finger. "Red hair and yellow dresses. That's a damned subtle warning, Honor."

"I'm three times a widow," she said dryly. "How blatant did I need to be?"

"I reckon you have a point there," he said, his lips twisting in a smirk. He pushed to his feet and put some distance between them, leaning against the barn's rough wall and folding his arms. "So, why stop it now? Why homespun gray?"

She shrugged. "It feels right."

As the conversation lagged Honor returned her attention to the kittens, thankful for their noisy play which interrupted the uncomfortable silence. At the far end of the barn the hog snorted and a chicken squawked, the familiar barn sounds Honor normally found soothing. Not today, however. Not with a predator among them. "What do you want, Luke?"

He pushed away from the wall. He braced his hands on his hips and when he spoke, his voice rumbled across her nerves like distant rolling thunder. "Even in gray, you're still dangerous, sunshine."

"But I don't scare you."

He chuckled then, sadly and softly, as if the joke were on him. "I'm the Bravest Man in Texas, lady, and you bring me to my knees."

She closed her eyes, the ache in her heart almost beyond bearing. "Please, Luke, just go. I'm too tired to battle with you any more."

He sighed and began to walk away, his footfalls soft but audible, and Honor began to breathe again. She pulled the nearest kitten into her arms and gently stroked the downy fur, seeking comfort more than offering it. Hinges squeaked, a wooden gate rattled. Then it slammed shut. His footsteps returned. Luke was coming back.

"You don't have to fight," he said. "All you need

to do is listen. And I want you to listen with your ears and your brain, Honor. I'm fixing to do some hard talking and you'll want to shut me out. Don't do it. Neither one of us is leaving this barn until we settle this."

Honor looked up. He stood beside a support post, his right hand holding the rough-hewn pine in a white-knuckled grip.

"Then allow me to ask you once again," she said, glaring at him. "What is it you want, Captain Prescott?"

"What I want has little to do with it." He glowered right back. "What's going to happen is that you and I are going to throw a wedding."

It caught her by surprise. "For whom?"

"For you and me."

"Excuse me?"

"We're adding another event to the jubilee agenda."

Cradling the calico kitten in her arms, Honor lurched to her feet. "I'm not going to marry you!"

"Well, that depends on the timing," he grimly declared. "If we can get the job done without doin' the I dos, we'll do it."

Honor gave her head a quick shake. Her entire body trembled. "What did you just say?"

"Why don't I start at the beginning."

"Why don't you pack up your things and leave?"

He thumbed his hat back off his brow. "Look, Honor. I intend to prove your father is a traitor to Texas if it's the last thing I do. It's the most important thing in my life." Honor flinched at his words, but she didn't think he noticed. He continued, "Rafe made it back from the capital today, and he brought news that we've hit a little snag in the plan."

Feeling the need to defend herself, Honor drawled in an exaggerated twang, "Well, ain't that a shame."

"You'll likely think so once I tell you how I intend to solve it. This affects you."

Honor turned away. Looking at him was pure torture. The man speaking to her now was not the same man who had loved her so sweetly in the cabin. He had been warm like summer sunshine and as gentle as a mourning dove's coo. This Luke Prescott was a stranger. He wore a mask of steely determination with no hint of mercy in his eyes. He was, she thought, as unmovable as the hills of central Texas.

"We will pass the word that we'll marry at the party, and that will bring all the players to the game. Soon after his arrival, your father will receive false information powerful enough to ruin Texas's chances for annexation and in effect hand the Republic of Texas over to England. I intend to make it easy for him to pass the intelligence on to the British chargé, and I'll be ready to catch him in the act when he makes the attempt. I give you my word I'll do my best to spring my trap before the vows are spoken, but if it doesn't work out that way I'll expect you to play along."

Dear Lord, it was happening all over again. A forced marriage. Unrequited love. "I won't do it. I won't marry you. You can't make me."

"But I can pay you."

"What?"

"I'm willing to pay a fair price for your cooperation, Honor. I've heard you and Luella talking and I know you're having trouble coming up with hard money. You do this for me and I'll pay you in cash. You'll have the means to leave Texas. As soon as the weekend is over, you can hightail it back east and start selling hats. Just think, a short time from now all your dreams will come true."

She almost laughed at that, but managed to bury the hysterical giggle that bubbled at the base of her throat. As silence stretched between them, Honor slowly lowered the kitten to the floor. He could not have said more clearly that he did not and never would love her. She felt battered and bruised and too proud to show it. Luke removed his hat from his head and absently reshaped the brim.

"Why are you doing this?"

"I told you. Your father is a traitor and he must be stopped."

"Isn't there another way?"

He replaced his hat on his head but didn't reply. Honor murmured, "You have no idea what you are asking of me."

His gaze snapped up to meet hers. Dark gray shards of ice, hard and angry and something else, too. Pain? she wondered. Surely not. She couldn't hurt him. He'd have to care for her before she could have the ability to hurt him. "Why must we make it a real marriage? Couldn't we fake it, go through the motions but avoid the legalities?"

"You mean rig the wedding like you did the raffle?" Luke pushed away from the support post and began to pace. "I can check into it. Might work."

"You'd agree to it? A false marriage?"

He halted abruptly and drilled her with an enigmatic stare. "Are you pregnant?"

Heat flooded her face. "No."

Luke closed his eyes. When he opened them again, he'd wiped them free of any emotion. "All right, how 'bout we try this. We'll have a fake preacher and a real preacher both standing by, and unless I discover a reason it won't work, we'll do it your way. Otherwise, we'll stick to my plan and annul the marriage as soon as feasible. All right?"

Honor choked back a sigh and nodded.

"I'll put the word out about the wedding right away. Don't fret about it, Honor. Either way it works out, real wedding or fake ceremony, I promise you'll leave Texas a wealthy woman."

"A *free* woman," she insisted.

Except for her heart. She'd be leaving that behind.

12

"Please, Cap'n Luke," Jason Best pleaded. "I'm feeling perky as a new pup. A ride into town won't hurt me none. Please let us go? I want to see Brown Baggage run something fierce."

The child and his brother stood just inside the doorway of Luke's room at Lost Pines. Hope filled Jason's expression, but the pessimistic twist to Micah's lips told him the older boy entertained a more realistic view of the situation. Luke slipped his candy tin into his jacket pocket and donned his hat. "I'm sorry, Jason. I know you've had three weeks' healing time, but that infection set you back some. You'll need a little more time taking it slow. I also know what a good jar or two would do to your shoulder. Town will be packed full of people today and your mother and I agree there's no need to take any more chances. We want you hale and hearty for the jubilee. You'll see Brown Baggage race then."

"But Cap'n Luke, I want to see her race today. Mr. Malone says she's the fastest and the smartest horse he's ever worked. He says she's even better than Starlight."

"Aw, Jace, give it a rest," Micah said. "They're not gonna let us go so you might as well just get happy about it. Besides, the monthly race day in Bastrop ain't all that much fun. Remember what happened last time when we talked Nana into taking us?"

Jason's sigh was heavy. "Yeah. Two fistfights for us and then a tongue-lashing from Nana."

"Would've been a real lashing if we hadn't told her what the fights were about." Micah glanced over at Luke. "We couldn't let those boys get by with talkin' that way about Honor."

Luke suspected that before the day was done, he might be tempted into a fistfight or two himself. The purpose of the trip into town was more than a way to announce Starlight's demise. Honor Duvall was returning to town today, under protest and at Luke's insistence. While he and Rafe stirred up interest in Brown Baggage at the races, Honor had an appointment with Mrs. Mary Litty, the local doctor's wife and the town's best seamstress. According to Luella, Mrs. Litty's talent and speed with a needle were well known. It was a good thing, because the party was ten days from today and Honor didn't have a wedding dress to wear.

Luke ruffled Jason's hair on the way out the door. "I'm sorry, son, but Micah's right. Y'all are staying home this time. Your mother and I need to know you're safe and sound here where no one's going to hurt you."

"But Cap'n Luke, I heard you telling Honor just last night that you thought we were safe now."

"I think you're safe because I have a trio of Texas

Rangers staying here helping me get ready for the party."

The boys followed him downstairs where Rafe and Honor waited. Luke looked at the lady and scowled. She was wearing that blue dress again and it bothered him something fierce. It bothered him even more that it bothered him at all. "You folks ready?" he asked gruffly.

Rafe nodded. "I have Brown Baggage tied to the back of the wagon. Thought I'd go with Honor. I noticed you have Red Pepper saddled up and ready to ride."

That's because the thought of spending the two-hour wagon trip into Bastrop seated next to Honor Duvall made Luke cringe inwardly. She already had him wound tighter than an eight-day clock. "Let's go, then."

Honor gave her sons a hug and exchanged a few brief, private words with Luella. Within minutes, they'd left Lost Pines behind. The morning air was warm, the sky a ribbon of brilliant blue above the road cut through the pine forest. Luke rode ahead of the wagon, attempting to listen to forest sounds that included the full-throated chant of redbirds rather than the sweet, trilling laughter Rafe Malone managed to coax from the widow. He enjoyed only limited success.

The woman was driving him nutty as a pecan pie. Considering her past experience, he understood why she'd be stubborn about getting married again, but that didn't mean he had to like it. The fact that he didn't like it bothered him, too. Why did he care so much? The answer hovered like a ghost at the edge of his mind, but Luke didn't have the guts to face it. Instead he sulked all the way into town. Which made him grumpy. He hated sulking in others and even more so in himself.

He led the wagon into Bastrop and as they made their way down Main Street, he heard the rumbles of excited voices and spied the scurrying as the townsfolk took note of the newcomers.

"She's back already!" said a gray-haired matron. "It's been little more than a month since the raffle."

A mother dressed in drab-colored homespun nudged her adolescent daughter. "Why just look at that. A blue calico dress."

"Hey, boys!" yelled a wrangler to the patrons inside the Golden Slipper. "Guess what! The Widow Duvall just rolled into town." Almost immediately, men spilled out into the street.

Luke reined in his horse until he rode beside the wagon. He watched with pride as Honor sat up straight and lifted her chin, pasting on a serene smile and nodding at openly curious stares. He doubted if anyone else could see that her black-booted foot tapped the wood beneath her at a mile-a-minute pace.

Rafe pulled the wagon to a stop in front of the livery barn. Luke turned Red Pepper over to a yard boy in greasy bib overalls, then approached the wagon where his friend was busy loosening Brown Baggage's tether. He spoke to Honor. "Are you ready?"

She didn't move from her seat. "No, I'm not. Pretending to want a new dress, to want this wedding, will require all my dramatic skills. I still don't think we need—"

"Hush. You made your point." Luke climbed up on the wagon and sat down beside her. Her protests, along with the memory of the laughter she'd shared with Rafe, stuck in his craw. He rested his finger against her lips and said, "I'm not certain you can pull it off either, so I reckon I ought to do my part to help out." Sliding his finger down to her chin, he tipped it upward, lifting her face. Then, smack-dab in the middle of Bastrop, in public view of anyone who cared to watch, the Bravest Man in Texas kissed the notorious Widow Duvall.

And kept on kissing her. He kissed her until all sound around them ceased. He kissed her until he damned near forgot who and where he was. Abruptly, he pulled away, muttering a curse as Malone's amused drawl floated from beside the wagon. "Well," he said, "I reckon that'll get the clothesline talk a'goin'. Tongues will fly so fast they're liable to catch fire."

Mine's already on fire, Luke thought.

Feminine twitters coming from the doorway to the dry goods across the street proved him right. Luke cleared his throat and flashed the ladies a rakish grin, hoping no one noticed he forced it. Honor simply looked dazed.

Luke clambered down from the wagon, then grasped Honor about the waist and swung her to the ground. To Rafe, he said, "After I see Honor situated I'll stop by the Golden Slipper to spread the word about Brown Baggage. I'll meet you at the track in probably, what, half an hour?"

Staring at a stunned Honor, Rafe absently replied, "Sounds good to me."

Taking Honor by the elbow, Luke led her across the street toward the mercantile. She walked stiffly beside him, repeatedly attempting to shrug off his touch. "I can't believe you are doing this to me," she grumbled beneath her breath.

Well aware of the faces pressed against the store window, Luke leaned close to her and said, "Settle down, sunshine. You can blame this one on Luella, not me. She's the one who accepted Mrs. Litty's offer on your behalf."

"My green silk would do fine for the occasion." Her voice quavered a bit as she added, "I really don't want to do this. It's difficult being a woman of my reputation. This is even worse than facing them for the raffle. This is much more intimate."

The flicker of vulnerability in her eyes all but broke his heart. That wasn't like Honor Duvall. "Hey now, buck up, gal. You've got more guts than you can hang on a fence. You're not gonna let a gaggle of busybodies do you in, are you?"

She gazed toward the plate-glass window where at least a dozen faces crowded to get a good look at the entertainment. "I'll probably spill something or break something. I'm always at my most clumsy when I'm nervous."

Yeah, but she didn't flinch when she was angry. Telling himself he did it for her sake alone, Luke planted a quick, hard kiss on Honor's mouth. Then he sent her toward the door with a pat on the behind. There, that ought to do it, he thought, his palm burning with the memory of soft, well-rounded, and yielding flesh.

She looked back over her shoulder, eyes burning like the skin on his hand. "If I had a gun in my hand I'd shoot you, Prescott."

"You might even hit me, too." He chuckled as the shop's welcome bell tinkled when she pushed inside. Mrs. Litty, a pretty woman with long dark hair and kind eyes, approached immediately. "Here you are right on time. It's so nice to see you again, Mrs. Duvall, Captain Prescott." She took Honor's hands in hers. "I know I told Luella you should bring your fabric selection to my home, but in all honesty, I couldn't wait. I absolutely adore weddings, and all the to-do surrounding them. Thank you so much for allowing me the honor to help you with your gown.

I'm in heaven when I get to sew a wedding dress. Now, since I'm here, may I assist you in selecting the cloth?"

As Honor conversed stiffly with Mrs. Litty, Luke glanced around the store. At least twenty people crowded the small mercantile, milling around display tables and cabinets, pretending not to stare at Honor but doing exactly that. A young man in a fancy black suit removed a bottle from a shelf and pretended to read the label while he actually gawked at Honor's bosom. Luke took a step toward him and gave him a menacing glare. The bottle slipped, crashed to the ground, and the pungent scent of vinegar billowed up in an invisible cloud.

Honor looks so cute with her nose wrinkled up, Luke thought as the ladies stepped over the widening pool of vinegar. Mrs. Litty ushered Honor toward a table piled high with bolts of fabric. A trio of women sidled up beside them and began offering suggestions and opinions.

Fearing snide remarks and hurtful comments, Luke listened in on the conversation, ready to jump to Honor's defense. But the ladies' comments were welcoming and friendly, even complimentary. Luke watched the surprise dawn in Honor's eyes, and then the smile spread across her face. When one of the ladies said something that made her laugh, he couldn't help grinning.

See, sunshine? Didn't I tell you not to worry? She wasn't the social pariah she believed. He sensed Luella's fine hand in smoothing the mercantile waters, and he decided to pick Luella up a bottle of good whiskey as thanks. If only Honor would give people a chance to get to know her, they'd learn that the notorious Black Widow was actually a warmhearted kitten. Who could tell, maybe he'd helped her a little. Maybe being linked with him and his celebrated, if undeserved, reputation offset the infamy in hers. The idea made him feel good.

Good and foolish, Prescott. She was leaving Texas in less than two weeks. It didn't matter whether the ladies of Bastrop liked her or not.

Luke's mood turned sour. Since the doctor's wife had matters safely in hand, he thought it best to beat a retreat. "Honor, if you don't need me anymore ..."

Mrs. Litty held up a length of peach satin in her outstretched hands and answered. "Run along, Captain. We'll be fine, right, Mrs. Duvall?"

Honor glanced at him, her whiskey eyes warm and happy, her shy smile soothing to his ill humor. She nodded. Luke found that he wanted to kiss her again. He cleared his throat. "Good. I'll see you later this afternoon then. At your home, Mrs. Litty?"

"That'll be fine, Captain."

Tipping his hat to the women, he turned to leave the mercantile. At the doorway, he paused a moment and frowned, a picture of the satin in Mrs. Litty's hand flashing through his mind. "Hey, Honor honey?" he called back, loud enough for everyone in the store to hear. "Pick up some lemon drops before you leave here, would you please? And don't forget, I want your wedding dress to be yellow. Mrs. Litty, she may be stubborn about this, but it's important to me. I'm trusting you to see she picks the right thing. When Honor Duvall becomes my wife I want her dressed in yellow."

"Luke!" Honor protested.

"Yellow, Honor."

Her glower promised retribution and Luke cockily blew her a kiss. Whistling, he left the store feeling certain he'd get his way this time. She'd do it to please the friendly mercantile ladies, not him, but that didn't matter. Honor Duvall should always wear yellow.

"I want the blue satin, Mary." Honor stood on a box in the Littys' spare bedroom dressed only in chemise and drawers. The doctor's wife was armed with a tape measure and a frown.

"Absolutely not. I won't be responsible for your groom's disappointment when he sees his bride on his wedding day. There, that should do it." Mary jotted a measurement down on a piece of paper. "I must say you'll be a pleasure to sew for. I've never done a dress for someone with such enviable measurements. I must remember to take care with the bodice seams as they'll take the most strain. Ordinarily when I sew for a woman with a bosom as big as yours, her waist seams take just as much stress." She stepped back and studied Honor, tapping pursed lips with an index finger. "I'll think I'll lower the neckline of that design you chose. Since we're bowing to Captain Prescott's wish on color, I think it's appropriate you battle back using your natural weapons. Your husband will get his yellow dress, but I've a notion it'll annoy him to see every man at the party eyeing his wife's substantial charms."

Honor couldn't help laughing. "Mary Litty, you are indeed wicked."

"No, I'm a woman who has learned how to deal with men. Now, I think we're through here. Why don't you go ahead and get dressed while I put on a pot of coffee."

Honor smiled as she donned the calico. Had anyone told her a week ago she'd spend a thoroughly enjoyable day today with the women of Bastrop, she'd have claimed that person had lost his mind. As she sat on the bed and bent to tie her shoes, she heard a knock on the door and the deep-pitched tone of a male voice.

Had Luke finished earlier than expected? She hoped the race had gone all right and that Brown Baggage had run as well as Rafe anticipated. If so, Honor intended to rid her conscience of the nagging regret for rigging the raffle by offering the quarter-miler to the true winner before she left Texas.

Honor snapped her fingers. She kept forgetting to retrieve that ticket from its hiding place and find out who the winner was. She needed to discover exactly whom she had cheated. She hadn't had the nerve to check the name before.

A knock sounded again, but this time Mary Litty called, "Honor? Come on out just as soon as you are ready. I have a wonderful surprise for you."

Brown Baggage must have won. Maybe she even ran better than expected. *I won't need to feel like a thief anymore.* Honor tied a bow in the end of her shoelaces and stood. She felt as if a hundred-pound burden had been lifted from her shoulders. Smiling wasn't difficult as she opened the bedroom door and stepped down the short hallway into the Littys' small parlor.

"Surprise, Honor, my dear!"

Honor froze. This moment came right out of her nightmares. "Hello, Father."

"Y'all ready, boys?" The starter's voice sounded above the buzz of the crowd.

Luke watched Rafe Malone swing young Billy Wilson into the saddle on Brown Baggage's back and wished one more time that Jason was healthy enough to ride. "Remember, don't let her swing wide on the turn," Rafe said. "That's where we'll win or lose this one." He handed the boy the reins and added, "And be spare with the quirt. Whipping distracts the lady."

Billy nodded, indicating he was set, and Rafe backed away. "We're ready."

"So are we," called the owner of their opponent, a pretty mare almost two hands taller than "BB," as Honor's sons had taken to calling their racer.

"Take your places."

As the horses took their position at the post, Rafe and Luke hurried to find a spot to watch the race near the finish line. The starter raised a pistol into the air, squeezed the trigger, and the horses broke quickly away. Immediately, they drew even, then Brown Baggage took the lead by a head. Luke tensed as the other horse challenged, gaining ground, and slowly pulled ahead. As the horses approached the pole, Brown Baggage was behind by a length. "It's yours, sweetheart. Do it here," Luke urged.

Rafe's mouth lifted in a slow grin when Brown Baggage made up the difference going around the turn. She came out of it ahead by a neck. "That's it. The mare will never catch her now. I think she'd win on a straight course, too, but this turn hedged our bet." The thunder of their hooves rose above the noise of the cheering crowd as they raced toward the finish. Brown Baggage won by two lengths.

Luke slapped Rafe on the back. "You did it!"

Rafe shook his head. "Billy did a good job, but I don't doubt Jason would have ridden a better race. Do you think there's a chance he'll be ready to ride by the jubilee? I want to beat Houston's horse so bad I can taste it."

"I doubt if we'll be able to hold Jason back."

The two men moved through the crowd, accepting backslaps and congratulations and hawking the upcoming race against Houston's quarter-miler. "I want to give her a good rubdown," Rafe told Luke. "Why don't you go on to the Golden Slipper and start buying drinks with our winnings. That's the best way to spread the word about the new racing legend to come out of Lost Pines. You can't ask for a better opportunity to make the announcement about Starlight."

"You'll meet me there later?"

"Yeah."

Luke watched his friend lead the horse away toward the livery stables and knew more than a horse race had taken place here today. It was so good to see Rafe excited about something again. Ever since he'd moved over to Lost Pines to help with guard duty and work with the horses, he'd seemed more like himself than he had in months. Luke suspected he'd finally begun to put Elizabeth behind him. Just goes to show, getting over a woman takes a little time.

Luke believed he'd need to remind himself of that fact in the months to come. Just because he didn't love Honor—couldn't love Honor—didn't mean he wouldn't miss her once she was gone. He even missed her already. She'd been on his mind all dad-gum morning.

She stayed on his mind throughout the afternoon, too. While he announced Starlight's demise and bought a round of drinks for the men at the Golden Slipper, he wondered what fabric she'd chosen for her gown. When he toasted the Heroes of the Republic, he imagined her gowned in a variety of wedding dress designs. While he finished off a bottle waiting for Rafe to finally show, he fantasized about stripping a ruffled yellow organza fancy from Honor's delectable body.

After the sixth or seventh toast, he got maudlin and his leg started aching, and finally a new friend poured enough coffee down him to sober him up. By the time he finally gave up on Rafe and presented himself at the doctor's front door, he was much later than he'd intended. Nor was he thinking clearly. Mrs. Litty had to repeat herself twice before he understood what she was saying. "Like I told you, Captain Prescott, Honor left some time ago. Hours, in fact. They waited for you for a little while, but then they said they had to go."

"Who's they? Honor and Rafe?"

"No, I never saw Mr. Malone. It was her father. Honor left here with Congressman Armstrong."

Honor sat stiffly beside her father in a carriage that rolled along the trail toward Lost Pines. The afternoon was hot and humid, the air heavy with the earthy scent of the forest. They rode for almost an hour in grim silence, the sounds of birdsong, the squeak of a wheel, and the occasional nicker from one of the horses filling the emptiness.

Her thoughts whirled like a vicious spring storm, and her emotions ran the gamut from hopelessness and despair to numbness, fear, fury. She'd been a fool to allow her father to whisk her away from the Littys'. She should have screamed or fought or done anything to escape him. Instead, she'd followed him meekly. "Just like the old days," she muttered to herself.

Richard turned his head. "What was that, my dear?"

Honor shivered at the sound of his voice. Even though she'd known of his pending arrival, she'd been unprepared to see him. It was too soon. The party was still ten days away. "Why have you come? Why won't you leave me alone?"

"You've been a disobedient child."

"I'm not a child and I don't want—"

"Really now, Honor," he interrupted, amusement

248

glittering in his hard green eyes. "When has it ever mattered what you want?"

She sucked in a sharp breath. "I despise you."

"I'm not all that thrilled with you, either." He manipulated the reins to guide the horses around a fallen tree partially blocking the trail. "Convincing that Ranger to marry you—that's quite a drastic rebellion. One that has caused me no end of bother. Lord Kendall was with me at Washington-on-the-Brazos when I received news of your upcoming nuptials. Neither one of us was too pleased."

Honor gripped the seat cushion. Marcus Black was in Texas? Already? "You said he wouldn't be here until midsummer."

"He's anxious to wed you."

Honor gazed blindly into the trees, her mind racing as she tried to think a step ahead of her father. She asked herself again why an English viscount wanted to marry her. She'd met Marcus Black only that once when she and Armand shared supper with him in Nacogdoches over a year before.

She thought back to the dinner, trying to remember details of what had transpired. She recalled that during the meal, Black had mentioned that lumber was his primary business and the source of much of his family's wealth. He'd also asked numerous questions about Armand's holdings, Duvall Pinery and the isolated forest land dubbed Lost Pines. Maybe that was it. Maybe he wanted her because she now owned so much of the Lost Pines forest. Perhaps he planned to rehire the workers and bring the business that had fallen apart after Armand's death back into production.

But he didn't need to marry her to do that, Honor realized. Her father could sign over tree harvest rights to Black if he chose. None of this made sense. "Why is Marcus Black in Washington-on-the-Brazos? Why is he in Texas this soon?"

"Use his title, Honor," Armstrong snapped. "It's his due. He's not at the capital, he's here. He met me in Bastrop this morning. We considered taking care of your marriage by proxy, but Lord Kendall wished to see for himself the wealth of the Lost Pines forest."

"He's in Bastrop!"

"We'd hoped to see the matter done today, but the minister refused to accompany us because of a funeral service he had scheduled for late afternoon. Once I heard of the spectacle you and the Ranger made of yourselves this morning, we decided I should escort you home immediately. Lord Kendall will bring a preacher to Lost Pines tomorrow morning and you will repeat your vows then. To him." He laid his hand on her leg and squeezed her knee. "Do you understand? To him!"

Tomorrow morning! Oh, Lord, help me.

"Why?" Honor asked. "Why does an English viscount want to marry a Texian widow? It must be more than the trees. Black was on his way back to London when I met him. How did he learn about Armand's death? Did you write him? What have you cooked up this time, Father? What would you gain from such a marriage?"

He ignored her questions. "This horse race extravaganza you have planned in honor of Houston will go on, of course. It will be a good campaign opportunity."

Honor wrenched her leg from his grip. "I demand to know why, Father. Why Marcus Black? What does he have that you want? He's an Englishman. He can't help you win the election."

"Never presume to demand anything of me, daughter," said Armstrong in a voice as cold as a west Texas winter. "I will tell you this much, just in case you're not convinced of my sincerity. The election is not the issue. With the help of your husbands' funds, I am well on the way to winning that already. You see, child, the presidency of the Republic of Texas is simply a stepping-stone to what I truly desire, what I've wanted all my life. This marriage is simply my insurance that all parties involved hold to the agreement."

"Insurance." Impotent fury coursed through her. "This marriage is my life!"

"That is of little consequence to me."

"What does Black get? What are you doing for him, Father? Spying for England?"

Richard Armstrong yanked back on the reins and the carriage rolled to a stop. Twisting in his seat, he backhanded her hard. "Dare even whisper that word again and I'll kill both those boys. The old woman, too. You understand me? I won't allow you to ruin this for me."

Honor's ears rang and her cheek stung from the force of his blow. She recalled similar blows in the past. Tears burned in her eyes and despair clutched her heart. Time had run out. She'd waited too late to make her escape.

Or had she?

Honor met her father's furious gaze as hope overcame her discouragement. Luke. Luke wouldn't allow this to happen. He might not love her, but he cared for Texas and he'd promised to protect her.

But he was back in Bastrop. What if he didn't get here in time? She'd have to find a way to cause a delay. But how? Too bad she hadn't married Luke when he asked. She wouldn't be in this position now if—

Honor's eyes widened as the idea burst in her brain. It was drastic. Desperate, even. But then, so was she. Honor sent Luke a silent apology as she swallowed hard and prayed she'd tell her lies well. "You're too late, Father. I can't marry Marcus Black. You see, Captain Prescott and I are already married."

For an instant, his expression grew dark as the forest at night. Then he laughed. "Don't be a fool, Honor. The news that you'll marry at the jubilee is on lips all across the Republic."

Nerves danced in Honor's stomach, but she ignored them. She squared her shoulders and lifted her chin. "We'll be repeating our vows at the jubilee. Repeating is the operative word. Luke is an old-fashioned man. He insisted on marrying me as soon as we made love."

"You bedded the man?"

"I did."

"I don't believe it. Armand always said you were the coldest bitch he'd ever found between the sheets."

A wash of hatred crashed over her, but Honor buried it with a controlled smile. "Intimacy with Luke Prescott has nothing in common with the abuse I endured at the hands of Armand Duvall. I chose my own husband this time around. I used all my womanly weapons and wiles to bind him to me. I may even now be carrying his child. You might as well turn your horse around and think of another way to achieve your goals."

He spoke in a soft, menacing whisper. "A child? That would ruin everything." He thrust a bold hand against her abdomen and she shuddered at his touch. "Bah, it's early yet. We can fool Kendall if we must."

"We won't need to fool Kendall. I'm already married."

"You lie," Armstrong snapped. "You wear no ring. I see no proof."

"I have proof at home," she replied, having anticipated the charge. She sent a quick prayer heavenward that all would go as planned and added, "I'll be more than happy to show you."

"I could always kill him."

"Luke Prescott is the toughest, smartest, bravest man in Texas. Do you really think you'd succeed where so many others have failed? Besides, killing him would be a mistake. Think of who he is, a bona fide hero. He loves the Republic of Texas second only to me, and he even supports your candidacy. I've told him nothing about the ... problems you and I have had. Luke would campaign for you if I asked. You need not spend the fortune you stole from me to buy the election if you have Luke Prescott on your side."

Money, Honor knew, was always a good argument to use with her father.

Pursing his lips, he held her stare as he obviously considered the argument. He opened his mouth to speak when the thudding thunder of a fast-approaching horse interrupted him. Honor caught her breath as she twisted around to look behind them. Luke? No, he'd give her away. She needed time to explain what she'd done!

But the rider wasn't Luke. Rafe Malone yanked his mount to a halt beside the carriage. "Honor! Am I happy to see you. Luke is tearing up Bastrop trying to find you."

Honor gave him a meaningful stare as she smiled and said, "My husband probably isn't too happy with me, is he?"

Rafe tugged off his hat and wiped his brow with his sleeve, his gaze never leaving Honor's. "Uh, no," he said after a long pause. "That's a pretty fair statement. Luke sent me on to Lost Pines hoping you'd taken it in your mind to head home. You shouldn't have left town without telling ... your husband."

Honor closed her eyes briefly as relief washed over her. Rafe must have tracked her from town. How had he known she was in trouble? Had he seen her? It didn't really matter, she realized. What mattered was that she was no longer alone.

Putting on his politician's facade, Armstrong patted Honor's knee and smiled at Rafe. "I'm afraid it's my fault. I wanted some time to myself with my daughter, you see. It's been too long since we had the opportunity to chat. I'm Honor's father." He leaned over and stretched out his hand toward Rafe. "Richard Armstrong."

"The Richard Armstrong who is running for president?" Rafe asked.

"I have not yet officially announced my candidacy."

"Well, I'll be dipped!" Rafe exclaimed, reaching to pump the candidate's arm. "I'm Rafe Malone. I'm a friend of the Prescotts. Didn't know you were Honor's father."

Armstrong briefly shifted his stare to Honor. "My daughter is often reluctant to mention her family connections," he said.

Rafe appeared not to hear the menace in his words, but Honor knew Gentleman Rafe Malone was more observant than that. "I'm sorry to have caused worry, Rafe," she said. "I certainly didn't mean to. You said Luke is still in town?"

Rafe nodded. "Yeah. I imagine he'll be along directly."

"Perhaps you should return to Bastrop and relieve his worry, Mr. Malone," Armstrong suggested.

"No need. He told me to see Honor safely home if I caught up with her. Besides, I don't want to be late for dinner. Yesterday Mrs. Best promised to bake a peach pie for dessert." He winked at Richard Armstrong, and added, "We'll come out ahead if we get our share before Luke gets home. He has a special liking for peach pie. I'm warning you up front, Captain Luke Prescott doesn't like to share."

13

Red Pepper's hooves pounded the road, thundering toward the turnoff leading to Lost Pines. Luke's gaze searched the wall of loblolly pine for the gateposts that marked the lane, the lump of fear that had lodged in his chest at the mention of Honor's father's name climbing to his throat as he neared her home. What if she wasn't there?

They'd cut a good twenty to thirty minutes off the trip. Once he made it home and found Honor safe and sound, he'd see Red Pepper treated like a king. I'll slip you a lemon drop or two, boy. The gelding enjoyed the candy as much as his master.

If Armstrong had hurt her he'd kill him with his bare hands.

Thank God for Rafe. Luke's friend had left a note for him at the livery explaining how young Billy Wilson had spied Honor riding out of town with the con-

255

gressman. The direction they had taken suggested they were traveling toward Lost Pines and Rafe had written that he intended to follow. Luke had breathed a big sigh of relief at that. He could trust Rafe Malone to keep Honor safe once he caught up with her and Armstrong.

Luke spied the wrought-iron arch that read Lost Pines. He pulled Red Pepper up, and as the great horse slowed, Luke asked himself how to play this one. With caution? Both barrels blazing in a frontal assault? As always, he listened to his gut and made his decision, praying his panic hadn't ruined his judgment. After making the turn, he gave Red Pepper an extra kick. They flew up the gently sloping hill toward the house where he prayed he'd find the woman he . . .

Luke couldn't finish the thought.

The clearings on either side of the road sparkled with brilliant wildflowers beneath the afternoon sun. He looked right past this beauty, his attention locked on Lost Pines's broad cypress doors.

He ran Red Pepper right up to the front steps, then reined him in hard. His heart slammed against his ribs as he bounded up the stairs, hardly feeling the twinge of pain in his leg. He threw open the front door, bellowing, "Honor!"

Her voice chimed like bell music. "In the parlor, darling."

Sweet relief flooded his limbs. She was alive. Thank God, she was alive. Luke moved instinctively toward the sound of her voice, pausing only when Rafe strode from the room and shot him a hard, warning look. "Your wife was getting worried, Captain Prescott. She expected you some time ago."

My wife? Luke held his friend's stare as the hair on the back of his neck stood at full attention. Looking into Rafe's eyes, he gave a slight nod and silently, thankfully acknowledged the warning. At the parlor doorway he paused, drinking in the sight of her. *Hell, sunshine, you scared me half to death.*

She beamed a smile of welcome so bright it all but blinded him to the presence of the other man in the room. "Please don't be angry at me, Luke," she said, coming toward him. "I know I should never have left town without you, and I promise I won't do it again." She threw herself into his arms, tugged his head down to hers, and captured his lips in a breath-stealing kiss.

Luke thought he must be muddled from lack of air when she finally drew back and flashed him a sunny smile. She hooked her arm through his and said, "We have a visitor. Luke, allow me to introduce my father, Richard Armstrong. Father, this is my husband, Captain Luke Prescott."

Luke, usually so quick on the uptake, was thinking at molasses speed. Still looking at Honor, he noticed the faint mark of a fist on her face and it was all he could do not to level her bastard father here and now. He promised himself the pleasure of returning the attention with interest at a later time. Giving his head a little shake, he turned to Armstrong and extended his free hand. "Welcome to Lost Pines."

The politician's handshake was firm. He watched Luke closely as he said, "So, Captain, I understand you married my daughter. It would have been nice for her family to be informed. I fear this news has created a bit of a difficulty."

"A difficulty?" Luke repeated, keeping his face a blank, uncertain how to play the hand currently being dealt. He nodded when Honor lifted a water pitcher and a glass, wordlessly offering him a drink.

"Yes." Armstrong's tone vibrated with disapproval. "It was bad enough that I was entertaining her fiancé when I received an invitation to her wedding to another man. Now, I arrive at my daughter's home to learn that the wedding will be but a public repetition of vows already spoken!"

Luke accepted the water from his "wife" and took his time taking a sip, not knowing how he should respond. Tension radiated from Honor like heat from a stove. What did she want him to say? Seeking some sort of hint, he arched an eyebrow at Honor. "Fiancé?"

She glanced at her father, then offered Luke an embarrassed smile. "Sweetheart, I'm sorry. I know I should have told you. It was wrong of me to keep such information from the man I love."

Luke's heart gave a funny little hitch at that. He tossed back the rest of his water, then said, "So what's the problem, Congressman?"

Richard Armstrong clasped his hands behind his back, his expression grave. "The problem is that Marcus Black, Lord Kendall, an old and dear friend of mine, is traveling to Lost Pines in the morning for the purpose of marrying my daughter."

Now this marriage business made some sense. Luke put his arm around Honor's shoulder. "Sorry, sir, but I'm afraid Mr. Black is gonna have to be disappointed. Bigamy is illegal in the Republic of Texas."

"Well, I am not convinced that bigamy is the issue. By her own admission, my daughter is not always honest. I'm an attorney by profession, Captain Prescott, and that makes me cautious. As you likely have realized, large sums of money are involved here. I'm afraid I'll need proof of this marriage."

Disgust laced Luke's voice. "I don't care about your daughter's money."

"I hope that's true. But if you'll look at the situation from my point of view, you'll understand my hesitation. Honor is engaged to be married to Lord Kendall and I receive an invitation to her wedding to another man. Upon my arrival I'm told the wedding has already taken place, but my daughter can't produce the proper legal documents."

"Only because I couldn't find the key, Father," Honor said. She implored Luke with a look. "I tried to get our marriage paper out of your lockbox to settle the question once and for all, but I couldn't remember where you put the key. Would you go get it please? I left the box on the table in our bedroom. The one beneath the wildflower painting."

"Now?"

"Yes, please."

"Sure," Luke replied, not sure of anything at all. She wanted him to go upstairs, but why? Leave it to Honor Duvall to do something unexpected. He just hoped he was talented enough to hang on until the end of the ride. As he turned to leave the parlor, another thought occurred to him. Where were the boys? Was Armstrong holding Micah and Jason, somehow using them against Honor? "Are the boys upstairs?"

"They're not here," Rafe answered from the doorway. "Luella got the notion to visit Molly Parker over at Paradise plantation and the boys talked her into letting them go along. They'll be back in a few days."

Luke nodded, interpreting Rafe's meaning with ease. Molly Parker was the whore who'd relieved both Rafe and Luke of their virginity when they weren't much older than Micah. Paradise was the tongue-in-cheek name Luke used for Rafe's cabin. Luella had taken the boys to hide out at Rafe's place. Good. Three fewer people to worry about. Fretting about Honor took all his energy as it was.

Luke hurried upstairs to the master suite. He didn't have a lockbox, so he didn't know what to expect.

Drawing his gun, he listened at the door. Nothing. Cautiously, he pushed the door open and quickly scanned the room. No one.

His gaze sought the wildflower painting on the opposite wall and the table beneath it. On the table, an inkwell and pen sat beside two sheets of paper, paper that hadn't been there when he'd left the room that morning.

Luke picked up the first page and read the sentence scrawled across it. *Please, Luke,* Honor wrote, *save me from my father.* A large blot of ink on the paper was still wet and it dripped as he held the page. Like an indigo teardrop, he absently observed.

He lifted the second piece of paper and scanned it. Shock washed through him like a cold fever. He stumbled toward the bed and sat on the edge.

Honor's handwriting. Honor's signature. All it lacked was his own John Henry to make it a legal and binding document. She'd dated it weeks ago, the day he'd proposed to her after taking her to bed, but she'd obviously written it today. A marriage bond. Son of a bitch.

Luke's eyes drifted shut. He hadn't seen a marriage bond for maybe ten years, when they were a common way for a man and woman to tie the knot. Back then, preachers were scarce in Texas and lovers didn't want to wait for months and sometimes years to set up housekeeping. They'd write out a marriage bond promising to speak vows before a cleric at the first opportunity or forfeit a specified sum of money to their partner should either refuse to do so. With more men of the cloth around in recent years, the practice had died out.

No greater proof of Honor's desperation existed. No better demonstration of her trust could he imagine.

Luke would be damned if he'd let her down. Not this woman. Not this time.

He snatched the pen from the well on the bedroom desk and scratched his name in the appropriate spot. Pursing his lips, he sent a gentle stream of air across the ink in order to help it dry. Legally, he had just become the notorious Widow Duvall's fourth husband. His mouth twisted in a wry smile and he muttered, "Maybe I'm not such a coward after all."

Honor met him at the parlor door downstairs. Anxiety glittered in her eyes and etched fine lines across her brow. Luke didn't say a word, just did what came naturally to a newly wedded man. He kissed his bride.

Armstrong cleared his throat. Luke kissed her for another full minute before lifting his head and drawling, "Sorry, I reckon I got carried away. Since essentially we are still on our honeymoon, I tend to do that a lot." He gave her a wicked wink that Armstrong was certain to see, then bussed her on the tip of her nose. "Why don't you let me talk to your father a bit in private, Honor. Take Malone to the kitchen and sweet-talk him into making some biscuits to go with the leftovers of my stew from last night. He bakes a mean biscuit."

"We ate supper an hour ago, Luke, and I didn't serve that stew." Her eyes said, *Thank you. You saved me.* "Micah tried to give it to the pigs this morning, but I think they turned up their noses at it, too."

"That's it. Those pigs are bound for bacon." Luke's eyes replied, *Glad to help, sunshine. I'm truly glad to help.*

"They've always been bound for bacon."

"But not quite this soon."

"We had beefsteak this evening. I saved you a plate." *Luke, I want you to know . . .*

"I'll get it later." *Later, Honor. We'll talk later.*

261

Armstrong cleared his throat. "Prescott? You have my proof?"

Luke gave Honor a quick kiss on the brow, then gestured for her to leave the room. When Rafe moved to leave with her, Luke said, "Hold on there, Malone. Why don't you keep us company for a bit? I was just kidding about the biscuits. Believe me, Honor needs no help. Whatever she cooks up, a man would be a fool to turn down."

Honor's hand smoothed the eiderdown covering Armand Duvall's bed. No, not Armand's. Luke's bed. Her husband's bed. And her bed once again. Oh, God.

The whisper of a sound, just a soft brush of wood against wood, floated past her and she knew Luke was there. She absorbed his presence, the scent of him, the charge that shimmered in the air whenever he was near. She took comfort in his proximity even as she dreaded the conversation looming before her.

The door clicked shut. Seconds passed as neither spoke. Finally, Luke broke the silence. "I wasn't certain I'd find you here."

Honor swallowed. Emotions nipped at her control. "I wasn't certain you'd want me here."

"God, Honor, I've wanted you here since the day I arrived."

She had no idea how to reply to that. Luke crossed to the bureau and began to empty his pockets. Honor heard the tinny whack of his candy tin against the marble-topped table, and felt compelled to speak. "My father expects me to be with you. Knowing him, he's liable to find an excuse to knock on the door." With her fingers laced, she squeezed her hands together and turned to face him. "I'm sorry, Luke. I didn't know what else to do."

He gave her a long, searching look. "A marriage bond was some pretty quick thinking."

"It's how I married Franklin."

"Franklin?"

"Franklin Tate. My first husband."

Luke nodded sagely, his dark eyes narrowed to flinty slits. "The first one. You know, you never have told me how he died."

Honor wasn't about to tell him now, either. Not tonight. "Luke, about the bond—"

Luke tossed his wallet on the chest. "It didn't hurt anything, Honor. Your father told me he'll still attend the party, so my plan isn't affected." His hand slipped inside his jacket, and he removed a folded set of documents from his pocket. "Rafe and I had a little meeting with your father. Do you remember that Rafe once practiced law?"

She nodded.

"He's even better at legal thievery than he was at the other kind. I showed Rafe your legal papers last week, so he knew how your father managed to get control of your funds. Did you realize you signed your community property rights back to your husband each time you married?"

"Not the first two times. I was young. If my father said sign here, I signed. With Armand, well, I wasn't strong enough to fight, yet."

"Times have changed, haven't they, sunshine?" Luke said with a tender smile. "Rafe was able to follow the complicated path that resulted in your father controlling all your funds. He was also able to figure out how to break his hold on you."

"Rafe knows how to break Armand's will?"

"No. The will isn't the problem, Honor. The contract Duvall had with your father putting him in control of the disbursement of your funds is what has caused the trouble."

"But I had a lawyer look at the papers. He said there was nothing I could do."

Luke shook his head. "He was wrong. Rafe knew what to do. He and I did some dickering with your father. What Armstrong thinks he agreed to and what he got are two different things." He tossed her the pages, saying, "Think of this as a wedding gift."

The folded papers crackled as Honor flipped them open. The signature scrawled across the bottom of the first page drew her eyes like a magnet. Richard P. Armstrong. "What is this?"

"Honor, your father played it too smart for his own good." Wicked satisfaction gleamed in Luke's eyes. "Legally, when we signed the marriage bond, your assets became mine. Your father believes he secured my agreement to an arrangement similar to what he had with your other husbands. He didn't read the documents closely enough."

Honor's heart gave a lurch. "So now *you* have control over my money?"

"Read the second page, sunshine. The third paragraph. Every time it says 'The party of the third part' substitute your name. Rafe wants his legal fees paid with your kisses and I told him to soak his head."

Honor hardly comprehended the words she read. The pages spilled to the floor. "Me? You've turned it all over to me?"

"Financial freedom." Luke's lips slid into a smile.

Honor's hands began to shake. Her mind whirled. Luke Prescott had just given her her most treasured dream. Liberty. Her independence. He'd handed her the means to go wherever she wanted, to live wherever she pleased, however she pleased. With whomever she pleased. She couldn't believe it. Her stomach fluttered with the wings of a million fireflies. Is this how it feels when wishes come true?

"Why? Why did you do this, Luke?"

"Why shouldn't I?" He shrugged, casually flipping a coin in the palm of his hand. "I helped this country fight a war for independence. I reckon I can sign a paper or two to further the cause on a more personal basis."

She gave her head a little shake of confusion. Luke tossed the coin to the bureau and sauntered toward her. He took her hand, touching her for the first time since entering the room. His rough thumb slid across her skin. "For all your railing and haranguing against the Republic, Honor, I look at you and I see Texas. The two of you are close in age. You both can fuel men's dreams with a single glance. You are strong and generous and demanding, and both a little wild."

He paused and stared deep into her eyes. "And you've been struggling against oppression for years. Richard Armstrong is your Mexico, Honor. He took control of your money out of greed, and in doing so, took away your liberty, denied you your personal freedom. He controlled your entire life with his rigid rules and domineering demands, all because it served his purposes. It didn't matter what you wanted."

Abruptly, he dropped her hand. He took a step away and his gaze made a slow sweep of her contours. "Well, he got away with it when you were young, but you've grown up. Just like Texas grew up. Santa Anna and the Mexican government failed to take that into consideration when they laid down their laws. So did your father. You had to go to war. You had no choice." He gestured toward the documents lying on the floor and offered an enigmatic smile. "Those papers are your Alamo, sunshine. I was proud to stand with you in battle."

Honor's gaze fastened on the documents. Slowly she bent to pick them up, then set them neatly on the bedside table. Luke's words had shaken her, touched a chord deep within her she never knew existed. She clutched his words to her soul, and tried to express her fear. "But the Alamo fell. Everyone died."

A mask dropped over his face, but not before Honor saw the flash of anguish in his eyes. "Not everyone," he said flatly, than gave his shoulders a shake. He moved across the room to where the French doors stood wide open. "It's getting kinda cool in here, don't you think?"

"No, please," Honor said, stepping toward him. The chill that settled into her bones had nothing to do with the cool night air streaming in through the open doors. "I can't be here all closed in. It traps me."

Luke lifted his hands away from the doors and faced her, his smile sadly crooked. "We're a hell of a pair, aren't we? I'm surprised there's room in this suite for you and me and all of our ghosts." He grasped her fingers and lifted them to his mouth. Dangerous emotions skidded across his eyes. Grazing her knuckles with his kiss, he asked, "Care to cuddle up beneath the covers and try to chase them away for a while? It is our wedding night, after all."

Honor sucked air past her teeth. She needed to be held by this man. Needed it like oxygen. But the love she felt for him compelled her to ask, "Is that to be my payment, then?"

"Payment? Payment for what?"

She waved a hand toward the documents. "For you signing the bond. For saving me from my father."

Luke's eyes snapped with hostility. He bit out his words. "Dammit, woman, that tongue of yours can slice raw meat. I wasn't asking you to whore, Honor. I meant both of us taking a little comfort, a little bit of good feeling to balance all the ugly. What I was asking . . ."

As his sentence trailed off, Honor sensed the change in him. Deep within her, hope sparked to life. "What were you asking, Luke?"

He didn't reply, but stood silent and stiff as a sentinel. A vein throbbed at his temple. His jaw muscles clenched. Honor held her breath and strained to read his belligerently hooded eyes, wishing desperately to see the emotion she longed for most of all. She took a step forward and stared into his soul. All she needed was one sign. Even a hint. She saw frustration and anger, sorrow and chagrin. Admiration. Respect. Even lust.

But she never saw love. Not the deep and desperate emotion she feared was shining from the depths of her own eyes.

Honor dropped her gaze and Luke muttered a curse. "I guess I was asking you to stay with me. After the jubilee, if I can succeed in bringing down your father without getting myself killed, I'd like to make this marriage a real one."

Her heart shattered. She hadn't seen love in his eyes. Clearing her throat, she asked, "Why?"

Luke winced. "Ah, shoot, Honor. You know the reasons."

"No, I don't. Tell me." She needed to hear him not say the words. In that, she'd find the strength to refuse him.

He closed his eyes. "I'd make you a good husband. I'd be the best father I could be to those boys and any children of our own we might have. I'd respect you and your independence, and I'd do my best never to hurt you." His eyelids lifted and his steel-gray stare bored a hole through her soul. "But I can't promise any more. I won't love you, Honor. I can't."

Her heart was one of his lemon drops, spilled to the ground and crushed beneath his bootheel. *Why can't you love me?*

She wouldn't beg. Pride came to her rescue, providing insulation from the pain knifing through her. It allowed her to lift her head and say, "And I can't stay. Our marriage can be no more than the pretense we meant all along."

For a long moment he held her gaze and Honor willed herself not to betray her injury by either look or action. What he was thinking, she could not tell. Beyond a fleeting flash of regret, his expression betrayed no emotion. Then abruptly, he nodded. "You'll stay until after the party?"

"Of course I will. I'll do everything I can to help you expose my father, Luke. You've given me my freedom. I'll do anything I can to help you."

Luke grimaced as if her gratitude had left a bad taste in his mouth. "This fellow your father wanted you to marry will arrive in the morning, but I hope he'll turn right around and leave. Your father wants to stay at Lost Pines until the party. We'll have to play the happily married pair for the next ten days. Will you be able to pull that off?"

"Yes." It would be both her heaven and her hell.

After that, they found little to talk about. She murmured some inanity about what to serve for breakfast the following morning, then disappeared into the adjoining room to change into her nightclothes. When she returned, Luke had removed the eiderdown from the bed to make a pallet on the floor. He noticed her frown and said, "Don't worry about me, Honor. I've slept in a lot worse places. This fancy rug is almost as soft as the mattress anyhow."

Honor glanced from the pallet to the bed and back to the pallet. *Both my heaven and my hell.*

"No," she said with a decisive shake of her head. "You'll not sleep on the floor and neither will I. We can share the bed."

"I don't think that's such a good idea."

Honor gestured toward the bed. "There is a saying about making one's bed and lying in it. When I wrote out that marriage bond, I knew that I sentenced myself to sleeping with the ghosts in this room. But I can't do it alone, Luke. I cannot sleep in that bed alone, and the floor isn't demon-free, either. There's no reason why we can't share. We've done it before."

Luke stared at the bed, his face as hard as granite. Honor held her breath as she waited for him to reply. A lifetime seemed to pass before he matter-of-factly said, "I don't know what Armand Duvall did to you here in this room. Seeing how you react to being here, though, makes me think I'd probably kill the bastard if he weren't already dead."

"You'll stay with me?"

He nodded and Honor exhaled with relief. She slipped beneath the sheets, lying stiff as a fence post as Luke blew out the lamps. She heard the rustle of clothing, and then, beside her, the bed dipped. Her body quivering, she waited for him to touch her. And waited and waited and waited.

"Luke?"

His hand brushed hers and he linked their fingers. "You think it would help to talk about Duvall?"

In the darkness, she scowled. "I'd rather not."

"Talking might scare your ghosts into somebody else's bedroom."

She scooted a little closer to him. "Has it worked for you and yours?"

"Hell, sunshine, I've never been brave enough to try."

She inched even closer, his body heat drawing her

like a moth to a flame. "But you're the Bravest Man in Texas."

"That, Mrs. Prescott, is the biggest demon of all."

Mrs. Prescott. Rafe had called her that earlier, but this was the first time Luke had used the name. It settled into her heart like sunshine on a winter morning. With her husband lying beside her she felt almost strong. Strong enough, she thought, to face a ghost or two.

"Armand had a special waterproof sheet he'd spread across the bed. He'd bathe me in bath salts, his own special mixture." Luke's grip tightened on her hand. She continued, "It was all quite ... ritualized. Physically, he never hurt me—well, except for the burns from his salts—but mentally, it was a nightmare. He'd surround the bed with things he'd call his toys." She fell silent, remembering. A shudder raked across her skin and she said in a whisper, "He always called me Mother. Then he'd make me bathe him."

"He was a sick son of a bitch." Luke pulled her against him and pressed a kiss to her brow. "How did you stand it?"

"Don't you mean, why the hell didn't I leave?" she asked, a defensive note creeping into her tone.

He gave her a squeeze. "You are the strongest woman I know, Honor. There's not a doubt in my mind that you did the best you could with the situation you were handed."

She thought about it for a moment. "If it had just been me, if I hadn't had Luella and the boys to consider, I'd have left him following the first night he summoned me to this room. But he was good to my family. Luella was ill when we married, very ill. She'd survived the yellow jack, but then she caught pneumonia. Between that and her rheumatism, she seldom left her room for an entire year. Armand was kind to her.

He brought a doctor to Lost Pines time and again, and he never mistreated my sons. He hired a tutor when I asked him to. The boys were happy here.

"Finally, though, I'd had all I could stand. One night I refused him. He was in the bath and I threw his tin of salts in his face and left. I had Luella and the boys pack their things. Luella insisted I tell him we were leaving and that's when I found him. He'd drowned in the bathtub. I don't know what he'd put in that batch, but it was as bad as my rhubarb pie."

"What do you mean?"

"I think the bath salts acted like a poison. Or maybe they somehow made him fall asleep. People don't drown while bathing without a reason. It had to be the salts." She blew a long sigh. "It took me too long to stand up to him. I thought I had to stay in the marriage, you see. I knew the problems I dealt with were no more than many women face. Marriage is such a trap. Women are powerless in a marriage. They—"

"Hold on there," Luke interrupted. "I have to call you on that one. Women have plenty of pull in a marriage. Rachel had me jumping to her tune with little more than a smile. She had more say-so over me than any of my Ranger bosses ever dreamed of having."

"But you loved her."

"Yes," he said softly. "I loved her."

Concealed by the darkness, a single tear spilled from her eyes and slid down her face. "That's beyond my experience, Luke. I only know what I've lived, and what I've lived has made me swear off loveless marriages."

He didn't speak for some moments. When finally he opened his mouth, she wished he'd kept it shut. "No wonder you don't want another one."

After that, there seemed little to say. He had loved Rachel. He couldn't love her. He'd said so twice.

Luke remained silent, his bare chest rising and falling steadily. His hand gently stroked her unbound hair. They lay like that for some time, and as the minutes passed, Honor became acutely aware of his nudity beneath the covers. But despite their proximity and relative lack of clothing, the mood that enveloped them wasn't sexual. It was melancholy and regretful. It was full of loss, deep and injuring.

Honor furiously blinked her tears away. Heaven and hell, she silently repeated. "I think I'll try to sleep now."

Luke cleared his throat. "Honor, I . . ." He heaved a sigh. "Sweet dreams, sunshine."

She rolled away and lay on her side, her back toward him, and attempted to clear her mind. Eventually, she dozed, but her rest was fitful. She heard the downstairs hall clock chime eleven and then midnight. Once she awoke to find her legs intertwined with Luke's. After that, she tossed and turned and never fell back to sleep.

Just as the clock struck three, she felt Luke's body go rigid.

14

As Luke lay in the darkness next to his bride, the truth floated across his mind like an apparition. He shied away from it, refusing to believe in the specter's existence, erecting all his defenses. But the scent of her, the brush of silk that was her skin against him, the silent sigh of her breathing, proved stronger weapons than his will.

He could love Honor.

The knowledge was a kick in the gut. It was one thing to want, to need, to desire, but it was something else entirely to love. He couldn't do that again. Love was the power that ruined him, the brush that painted a yellow stripe down his back. Bravest Man in Texas be damned.

Luke Prescott was the Coward of the Alamo.

Suddenly cold, he rolled from the bed. Moonlight cast faint beams of silvery light through the open

French doors as he pulled on his trousers. Padding across the floor, he approached the hearth and hunkered down to light a fire.

Thoughts pounded his brain like grapeshot. How had he let his guard down? Honor Duvall was a threat, after all. Thank God she was so strong. Had she accepted his proposal, accepted this marriage, he'd have been lost.

A ribbon of heat brushed his cheek. Luke stared at the flickering flames and wondered why he'd allowed her so close. He'd believed he'd never love again. He'd thought he could live on the fringes of her family forever. He'd been a damned fool.

I could love her.

He wouldn't allow it to happen. This thing between them could go no further. He had to stop it now. Put an end to it forever. One weapon would kill any feeling she imagined she had for him. The truth would drive her away without fail.

Honor's voice drifted from out of the darkness. "You must be cold."

God, if she only knew.

Luke summoned the courage to turn to her and say, "Yes, I'm cold. I've been cold for seven hellish years. I figure after all that's happened I owe you an explanation." He swallowed hard. "It's time I told you about the Alamo."

"The Alamo?" she repeated.

"Yeah. The Alamo is the reason I'm here. It's the reason for everything. Will you listen, Honor?"

She lit the bedside lamp and said, "Of course I'll listen."

As Luke took a moment to decide where to begin, she added, "But come back to bed, will you, please? I'm starting to get a bit shivery here by myself."

He didn't want to. He didn't want to see her or

274

touch her or smell her while he confessed the truth. But aware of her demons, he couldn't deny her request. He needed the closeness as much as she. He'd face some demons of his own while telling this story.

He returned to the bed and without undressing sat with his back against the headboard. Honor snuggled against him. Draping his arm around her, Luke tried to decide where to start. Finally, he drew a deep breath, exhaled a heavy sigh, and began to speak. "My first fighting was with Ben Milam in December of thirty-five when we took Bexar back from the Mexicans. In January, I headed home—some good cotton land I had over toward Gonzales. But in late January, I heard that James Bowie had arrived in Bexar and decided to transform the old San Antonio de Valero Mission, the Alamo, into a Texian fortress. Everyone knew the Mexicans would be back, and in my egotistical stupidity, I decided Jim Bowie couldn't do the job without me. I left my family and joined the garrison at Bexar. Then Santa Anna brought his army to town—five thousand men to our less than two hundred."

Luke leaned his head back and shut his eyes. "I'll never forget the sight of the banner as it unfurled from the San Fernando Cathedral bell tower. Blood red, it was. The sign that no quarter would be given. Sent shivers up the spine of every man jack among us. Travis, bold son of a bitch that he was, ordered a cannon shot for an answer. We'd stay at the Alamo and defend her unto death.

"The siege began on February twenty-fourth. They peppered us with skirmishes. The excitement kept us awake the first few nights."

Long rifle over the wall, pull the trigger, take the kick. Nose stinging at the acrid black powder smoke

275

bleeding from the pan and barrel. Reload and do it all over again.

Remembering, Luke felt the numbing weariness of it all. He absently stroked Honor's arm as he continued. "Travis started sending out emissaries to appeal for aid. Sutherland, Smith, Baylor. Jim Bonham went out twice. Each day Santa Anna's forces continued to swell." Luke fell silent then, as the telling took him back to the mission.

Rain. Hailstones cracked against the limestone and adobe walls, joining the steady crackle of gunfire in a purgatory of noise. The stench of blood and festering flesh. Of fear. Luke knelt on the floor of one of the cavelike rooms inside the Alamo's sprawling barracks, a sense of despair overwhelming him. They were done for. The battle surely lost. Oh, they might stave off this day's attack, but what of the next and the next and the next? What chance did the men of the Alamo have of holding off thousands?

None. Fear created a spasm in his bowels. The stench of death moved from beyond the fortress walls into this very room and Luke choked on it, tasting bile.

Rachel. When the Mexicans took the Alamo, they'd head east toward Gonzales. Toward his family. He never should have left her. Rachel's father wouldn't leave the farm. The man was stubborn as a hill-country mule. The Mexicans would come and they'd kill 'em. Or worse. God, Rachel. Run. Take my babies and get out of Santa Anna's way.

He yanked his long arm from the loophole and sank to the ground, cradling the gun in his lap. He couldn't do it anymore.

Slowly, anger replaced his despair. He had to do it. He had to keep killing and killing and killing until the very end. Every Mexican he killed was one fewer to march to Gonzales. One fewer to hurt his Rachel.

Damn Jim Bowie for not destroying the Alamo when Houston ordered it done. The General had been right. The Texians in San Antonio de Bexar should have fallen back and reinforced Houston and Colonel Fannin. Damn that half-baked zealot Travis, too. Him and his fiery words, selling the men on whiskey patriotism.

And damn me for listening to him.

"Ah, Rachel, I'm so sorry," he whispered, aware of a hand touching him, his mind still locked in the past.

The rawhide and wood door swung open to reveal the zealot, himself, standing in the entrance. "Men," Colonel Travis said. "I want to send another courier to Sam Houston. I'm asking for volunteers."

No one spoke up. Luke straightened, his mind racing. None of the messengers had made it back. Courier service was likely to be a death sentence. But if he made it through, he could warn Rachel.

Luke moved like lightning, fearful someone else would bet him to the punch. "I'll do it, Colonel Travis. I'll take the message to Sam Houston."

"You are a brave man, Prescott," the commander said.

Those inauspicious words had cruelly echoed in Luke's mind every day for the next seven years.

Luke clasped Honor's hand as he cleared his throat and continued. "I volunteered to take a message from Colonel Travis to General Houston at Gonzales. I waited until dark and crawled my way out down the irrigation canal. The size of the Mexican army shocked me. I'd never seen that many men in any one place in Texas. I stole a horse and rode east as fast as the nag would run."

He stopped speaking and drew a shuddering breath.

"But I had worried about my family for days. I took a detour, Honor. I went home. I went home and told my wife the Alamo was about to fall and the Mexicans were coming. I told her to pack up the kids and flee. I told her to go to her aunt's in Louisiana. I k—k—" He stopped and cleared his throat. "I kissed them all good-bye and rode for Gonzales." He sucked in a breath. "I never saw them again."

Honor lifted their linked hands and pressed a kiss to his knuckles. "It wasn't your fault they died, Luke. You did the right thing."

"No," he said flatly. "The Mexicans' march didn't take them past our farm. They would have been safe. I sent them on that god-awful Runaway Scrape that ended in their deaths. I killed them."

"Oh, Luke."

"I failed the men left in the Alamo, too. By now better than three hundred fifty volunteers waited in Gonzales for Sam Houston to arrive and take command. I tried to get them to march for Bexar without him. I talked until my voice gave out, but the damned officers held them back. I didn't convince them. I knew they were the Alamo's last hope and I couldn't get them off their damned asses."

Honor shook her head. "You must have been frantic."

Disgust laced his voice as he said, "That didn't keep me from finding a bath, blankets, and a nice soft bed. Hot food in my gullet. I spent the afternoon of March sixth playing cards with some of the officers. I tried to tell myself a little friendly persuasion was in order."

Abruptly, he shoved away from her and lurched from the bed. He faced her, his fists clenching at his sides. Black defeat rolled over him in waves. "Honor, while I was smoking a goddamned cigar, Santa Anna was burning my comrades' bodies! While I drenched my troubles with Tennessee whiskey, my wife and son and daughter drowned trying to cross the Colorado River!"

Tears rolled down Honor's face. "It wasn't your fault, Luke. You told me before it was an accident. You could have been right there with them and the same thing would have happened."

"But I wasn't with my family, was I? I wasn't at the Alamo, was I? You want to know why, Honor? Do you want to know why?"

Self-directed venom erupted from the pit of his guilt. "Because I was afraid. I volunteered to be a courier because I was scared of dying. I was gutless, spineless. It's the deep, dark secret, lady. The Bravest Man in Texas is nothing more than a yellow-bellied coward."

His voice echoed in the silence, then Honor folded her arms and boldly held his gaze. "Bullshit."

Shock at her curse brought him up short. He gawked at her. She sat cross-legged in the middle of the bed, her eyes bright with anger instead of tears. "Yes, you heard me right. You're not a coward, you're a fool. I've said it time and again and it's still true. Let's start with the act of volunteering, shall we? I gather this was well into the siege? The Mexicans surely had the Alamo surrounded—with five thousand men, let's not forget. You mentioned crawling your way out. I guess because you were on your hands and knees that adds to the cowardice argument, hmm?"

"Honor," he warned.

Sarcasm riddled her voice. "Then you stole a horse. Yes. It is a cowardly act to steal, isn't it. And wasn't it a good thing none of the other couriers had made it back. That way you didn't have to know ahead of time how truly frightening the experience would be."

"Stop it."

She went up on her knees. "You are an idiot, Luke Prescott. Do you honestly think you were the only man in the Alamo who was afraid to die? You wanted to protect your family, to keep them safe. You saw your chance to do it and you took it. That's nothing to be ashamed of."

"Good men died that day. Better men than I."

"Good men die every day! So do bad men. Everybody dies. It's life. We live and we die. Believe me, I know."

Luke relaxed his fisted hands. "Honor, you're a woman. You don't understand."

Her dark eyes crackled with angry fire. "Now you're making me mad, Prescott."

"I'm sorry. That was a stupid thing to say."

"Well, it's a night for that, I guess." The vinegar seemed to drain from her as she crawled off the bed and moved to stand in front of him. She took his hands in hers and brought them to her mouth for a kiss. "Luke, I haven't known you very long, but I feel I know you very well. You wanted to keep everyone safe and that's what you tried to do. You did your best. That's all anyone can do."

She gave his hands a little shake. "Listen to me, honey. Listen close. When you volunteered to leave the Alamo, maybe you were a little afraid. But you also thought you could help, didn't you?"

"Yeah. But I was wrong. I couldn't get the army to listen to me."

"And maybe that's a good thing. Have you ever considered that? What would have happened if Houston had met the Mexicans at San Antonio de Bexar instead of San Jacinto? Somehow I doubt if the Texian army would have emerged victorious from a battle that lasted eighteen whole minutes."

Luke closed his eyes. "But Honor—"

"And if the army had listened to you and marched toward Bexar, I doubt if you'd have spent the past seven years trying to atone for your 'failings.' You wouldn't have lived to make the effort. How many men died at the Alamo? Around a hundred and fifty?"

"One eighty-nine."

"And how many lives did you save during your years as a Texas Ranger? How many men and mothers and children and doctors and teachers and preachers did your heroic deeds keep safe? Two? Four? Two hundred? Two thousand? Do you see my point, Prescott? Has anything I've said gotten through that thick skull of yours?"

"I wasn't trying to be a hero."

"I'm sure you weren't. More likely you were trying to get yourself killed."

She squeezed his hands tightly. "It's awful that you lost your wife and children, Luke. My heart aches for you. But you know something? You've talked about Rachel a time or two. From what you've said, I don't think she was the kind of woman to blame you for what happened, was she?"

He heaved a sigh. "No. Rachel wouldn't do that. But if I had done my duty and gone straight to Gonzales, my children wouldn't have died."

Honor flung away his hands. "You did your duty to your family. You'll have to excuse me, but I personally think that's just as important as your duty to a cause. Texas isn't a place for you, it's a religion."

"Honor, that's not—"

"I'm not stupid, Luke. I know that's why you stayed at Lost Pines. It had nothing to do with me or my sons or the horses I offered. None of this had anything to do with me." She mocked him with her tone. "You have to catch a traitor for Texas. Maybe the Alamo ghosts will tally that up in the redemption column. Another great, grand service for Texas to atone for your sins."

She closed her eyes and shuddered. "Always Texas! God, I hate this place. You don't want me because all you can think about is serving the great Republic of Texas."

"Damn you, Honor!" Fast as a rattler strike, Luke's hand snaked out and grasped her wrist. He yanked her close so that they stood chest to chest. His voice was harsh and angry, tormented. "I want you so bad it's near eating me alive. I'm hard all the time for you, Honor. All I have to do is think of you and it happens."

He yanked her hand upward and laid it over his heart. "But this is where I really want you. I ache with the need. In my mind's eye I can see what we'd have together. It's a glimpse of heaven from my everyday hell. When you smile at me, I want it so bad I can taste it."

"Luke," she breathed.

He released her hand. She left it where it was, lying on his heart. Reaching out to him. Luke traced a gentle finger along her cheek. "I can't have it. I can't have you, Honor. I can't love you."

"Why? I don't understand!"

"Because I'm not worthy. I'm a goddamned coward! I'm too afraid. I'm too afraid I'll kill you, too."

"Oh, Luke. You can't have that fear, it's taken already. It's mine. I'm afraid I'll kill you like I did the others." Tears spilled down her cheeks. "We are such a pair of fools."

"Sunshine, don't cry. Please, don't cry." He bent toward her and kissed the wetness from her cheeks. Honor lifted her face and their lips met and fused.

Luke kissed her with all the passion bottled up inside him. She returned his kiss with such emotion it touched his soul. As they tumbled back onto the bed, he abandoned all effort to resist the desire he felt for this woman. His wife, if only for tonight.

Luke made love to Honor. With each stroke of his hands, his lips, his tongue, he loved her. With every murmured word and each brush of his skin across hers, he loved her. And when he slipped into her welcoming sheath, stretched her and filled her and stroked her to completion, when he poured his life-force into her, he loved her. When he cradled her next to him, their hearts still pounding, their bodies both glistening from exertion, his lips pressing gentle kisses to her brow, he loved her.

But through it all, the words never passed his lips.

A doe picked her way along the line of trees just south of the arched gatepost that spelled out the words Lost Pines. Waiting to intercept Lord Kendall, Richard Armstrong targeted the deer in his gunsights and feigned pulling the trigger. The animal flicked up her tail and tore off into the trees, a spotted fawn following behind her.

Brawny sunbeams radiated down upon the forest, foretelling a hot and muggy afternoon. Armstrong sucked in a deep breath and smelled Texas. He yearned for the urban, dirty scents of London.

If Honor's bit of rebellion mucked this up for him, she'd live to regret it.

Richard heard the sound of approaching horses minutes before he saw them. Lord Kendall sat his blooded bay, every inch the titled lord. He was broad of shoulder and whipcord lean, with an aristocratic nose and mysterious amber eyes. Dressed in a fitted frock coat and gold tweed vest, the viscount chatted casually with his companion as they approached Lost Pines.

Richard stepped out into the road. Upon reaching him, Lord Kendall reined in his mount. Arching a curious brow, the Englishman introduced the minister.

"We've had a change in plans, I'm afraid," Richard explained as they exchanged handshakes. "Reverend, if you'd care to ride on up to the house, my daughter is expecting you. I believe you'll find sufficient food and drink to refresh you from your ride." To Kendall, he said, "May I have a private word with you, please?"

Lord Kendall nodded, his eyes narrowing. He flicked at his thigh with the tip of one rein, not speaking until the minister disappeared from sight. "I trust all is well?" he asked, the British tones clipped and cool.

"It will be." Armstrong dismissed a shiver of unease and silently cursed his daughter. "I've been forced to alter our plans, and while it took creative thinking, I'm certain you'll be pleased with the changes. Shall we walk a bit?"

Saddle leather creaked as the viscount dismounted. Lord Kendall secured his horse to the nearest tree, then followed Armstrong's lead. Richard removed his handkerchief from his jacket pocket and wiped the perspiration from the back of his neck. Aware of Lord Kendall's impatient gaze, he blurted out, "My daughter married the Ranger. They intend to repeat their vows at the ceremony the day of the horse race."

Lord Kendall halted abruptly and drilled him with a look. "What?" he said coldly. "Honor is mine."

"Don't worry. Knowledge of the marriage is limited to a few. I've figured out how to work this to our advantage." Armstrong rested his hand against a loblolly's rough bark and glanced up toward the mockingbird flitting from branch to branch. Casually, he continued, "In nine days they will play host to the cream of Texas society. Every man of influence in the Republic will attend. I cannot ask for a better forum to further my candidacy. The events of the day will be discussed across the country for months to come."

Lord Kendall stepped carefully toward Armstrong, his desire to protect the vivid shine on his riding boots obvious. "I want your daughter. I didn't come this far to find her encumbered all over again."

"You'll have her. That hasn't changed. Honor's marriage to you is my protection that you'll hold up your end of the bargain."

"I've assured you—"

Shaking his head, Richard interrupted, "Life has taught me a few things, Lord Kendall, and one of those is to cover my backside. I'll have that title you've promised. I'll have the estate. Honor's marriage to you provides me that insurance, especially once you plant a child in her. You and I are both strengthened by family ties, each at risk should one of us fail to uphold his end of the agreement. Double-crossing family members is more difficult than doing so to strangers. Believe me, I have vast experience in that regard."

"Still, that hasn't stopped you from doing it, has it? You've betrayed your daughter repeatedly."

"Not really." Armstrong scowled and kicked at a pinecone with the toe of his boot. "She made money each time I married her off. We're wealthy now because of it. And I did get rid of Duvall once I learned how he was mistreating her."

"Don't fool yourself, Armstrong. You weren't rescuing her. You had that man Mullins sneak into Lost Pines and drown Duvall so your daughter would be free to marry me."

Geralyn Dawson

"I didn't tell him how to kill Duvall, just to kill him. Mullins was a useful man. I was sorry to read that he'd died. And as for Honor, despite what you think, I am rescuing her. I know how you treat your possessions. Honor won't be mistreated by you like she was with Duvall."

His gaze snagged on Kendall's elegant riding gloves and he made a mental note to order some for himself. "Anyway, that's neither here nor there. Our situation has not changed. You need a wife. You can use a fortune in lumber." He squared his shoulders and lifted his chin. "And, you crave the political power that association with the president of the Republic of Texas will bring you. Family ties will serve us both, bringing the appearance of propriety to a situation that has none."

"Considering the creation of a family tie at this juncture would mean committing the crime of bigamy, can I assume you intend to deal with Honor's fourth husband like you did with the third? How do you intend to make the Ranger's death look like an accident?"

"Oh, it doesn't need to look like an accident. Captain Prescott shall be revealed as a traitor to his country. Did you know, Lord Kendall, that he has been spying for Mexico for years? He was at the Alamo, you see, shortly before the fall. Folks will believe he had safe passage through the Mexican lines when he left. People will be shocked to learn that the Bravest Man in Texas is actually a blackguard of the first water."

Above them, a mockingbird chattered as Lord Kendall pursed his lips and considered the plan. "He'll deny it, of course, so what proof will you offer? Prescott is a well-known figure. You can't be certain they'll hang him on the spot."

"Ah, but that's the beauty of my scheme, my friend. What political crime is more vile than treason? I can think of only one."

Marcus Black, Lord Kendall, appeared to draw a blank.

"Assassination, sir." Armstrong rubbed his hands together in glee, his excitement prodding him into a walk. "Imagine the reaction of the citizens of the Republic of Texas when they learn that their Texas Ranger hero has assassinated President Sam Houston. They'll be relieved to know I"—he thumped his chest—"made the villain pay for his crime even as he committed it. I'll be revered as the man who killed the villain and as the father who rescued his daughter on the eve of her marriage to a fiend."

Lord Kendall tugged on the fingers of one glove, nodding.

Armstrong laughed. "I'll win the election in a landslide and conduct the country's business in England's best interest. There will be no annexation by the United States. Plus, I don't doubt that Honor will be too distraught to resist your efforts to take her to England."

The viscount lifted his face toward the sky and squinted into the hot Texas sun. "You propose to kill President Houston."

Armstrong nodded smugly. "And make it look like Luke Prescott did it."

15

Party preparations filled Honor's days. Loving Luke Prescott consumed her nights. They spoke neither of the future nor of the past, but lived each day as it came. They lived each night as if it were their last.

Honor moved her things into the master suite, and once the bedroom door closed behind them, they didn't speak until the sun rose the following day. They communicated by action alone. Despite the lack of words, or more likely because of it, Honor felt more loved during those ten days than she'd felt in her entire life. Luke brought her roses one evening. He fed her pieces of ripe, juicy peaches another. Each night he slew another ghost for her, until she grew strong enough to kill the last one herself.

On the last night of their ten-day Eden, Luke entered their room to find the tub filled with steaming water, a glass of whiskey and a full tin of lemon drops on the table to one side. Honor knelt at the other. She held a bar of sandalwood-scented soap and a washcloth. She wore a smile, a silk robe, and nothing else. A smile flirted at Luke's mouth as he stripped off his clothes. He sank into the tub with a sigh and offered himself up to her ministrations with a groan. By the time they abandoned the bathing chamber for the bed, the water was ice cold, the floor sopping wet, and Honor's robe lay ripped in two pieces.

Through it all, they never said a word.

He woke her twice more to make love to her. Honor woke him once. She was surprised they slept at all. This was, after all, their final night together. She and Luke were saying good-bye.

Their guests would arrive throughout the day. Plans called for a late-afternoon barbecue dinner and dancing into the night, followed by the race between Brown Baggage and Sam Houston's horse the next morning. The wedding ceremony was the last event scheduled. Not that it would happen. Luke intended to bait his trap as soon as all the principal players arrived at Lost Pines. This was the day he'd waited for. This was the day he'd trick her father into revealing his treachery. This was their last night together.

Honor wanted nothing more than to hold off the dawn.

It was beyond her power. Honor opened her eyes as the first rays of sunlight pierced the eastern sky, well aware she lay alone in bed. She sat up, clutching the sheet to her naked breasts. Her gaze went unerringly to the balcony and Luke.

Clad only in buckskin pants, he stood facing her, his eyes shut, his face lifted toward the sky. The rising sun revealed a man in turmoil, a man in torment. Tensed muscles rippled across his torso. His hands clenched the balcony railing in a white-knuckled grip and harsh lines furrowed his brow.

The sun broke above the trees in a yellow ball of fire. Honor absently noted that the sky had dawned clear for the first time in over a week. She said, "Luke, what's wrong? Is it your leg?"

Slowly, he lowered his face and looked at her, his eyes a gray ache. Honor understood. It wasn't his physical wounds that pained him, but his emotional ones. The hurt was in his heart, not his leg. She couldn't address that problem. It went against their unspoken rules for these days and nights out of time.

Instead, she slipped from the bed and casually donned the nightgown she'd left lying across the back of a chair. "Are you worried about today? Are you concerned my father won't return?"

Luke gave his shoulders a shrug as if shaking off the concerns of the night. He assumed the matter-of-fact daytime manner they'd adopted with each other and sauntered back into the room. "No, I know Armstrong will be here. Marcus Black, too, whether I like that idea or not. In fact, I'll be surprised if they're not some of our first arrivals. The trip they took up to the Brazos River valley was just an excuse to get away from here."

Richard Armstrong, the jilted bridegroom, and the preacher had visited at Lost Pines an uncomfortable two days before departing, the minister headed for town and the others ostensibly heading north to see a man about a land purchase. Once her father disappeared from sight, Honor waited a whole fifteen minutes before heading off to Rafe's to tell Luella and the boys it was safe to come home.

After that, preparations for the party intensified. Every day more friends of Luke's arrived at Lost Pines. If the outlaws and renegades across the country knew how many Texas Rangers currently occupied Honor's bunkhouse, the crime spree certain to follow would rattle the Republic.

"Tell me again the boys will be safe?"

Luke dragged a hand through his hair. "Honor, I have five Rangers assigned to watch out for Micah and Jason. Even Luella has a bodyguard."

"So everything is ready then?"

He nodded and went to the wardrobe for a shirt. "All the players are in place."

"I hope I do my part without messing up."

Luke slipped his arms into the sleeves of a blue chambray shirt and smiled. "Honor, your capacity for deceit is downright scary. I have no doubt you'll pull your part off without a hitch. Besides, your main job is to be clumsy. Let's face it. That's not much of a stretch."

She wanted to hit him, but settled for sticking out her tongue.

Luke laughed. "C'mon, brat. Hurry up and get dressed. We have lots to do before breakfast."

Downstairs they found Luella already hard at work directing the boys in their chores. Spying Luke, she scowled. "Captain Prescott. I know this week has been particularly rainy, and I'm aware that you and your Ranger friends have serious business to discuss. But it wouldn't hurt a one of you to take a second and wipe your feet before stepping into this house."

"Yes, ma'am. I'll pass the word along."

"See that you do."

Outside, Honor and Luke parted ways. He headed for the bunkhouse while she hurried to the kitchen, giving a grateful glance above to the clear blue sky, a welcome change after rain for five straight days.

In the kitchen she greeted the trio of town ladies hired a week ago to help with party preparations.

They, she, and Luella had been baking for days. Their breads, pies, cakes, cobblers, and puddings, along with the contributions provided by the guests, would supplement the beef, pork, and venison being roasted by the men. Two hours later, when Honor returned to her bedroom to don her party dress, the food, the house—everything was ready.

But Honor wasn't ready. She wasn't ready when she observed Luke greeting the British chargé d'affaires, Charles Elliot, with a handshake and a grin. She wasn't ready when she heard her father's voice rumble from the parlor. She wasn't ready when a shout from the front porch hailed Sam Houston and promised to place a bet on the sorrel he brought with him.

Most especially, she wasn't ready when Luke knocked on the bedroom door and said, "Honor. It's time."

It didn't matter whether she was ready or not. Her time had just run out.

Anticipation thrummed in Luke's veins as he twisted the doorknob and stepped inside Honor's bedroom. He took one look at the woman seated at her vanity braiding her glistening hair and his mood sank like a stone in a well. He hadn't realized until that very moment how much he'd wanted to see her dressed in yellow again.

The ruffled blue gingham gown she wore was pretty, the woman wearing it so beautiful she made him ache, but he missed the Honor who wore yellow. In it, she was happy, confident, and full of laughter. He had taken that from her, and the knowledge made him feel guilty.

He cleared his throat and forced his attention back to the matter at hand. "Everyone's here. I told Rafe to pass the message, so it will all start happening soon. Are you ready?"

He watched her wrap the braid in a coronet around her head and pin it. Bravely, she met his gaze in the mirror and said, "It's time to see this trouble ended. Time for me to get on with my life."

Luke winced at the verbal arrow, certain she included him in her definition of trouble. She stood and turned to face him and for a long moment neither of them moved. Through the open windows came a symphony of sounds—adult laughter, the squeals of frolicking children, the distant song of a harmonica. He smelled her perfume, a light teasing blend of lavender and heaven.

Luke swallowed hard. He should say something, try one more time to explain. Except he didn't know how to explain anything, even to himself. The unplanned words burst from his mouth. "I want your promise that if a child comes of our time together you'll send word."

She closed her eyes and nodded once abruptly. Then she moved to brush by him.

Luke caught her arm, stopping her. "Honor, I want you to know .."

Her eyes glowed sad and seductive like whiskey in a lonely man's glass. "Yes?"

He foundered, searching for words, until he was saved by a scream. He exhaled in a whoosh, feeling guilty at his relief. "That's Betsy," he said as the shrill feminine squeal continued. "McCutcheon must have arrived, supposedly just returned from a Mexican prison."

"When did he actually come home?"

"Couple of months ago. C'mon, we've gotta go."

On the way out the door, Honor rose on her tiptoes and kissed his cheek. "Good luck, Captain Prescott."

She started to walk down the hall when, on impulse, he grabbed her arm again. Pulling her back against him, he took her mouth in a fierce, fervent kiss. "You're a hell of a woman, Mrs. Prescott," he whispered against her ear. "I'm proud to have you with me in this fight."

As they broke apart, she searched his gaze as if looking for more than bare meaning in his words. Luke wondered what she found. He, himself, couldn't say.

By the time they made it downstairs and out onto the porch, Betsy's screams had ended. Luke and Honor found her wrapped in a man's arms, swallowed by kisses. When the lovers finally broke apart, tears streamed down Betsy's face. "Oh, Jimmy, I thought for sure Santy Anny had killed you dead."

Word quickly circulated through the crowd that James Patrick McCutcheon had been a prisoner of Santa Anna, one of the Texians captured during an ill-fated raiding expedition into Mexico. After giving his wife another hug, McCutcheon spoke in a voice loud enough for those around him to hear. "I was released from a prison in Salado, Mexico, to deliver a letter for President Houston from Santa Anna. They told me in Gonzales that the Raven was headed this way, so here I am."

Houston emerged from the crowd. A tall, fair man with a regal bearing befitting his position as president, Sam Houston turned serious blue eyes upon the newcomer and said, "Sir, you have a message for me?"

Honor stepped forward and gave Sam Houston her most dazzling, irresistible smile. "Mr. President, you are more than welcome to adjourn to my library to conduct this business. Luke, would you show the president the way? I'm certain you'll want your advisors with you, so I'll send my father along, also."

Looking somewhat dazed, Houston nodded. He followed Luke without protest. Rafe fell into place beside Luke as they marched toward the house. He leaned over and murmured, "That smile's a lethal weapon."

"You should see the rest of her arsenal."

"I'd like that."

"Do it and die."

Rafe chuckled and dropped back to assume his assigned position during the next phase of the plan. Luke's gaze searched for Honor and found her talking to her father. "Good girl," he whispered when Armstrong strolled toward the house.

The former Texas Ranger followed his president and the former prisoner into Lost Pines's library. He gestured for Houston to take the seat behind the broad mahogany desk, and offered the black leather wing chair to McCutcheon.

Following the introductions, Houston leaned back in his chair and folded his arms across his stomach. His bushy gray eyebrows dipped in a frown. "Pardon my saying so, James, but you look like a cadaver in buckskins."

Jimmy shrugged. "A Mexican prison don't exactly offer the comforts of home, sir."

"How are our men doing? I fear negotiations for their release are proceeding slowly."

Luke listened silently while Houston, McCutcheon, and Armstrong discussed men and conditions in the Mexican prison. He had heard the stories two months earlier when McCutcheon dragged himself home following a daring escape from prison. Even after two months of Betsy's good cooking, Jimmy remained thin and gaunt. He was haunted by memories and his fears for those left behind who still faced starvation, disease, and death. Politically, he opposed Sam Houston, but he didn't betray it here today. In fact, he appeared to be enjoying the experience of fooling his president as he brought the conversation around to the letter.

"I don't know why Santy Anny chose me to deliver his message, but I'm damned glad he did." He reached into his jacket pocket and withdrew a paper sealed in gold wax. "From the president of Mexico to the president of the Republic of Texas." He passed the page to Houston, adding, "If you don't mind, sir, now that I've done my duty I'd like to see to my wife."

Houston excused McCutcheon with a sincere and formal expression of thanks. When the door shut behind Jimmy, Houston calmly broke the seal.

Eager tension crawled up Luke's spine as he watched Houston read the letter. He'd waited for this opportunity for the past seven years. Despite the president's familiarity with Santa Anna's signature, Luke didn't worry he'd identify it as false. Along with his other talents, Rafe Malone was a damned fine forger.

"Good Lord!" The president dropped the letter onto the desk and thoughtfully stared out the window. Finally, he returned his attention to the silent room and said, "Gentlemen, we have a problem."

"What's that, Sam?" Armstrong asked.

When Houston gestured for Armstrong to read the letter, Luke gritted his teeth to keep from grinning. Honor's father's lips pursed. He sucked in an audible breath. "This has far-reaching implications," he said, gesturing with the letter. "One of the greatest issues currently facing our country is that of annexation. If Mexico is finally willing to recognize Texas's independence, consider how that might affect the question. Without the constant threat of war from Mexico, Texas won't need the protection of the United States nearly as badly. Our citizens might prefer to remain a republic." He handed the letter to Luke. "This could be a great blow to your plans for annexation, Mr. President."

Luke scanned the sheet in his hand, scowled, and fired his first salvo. "I don't believe this, Sam. We can't trust Santa Anna as far as we can throw him."

"You are right about that, Prescott." Houston rose and stood beside the window, pushing back the green velvet draperies to peer outside at the jovial crowd. "Gentlemen, what do you suggest?"

Frowning, Armstrong sank into the chair that McCutcheon had vacated. "You will need to release this information with a most delicate touch. You should first canvass the reactions of Congress, and then—"

"Wrong," Luke interrupted, enjoying Armstrong's outraged glare. "You need to ignore this letter, pretend you never got it. You can't allow something that's more than likely a hoax to ravage the future of Texas. You have to keep this letter a secret."

"You can't do that," Armstrong protested at once. "The citizens of Texas have a right to know about so significant an offer."

"Only if it's the truth. Only if we can prove Santa Anna means to honor his promise." Luke turned to Houston. "Confirm the information first, Sam. Keep it secret until then."

Sam Houston slowly nodded and resumed his seat. "Yes. I think you may be right. This proposal smells like fresh-branded hair." He rocked forward in his chair and lunged to his feet again. "Lock this away for me, please, Luke. I'll sidestep the questions that are certain to be asked, and we'll keep the contents of this letter a secret for now. Are we agreed?"

Both men nodded, Armstrong's scowl displaying his reluctance. Luke accepted the letter and threw back one corner of the fringe-trimmed rug. Kneeling, he opened Armand Duvall's floor safe and deposited the letter in it.

As he stood and replaced the rug, he eyed his father-in-law. "Sam, just so we're all clear on it. By 'secret' you mean among the three of us, correct? Not my wife or any of the other dignitaries here today. Especially not Richard's traveling companion."

To Houston, he explained, "Richard's friend is an English peer, Marcus Black, Viscount Kendall. Can you imagine what the Brits would do if they learned about Santa Anna's letter? Why, they'd spread the story just to snatch the power of a decision right out of your hand, Sam."

"Now, Prescott—" Armstrong started to protest.

Rubbing his chin with his palm, Houston scowled and interrupted him. "Hell, the blasted British will do anything to prevent annexation. They wouldn't think twice about using possibly false information to influence public opinion. They might not want to fold us into their empire, but they're dead set on preventing the westward expansion of the United States."

The president pinned Armstrong with a glare. "What are you doing keeping company with the enemy? Be careful, my friend." He crossed to the section of carpet that hid the floor safe and stomped his foot down hard. "Annexation is the right thing for Texas. I'm convinced it's the only way we'll survive over time. We're broke as church mice. We're fighting the Indians and the Mexicans and a land that requires a man's soul to bring in a crop. We need our neighbor's help. We need annexation. If the British got hold of that letter, they would destroy Texas."

Richard Armstrong leaned against the porch railing at the far west corner of the veranda and watched his daughter pour boiled-down sorghum molasses onto greased platters for the taffy pull. Children and young adults lined up to participate in the game of pulling and folding the sticky substance. Honor laughed along with her guests and blushed prettily when her Ranger husband made an innuendo-filled remark about partnering her in the amusement.

Frustration flickered inside Richard at the nearly constant compliments he had received this day concerning his delightful daughter. The fact that she'd waited until now to abandon her standoffish ways stuck in his craw. Stubborn girl. People liked her when she wasn't trying to play the infamous widow, and it proved something he'd always known. With a little effort, she could have helped his own reputation rather than cast a shadow on it. Curse her for her defiant ways.

A wooden floorboard creaked as Lord Kendall sidled up beside him. The Brit followed the path of his gaze and remarked, "She's beautiful. She'll make a fine viscountess."

"Shush." Richard whipped his head around to make certain Kendall had not been overheard. "You'll keep quiet about that. In fact, it will be best if we are not seen speaking together at all. Something has occurred."

Kendall's eyes narrowed. "Will this occurrence affect our plan?"

"No." Richard motioned Kendall around the side of the house. When he was certain they'd not be overheard, he said, "We're still set for the morning. Shortly before the horse race, in fact."

"Where?"

"I plan to make certain that Prescott and Houston watch the race from the upper front balcony in full view of the track. You'll have a nice angle for your shot from the bedroom door. I'll be with Houston and Prescott, of course, but I'll have no trouble hiding my pistol."

"And the reason for the argument between them?"

"It's what I explained before. Prescott kills Houston when he's confronted about secret information the president received that named Prescott as a spy for Santa Anna."

"Brilliant," Kendall said.

"I thought so." He paused, then added, "Speaking of secrets, I am in possession of information our superiors will be grateful to learn."

Kendall's eyes lit with interest as Armstrong related the details of Santa Anna's message. "This offer is vital to England's interests. You must see that your contact receives it immediately." He paused for a moment, thinking out loud. "It will do us no good if Houston denies it, however. You need the letter as proof, Armstrong."

"I already reached that conclusion. Appropriating the letter should be easy since I know the combination to the safe. With any luck I'll find the opportunity to retrieve it today. I'd prefer no unnecessary distractions tomorrow."

Lord Kendall steepled his fingers in front of his face and tapped his mouth. "That's smart thinking. Rather than waiting for your regular contact, perhaps you should send it under cover through regular diplomatic channels. The diplomatic pouch will reach London straightaway. Elliot is here today, and under the circumstances, I think you should use him."

Before Richard could agree, a child's ball came sailing past him. As Micah Best bounded onto the porch to retrieve the toy, the two men went their separate ways. For the next few hours, Richard paid close attention to the comings and goings inside the house.

His opportunity arose when a political opponent of

Sam Houston's began a loud and public debate with the president. With the party guests' attention captured by the flamboyant men, Armstrong slipped into the house and found the front hallway deserted. Casting a furtive glance around, he stepped into the library and silently closed the door behind him. The click of the lock sounded like a gunshot to his ears and made him flinch. He put his ear to the door and listened hard.

Richard wasn't accustomed to working in such an overt manner, preferring legal maneuvering over naked theft. For anything dirtier, he hired a gun. But for the delicacy of this weekend's work, he had refrained from such a move. When a man intended to assassinate a president, the fewer who knew it the better.

Hearing only silence from the other side of the door reassured him. He turned to the business at hand, anxious to make every second count. After removing a sheet of paper from the desk, he threw back the rug and knelt beside the safe. With three quick twists of his wrist, the lock released. Raising the door, he quickly removed Santa Anna's letter and replaced it with the plain sheet of paper which he folded in a manner similar to the valuable document. It wouldn't pass more than the most cursory examination, but he doubted if Prescott would do that much in the press of his duties as host.

Minutes later, he rejoined the crowd, the letter from Mexico included in a sealed message addressed to Mr. Huntington-Smythe in London, England, and tucked safely in his jacket pocket.

"My my my. I do love Mr. Litty dearly, but at the moment, Honor, I can't help but envy you."

Seated on a quilt in the negligible shade of a loblolly

pine along with the members of the Bastrop Sewing Circle, Honor looked up from the wedding gift she'd reluctantly opened to see Luke making his way toward her. Confident and commanding, he sauntered slowly but steadily in her direction.

"He is certainly a man's man," another woman observed.

"I don't know of a woman that'd throw him back, either," said a young mother.

Honor looked at her husband, seeing him through the other women's eyes. From the tip of his hat to the soles of his black leather boots, Luke Prescott oozed masculinity. The gray felt brim shadowed slate-colored eyes gleaming with intelligence and a roguish spark. His chiseled cheekbones and determined jaw defined a man of power, a man of pride. His shoulders stretched halfway across Texas and his easy-hipped swagger—

Honor broke away from her musings and smiled. Luke's walk betrayed not even a hint of a limp. His body was healed.

If only his heart would follow suit.

She winced a little inside. Dear Lord, she would miss him. She wondered if he'd haunt her dreams until the day she died. Probably. Life was cruel that way. Her bed would be empty, while her mind remained filled with Luke Prescott—a nightly reminder of all she'd lost. And she didn't mean the lovely wedding gifts she'd be returning to the generous givers the following morning.

Setting aside the box containing a finely embroidered tablecloth, she stood up. Luke was now twenty feet away. Their gazes met. Excitement flared in his eyes as he sent her a silent message. When he stopped to speak with President Houston, she realized what that message was.

It had happened. Her father had taken the bait. The first step of Luke's plan had succeeded.

Honor's heart pounded as her husband and Sam Houston conducted a brief and private conversation. When the two men parted, Luke turned toward her once more. His manner cocky, a roguish grin upon his face, Luke strode toward her to present the signal for Honor to proceed with her final contribution to the plan.

She licked her suddenly dry lips. Beside her, Mary Litty sighed and repeated, "My my my."

Luke didn't speak. He simply took her hands in his and tugged her against him. He lowered his head and took her mouth in a sizzling, zizzling kiss, right in front of Mary Litty, the members of the Bastrop Sewing Circle, and the president of the Republic of Texas.

She melted. He muttered a groan. Finally releasing her, he took a step away, winked at her, and left.

"He never said a word!" Mary Litty exclaimed.

"He does his best work that way," Honor breathed when she'd sucked in enough air to speak. Leave it to Luke Prescott to use a kiss for a signal.

She would miss him so very much.

The heat of a blush stung her cheeks as Honor cleared her throat. "If y'all will excuse me, I believe I'm needed elsewhere. The gifts are all wonderful and Luke and I appreciate your thoughtfulness." She glanced at her mother-in-law. "Luella, would you ask the boys to carry them inside, please?"

Luella nodded while one of the circle members sighed. "Thanks for the entertainment, Honor dear. Won't we have a mouthful to discuss at next week's meeting."

Honor's embarrassment lingered as she crossed the near pasture almost ten minutes later, her destination the group of men watching Sam Houston's racehorse lope around the track. Fixing her gaze on Charles Elliot, she recalled her husband's instructions when outlining the plan. "Flirt a little if you have to. Bat those long curling eyelashes. Show him that smile you have." He'd scowled then and warned, "But don't let him touch anything."

Calling out greetings and hellos, Honor joined the group. With the skill of a good cow pony, she soon cut Charles Elliot from the herd. "Believe me, Mr. Elliot," she said, flashing a winsome smile as they walked toward the stables. "You'll be making a mistake if you don't place your money on Brown Baggage. As you'll see in a moment, she's not as pretty as Houston's horse, but I promise you, she can run."

A smile trifled with the corners of his generous lips and his sapphire eyes glittered. "I learned years ago not to judge by looks alone, Mrs. Duvall. Of course, in your case, I'm certain I would be safe in doing so. You are undoubtedly as beautiful in character as you are of face."

Honor laughed and accepted the arm he offered. "You sound more like a courtier than a diplomat, Mr. Elliot."

"Now, madam," he said, the defensive note in his voice at odds with the teasing glimmer in his eyes. "I'll have you know I always tell the truth."

Honor suddenly got serious. "Is that so? Then allow me to ask a question. Do you consider Luke Prescott a friend?"

Elliot stopped and stared down at her. "I do."

"Good. In that case, come let me introduce you to my Brown Baggage." She led him into the stables.

At his first sight of the stocky quarter-miler, Elliot gave her a disparaging look. Still, he listened closely when Honor launched into praising her horse. "All right. All right," he said some minutes later, holding up his hands in surrender. "You've convinced me. Come tomorrow, I'll bet my money on this bit of baggage. I'd like to know one more thing, however. What difference is it to you where my money goes?"

Honor lowered her voice and spoke from the heart. "Luke told me about your visits during his recovery. It was a difficult time for him and you helped. You went out of your way for a man you barely knew. This is my way of saying thank you. I know my horse will win."

Elliot shrugged. "Luke is a good man. My visits with him were a pleasure. I need not be rewarded for something I enjoyed."

"Very well. Then consider this a thank you for attending our party. It means more to Luke than you could ever guess. We've heard of your argument with Houston, and we know you made the decision to come to Lost Pines after we expanded the occasion to include our wedding along with the activities honoring the president."

Elliot folded his arms and studied her. "If that's the case, then you should also know I'd bet against Sam Houston's horse even if a knobby-kneed nag ran against her. What are you up to, Mrs. Duvall?"

Honor returned his scrutiny, and abruptly, she made a decision. "Luke told me I'd not need subterfuge in dealing with you. Now that I've met you, I tend to agree with my fiancé." She looked him in the eyes and said, "I'd like to request a favor of you, sir. I'm going to leave the stables in a few moments, but I'd like you to remain here until you are contacted by either my father or Luke."

"What is this about?"

"Nothing to compromise you, I swear." Honor began to pace. "It's family business, Mr. Elliot. Very important family business. I don't doubt you'll be free to rejoin the party within half an hour."

"This is a strange request. Luke knows about it?"

"It's Luke's idea, for the most part, anyway."

"Very well, then. I can look over the fine horseflesh in your stables a bit longer. I don't see what it would hurt."

"Thank you, Mr. Elliot."

"Charles."

"Thank you, Charles." Honor squeezed his hand and turned to leave, her breast brushing against a support post as she did so. She felt the tug at her bodice, but before she could stop, she heard the telltale rip. Blue cotton and white linen fell prey to an exposed nail. Honor looked down to see the pink flesh of her breast exposed to the entire left side of the stables, Charles Elliot included.

Mortified, she yanked the cloth free and snatched it to her chest, managing to cover most of what she'd inadvertently revealed. Elliot finally turned away in a belated gentlemanly move. As she ran from the stables, she heard a whispered curse and prayed Elliot had not heard the sound.

It was bad enough that she knew at least a half dozen Texas Rangers were hidden in the stables. If Elliot realized it, her clumsiness had given the game away.

Luke met her halfway to the house. He clutched her tight. The grinding of his teeth was audible. "Honor, what happened to you?"

"I not only have two left feet," she wailed into his shirt, "I have two left breasts!"

"What? Honor, did Elliot do this? I'll kill him."

"No. It was a nail. I think it's all right because the Ranger groaned very quietly."

"Groaned?" Luke growled low in his throat. "Let's

get you to the house. This might not take long and I want to be there when it happens."

Honor loosened her death grip on his shirt. "No, I can change my dress on my own. You go on and take care of business."

"I don't mind—" He broke off abruptly at the sound of a mourning dove's coo. "That's Rafe. Your father's on his way to the stables."

Emotion rushed through her, frothy and violent like the Colorado after a week of spring rain. With one arm clutching her dress to her chest, she stood on her tiptoes and pressed a kiss against Luke's cheek. "Good luck, Luke. I hope this brings you the peace you've been looking for. Now, go on. Go do your duty to Texas."

She backed away from him. Luke stared toward the stables, then back at her. "You can come with me. You *should* come with me. He's your enemy."

He's my father. She had a sudden memory of a young Richard Armstrong laughing as he lifted his daughter and swung her around in a circle before leaning over to kiss his wife. "I can't. You do this without me. Do it for me."

He nodded. As he moved past her, his right hand flipped back the tail of his jacket and rested on the butt of his Paterson. The sight caused Honor's heart to clench and his name burst from her lips. "Luke, wait! You have to know. I have to tell you."

He paused and looked at her. "Yeah?"

A single tear as hot as molten lead spilled from her eyes. "Be careful, Luke. I love you."

16

I love you.

Honor's words echoed in Luke's mind as he made his way toward the stables. They clung there like frightened kittens, their claws digging hard into a surface resisting their purchase. Dear God, help me.

Rafe Malone waved at him to hurry, and for the first time in well over half a year, Luke picked up his feet in a run. He had the vague impression he was fleeing her declaration as much as he was running toward his destiny.

At his approach, Rafe placed his fingers to his lips, his eyes gleaming like emeralds beneath the slouch of his hat. He and Sam Houston stood against the stable's south wall, their ears pressed to knotholes in the wood. The president stood stiff as a fence post, his face set in angry lines, a cold rage burning in his eyes. Betrayal hit a man hard.

Rafe moved aside, offering Luke a chance to listen himself. The muffled voices became clearer as Luke put his ear to the wall. Charles Elliot was speaking. "I want you to know I didn't touch your daughter. She snagged her gown on a nail."

"Oh, I don't doubt that. Honor has been clumsy all her life. When I saw her leave the stables, I assumed she was at fault for her disheveled condition. You mistook my question. What I want to know, Mr. Elliot, is how soon your next correspondence to England will be sent."

After a moment's pause, Elliot said, "And what concern is that of yours?"

"I've a letter requiring immediate delivery. Diplomatic channels will likely be the swiftest route in this instance."

"And what is the nature of this letter?"

"It's private."

"I'm sorry, Mr. Armstrong, but I cannot possibly accommodate you. My mail pouch is reserved for the business of the Crown."

A note of menace crept into Armstrong's tone. "Believe me, sir, you will never in your career handle a missive more vital to Britain's concerns than this. If you refuse me, I can promise you your career will be over by the bloody Fourth of July."

"Making threats is poor diplomacy."

"I'm no diplomat. You see this delivered to Lord Huntington-Smythe at once, or I'll have your balls for breakfast."

Houston jerked his head away from the wall, his bushy brows lowered over icy blue eyes. He motioned that he'd heard enough.

"Black isn't in there?" Luke whispered to Rafe as they made their way toward the stable door.

"No. I saw him over by the ale kegs a short while ago."

Luke nodded. He'd deal with Black later. Drawing his gun, he made his way to the stable door. At a signal from Houston, he threw it open wide and hollered, "Now!"

The sound of a dozen cocking guns cracked like thunder in the stable's gloom. "What is this?" Armstrong shouted, shoving the letter into Elliot's hands.

"Isn't it obvious?" Elliot dryly asked. "It's the bloody Texas Rangers."

Sam Houston marched into the sunlight-striped space, his bearing regal as a king's. "Richard Armstrong, as president of the Republic of Texas, I hereby place you under arrest. The charge, you sorry son of a bitch, is treason."

As the men hidden throughout the stables emerged from their various places of concealment, Armstrong's eyes shifted in panic and his face bled white. "No! It's a mistake! President Houston, whatever you've assumed is wrong! Give me the opportunity to explain."

"Oh, you'll have your opportunity. Before the whole government of Texas, in fact." He looked to the Texas Ranger captain. "I want Armstrong taken to the capital for incarceration. See that he remains alive. We'll hang him in our own good time."

"No! I'm innocent! You can't do this!"

"Oh, but I can," Houston said. "I am the president of the Republic of Texas. I can do what I damned well please to the likes of you." He motioned for the Rangers to take Armstrong away. Two men grabbed him by the arms and all but dragged him, struggling and shouting, toward the door.

There, to Luke's surprise, Honor blocked their way. She wore a shawl he recognized as Luella's covering her ripped bodice and in the shadowed light of the barn, her face appeared drawn and devastated. Luke's gut churned as the Rangers halted and his wife calmly met her father's angry glare. "You," Armstrong jeered. "You set me up, didn't you? You did this to me. My own daughter."

She didn't respond at first, just searched his gaze—looking for what, Luke couldn't tell. When she finally spoke, he heard the heartbreak in her voice. "Luke told me I should be here to see this and he was right. All my life I loved you, Father. I tried so hard to make you happy after Mama died. I tried so hard to win your love. I married Franklin, and Philip, and Armand. I—"

"You betrayed me. You betrayed me and now I've lost it all. Everything I've worked for. Everything I ever wanted. How could you do that to me? My own flesh and blood!"

Honor's fingers turned white with her tight grip on her shawl. "What have you lost, Father? You once told me the presidency of the Republic was a stepping-stone. A stepping-stone to what? Let me understand why you did all this."

"What did I want?" The question exploded from his mouth. He wrenched himself from the Rangers' grip. "I wanted what should have been mine from the beginning. I wanted what I've been denied all my life because of six lousy minutes. The title, the lands. I wanted my father to finally acknowledge that the stronger, smarter, better twin was born second. I was to be an earl, Honor. My father is but a mere baron. I was to own the estate they've always coveted. They'd have hated it. They'd have envied me." He thumped his chest. "Me! The second son, unworthy of his father's attention. It was to be the culmination of all my dreams."

Luke took a protective step nearer to Honor as

Armstrong talked, his gaze switching between the angry man and his obviously shocked daughter. She asked, "How was spying going to get you that?"

"Black wanted the power I could give him as president of the Republic."

Sam Houston gestured toward a trio of Rangers and the doorway. No one needed to ask what he wanted, and the men left in search of Marcus Black. Luke wanted to go with them, but he wasn't about to leave Honor.

"I had no idea you harbored such resentment toward your family, Father," she said, shaking her head in wonder. "So you did all this out of sibling rivalry? You tried to ruin my life in order to taunt your father? In a way, you treated me with the same contempt he showed you. Have you ever thought about that? Look at what you've done in order to get your father's notice. You betrayed your country."

Honor gestured toward the ring of Rangers observing them in silence. "These men undoubtedly think that's the worse sin you could have committed. I tend to take matters a little more personally."

Honor's chin came up and Luke could see the tears shimmering in her eyes. "You went too far when you hired Wild Horse Mullins to hurt my boys. I couldn't forgive that. I can't forgive it. Mama would understand. And I won't feel guilty for my part in revealing your treachery."

"Your mother wouldn't understand," he insisted, his expression fierce. "She'd be ashamed of you, Honor Armstrong! Ashamed."

"No, she'd be proud of my strength, and in a way, I guess I have you to thank for that. I had to toughen up in order to deal with your evil." She paused a moment, her scornful gaze sweeping over him. "Goodbye, Father. May God forgive you. I don't know that

I ever will." With that, Honor turned her back and stepped out into the sunshine.

For a moment following her departure, silence reigned in the stable. Then Sam Houston observed, "Damn fine woman you're marrying, Prescott."

"Damn fine," Luke agreed. When the Rangers moved to drag the protesting Armstrong away, Luke held up a hand. "Wait. Let him go for a second."

Quick to obey their former captain, the Rangers did as Luke asked. He stepped up to Armstrong and stared him in the eyes. "I owe you for my family," Luke said. He slammed his fist into Armstrong's stomach. The man bent over double and the Rangers dragged him upright. Luke blew a stream of air across his knuckles and smiled an evil grin. "I owe you for my wife."

The punch he threw to Armstrong's chin knocked the bastard cold. "Get him out of here, men, before I forget my president's instructions and kill him."

Richard Armstrong was hauled from the stables like the load of horse dung he was.

Luke rubbed his pleasantly sore hand and addressed the British diplomat. "We'll take the letter, if you don't mind, Charles."

Elliot offered it up immediately. "It seems that I am caught in something of a snare."

"No," Sam Houston said, scanning the note Armstrong had written to accompany the stolen letter. "We know you are innocent of this skulduggery. It is the spymaster, Lord Huntington-Smythe, who is responsible for placing agents in Texas. If you know other agents' identities, Mr. Elliot, whether one man or many, you might pass along a warning that I've put my best man on the job to track them down." He motioned to one of the remaining Rangers. "Can I borrow your badge, please?"

Taking the five-pointed star in his hand, he pinned it to Luke's jacket. "Captain Prescott, I'll expect you back to work just as soon as your honeymoon is over. You have served Texas well over the past seven years. Today you've done a service beyond measure. I don't doubt that history will prove you single-handedly preserved the future for generations of Texians. You have my utmost gratitude. Welcome back to the corps." Leaning close, he added in a voice only Luke could hear, "Let the Alamo go, Luke. You were meant to survive for today."

Rafe Malone let out a whoop and the Rangers joined in. Luke shook his president's hand and waited for much-sought peace to wash over him.

He waited in vain.

Houston clapped him on the back and they walked out of the stable into the sunshine, where they watched as four Texas Rangers escorted Richard Armstrong toward the buckboard that would transport him off the premises. "Since the letter was a fake, I don't know if, legally, we'll be able to hang Armstrong like he deserves. After what I saw here today, I don't doubt an investigation into his past will yield more evidence against him. Either way, his reputation is ruined." Houston tossed Luke an oblique glance. "Guess Richard and his daughter have switched places where reputation is concerned."

"That's the way it should have been from the start."

As word of Armstrong's downfall spread, Luke was surrounded by friends and acquaintances wanting to express their shock, appreciation, and congratulations. He accepted the accolades with a grim smile; his good cheer went no deeper than his skin. As the merriment grew around him, Luke felt a panic kindle to life inside him.

Atonement. Redemption. The goals he had fought

toward for so long. Is this how it was supposed to feel? This ... empty?

I love you.

He slowly perused the crowd looking for Honor. He was torn between the desire to hold her in his arms and the need to run from her as fast and as far as he could go. One of the Rangers informed him Black had yet to be located and Luke elected to join the search. He wanted to be present for that confrontation when it came. I have a word or two to say to the Englishman, also, he thought, making a fist with his right hand.

As he moved through the throng of people, looking for Black, his thoughts drifted to Honor and the events of the day. He did his best to forget all the nights spent in her arms. He'd have to forget. He had no choice.

Redemption wasn't possible.

Luke's step faltered and he halted and gazed up at the serenely blue sky. He'd hung his hope on the idea that serving Texas in a significant manner would atone for failing the Heroes of the Alamo. He'd succeeded. He'd saved Texas. The man who understood his feelings better than any man alive, the very man who'd coined the battle cry Remember the Alamo, now told him to lay his ghosts to rest.

But it wasn't enough. He knew that now. It could never be enough. Rachel and the children were dead. His family was dead and saving his country from a traitor wouldn't bring them back to life.

By the time he'd searched the entire front pasture for Honor and headed back toward the house to search it, he'd reached a decision. Early on, he'd promised Honor to accomplish his aim without going through with the farce of a wedding. It was time to keep his promise. Once Black had been dealt with he'd make an announcement to the crowd and explain what had transpired. He could be gone from Lost Pines by nightfall.

Honor stared at her reflection in the mirror and smiled. The yellow dress was as bright as a field full of wildflowers.

She lifted the torn gown from the floor and held it up before her. That robin's egg blue didn't complement her complexion nearly as well. She tossed the dress down and spun in a full circle. The buttercup skirt flared in a wave of brilliance that brightened the entire room.

It felt good to wear yellow again, she thought. It felt right. She wasn't a coward anymore, at least, not a total coward. She'd stood up to her father. She'd told Luke she loved him. But for all her newfound bravery, she wasn't courageous enough to stay with him as long as her love remained one sided.

She whirled away from the mirror and sat on the edge of the bed, her lift in spirits now evaporated. What a day. She should go back downstairs, but she hadn't quite summoned the nerve to do so yet. First, the embarrassing incident in the barn with Elliot, then the scene with her father. Honor sighed.

Although she'd defied him, vilified him, and prayed for his destruction, she'd found it difficult to watch his downfall. A part of her would always remember the man he'd been before the loss of her mother changed him. But mostly, she'd remember the man who'd forced her to act in defense of her children.

If only she could be so certain about other areas in her life. When Richard Armstrong left Lost Pines escorted by a detachment of Texas Rangers, the irony of the moment had not escaped Honor's notice. Now that her father was no longer a threat to her or her sons, she no longer needed to leave home.

But neither could she stay. Luke had given her financial freedom, and that meant access to Armand's bank accounts in New Orleans. She now had the means to flee and flee she would. Luke didn't love her; he wouldn't love her. No matter how strong she'd become over the past months, she knew she simply didn't have the courage to survive another marriage where she wasn't loved. That hurt to even think about. And the idea of remaining at Lost Pines, where the memories of his presence, his voice, his scent, would haunt every room, twisted her heart in two.

Would it be any better in Charleston? She had the idea that no matter where she lived or whom she lived with, she'd think of Luke each time she tasted a lemon drop, baked a pecan pie, spied a gray felt hat, or did a hundred other things. She closed her eyes and flopped back on the bed. How would she ever stand it?

"If this isn't a picture straight out of my fantasies."

Marcus Black! Honor's eyes flew open wide and she gaped in shock. Gone were the Englishman's fashionable clothes. He now wore plain dark trousers, a blue chambray shirt, and a leather vest, clothing similar to that of many of the Rangers at the jubilee. With the straw panama hat pulled low on his brow, she would not have recognized him had she not known his voice. A shiver raked down her spine as she vaulted off the bed and said, "What are you doing here?"

His narrow, mean eyes gleamed as he pulled a pistol from inside his jacket. "I'm here for you, Honor dear."

Her eyes focused on the gun. "For me?"

"My career is ruined. All the time I invested in him. All the effort. Your father—the incompetent imbecile—ruins it. But at least I'll have you. I decided to have you for my wife the first moment I saw you. Your father didn't understand it, of course. He thought I wanted your husband dead because I wanted Duvall's forest. Damn fool. Armstrong didn't appreciate what he had in you. I never should have trusted him with governmental affairs." He waved the gun toward the wardrobe. "Pack a bag quickly, Honor. The journey ahead of us is a long one. We'll marry aboard ship on the way to England."

Honor slowly made sense of what he'd said, her thoughts pushing through the honeycomb of confusion in her mind. He planned to take her to England? Marry aboard ship? What else was it he'd said? Get rid of Duvall? "You wanted Armand dead?"

"I thought murder preferable to bigamy. It's a more final solution, don't you agree? I had your father pay that Mullins fellow to murder the bastard. He hid in the house and waited for an opportune time. When he found Duvall sleeping in the bathtub, he held his head underwater until he drowned." He crossed to the wardrobe and began throwing dresses onto the floor. "Enough explanations, my beauty. Move a bit faster now."

Even as Honor absorbed the news of how Armand had died, a new worry sliced through her mind like a bowie knife. Murder preferable to bigamy? Where was Luke? Marcus Black knew she and Luke were already legally wed. Oh, God, had Black done something to him? Where was he? Why hadn't he come to her after he'd finished with Richard? Honor stared hard at the door.

"Honor!" Black snapped. She looked at him dumbly, and he said, "Very well. Forget the dresses. I'll buy you new ones in New Orleans, enough to last the trip. Your gowns are hopelessly out of fashion anyway."

He grabbed her by the arm and tugged her toward the door. "Not a word now, darling. The Rangers are looking for me, but so far my disguise has fooled them. We'll go out the back way past the kitchen. Do nothing to attract attention. I don't want to hurt you, but I will if you force me to."

She considered arguing with him, but decided her energies would be better spent trying to get away. Surely she could manage this. She was an intelligent woman. About eighty people milled around her front yard. Certainly she could catch the attention of one of them and communicate she needed help, especially since so many of the men wore the Texas Ranger star. Black's disguise surely wouldn't fool them all.

But Marcus Black, Lord Kendall, had prepared for their escape. A pair of horses stood hitched to a buckboard in an out-of-the-way spot behind the kitchen. A rope lay curled on a folded tarp.

"I apologize for the accommodations. Had I known of the need earlier, I'd have arranged something more comfortable." He shoved the gun into her side and motioned for her to climb onto the wagon. Then he bound her wrists and ankles and gagged her with his cravat.

Forcing her to lie down, he covered her with the tarp. "Be patient, my darling. This is only necessary until we're out of sight. Then you'll sit beside me where you belong."

The sounds of the party faded as the wagon rolled away from Lost Pines. Honor thought hard. She tried desperately to swallow her fear. It was the only thing she could swallow, so dry was her mouth. The sooner she escaped the better. The odor of muck hung heavy on the tarp. *I'd gag if I weren't already gagged.*

At that thought, she knew the bumps and jostles and bangs had beaten the sense right out of her.

Finally the wagon bounced to a stop and Black threw back the cover. He lifted her onto the seat beside him, untying her gag and freeing her limbs. Numb terror bound her more securely than ropes. If only she had caught one glimpse of Luke, to be assured he was still alive.

Honor laid her hand upon his arm, hoping to distract him with her touch and her voice. "Please don't do this, Lord Kendall. I wouldn't make you a good wife. I'm a rough-cut Texian. I make my own butter, plant my own corn, and shovel my own horse"—the word stuck in her mouth but she thought the circumstances called for it—"shit. I'd shame you before London society."

"Bah!" He whipped the reins and the wagon rolled forward. "You're the most beautiful woman I've ever seen. There are ways to refine you. You'll learn that I've never troubled myself with the opinions of society twits. They have no power. That lies in the hands of the men whose favor your father's idiocy may well have cost me. If I'm to be drummed from the circle, I may as well have the reward I desire."

Taking his attention off the trail, he studied her intently. "I own many beautiful things. Flawless jewels. Paintings by Lely. Grecian sculpture. The finest wines ever laid down. And now I own you." She shuddered. He threw back his head and laughed.

Honor seized the opportunity to jump from the wagon.

Picking up her skirts, she dashed for the trees, her heart pounding like her feet. She came close to making it, but Black was fast. He tackled her and she fell skinning her hands and knees.

"Now now, my dove. I'd hoped to avoid this sort

of nonsense." She fought him, scratched him, bit him as he carried her back to the wagon. He slapped her face before he threw her in its bed. The impact knocked her breath from her lungs. Binding her hands, then her feet, he spoke through gritted teeth. "Now you'll stay put."

No, she wouldn't. She refused to be defeated by this man. Honor was filled with determination to free herself. While he concentrated on driving the wagon, she twisted her body until she could pluck at the rope binding her ankles. Black wasn't much with knots, thank God, and she soon freed her feet. Immediately, she went to work on her hands, tugging on the knot with her teeth, thankful he paid her scant attention.

She'd loosened the rope considerably when the wagon slowed, attracting her notice. Honor glanced around and her throat constricted with fear. She recognized the outcropping of rock. He'd taken the opposite direction from what she'd expected. They were traveling the south road that led toward the river. She spied the deceptively slow-moving waters of the Colorado just ahead and the protest burst from her lips. "No! Lord Kendall, you can't do this! This is a low-water ford and it's been raining for a week. The river is way up. We'll never make it across. You'll get us both killed!"

She should have kept her mouth shut. Even as she freed her hands, even as she prepared to jump from the wagon, Marcus Black whipped the reins, urging the horses into the river, then reached back and grabbed Honor by the hair.

Searching for Honor in the crowd proved time consuming and finally impossible for Luke. The news about Richard Armstrong had spread like a dry August prairie fire. Luke dodged as many questions as possible and accepted the congratulations with hurried grace. All the while, he kept his eyes focused on finding Honor. He managed to corner Jason and Micah as they watched a neighbor pack black powder into the bottom of an anvil. "You ever seen somebody shoot the anvil, Cap'n?" Jason asked.

"He's gonna put it on that tree stump and light a fuse," Micah added. "Blows that sucker plumb high into the air. Sounds like a cannon when it goes off, too."

"I know it's exciting, boys, but tell me, have you seen your mother around?"

The boys looked at each other and shrugged. "Not for a long time," Micah answered.

Luke left them to their explosions and continued his search, veering off his path when he spied Luella. "Captain Prescott!" Her face wrinkled deeper in a smile. "Our hero! Come here, son, so I can thank you properly."

He allowed her no opportunity to express her gratitude, asking abruptly, "Have you seen Honor since she went to the house to change her dress?"

Luella pursed her lips and creased her brow in thought. "No, I don't believe I have. What's the matter, Luke? Do you think something is wrong?"

"No. I'm sure she's fine. She's probably still up at the house." She was probably hiding out, summoning her strength to face the barbecue guests on the heels of her father's arrest. He should have gone to her right away and helped her get through this, rather than jawing with the guests. God, Prescott, you are still such a cowardly bastard.

Luke made a beeline for the house. He bounded up the front porch steps, then rushed inside, calling her name. But Honor didn't answer. After making a quick search of the ground floor, he took the stairs two at a time. He checked her bedroom first, and then his own. "Honor?" He breathed a sigh of relief when he spied the torn blue gown lying in a heap on the floor.

Then he frowned. Near the wardrobe, clothes lay like colorful puddles. Honor never left her clothes on the floor, not even the ones he'd ripped off of her during some of their more athletic lovemaking moments. Damn. Now an itch began to nag at the back of his neck. "Honor?" he called, not expecting an answer.

He stepped outside onto the veranda. "Honor!" he shouted as loudly as he could. He gripped the railing and leaned forward, straining to listen, willing himself to hear her voice. "Come on, sunshine, answer me."

From the corner of his eye, he saw it. A flash of color where color didn't belong. Jerking around, he scanned the Colorado River. Well upstream, a man whipped his horses, the front wheels of a wagon rolling steadily into the water. Something yellow squirmed in the wagon's bed. A yellow dress!

"Honor!" Luke froze in horror as the horses moved into the river. They'd never make it. The water was too deep, the current too strong, after the recent heavy rains.

And Honor wasn't much of a swimmer.

Not again. This couldn't happen again. She couldn't die. Not Honor. Not his wife.

Not his love.

He let out a howl of despair from the depths of his soul even as he started to move. No time for the stairs. He climbed over the balcony and shinnied down a column, jumping the last few feet. His bad leg buckled when he hit the ground.

Getting up, he glanced toward the river. The horses were swimming now, pulling hard, and Luke willed the animals to fight the current. But before his fearful eyes, they lost headway.

Luke ran toward the river, arms and legs pumping, aching, lungs swelling against his ribs. He whipped his head around looking for help and spotted a boy about Micah's age. He yelled, "Boy, fetch Rafe Malone. Fetch help. Honor's in the river."

Praying the child would do as he was told, Luke rushed toward the path that led down the bluff to the river, watching the water the entire way. He spied the wagon, floating now, drifting downstream. Toward a large boulder. It hit hard. Luke heard Honor's scream in his heart.

The driver—Marcus Black, Luke now saw—flew from the wagon, flung against the rock like a rag doll. He dropped into the water and Luke didn't see him come up. Honor tumbled over the side, her hands clawing for a hold, grabbing the side of the wagon.

"Hang on, sunshine!"

Honor held on and held on and held on. The horses kept swimming. They might make it. Even as his hopes rose, Honor's grip slipped and she disappeared below the surface of the muddy, churning, rain-swollen waters of the Colorado River.

His heart in his throat, Luke reached the edge of the bluff at last. His gaze fearfully searched the water upstream. There. She had her head up, but she was moving fast. He wouldn't have time for the path.

"Good girl. Keep fighting!" Luke eyed the distance, judged the speed of the current, backed ten steps off the edge of the bluff, then took a running jump.

He seemed to fall forever. At the last moment, just before he hit the water, he saw a boulder lying just below the surface. Ah, hell. He banged against it, bad leg first. White hot pain exploded, consuming him in its fury. He fought to stay conscious. Fought to stay afloat. Honor.

Where was she? Had he missed her? There, a flash of color some ten yards upstream. With his leg worse than useless, he worked the water with powerful arm strokes to slow himself down. One chance, Prescott. You have one chance to save her.

He damn near missed her. She rammed into him, her legs kicking his painfully before she bounced off. He reached out desperately and grasped a handful of her skirt. "Luke," she gasped, spitting water. He pulled her into his arms and ignored the pain radiating from his leg.

"I've got you. No, don't grab my neck. Trust me, sunshine. Roll over on your back and let *me* hold *you*. There you go." Luke took a look around him.

The water pushed them to a wider spot in the river, maybe two hundred feet across. The cliff side was closer, and Luke felt his strength fading fast. Should he swim for the far side and the gently sloped bank they could crawl up on their own? Or go for the steep side where they'd need help getting from the water? Something beneath the boiling surface banged against his leg and made his decision for him. "Kick your legs, Honor. We're gonna swim for the cliffs. You gotta help. Help me watch for Rafe."

"I'm afraid. I'm not a good swimmer." She sounded as desperate for a good lungful of breath as he was.

"I'll keep you afloat, just kick your legs." Be my legs. The battering current sucked energy from Luke's body like ale from a tap. Honor thrashed in the floodwaters. He kicked as hard as his bad leg would let him, aiming for the riverbank. Treacherous currents hammered his whole body, tore at his grip on her, swept them downstream.

Finally, he got them close enough to grab at a small

tree growing from the base of the cliff, leaning out over the water. He saw his numb fingers close around a branch washed smooth by the river. Lord, just let him keep hold on Honor and this limb.

The water was freezing and Luke's whole body was going numb. Honor's skin was cold, but he felt warmth flow from deep inside her. "That's my sunshine."

Above the water's rush, a sharper sound roused him. A voice, shouting. Rafe!

He couldn't make out words, but he yelled in answer. He'd never seen anything more welcome than the rope that tumbled over the rocky ledge to dangle beside them.

"All right, Honor. Here we go." He fought the water as he looped the rope around her chest, tied it with fumbling cold fingers, and handed her the slack hanging from above. The knots had to hold. Awkwardly, he looped one more into the wet rope.

"Hang on tight so it won't hurt so much. Keep your shoulders square; we don't want you slipping out. Rafe'll have you safe quick as a hiccup. I'll be right behind you." He yanked twice on the rope.

"Luke?" she cried as Rafe pulled her from the water.

Clinging to the limb, he watched her ascend. Then his hand was empty, ripped from the tree by a blow from behind him. A million needles of blazing hot pain stabbed him as the water swept him downstream, tumbling him around a sunken log.

He was tired, too tired to care any longer. Too tired to think. The water pulled him down, spit him up, tugged him down, the old shame and self-doubt singing a siren song in his mind.

It was easier to quit, to find peace. So damned easy. Easier than fighting. Why not let it happen? Maybe now, after seven interminable years, the time was finally right. Now, today, his would be an honorable death. He'd made up for his shortcomings as best he could. Today he'd done a great service to his country. This time he'd saved the woman he loved.

The woman he loved. *Hell, sunshine, I wish I'd had the chance to tell you.*

The chilly spring water even felt warm as it embraced all of him. It cradled him, offering surcease, promising sanctuary. With an odd sense of euphoria, he sank toward oblivion.

But suddenly, something barred his way. An icy flicker. The tiniest prickle. A pinpoint deep in his soul. Sharp and bitter cold. Fear. *I'm afraid to die.*

He jerked his eyelids open. Muddy water red as blood blocked his vision. Arching his back, he lifted his head from the water, sucking in a reviving breath. He couldn't believe it. How many times in the past seven years had he faced dying and felt no fear at all? Twenty? Forty? Hell, more than he could remember anyway. And now, as the currents of the Colorado strained to suck him under, his gut was clenched with fear. Even stranger, he didn't feel the least bit like a coward for being so scared. Why? Why now?

The answer came to him with the crystal clarity of a single word. Honor.

He was afraid because he'd allowed himself to feel again, to care again, to love again. He was afraid today just as he'd been afraid at the Alamo, because it was a natural, intelligent reaction.

Flailing his arms, Luke quit battling himself and began to battle the Colorado River. He realized the only people not afraid to die were those who had nothing to live for. He didn't qualify. He had something to live for. Someone to live for.

To hell with dying an honorable death. He wanted to live with Honor.

Luke kicked hard, ignoring the agony in his leg. Slowly, stroke by long, agonizing stroke, he fought his way toward the riverbank. At times he thought he heard Honor call his name. He kicked and stroked for a lifetime or maybe a few minutes. A bend in the river swept him toward the shore, and finally Luke made landfall. He crawled out of the Colorado and plopped facedown on a muddy rock, sucking in air like a flood-stranded fish.

"Luke!"

This time he knew he heard Honor's voice. Summoning what was left of his strength, careful not to roll off the rock, he turned onto his back and gazed above him. She was a vision in mud and dirty yellow running along the edge of the bluff some twenty feet above him. "Luke!" she cried, joy ringing in her voice as she spotted him. She dropped to her hands and knees and leaned over the top of the rise. "Oh, Luke, thank God. Are you all right, honey? Please, darling, tell me you're all right."

Peace washed over Luke, warming his heart and soul even as rays from the sun warmed his soaked body. He smiled up at Honor and his voice came loud and strong. "I'm better than I've been in years. I love you, Honor Prescott."

At first, all he heard was the rush of the water. "You love me?" she finally asked in wonder.

"Yeah."

"You mean it? You really love me?"

"Honor, my love for you is as big as Texas."

She closed her eyes and rolled back out of sight. Almost immediately, she appeared again. "Will it last, Luke? You sure you didn't hit your head on something?"

The woman wouldn't just take his word for it? "Honor, I swear on my brand-new Texas Ranger's badge that I'll love you as long as there are mosquitoes in Texas."

"That's forever, then."

He could see her chin tremble. "Yes, sunshine, that's forever."

17

Luke sat beneath the shade of a pecan tree in Luella Best's favorite rocker, his leg propped on a crate, his fingers ruffling the edges of the cards in his hand. He had stayed off his feet as much as possible this morning, wanting to rest his leg before the big event.

He'd not even bothered to stand a little while ago to watch the horse race, gauging Brown Baggage's progress by the expression on Sam Houston's face. Honor's horse had won, of course, beating the president's challenger by a west Texas mile in a quarter-mile race. Brown Baggage's reputation had been made in that moment, eclipsing Starlight's, as Rafe had predicted.

Luke tossed down a card and asked the dealer, Rafe Malone, for another. He picked up a jack of spades and casually said, "Thanks, friend."

Rafe met his gaze and grinned, obviously aware that

Luke was speaking about more than the card he'd been dealt. They'd had a long talk last night after the ball, he and Rafe. It looked as if they might give the horse-breeding business a try. Luke had decided to make his retirement from the Texas Rangers permanent. A family man had no business putting himself in harm's way on a regular basis. Experience had taught him that. Also, Rafe said he was ready to try something new now that he'd recovered from his broken heart.

The card player next to Luke called the hand and won the pot for the third time in a row. "Dadgummit, Micah," Luke said, playfully knocking the boy's hat off his head. "Why don't you go eat again or something. The rate things are going, I'll be broke before I see my bride."

"What's taking them so long, Cap'n Luke?" Jason asked from his position behind Luke's shoulder.

Luke had forgotten the boy was there. "Now I know why Micah keeps winning. You are spying on my cards. Is that any way to treat the man who got your mama to promise to sell her hat shop and stay in Texas?" He gave the boy a playful cuff on the shoulder and said, "Go stand by your brother, squirt."

"What is taking so long, Luke?" Rafe inquired, gazing toward the house with a frown. "I thought the wedding was supposed to start thirty minutes ago."

Luke shrugged. "I don't know."

One of the other card players rubbed his Ranger's badge with his knuckles. "Maybe she's chickened out. Or got some good sense."

Luke drilled him with a glare. "Maybe you oughta deal the cards and shut your mouth, Duane."

Just then, Luella's voice rang out from the front porch. "Jason! Micah! Come along, boys. Your mama needs you."

331

"Maybe I should go check on things," Rafe said, his brow dipping in concern as the boys scampered off.

Luke wasn't worried. "No, there's nothing to worry about. Armstrong is in jail. Marcus Black is dead. And Honor loves me."

"And you love her."

"Who'd have ever thought it?"

"Me. I knew it right off. You should have seen the look on your face when you won that raffle, Prescott. You were a goner then and there."

Smiling, Luke tossed his cards in his friend's smirking face. Just then, the boys came shooting out of the house, Luella Best hobbling slowly behind. Luke got up, intending to give her his seat. Maybe he should go check on Honor. It wasn't like her to be this late doing anything. He'd ask Luella what she thought.

But the news reached him before Luella did.

A lanky, bowlegged cowboy waved a handful of red papers in the air and hollered out for quiet. "Listen up, folks," he said, excitement shining in his eyes. "You're not gonna believe this. She's gonna do it again. Gonna give away another racehorse. She's givin' away the tickets. She told me to tell y'all she's holding a wedding raffle."

"What!" Rafe Malone exclaimed, shooting to his feet. "She can't do that! We need those horses! Luke, tell her she can't do that!"

A crooked smile tilted the corners of Luke's lips. He leaned against the pecan tree and folded his arms. "I'm not telling her anything. They're her horses. She can do with them whatever she wants." Secretly, he was a bit worried. He wondered why she hadn't said anything about a raffle to him last night.

If she gave Saracen away, their breeding business would take a blow. He didn't think she'd do that. His money was on her offering up Brown Baggage. It made sense. Honor had told him weeks ago she'd drawn a true winning ticket before rigging that first raffle so that he won. Now that she owned another winning racehorse, Luke would bet his last lemon drop she intended to give it to the actual raffle winner.

Micah and Jason walked through the crowd passing out tickets. Jason walked by the card players. "Here you go, Cap'n Luke. Honor said for me to be sure you got a ticket."

"Oh, she did, did she?" Luke swallowed a laugh. Suddenly, a remark she'd made early this morning made sense. "She said she had a surprise for me. What do you want to bet I win again."

"No," Rafe said, taking a ticket for himself. "Honor wouldn't do that. She's too honest to rig her own raffle."

Luke fought down a snort and didn't bother to answer because his bride had just walked out onto the porch. The words he'd said about her wearing yellow when she married him came back to him. His throat grew so tight he couldn't have choked out a word if he'd had to.

She wore lemon yellow taffeta with white flowers embroidered on the skirt. The sleeves were little wisps of fancy, cut off the shoulders, and the neckline plunged entirely too low for Luke's peace of mind. Combs wired with buttercups and angel's-trumpet pulled her hair away from her face, and it fell scandalously free in Luke's favorite style, long curls past her shoulders down almost to her waist.

"May I have your attention, please?" she asked. She held up a red ticket. "Does everyone have a raffle ticket?"

Scattered no's sent Jason and Micah running. Luella, having made her way over to Luke, took a seat in the rocker and asked, "How 'bout you boys? Y'all fixed up?"

"I have my ticket," Luke said.

"Me too," Rafe chimed in. "Although, I think I should get more than one. I bought fifty of 'em last time, you know."

"Well, Mr. Malone, I have to agree with you." She cupped her hand beside her mouth and called, "Hey, Honor. Send the boys over this way."

Rafe ended up with ten raffle tickets, and he turned to Luke with a smug smile. "I'm gonna win this time. You just wait and see."

"I'm seeing enough," Luke replied, unable to drag his gaze off Honor.

"Now," she said loudly, smiling out at the crowd. "In a few short minutes Captain Luke Prescott of the Texas Rangers and I will stand before Reverend Martin and repeat our wedding vows. As most of you know, it was a raffle drawing that brought Luke and me together to begin with. In honor of that occasion, and because this is the happiest day of my life, I thought it appropriate to hold another raffle drawing as a way of celebrating this most wonderful of days, our wedding day."

"What's the prize?" called a hopeful voice from the back of the crowd.

"I'm glad you asked that." Honor met Luke's gaze and held it. "The winner of the wedding raffle will take home—"

"The bride!" shouted one of the Rangers.

"Only if she draws my name!" Luke hollered over the laughter and cheers of the crowd.

A young man called in a scornful tone, "If that happens this raffle is rigged! Someone will have to arrest her."

"I volunteer," shouted all the Rangers in the crowd.

Luke started laughing as a blush climbed Honor's face. "No," she said, "this will be a legitimate raffle and the winner will receive the best racehorse in Texas—Brown Baggage."

The crowd hushed, all except Rafe, who yelped and sank to the ground where he buried his head in his hands. "She can't do this to us. First Starlight. Now Brown Baggage." He looked up at Luke. "Do something."

Luke shook his head. "Don't worry, Rafe. You don't need to. I'm gonna win this raffle. She all but told me so this morning. Said she had a special gift for me."

Honor called, "Reverend Martin, would you please come up and draw the winning ticket?"

The reverend made his way through the crowd to the front porch steps. He reached into his jacket and removed a pair of spectacles. When he'd climbed the stairs to the porch, he said, "Before I do this, allow me to tell you, Miz Honor, that Luke Prescott is not only the Bravest Man in Texas, he's also the Luckiest Man in Texas. You make a beautiful bride."

The crowd cheered as he reached into the box she held above his head and removed a red ticket. Silence fell like a curtain over the guests; the only sound to be heard was the scolding of a chickadee from high in the pecan tree. As Reverend Martin cleared his throat, Luke began to limp forward, ready to claim his prize.

"The winning number is five, nine, three, two, seven," the reverend called out.

Grinning, Luke glanced down at the ticket in his hand. Four, eight, three, seven, one. "What!" he bellowed.

"Hell's bells," Sam Houston complained, ripping his coupon in two.

Luke watched Honor in shock as the seconds dragged past and no one claimed the prize. Her brown eyes twinkled and a smile played at her lips. What scheme was the little outlaw up to this time?

Outlaw. Luke's chin dropped. Well, I'll be a son of a gun. Fifty tickets. "Rafe, check your numbers."

"Why bother. We've just lost the best horse—"

"Gentleman Rafe Malone, check your numbers!"

He did, slowly searching through the tickets remaining in his hand. His head jerked up. "Five, nine three, two, seven? Is that it?"

"Five, nine, three, two, seven," Honor called, looking smug as a well-fed cat.

Rafe surged to his feet and rushed toward the porch. "It's me! I won!" He yanked Honor into his arms and planted a kiss right on her mouth. "I won the wedding raffle."

Reaching the porch a few steps behind Rafe, Luke shoved him gently aside and took Honor's hands in his. "No you didn't, Malone. You may have won the horse, but I won the prize."

Twenty minutes later Honor blinked back tears as Luella walked proudly up the flower-strewn path toward the gazebo where Luke waited with Reverend Martin and his groomsmen, Rafe Malone and Micah and Jason Best. Accepting the arm of the president of the Republic of Texas, Honor stepped forward to meet her groom.

He looked so handsome. So happy. A little nervous. Honor smiled, wanting to laugh, her soul filled with joy. All her life she'd dreamed of marrying a man who looked at her the way Luke was looking at her now. All her life she'd dreamed of finding love. Oh, Mama, I'm so happy. Finally, so very happy.

Luke took her hands in his. Leaning toward her, he whispered, "Are you as scared as I am?"

Honor giggled. "You can't be scared. You're the Bravest Man in Texas."

Luke kept his voice low, speaking to Honor alone. "Nah, the reverend had it right. I'm the luckiest. You gave me the courage to love again, Honor, and I plan to show my appreciation every day and every night for the rest of our lives."

"You gave me the same gift, Luke. I was afraid to risk my heart so I built walls around it. You scaled those walls without even meaning to. I didn't want to love you, but I couldn't help myself. I love you now, Luke, and I'll love you forever." She smiled and added, "As long as there are mosquitoes in Texas."

Reverend Martin cleared his throat. "Are y'all done or do you want to do the traditional ceremony, too?"

"Git at it, Preacher," Luke replied, giving Honor's hands a squeeze. "I reckon we've covered the major points, but we might have missed a little one or two."

Honor didn't think they had. In fact, she hardly listened to what the minister was saying, so mesmerized was she by the light of love shining in Luke's eyes. Luke didn't pay much attention, either, as his action proved. While the minister droned on, he leaned toward her again and whispered, "Hey, what about that gift you promised. I thought it was the horse."

She gave her head the slightest of shakes and spoke out of one side of her mouth. "Nope. You'll get your gift later."

Luke thought about that a moment. "What is it?"

Honor looked at him directly. Wasn't that just like a man, never quiet in church. When he held out his hand toward Rafe for the ring he would put on her finger, an imp of mischief rose up inside her. She mouthed the words. "Yellow corset."

Both men saw it. Rafe dropped the ring. "Dammit, Malone!"

"Mr. Prescott!" Reverend Martin scolded as Honor bit back her laughter.

They repeated their vows—the traditional ones—without further incident. The reverend pronounced them man and wife and told Luke he could kiss his bride. Honor's heart took flight. She lifted her face, her blood thrumming in joy and anticipation, as he bent his head toward hers.

Abruptly, Luke stopped and both his gaze and his tone grew serious. "Wait a minute. There's one more thing I want to know. You never told me about number one."

"What?"

"Your first husband. I want to know how he died."

Honor's breath caught. Heat crept up her spine and her neck and flooded her cheeks. Her teeth nibbled at her lower lip.

"Right now, Honor Prescott. I'm not kissin' you until I know how Franklin Tate kicked the old bucket."

She sniffed haughtily. She wanted a kiss. She wanted a lot more than a kiss. "Well, fine. But don't think that just because you know the truth, it'll excuse you from any duties." She crooked her finger. Luke put his ear to her lips. In two short sentences, she told him.

Luke's dark eyes were round as he slowly straightened. A wide smile of admiration stretched across his face. "Lucky son of a gun. And I always thought I wanted to die with my boots on."

A Gift of Love

Judith McNaught
Jude Deveraux
Andrea Kane
Kimberly Cates
Judith O'Brien

A wonderful romance collection in the tradition of *New York Times* bestsellers *A Holiday of Love* and *Everlasting Love*, A GIFT OF LOVE is sure to delight romance fans and readers alike.

❏ A GIFT OF LOVE 53661-3/$6.99

The enchanting new novel from the
author of the *New York Times*
bestseller *Until You*

JUDITH MCNAUGHT

REMEMBER WHEN

Judith McNaught creates an unforgettable world
filled with her "very special brand of dazzling wit,
passion, and tender sensuality."—*Romantic Times*

COMING MID-NOVEMBER IN HARDCOVER
FROM POCKET BOOKS

POCKET
B O O K S

1131-02

JUDE
DEVERAUX

*America's
favorite historical
romance author!*

Join the *New York Times* bestselling author
as she transports us from modern-day
Virginia to the high mountain deserts of
1873 Colorado, with a vibrant new tale
about a feisty lady and the man she was
meant to love.

LEGEND

Now available in hardcover
from Pocket Books

POCKET
B O O K S

1273